The Dream Doctor

It was Mrs. Brainard, tall, almost imperial in her loose morning gown her dark eyes snapping fire at the sudden intrusion.

THE CRAIG KENNEDY SERIES

THE
DREAM DOCTOR

BY
ARTHUR B. REEVE

FRONTISPIECE BY
WILL FOSTER

WILDSIDE PRESS
BERKELEY HEIGHTS • NEW JERSEY

Another great publication from...

Wildside Press
PO Box 45
Gillette, NJ 07933-0045
www.wildsidepress.com

First Wildside Press edition:
September 2000

Contents

The Dream Doctor

The Dream Doctor

I

The Dream Doctor

"JAMESON, I want you to get the real story about that friend of yours, Professor Kennedy," announced the managing editor of the *Star*, early one afternoon when I had been summoned into the sanctum.

From a batch of letters that had accumulated in the litter on the top of his desk, he selected one and glanced over it hurriedly.

"For instance," he went on reflectively, "here's a letter from a Constant Reader who asks, 'Is this Professor Craig Kennedy really all that you say he is, and, if so, how can I find out about his new scientific detective method?'"

He paused and tipped back his chair.

"Now, I don't want to file these letters in the waste basket. When people write letters to a newspaper, it means something. I might reply, in this case, that he is as real as science, as real as the fight of society against the criminal. But I want to do more than that."

The editor had risen, as if shaking himself momentarily loose from the ordinary routine of the office.

"You get me?" he went on, enthusiastically. "In other words, your assignment, Jameson, for the next month is to do nothing except follow your friend Kennedy. Start in right now, on the first, and cross-section out of his life just one month, an average month. Take things just as they come, set them down just as they happen, and when you get through give me an intimate picture of the man and his work."

He picked up the schedule for the day and I knew that the interview was at an end. I was to "get" Kennedy.

Often I had written snatches of Craig's adventures, but never before anything as ambitious as this assignment, for a whole month. At first it staggered me. But the more I thought about it, the better I liked it.

I hastened uptown to the apartment on the Heights which Kennedy and I had occupied for some time. I say we occupied it. We did so during those hours when he was not at his laboratory at the Chemistry Building on the University campus, or working on one of those cases which fascinated him. Fortunately, he happened to be there as I burst in upon him.

"Well?" he queried absently, looking up from a book, one of the latest untranslated treatises on the new psychology from the pen of the eminent scientist, Dr. Freud of Vienna, "what brings you uptown so early?"

Briefly as I could, I explained to him what it was

that I proposed to do. He listened without comment and I rattled on, determined not to allow him to nega- tive it.

"And," I added, warming up to the subject, "I think I owe a debt of gratitude to the managing editor. He has crystallised in my mind an idea that has long been latent. Why, Craig," I went on, "that is exactly what you want—to show people how they can never hope to beat the modern scientific detec- tive, to show that the crime-hunters have gone ahead faster even than—"

The telephone tinkled insistently.

Without a word, Kennedy motioned to me to "lis- ten in" on the extension on my desk, which he had had placed there as a precaution so that I could cor- roborate any conversation that took place over our wire.

His action was quite enough to indicate to me that, at least, he had no objection to the plan.

"This is Dr. Leslie—the coroner. Can you come to the Municipal Hospital—right away?"

"Right away, Doctor," answered Craig, hanging up the receiver. "Walter, you'll come, too?"

A quarter of an hour later we were in the court- yard of the city's largest hospital. In the balmy sun- shine the convalescing patients were sitting on benches or slowly trying their strength, walking over the grass, clad in faded hospital bathrobes.

We entered the office and quickly were conducted by an orderly to a little laboratory in a distant wing.

"What's the matter?" asked Craig, as we hurried along.

"I don't know exactly," replied the man, "except that it seems that Price Maitland, the broker, you know, was picked up on the street and brought here dying. He died before the doctors could relieve him."

Dr. Leslie was waiting impatiently for us. "What do you make of that, Professor Kennedy?"

The coroner spread out on the table before us a folded half-sheet of typewriting and searched Craig's face eagerly to see what impression it made on him.

"We found it stuffed in Maitland's outside coat pocket," he explained.

It was dateless and brief:

Dearest Madeline:

May God in his mercy forgive me for what I am about to do. I have just seen Dr. Ross. He has told me the nature of your illness. I cannot bear to think that I am the cause, so I am going simply to drop out of your life. I cannot live with you, and I cannot live without you. Do not blame me. Always think the best you can of me, even if you could not give me all. Good-bye.

Your distracted husband,
PRICE.

At once the idea flashed over me that Maitland had found himself suffering from some incurable disease and had taken the quickest means of settling his dilemma.

Kennedy looked up suddenly from the note.

"Do you think it was a suicide?" asked the coroner.

"Suicide?" Craig repeated. "Suicides don't usually write on typewriters. A hasty note scrawled on a sheet of paper in trembling pen or pencil, that is what they usually leave. No, some one tried to escape the handwriting experts this way."

"Exactly my idea," agreed Dr. Leslie, with evident satisfaction. "Now listen. Maitland was conscious almost up to the last moment, and yet the hospital doctors tell me they could not get a syllable of an ante-mortem statement from him."

"You mean he refused to talk?" I asked.

"No," he replied; "it was more perplexing than that. Even if the police had not made the usual blunder of arresting him for intoxication instead of sending him immediately to the hospital, it would have made no difference. The doctors simply could not have saved him, apparently. For the truth is, Professor Kennedy, we don't even know what was the matter with him."

Dr. Leslie seemed much excited by the case, as well he might be.

"Maitland was found reeling and staggering on Broadway this morning," continued the coroner. "Perhaps the policeman was not really at fault at first for arresting him, but before the wagon came Maitland was speechless and absolutely unable to move a muscle."

Dr. Leslie paused as he recited the strange facts, then resumed: "His eyes reacted, all right. He seemed to want to speak, to write, but couldn't. A frothy saliva dribbled from his mouth, but he could not frame a word. He was paralysed, and his breathing was peculiar. They then hurried him to the hospital as soon as they could. But it was of no use."

Kennedy was regarding the doctor keenly as he proceeded. Dr. Leslie paused again to emphasise what he was about to say.

"Here is another strange thing. It may or may not be of importance, but it is strange, nevertheless. Before Maitland died they sent for his wife. He was still conscious when she reached the hospital, could recognise her, seemed to want to speak, but could neither talk nor move. It was pathetic. She was grief-stricken, of course. But she did not faint. She is not of the fainting kind. It was what she said that impressed everyone. 'I knew it—I knew it,' she cried. She had dropped on her knees by the side of the bed. 'I felt it. Only the other night I had the horrible dream. I saw him in a terrific struggle. I could not see what it was—it seemed to be an invisible thing. I ran to him—then the scene shifted. I saw a funeral procession, and in the casket I could see through the wood—his face—oh, it was a warning! It has come true. I feared it, even though I knew it was only a dream. Often I have had the dream of that funeral procession and always I saw the same face, his face. Oh, it is horrible—terrible!'"

It was evident that Dr. Leslie at least was impressed by the dream.

"What have you done since?" asked Craig.

"I have turned loose everyone I could find available," replied Dr. Leslie, handing over a sheaf of reports.

Kennedy glanced keenly over them as they lay

spread out on the table. "I should like to see the body," he said, at length.

It was lying in the next room, awaiting Dr. Leslie's permission to be removed.

"At first," explained the doctor, leading the way, "we thought it might be a case of knock-out drops, chloral, you know—or perhaps chloral and whiskey, a combination which might unite to make chloroform in the blood. But no. We have tested for everything we can think of. In fact there seems to be no trace of a drug present. It is inexplicable. If Maitland really committed suicide, he must have taken *something*—and as far as we can find out there is no trace of anything. As far as we have gone we have always been forced back to the original idea that it was a natural death—perhaps due to shock of some kind, or organic weakness."

Kennedy had thoughtfully raised one of the lifeless hands and was examining it.

"Not that," he corrected. "Even if the autopsy shows nothing, it doesn't prove that it was a natural death. Look!"

On the back of the hand was a tiny, red, swollen mark. Dr. Leslie regarded it with pursed-up lips as though not knowing whether it was significant or not.

"The tissues seemed to be thickly infiltrated with a reddish serum and the blood-vessels congested," he remarked slowly. "There was a frothy mucus in the bronchial tubes. The blood was liquid, dark, and didn't clot. The fact of the matter is that the autopsical research revealed absolutely nothing but a general disorganisation of the blood-corpuscles, a most peculiar thing, but one the significance of which none of us here can fathom. If it was poison that he took or that had been given to him, it was the most subtle, intangible, elusive, that ever came to my knowledge. Why, there is absolutely no trace or clue—"

"Nor any use in looking for one in that way," broke in Kennedy decisively. "If we are to make any progress in this case, we must look elsewhere than to an autopsy. There is no clue beyond what you have found, if I am right. And I think I am right. It was the venom of the cobra."

"Cobra venom?" repeated the coroner, glancing up at a row of technical works.

"Yes. No, it's no use trying to look it up. There is no way of verifying a case of cobra poisoning except by the symptoms. It is not like any other poisoning in the world."

Dr. Leslie and I looked at each other, aghast at the thought of a poison so subtle that it defied detection.

"You think he was bitten by a snake?" I blurted out, half incredulous.

"Oh, Walter, on Broadway? No, of course not. But cobra venom has a medicinal value. It is sent here in small quantities for various medicinal purposes. Then, too, it would be easy to use it. A scratch on the hand in the passing crowd, a quick shoving of the letter into the pocket of the victim— and the murderer would probably think to go undetected."

We stood dismayed at the horror of such a scientific murder and the meagreness of the materials to work on in tracing it out.

"That dream was indeed peculiar," ruminated Craig, before we had really grasped the import of his quick revelation.

"You don't mean to say that you attach any importance to a dream?" I asked hurriedly, trying to follow him.

Kennedy merely shrugged his shoulders, but i could see plainly enough that he did.

"You haven't given this letter out to the press?" he asked.

"Not yet," answered Dr. Leslie.

"Then don't, until I say to do so. I shall need to keep it."

The cab in which we had come to the hospital was still waiting. "We must see Mrs. Maitland first," said Kennedy, as we left the nonplused coroner and his assistants.

The Maitlands lived, we soon found, in a large old-fashioned brownstone house just off Fifth Avenue.

Kennedy's card with the message that it was very urgent brought us in as far as the library, where we sat for a moment looking around at the quiet refinement of a more than well-to-do home.

On a desk at one end of the long room was a typewriter. Kennedy rose. There was not a sound of any one in either the hallway or the adjoining rooms. A moment later he was bending quietly over the typewriter in the corner, running off a series of characters on a sheet of paper. A sound of a closing door upstairs, and he quickly jammed the paper into his pocket, retraced his steps, and was sitting quietly opposite me again.

Mrs. Maitland was a tall, perfectly formed woman of baffling age, but with the impression of both youth and maturity which was very fascinating. She was calmer now, and although she seemed to be of anything but a hysterical nature, it was quite evident that her nervousness was due to much more than the shock of the recent tragic event, great as that must have been. It may have been that I recalled the words of the note, "Dr. Ross has told me the nature of your illness," but I fancied that she had been suffering from some nervous trouble.

"There is no use prolonging our introduction, Mrs. Maitland," began Kennedy. "We have called because the authorities are not yet fully convinced that Mr. Maitland committed suicide."

It was evident that she had seen the note, at least. "Not a suicide?" she repeated, looking from one to the other of us.

"Mr. Masterson on the wire, ma'am," whispered a maid. "Do you wish to speak to him? He begged to say that he did not wish to intrude, but he felt that if there—"

"Yes, I will talk to him—in my room," she interrupted.

I thought that there was just a trace of well-concealed confusion, as she excused herself.

We rose. Kennedy did not resume his seat immediately. Without a word or look he completed his work at the typewriter by abstracting several blank sheets of paper from the desk.

A few moments later Mrs. Maitland returned, calmer.

"In his note," resumed Kennedy, "he spoke of Dr. Ross and—"

"Oh," she cried, "can't you see Dr. Ross about it? Really I—I oughtn't to be—questioned in this way —not now, so soon after what I've had to go through."

It seemed that her nerves were getting unstrung again. Kennedy rose to go.

"Later, come to see me," she pleaded. "But now —you must realise—it is too much. I cannot talk —I cannot."

"Mr. Maitland had no enemies that you know of?" asked Kennedy, determined to learn something now, at least.

"No, no. None that would—do that."

"You had had no quarrel?" he added.

"No—we never quarrelled. Oh, Price—why did you? How could you?"

Her feelings were apparently rapidly getting the better of her. Kennedy bowed, and we withdrew silently. He had learned one thing. She believed or wanted others to believe in the note.

At a public telephone, a few minutes later, Kennedy was running over the names in the telephone book. "Let me see—here's an Arnold Masterson," he considered. Then turning the pages he went on, "Now we must find this Dr. Ross. There—Dr. Sheldon Ross—specialist in nerve diseases—that must be the one. He lives only a few blocks further uptown."

Handsome, well built, tall, dignified, in fact distinguished, Dr. Ross proved to be a man whose very
face and manner were magnetic, as should be those
of one who had chosen his branch of the profession.

"You have heard, I suppose, of the strange death
of Price Maitland?" began Kennedy when we were
seated in the doctor's office.

"Yes, about an hour ago." It was evident that he
was studying us.

"Mrs. Maitland, I believe, is a patient of yours?"

"Yes, Mrs. Maitland is one of my patients," he admitted interrogatively. Then, as if considering that
Kennedy's manner was not to be mollified by anything short of a show of confidence, he added: "She
came to me several months ago. I have had her
under treatment for nervous trouble since then, without a marked improvement."

"And Mr. Maitland," asked Kennedy, "was he a
patient, too?"

"Mr. Maitland," admitted the doctor with some
reticence, "had called on me this morning, but no,
he was not a patient."

"Did you notice anything unusual?"

"He seemed to be much worried," Dr. Ross replied
guardedly.

Kennedy took the suicide note from his pocket and
handed it to him.

"I suppose you have heard of this?" asked Craig.

The doctor read it hastily, then looked up, as if
measuring from Kennedy's manner just how much
he knew. "As nearly as I could make out," he said
slowly, his reticence to outward appearance gone,

"Maitland seemed to have something on his mind. He came inquiring as to the real cause of his wife's nervousness. Before I had talked to him long I gathered that he had a haunting fear that she did not love him any more, if ever. I fancied that he even doubted her fidelity."

I wondered why the doctor was talking so freely, now, in contrast with his former secretiveness.

"Do you think he was right?" shot out Kennedy quickly, eying Dr. Ross keenly.

"No, emphatically, no; he was not right," replied the doctor, meeting Craig's scrutiny without flinching. "Mrs. Maitland," he went on more slowly as if carefully weighing every word, "belongs to a large and growing class of women in whom, to speak frankly, sex seems to be suppressed. She is a very handsome and attractive woman—you have seen her? Yes? You must have noticed, though, that she is really frigid, cold, intellectual."

The doctor was so sharp and positive about his first statement and so careful in phrasing the second that I, at least, jumped to the conclusion that Maitland might have been right, after all. I imagined that Kennedy, too, had his suspicions of the doctor.

"Have you ever heard of or used cobra venom in any of your medical work?" he asked casually.

Dr. Ross wheeled in his chair, surprised.

"Why, yes," he replied quickly. "You know that it is a test for blood diseases, one of the most recently discovered and used parallel to the old tests. It is known as the Weil cobra-venom test."

"Do you use it often?"

"N-no," he replied. "My practice ordinarily does not lie in that direction. I used it not long ago, once, though. I have a patient under my care, a well-known club-man. He came to me originally—"

"Arnold Masterson?" asked Craig.

"Yes—how did you know his name?"

"Guessed it," replied Craig laconically, as if he knew much more than he cared to tell. "He was a friend of Mrs. Maitland's, was he not?"

"I should say not," replied Dr. Ross, without hesitation. He was quite ready to talk without being urged. "Ordinarily," he explained confidentially, "professional ethics seals my lips, but in this instance, since you seem to know so much, I may as well tell more."

I hardly knew whether to take him at his face value or not. Still he went on: "Mrs. Maitland is, as I have hinted at, what we specialists would call a consciously frigid but unconsciously passionate woman. As an intellectual woman she suppresses nature. But nature does and will assert herself, we believe. Often you will find an intellectual woman attracted unreasonably to a purely physical man—I mean, speaking generally, not in particular cases. You have read Ellen Key, I presume? Well, she expresses it well in some of the things she has written about affinities. Now, don't misunderstand me," he cautioned. "I am speaking generally, not of this individual case."

I was following Dr. Ross closely. When he talked so, he was a most fascinating man.

"Mrs. Maitland," he resumed, "has been much

troubled by her dreams, as you have heard, doubtless. The other day she told me of another dream. In it she seemed to be attacked by a bull, which suddenly changed into a serpent. I may say that I had asked her to make a record of her dreams, as well as other data, which I thought might be of use in the study and treatment of her nervous troubles. I readily surmised that not the dream, but something else, perhaps some recollection which it recalled, worried her. By careful questioning I discovered that it was —a broken engagement."

"Yes," prompted Kennedy.

"The bull-serpent, she admitted, had a half-human face—the face of Arnold Masterson!"

Was Dr. Ross desperately shifting suspicion from himself? I asked.

"Very strange—very," ruminated Kennedy. "That reminds me again. I wonder if you could let me have a sample of this cobra venom?"

"Surely. Excuse me; I'll get you some."

The doctor had scarcely shut the door when Kennedy began prowling around quietly. In the waiting-room, which was now deserted, stood a typewriter.

Quickly Craig ran over the keys of the machine until he had a sample of every character. Then he reached into drawer of the desk and hastily stuffed several blank sheets of paper into his pocket.

"Of course I need hardly caution you in handling this," remarked Dr. Ross, as he returned. "You are as well acquainted as I am with the danger attending its careless and unscientific uses."

"I am, and I thank you very much," said Kennedy.
We were standing in the waiting-room.

"You will keep me advised of any progress you
make in the case?" the doctor asked. "It compli-
cates, as you can well imagine, my treatment of Mrs.
Maitland."

"I shall be glad to do so," replied Kennedy, as we
departed.

An hour later found us in a handsomely appointed
bachelor apartment in a fashionable hotel overlooking the lower entrance to the Park.

"Mr. Masterson, I believe?" inquired Kennedy, as
a slim, debonair, youngish-old man entered the room
in which we had been waiting.

"I am that same," he smiled. "To what am I in
debted for this pleasure?"

We had been gazing at the various curios with
which he had made the room a veritable den of the
connoisseur.

"You have evidently travelled considerably," remarked Kennedy, avoiding the question for the time.

"Yes, I have been back in this country only a few
weeks," Masterson replied, awaiting the answer to
the first question.

"I called," proceeded Kennedy, "in the hope that
you, Mr. Masterson, might be able to shed some light
on the rather peculiar case of Mr. Maitland, of whose
death, I suppose, you have already heard."

"I?"

"You have known Mrs. Maitland a long time?"
ignored Kennedy.

"We went to school together."

"And were engaged, were you not?"

Masterson looked at Kennedy in ill-concealed surprise.

"Yes. But how did you know that? It was a secret—only between us two—I thought. She broke it off—not I."

"She broke off the engagement?" prompted Kennedy.

"Yes—a story about an escapade of mine and all that sort of thing, you know—but, by Jove! I like your nerve, sir." Masterson frowned, then added: "I prefer not to talk of that. There are some incidents in a man's life, particularly where a woman is concerned, that are forbidden."

"Oh, I beg pardon," hastened Kennedy, "but, by the way, you would have no objection to making a statement regarding your trip abroad and your recent return to this country—subsequent to—ah—the incident which we will not refer to?"

"None whatever. I left New York in 1908, disgusted with everything in general, and life here in particular—"

"Would you object to jotting it down so that I can get it straight?" asked Kennedy. "Just a brief résumé, you know."

"No. Have you a pen or a pencil?"

"I think you might as well dictate it; it will take only a minute to run it off on the typewriter."

Masterson rang the bell. A young man appeared noiselessly.

"Wix," he said, "take this: 'I left New York in 1908, travelling on the Continent, mostly in Paris,

Vienna, and Rome. Latterly I have lived in London, until six weeks ago, when I returned to New York.' Will that serve?"

"Yes, perfectly," said Kennedy, as he folded up the sheet of paper which the young secretary handed to him. "Thank you. I trust you won't consider it an impertinence if I ask you whether you were aware that Dr. Ross was Mrs. Maitland's physician?"

"Of course I knew it," Masterson replied frankly. "I have given him up for that reason, although he does not know it yet. I most strenuously object to being the subject of—what shall I call it?—his mental vivisection."

"Do you think he oversteps his position in trying to learn of the mental life of his patients?" queried Craig.

"I would rather say nothing further on that, either," replied Masterson. "I was talking over the wire to Mrs. Maitland a few moments ago, giving her my condolences and asking if there was anything I could do for her immediately, just as I would have done in the old days—only then, of course, I should have gone to her directly. The reason I did not go, but telephoned, was because this Ross seems to have put some ridiculous notions into her head about me. Now, look here; I don't want to discuss this. I've told you more than I intended, anyway."

Masterson had risen. His suavity masked a final determination to say no more.

II

The Soul Analysis

THE day was far advanced after this series of very unsatisfactory interviews. I looked at Kennedy blankly. We seemed to have uncovered so little that was tangible that I was much surprised to find that apparently he was well contented with what had happened in the case so far.

"I shall be busy for a few hours in the laboratory, Walter," he remarked, as we parted at the subway. "I think, if you have nothing better to do, that you might employ the time in looking up some of the gossip about Mrs. Maitland and Masterson, to say nothing of Dr. Ross," he emphasised. "Drop in after dinner."

There was not much that I could find. Of Mrs. Maitland there was practically nothing that I already did not know from having seen her name in the papers. She was a leader in a certain set which was devoting its activities to various social and moral propaganda. Masterson's early escapades were notorious even in the younger smart set in which he had moved, but his years abroad had mellowed the recollection of them. He had not distinguished himself in any way since his return to set gossip afloat, nor had any tales of his doings abroad filtered through to New York clubland. Dr. Ross, I found to my surprise, was rather better known than I had supposed, both as a specialist and as a man about town. He seemed to have risen rapidly in his profession as physician to the ills of society's nerves.

I was amazed after dinner to find Kennedy doing nothing at all.

"What's the matter?" I asked. "Have you struck a snag?"

"No," he replied slowly, "I was only waiting. I told them to be here between half-past eight and nine."

"Who?" I queried.

"Dr. Leslie," he answered. "He has the authority to compel the attendance of Mrs. Maitland, Dr. Ross, and Masterson."

The quickness with which he had worked out a case which was, to me, one of the most inexplicable he had had for a long time, left me standing speechless.

One by one they dropped in during the next half-hour, and, as usual, it fell to me to receive them and smooth over the rough edges which always obtruded at these little enforced parties in the laboratory.

Dr. Leslie and Dr. Ross were the first to arrive. They had not come together, but had met at the door. I fancied I saw a touch of professional jealousy in their manner, at least on the part of Dr. Ross. Masterson came, as usual ignoring the seriousness of the matter and accusing us all of conspiring to keep him from the first night of a light opera which was opening. Mrs. Maitland followed, the unaccustomed pallor of her face heightened by the plain black dress.

I felt most uncomfortable, as indeed I think the rest did. She merely inclined her head to Masterson, seemed almost to avoid the eye of Dr. Ross, glared at Dr. Leslie, and absolutely ignored me.

Craig had been standing aloof at his laboratory table, beyond a nod of recognition paying little attention to anything. He seemed to be in no hurry to begin.

"Great as science is," he commenced, at length, "it is yet far removed from perfection. There are, for instance, substances so mysterious, subtle, and dangerous as to set the most delicate tests and powerful lenses at naught, while they carry death most horrible in their train."

He could scarcely have chosen his opening words with more effect.

"Chief among them," he proceeded, "are those from nature's own laboratory. There are some sixty species of serpents, for example, with deadly venom. Among these, as you doubtless have all heard, none has brought greater terror to mankind than the cobra-di-capello, the *Naja tripudians* of India. It is unnecessary for me to describe the cobra or to say anything about the countless thousands who have yielded up their lives to it. I have here a small quantity of the venom"—he indicated it in a glass beaker. "It was obtained in New York, and I have tested it on guinea-pigs. It has lost none of its potency."

I fancied that there was a feeling of relief when Kennedy by his actions indicated that he was not going to repeat the test.

"This venom," he continued, "dries in the air into a

substance like small scales, soluble in water but not in alcohol. It has only a slightly acrid taste and odour, and, strange to say, is inoffensive on the tongue or mucous surfaces, even in considerable quantities. All we know about it is that in an open wound it is deadly swift in action."

It was difficult to sit unmoved at the thought that before us, in only a few grains of the stuff, was enough to kill us all if it were introduced into a scratch of our skin.

"Until recently chemistry was powerless to solve the enigma, the microscope to detect its presence, or pathology to explain the reason for its deadly effect. And even now, about all we know is that autopsical research reveals absolutely nothing but the general disorganisation of the blood corpuscles. In fact, such poisoning is best known by the peculiar symptoms—the vertigo, weak legs, and falling jaw. The victim is unable to speak or swallow, but is fully sensible. He has nausea, paralysis, an accelerated pulse at first followed rapidly by a weakening, with breath slow and laboured. The pupils are contracted, but react to the last, and he dies in convulsions like asphyxia. It is both a blood and a nerve poison."

As Kennedy proceeded, Mrs. Maitland never took her large eyes from his face.

Kennedy now drew from a large envelope in which he protected it, the typewritten note which had been found on Maitland. He said nothing about the "suicide" as he quietly began a new line of accumulating evidence.

"There is an increasing use of the typewriting machine for the production of spurious papers," he be-gan, rattling the note significantly. "It is partly due to the great increase in the use of the typewriter gen-erally, but more than all is it due to the erroneous idea that fraudulent typewriting cannot be detected. The fact is that the typewriter is perhaps a worse means of concealing identity than is disguised hand-writing. It does not afford the effective protection to the criminal that is supposed. On the contrary, the typewriting of a fraudulent document may be the direct means by which it can be traced to its source. First we have to determine what kind of machine a certain piece of writing was done with, then what particular machine."

He paused and indicated a number of little instru-ments on the table.

"For example," he resumed, "the Lovibond tintom-eter tells me its story of the colour of the ink used in the ribbon of the machine that wrote this note as well as several standard specimens which I have been able to obtain from three machines on which it might have been written.

"That leads me to speak of the quality of the paper in this half-sheet that was found on Mr. Maitland. Sometimes such a half-sheet may be mated with the other half from which it was torn as accurately as if the act were performed before your eyes. There was no such good fortune in this case, but by measure-ments made by the vernier micrometer caliper I have found the precise thickness of several samples of paper as compared to that of the suicide note. I need hardly add that in thickness and quality, as well

3

as in the tint of the ribbon, the note points to one person as the author."

No one moved.

"And there are other proofs—unescapable," Kennedy hurried on. "For instance, I have counted the number of threads to the inch in the ribbon, as shown by the letters of this note. That also corresponds to the number in one of the three ribbons."

Kennedy laid down a glass plate peculiarly ruled in little squares.

"This," he explained, "is an alignment test plate, through which can be studied accurately the spacing and alignment of typewritten characters. There are in this pica type ten to the inch horizontally and six to the inch vertically. That is usual. Perhaps you are not acquainted with the fact that typewritten characters are in line both ways, horizontally and vertically. There are nine possible positions for each character which may be assumed with reference to one of these little standard squares of the test plate. You cannot fail to appreciate what an immense impossibility there is that one machine should duplicate the variations out of the true which the microscope detects for several characters on another.

"Not only that, but the faces of many letters inevitably become broken, worn, battered, as well as out of alignment, or slightly shifted in their position on the type bar. The type faces are not flat, but a little concave to conform to the roller. There are thousands of possible divergences, scars, and deformities in each machine.

"Such being the case," he concluded, "typewriting has an individuality like that of the Bertillon system, finger-prints, or the *portrait parlé.*"

He paused, then added quickly: "What machine was it in this case? I have samples here from that of Dr. Ross, from a machine used by Mr. Masterson's secretary, and from a machine which was accessible to both Mr. and Mrs. Maitland."

Kennedy stopped, but he was not yet prepared to relieve the suspense of two of those whom his investigation would absolve.

"Just one other point," he resumed mercilessly, "a point which a few years ago would have been inexplicable—if not positively misleading and productive of actual mistake. I refer to the dreams of Mrs. Maitland."

I had been expecting it, yet the words startled me. What must they have done to her? But she kept admirable control of herself.

"Dreams used to be treated very seriously by the ancients, but until recently modern scientists, rejecting the ideas of the dark ages, have scouted dreams. To-day, however, we study them scientifically, for we believe that whatever is, has a reason. Dr. Ross, I think, is acquainted with the new and remarkable theories of Dr. Sigmund Freud, of Vienna?"

Dr. Ross nodded. "I dissent vigorously from some of Freud's conclusions," he hastened.

"Let me state them first," resumed Craig. "Dreams, says Freud, are very important. They give us the most reliable information concerning the individual. But that is only possible"—Kennedy emphasised the point—"if the patient is in entire *rapport* with the doctor.

"Now, the dream is not an absurd and senseless jumble, but a perfect mechanism and has a definite meaning in penetrating the mind. It is as though we had two streams of thought, one of which we allow to flow freely, the other of which we are constantly repressing, pushing back into the subconscious, or unconscious. This matter of the evolution of our individual mental life is too long a story to bore you with at such a critical moment.

"But the resistances, the psychic censors of our ideas, are always active, except in sleep. Then the repressed material comes to the surface. But the resistances never entirely lose their power, and the dream shows the material distorted. Seldom does one recognise his own repressed thoughts or unattained wishes. The dream really is the guardian of sleep to satisfy the activity of the unconscious and repressed mental processes that would otherwise disturb sleep by keeping the censor busy. In the case of a nightmare the watchman or censor is aroused, finds himself overpowered, so to speak, and calls on consciousness for help.

"There are three kinds of dreams—those which represent an unrepressed wish as fulfilled, those that represent the realisation of a repressed wish in an entirely concealed form, and those that represent the realisation of a repressed wish in a form insufficiently or only partially concealed.

"Dreams are not of the future, but of the past, except as they show striving for unfulfilled wishes.

Whatever may be denied in reality we nevertheless can realise in another way—in our dreams. And probably more of our daily life, conduct, moods, beliefs than we think, could be traced to preceding dreams."

Dr. Ross was listening attentively, as Craig turned to him. "This is perhaps the part of Freud's theory from which you dissent most strongly. Freud says that as soon as you enter the intimate life of a patient you begin to find sex in some form. In fact, the best indication of abnormality would be its absence. Sex is one of the strongest of human impulses, yet the one subjected to the greatest repression. For that reason it is the weakest point in our cultural development. In a normal life, he says, there are no neuroses. Let me proceed now with what the Freudists call the psychanalysis, the soul analysis, of Mrs. Maitland."

It was startling in the extreme to consider the possibilities to which this new science might lead, as he proceeded to illustrate it.

"Mrs. Maitland," he continued, "your dream of fear was a dream of what we call the fulfilment of a suppressed wish. Moreover, fear always denotes a sexual idea underlying the dream. In fact, morbid anxiety means surely unsatisfied love. The old Greeks knew it. The gods of fear were born of the goddess of love. Consciously you feared the death of your husband because unconsciously you wished it."

It was startling, dramatic, cruel, perhaps, merciless—this dissecting of the soul of the handsome woman before us; but it had come to a point where it was necessary to get at the truth.

Mrs. Maitland, hitherto pale, was now flushed and indignant. Yet the very manner of her indignation showed the truth of the new psychology of dreams, for, as I learned afterward, people often become indignant when the Freudists strike what is called the "main complex."

"There are other motives just as important," protested Dr. Ross. "Here in America the money motive, ambition—"

"Let me finish," interposed Kennedy. "I want to consider the other dream also. Fear is equivalent to a wish in this sort of dream. It also, as I have said, denotes sex. In dreams animals are usually symbols. Now, in this second dream we find both the bull and the serpent, from time immemorial, symbols of the continuing of the life-force. Dreams are always based on experiences or thoughts of the day preceding the dreams. You, Mrs. Maitland, dreamed of a man's face on these beasts. There was every chance of having him suggested to you. You think you hate him. Consciously you reject him; unconsciously you accept him. Any of the new psychologists who knows the intimate connection between love and hate, would understand how that is possible. Love does not extinguish hate; or hate, love. They repress each other. The opposite sentiment may very easily grow."

The situation was growing more tense as he proceeded. Was not Kennedy actually taxing her with loving another?

"The dreamer," he proceeded remorselessly, "is always the principal actor in a dream, or the dream centres about the dreamer most intimately. Dreams are personal. We never dream about matters that really concern others, but ourselves.

"Years ago," he continued, "you suffered what the new psychologists call a 'psychic trauma'—a soul-wound. You were engaged, but your censored consciousness rejected the manner of life of your fiancé. In pique you married Price Maitland. But you never lost your real, subconscious love for another."

He stopped, then added in a low tone that was almost inaudible, yet which did not call for an answer, "Could you—be honest with yourself, for you need say not a word aloud—could you always be sure of yourself in the face of any situation?"

She looked startled. Her ordinarily inscrutable face betrayed everything, though it was averted from the rest of us and could be seen only by Kennedy. She knew the truth that she strove to repress; she was afraid of herself.

"It is dangerous," she murmured, "to be with a person who pays attention to such little things. If every one were like you, I would no longer breathe a syllable of my dreams."

She was sobbing now.

What was back of it all? I had heard of the so-called resolution dreams. I had heard of dreams that kill, of unconscious murder, of the terrible acts of the subconscious somnambulist of which the actor has no recollection in the waking state until put under hypnotism.   Was it that which Kennedy was driving at disclosing?

Dr. Ross moved nearer to Mrs. Maitland as if to reassure her.   Craig was studying attentively the effect of his revelation both on her and on the other faces before him.

Mrs. Maitland, her shoulders bent with the outpouring of the long-suppressed emotion of the evening and of the tragic day, called for sympathy which, I could see, Craig would readily give when he had reached the climax he had planned.

"Kennedy," exclaimed Masterson, pushing aside Dr. Ross, as he bounded to the side of Mrs. Maitland, unable to restrain himself longer, "Kennedy, you are a faker—nothing but a damned dream doctor —in scientific disguise."

"Perhaps," replied Craig, with a quiet curl of the lip.   "But the threads of the typewriter ribbon, the alignment of the letters, the paper, all the 'fingerprints' of that type-written note of suicide were those of the machine belonging to the man who caused the soul-wound, who knew Madeline Maitland's inmost heart better than herself—because he had heard of Freud undoubtedly, when he was in Vienna—who knew that he held her real love still, who posed as a patient of Dr. Ross to learn her secrets as well as to secure the subtle poison of the cobra.   That man, perhaps, merely brushed against Price Maitland in the crowd, enough to scratch his hand with the needle, shove the false note into his pocket—anything to win the woman who he knew loved him, and whom he could win.   Masterson, you are that man!"

The next half hour was crowded kaleidoscopically with events—the call by Dr. Leslie for the police, the departure of the Coroner with Masterson in custody, and the efforts of Dr. Ross to calm his now almost hysterical patient, Mrs. Maitland.

Then a calm seemed to settle down over the old laboratory which had so often been the scene of such events, tense with human interest. I could scarcely conceal my amazement, as I watched Kennedy quietly restoring to their places the pieces of apparatus he had used.

"What's the matter?" he asked, catching my eye as he paused with the tintometer in his hand.

"Why," I exclaimed, "that's a fine way to start a month! Here's just one day gone and you've caught your man. Are you going to keep that up? If you are—I'll quit and skip to February. I'll choose the shortest month, if that's the pace!"

"Any month you please," he smiled grimly, as he reluctantly placed the tintometer in its cabinet.

There was no use. I knew that any other month would have been just the same.

"Well," I replied weakly, "all I can hope is that every day won't be as strenuous as this has been. I hope, at least, you will give me time to make some notes before you start off again."

"Can't say," he answered, still busy returning paraphernalia to its accustomed place. "I have no control over the cases as they come to me—except that I can turn down those that don't interest me."

"Then," I sighed wearily, "turn down the next one. I must have rest. I'm going home to sleep."

"Very well," he said, making no move to follow me.

I shook my head doubtfully. It was impossible to force a card on Kennedy. Instead of showing any disposition to switch off the laboratory lights, he appeared to be regarding a row of half-filled test-tubes with the abstraction of a man who has been interrupted in the midst of an absorbing occupation.

"Good night," I said at length.

"Good night," he echoed mechanically.

I know that he slept that night—at least his bed had been slept in when I awoke in the morning. But he was gone. But then, it was not unusual for him, when the fever for work was on him, to consider even five or fewer hours a night's rest. It made no difference when I argued with him. The fact that he thrived on it himself and could justify it by pointing to other scientists was refutation enough.

Slowly I dressed, breakfasted, and began transcribing what I could from the hastily jotted down notes of the day before. I knew that the work, whatever it was, in which he was now engaged must be in the nature of research, dear to his heart. Otherwise, he would have left word for me.

No word came from him, however, all day, and I had not only caught up in my notes, but, my appetite whetted by our first case, had become hungry for more. In fact I had begun to get a little worried at the continued silence. A hand on the knob of the door or a ring of the telephone would have been a welcome relief. I was gradually becoming aware of the fact that I liked the excitement of the life as much as Kennedy did.

I knew it when the sudden sharp tinkle of the telephone set my heart throbbing almost as quickly as the little bell hammer buzzed.

"Jameson, for Heaven's sake find Kennedy immediately and bring him over here to the Novella Beauty Parlour. We've got the worst case I've been up against in a long time. Dr. Leslie, the coroner, is here, and says we must not make a move until Kennedy arrives."

I doubt whether in all our long acquaintance I had ever heard First Deputy O'Connor more wildly excited and apparently more helpless than he seemed over the telephone that night.

"What is it?" I asked.

"Never mind, never mind. Find Kennedy," he called back almost brusquely. "It's Miss Blanche Blaisdell, the actress—she's been found dead here. The thing is an absolute mystery. Now get him, *get him.*"

It was still early in the evening, and Kennedy had not come in, nor had he sent any word to our apartment. O'Connor had already tried the laboratory. As for myself, I had not the slightest idea where Craig was. I knew the case must be urgent if both the deputy and the coroner were waiting for him. Still, after half an hour's vigorous telephoning, I was unable to find a trace of Kennedy in any of his usual haunts.

In desperation I left a message for him with the hall-boy in case he called up, jumped into a cab, and rode over to the laboratory, hoping that some of the care-takers might still be about and might know something of his whereabouts. The janitor was able to enlighten me to the extent of telling me that a big limousine had called for Kennedy an hour or so before, and that he had left in great haste.

I had given it up as hopeless and had driven back to the apartment to wait for him, when the hall-boy made a rush at me just as I was paying my fare.

"Mr. Kennedy on the wire, sir," he cried as he half dragged me into the hall.

"Walter," almost shouted Kennedy, "I'm over at the Washington Heights Hospital with Dr. Barron —you remember Barron, in our class at college? He has a very peculiar case of a poor girl whom he found wandering on the street and brought here. Most unusual thing. He came over to the laboratory after me in his car. Yes, I have the message that you left with the hall-boy. Come up here and pick me up, and we'll ride right down to the Novella. Good-bye."

I had not stopped to ask questions and prolong the conversation, knowing as I did the fuming impatience of O'Connor. It was relief enough to know that Kennedy was located at last.

He was in the psychopathic ward with Barron, as I hurried in. The girl whom he had mentioned over the telephone was then quietly sleeping under the influence of an opiate, and they were discussing the case outside in the hall.

"What do you think of it yourself?" Barron was asking, nodding to me to join them. Then he added for my enlightenment: "I found this girl wandering bareheaded in the street. To tell the truth, I thought at first that she was intoxicated, but a good look showed me better than that. So I hustled the poor thing into my car and brought her here. All the way she kept crying over and over: 'Look, don't you see it? She's afire! Her lips shine—they shine, they shine.' I think the girl is demented and has had some hallucination."

"Too vivid for a hallucination," remarked Kennedy decisively. "It was too real to her. Even the opiate couldn't remove the picture, whatever it was, from her mind until you had given her almost enough to kill her, normally. No, that wasn't any hallucination. Now, Walter, I'm ready."

III

The Sybarite

WE found the Novella Beauty Parlour on the top
floor of an office-building just off Fifth Avenue on a side street not far from Forty-second Street.
A special elevator, elaborately fitted up, wafted us
up with express speed. As the door opened we saw
a vista of dull-green lattices, little gateways hung
with roses, windows of diamond-paned glass set in
white wood, rooms with little white enamelled manicure-tables and chairs, amber lights glowing with soft
incandescence in deep bowers of fireproof tissue flowers. There was a delightful warmth about the place,
and the seductive scents and delicate odours betokened the haunt of the twentieth-century Sybarite.

Both O'Connor and Leslie, strangely out of place
in the enervating luxury of the now deserted beauty-parlour, were still waiting for Kennedy with a grim
determination.

"A most peculiar thing," whispered O'Connor, dashing forward the moment the elevator door opened.
"We can't seem to find a single cause for her death.
The people up here say it was a suicide, but I never
accept the theory of suicide unless there are undoubted proofs. So far there have been none in this
case. There was no reason for it."

Seated in one of the large easy-chairs of the recep-

tion-room, in a corner with two of O'Connor's men
standing watchfully near, was a man who was the
embodiment of all that was nervous. He was alternately wringing his hands and rumpling his hair.
Beside him was a middle-sized, middle-aged lady in a
most amazing state of preservation, who evidently
presided over the cosmetic mysteries beyond the male
ken. She was so perfectly groomed that she looked
as though her clothes were a mould into which she
had literally been poured.

"Professor and Madame Millefleur—otherwise Miller,"—whispered O'Connor, noting Kennedy's questioning gaze and taking his arm to hurry him down
a long, softly carpeted corridor, flanked on either
side by little doors. "They run the shop. They say
one of the girls just opened the door and found her
dead."

Near the end, one of the doors stood open, and before it Dr. Leslie, who had preceded us, paused. He
motioned to us to look in. It was a little dressing-
room, containing a single white-enamelled bed, a
dresser, and a mirror. But it was not the scant
though elegant furniture that caused us to start back.

There under the dull half-light of the corridor lay
a woman, most superbly formed. She was dark, and
the thick masses of her hair, ready for the hair-
dresser, fell in a tangle over her beautifully chiselled
features and full, rounded shoulders and neck. A
scarlet bathrobe, loosened at the throat, actually
accentuated rather than covered the voluptuous lines
of her figure, down to the slender ankle which had
been the beginning of her fortune as a danseuse.

Except for the marble pallor of her face it was difficult to believe that she was not sleeping. And yet there she was, the famous Blanche Blaisdell, dead—dead in the little dressing-room of the Novella Beauty Parlour, surrounded as in life by mystery and luxury.

We stood for several moments speechless, stupefied. At last O'Connor silently drew a letter from his pocket. It was written on the latest and most delicate of scented stationery.

"It was lying sealed on the dresser when we arrived," explained O'Connor, holding it so that we could not see the address. "I thought at first she had really committed suicide and that this was a note of explanation. But it is not. Listen. It is just a line or two. It reads: 'Am feeling better now, though that was a great party last night. Thanks for the newspaper puff which I have just read. It was very kind of you to get them to print it. Meet me at the same place and same time to-night. Your Blanche.' The note was not stamped, and was never sent. Perhaps she rang for a messenger. At any rate, she must have been dead before she could send it. But it was addressed to—Burke Collins."

"Burke Collins!" exclaimed Kennedy and I together in amazement.

He was one of the leading corporation lawyers in the country, director in a score of the largest companies, officer in half a dozen charities and social organisations, patron of art and opera. It seemed impossible, and I at least did not hesitate to say so. For

answer O'Connor simply laid the letter and envelope
down on the dresser.

It seemed to take some time to convince Kennedy.
There it was in black and white, however, in
Blanche Blaisdell's own vertical hand. Try to figure
it out as I could, there seemed to be only one conclusion, and that was to accept it. What it was that interested him I did not know, but finally he bent down
and sniffed, not at the scented letter, but at the covering on the dresser. When he raised his head I saw
that he had not been looking at the letter at all, but
at a spot on the cover near it.

"Sn-ff, sn-ff," he sniffed, thoughtfully closing his
eyes as if considering something. "Yes—oil of turpentine."

Suddenly he opened his eyes, and the blank look of
abstraction that had masked his face was broken
through by a gleam of comprehension that I knew
flashed the truth to him intuitively.

"Turn out that light in the corridor," he ordered
quickly.

Dr. Leslie found and turned the switch. There we
were alone, in the now weird little dressing-room,
alone with that horribly lovely thing lying there cold
and motionless on the little white bed.

Kennedy moved forward in the darkness. Gently,
almost as if she were still the living, pulsing, sentient
Blanche Blaisdell who had entranced thousands, he
opened her mouth.

A cry from O'Connor, who was standing in front of
me, followed. "What's that, those little spots on her

4

tongue and throat? They glow. It is the corpse light!"

Surely enough, there were little luminous spots in her mouth. I had heard somewhere that there is a phosphorescence appearing during decay of organic substances which once gave rise to the ancient super-stition of "corpse lights" and the will-o'-the-wisp. It was really due, I knew, to living bacteria. But there surely had been no time for such micro-organisms to develop, even in the almost tropic heat of the Novella. Could she have been poisoned by these phosphores-cent bacilli? What was it—a strange new mouth-malady that had attacked this notorious adventuress and woman of luxury?

Leslie had flashed up the light again before Craig spoke. We were all watching him keenly.

"Phosphorus, phosphoric acid, or phosphoric salve," Craig said slowly, looking eagerly about the room as if in search of something that would explain it. He caught sight of the envelope still lying on the dresser. He picked it up, toyed with it, looked at the top where O'Connor had slit it, then deliberately tore the flap off the back where it had been glued in sealing the letter.

"Put the light out again," he asked.

Where the thin line of gum was on the back of the flap, in the darkness there glowed the same sort of brightness that we had seen in a speck here and there on Blanche Blaisdell's lips and in her mouth. The truth flashed over me. Some one had placed the stuff, whatever it was, on the flap of the envelope, knowing that she must touch her lips to it to seal it.

She had done so, and the deadly poison had entered her mouth.

As the light went up again Kennedy added: "Oil of turpentine removes traces of phosphorus, phosphoric acid, or phosphoric salve, which are insoluble in anything else except ether and absolute alcohol. Some one who knew that tried to eradicate them, but did not wholly succeed. O'Connor, see if you can find either phosphorus, the oil, or the salve anywhere in the shop."

Then as O'Connor and Leslie hurriedly disappeared he added to me: "Another of those strange coincidences, Walter. You remember the girl at the hospital? 'Look, don't you see it? She's afire. Her lips shine—they shine, they shine!'"

Kennedy was still looking carefully over the room. In a little wicker basket was a newspaper which was open at the page of theatrical news, and as I glanced quickly at it I saw a most laudatory paragraph about her.

Beneath the paper were some torn scraps. Kennedy picked them up and pieced them together. "Dearest Blanche," they read. "I hope you're feeling better after that dinner last night. Can you meet me to-night? Write me immediately. Collie."

He placed the scraps carefully in his wallet. There was nothing more to be done here apparently. As we passed down the corridor we could hear a man apparently raving in good English and bad French. It proved to be Millefleur—or Miller—and his raving was as overdone as that of a third-rate actor. Madame was trying to calm him.

"Henri, *Henri*, don't go on so," she was saying.

"A suicide—in the Novella. It will be in all the papers. We shall be ruined. Oh—oh!"

"Here, can that sob stuff," broke in one of O'Connor's officers. "You can tell it all when the chief takes you to headquarters, see?"

Certainly the man made no very favourable impression by his actions. There seemed to be much that was forced about them, that was more incriminating than a stolid silence would have been.

Between them Monsieur and Madame made out, however, to repeat to Kennedy their version of what had happened. It seemed that a note addressed to Miss Blaisdell had been left by some one on the desk in the reception-room. No one knew who left it, but one of the girls had picked it up and delivered it to her in her dressing-room. A moment later she rang her bell and called for one of the girls named Agnes, who was to dress her hair. Agnes was busy, and the actress asked her to get paper, a pen, and ink. At least it seemed that way, for Agnes got them for her. A few minutes later her bell rang again, and Agnes went down, apparently to tell her that she was now ready to dress her hair.

The next thing any one knew was a piercing shriek from the girl. She ran down the corridor, still shrieking, out into the reception-room and rushed into the elevator, which happened to be up at the time. That was the last they had seen of her. The other girls saw Miss Blaisdell lying dead, and a panic followed. The customers dressed quickly and fled, almost in panic. All was confusion. By that time a policeman had arrived, and soon after O'Connor and the coroner had come.

There was little use in cross-questioning the couple. They had evidently had time to agree on the story; that is, supposing it were not true. Only a scientific third degree could have shaken them, and such a thing was impossible just at that time.

From the line of Kennedy's questions I could see that he believed that there was a hiatus somewhere in their glib story, at least some point where some one had tried to eradicate the marks of the poison.

"Here it is. We found it," interrupted O'Connor, holding up in his excitement a bottle covered with black cloth to protect it from the light. "It was in the back of a cabinet in the operating-room, and it is marked 'Ether phosphoré.' Another of oil of turpentine was on a shelf in another cabinet. Both seem to have been used lately, judging by the wetness of the bottoms of the glass stoppers."

"Ether phosphoré, phosphorated ether," commented Kennedy, reading the label to himself. "A remedy from the French Codex, composed, if I remember rightly, of one part phosphorus and fifty parts sulphuric ether. Phosphorus is often given as a remedy for loss of nerve power, neuralgia, hysteria, and melancholia. In quantities from a fiftieth to a tenth or so of a grain free phosphorus is a renovator of nerve tissue and nerve force, a drug for intense and long-sustained anxiety of mind and protracted emotional excitement—in short, for fast living."

He uncorked the bottle, and we tasted the stuff. It was unpleasant and nauseous. "I don't see why it wasn't used in the form of pills. The liquid form of a few drops on gum arabic is hopelessly anti-quated."

The elevator door opened with a clang, and a well-built, athletic looking man of middle age with an acquired youngish look about his clothes and clean-shaven face stepped out. His face was pale, and his hand shook with emotion that showed that something had unstrung his usually cast-iron nerves. I recog-nised Burke Collins at once.

In spite of his nervousness he strode forward with the air of a man accustomed to being obeyed, to hav-ing everything done for him merely because he, Burke Collins, could afford to pay for it and it was his right. He seemed to know whom he was seeking, for he im-mediately singled out O'Connor.

"This is terrible, terrible," he whispered hoarsely. "No, no, no, I don't want to see her. I can't, not yet. You know I thought the world of that poor little girl. Only," and here the innate selfishness of the man cropped out, "only I called to ask you that nothing of my connection with her be given out. You under-stand? Spare nothing to get at the truth. Employ the best men you have. Get outside help if neces-sary. I'll pay for anything, anything. Perhaps I can use some influence for you some day, too. But, you understand—the scandal, you know. Not a word to the newspapers."

At another time I feel sure that O'Connor would have succumbed. Collins was not without a great deal of political influence, and even a first deputy may be "broke" by a man with influence. But now here was Kennedy, and he wished to appear in the best light.

He looked at Craig. "Let me introduce Professor Kennedy," he said. "I've already called him in."

"Very happy to have the pleasure of meeting you," said Collins, grasping Kennedy's hand warmly. "I hope you will take me as your client in this case. I'll pay handsomely. I've always had a great admiration for your work, and I've heard a great deal about it."

Kennedy is, if anything, as impervious to blandishment as a stone, as the Blarney Stone is itself, for instance. "On one condition," he replied slowly, "and that is that I go ahead exactly as if I were employed by the city itself to get at the truth."

Collins bit his lip. It was evident that he was not accustomed to being met in this independent spirit. "Very well," he answered at last. "O'Connor has called you in. Work for him and—well, you know, if you need anything just draw on me for it. Only if you can, keep me out of it. I'll tell everything I can to help you—but not to the newspapers."

He beckoned us outside. "Those people in there," he nodded his head back in the direction of the Millefleurs, "do you suspect them? By George, it does look badly for them, doesn't it, when you come to think of it? Well, now, you see, I'm frank and confidential about my relations with Blan—er—Miss Blaisdell. I was at a big dinner with her last night with a party of friends. I suppose she came here to get straightened out. I hadn't been able to get her on the wire to-day, but at the theatre when I called up they told me what had happened, and I came right over here. Now please remember, do everything, anything but create a scandal. You realise what that would mean for me."

Kennedy said nothing. He simply laid down on the desk, piece by piece, the torn letter which he had picked up from the basket, and beside it he spread out the reply which Blanche had written.

"What?" gasped Collins as he read the torn letter. "I send that? Why, man alive, you're crazy. Didn't I just tell you I hadn't heard from her until I called up the theatre just now?"

I could not make out whether he was lying or not when he said that he had not sent the note. Kennedy picked up a pen. "Please write the same thing as you read in the note on this sheet of the Novella paper. It will be all right. You have plenty of witnesses to that."

It must have irked Collins even to have his word doubted, but Kennedy was no respecter of persons. He took the pen and wrote.

"I'll keep your name out of it as much as possible," remarked Kennedy, glancing intently at the writing and blotting it.

"Thank you," said Collins simply, for once in his life at a loss for words. Once more he whispered to O'Connor, then he excused himself. The man was so obviously sincere, I felt, as far as his selfish and sensual limitations would permit, that I would not have blamed Kennedy for giving him much more encouragement than he had given.

Kennedy was not through yet, and now turned

quickly again to the cosmetic arcadia which had been so rudely stirred by the tragedy.

"Who is this girl Agnes who discovered Miss Blaisdell?" he shot out at the Millefleurs.

The beauty-doctor was now really painful in his excitement. Like his establishment, even his feelings were artificial.

"Agnes?" he repeated. "Why, she was one of Madame's best hair-dressers. See—my dear—show the gentlemen the book of engagements."

It was a large book full of girls' names, each an expert in curls, puffs, "reinforcements," hygienic rolls, transformators, and the numberless other things that made the fearful and wonderful hair-dresses of the day. Agnes's dates were full, for a day ahead.

Kennedy ran his eye over the list of patrons. "Mrs. Burke Collins, 3:30," he read. "Was she a patron, too?"

"Oh, yes," answered Madame. "She used to come here three times a week. It was not vanity. We all knew her, and we all liked her."

Instantly I could read between the lines, and I felt that I had been too charitable to Burke Collins. Here was the wife slaving to secure that beauty which would win back the man with whom she had worked and toiled in the years before they came to New York and success. The "other woman" came here, too, but for a very different reason.

Nothing but business seemed to impress Millefleur, however. "Oh, yes," he volunteered, "we have a fine class. Among my own patients I have Hugh Dayton, the actor, you know, leading man in Blanche Blais-

dell's company. He is having his hair restored.
Why, I gave him a treatment this afternoon. If ever
there is a crazy man, it is he. I believe he would kill
Mr. Collins for the way Blanche Blaisdell treats him.
They were engaged—but, oh, well," he gave a very
good imitation of a French shrug, "it is all over now.
Neither of them will get her, and I—I am ruined.
Who will come to the Novella now?"

Adjoining Millefleur's own room was the writing-
room from which the poisoned envelope had been
taken to Miss Blaisdell. Over the little secretary
was the sign, "No woman need be plain who will visit
the Novella," evidently the motto of the place. The
hair-dressing room was next to the little writing-room.
There were manicure rooms, steam-rooms, massage-
rooms, rooms of all descriptions, all bearing mute testimony to the fundamental instinct, the feminine longing for personal beauty.

Though it was late when Kennedy had finished his
investigation, he insisted on going directly to his laboratory. There he pulled out from a corner a sort
of little square table on which was fixed a powerful
light such as might be used for a stereopticon.

"This is a simple little machine," he explained, as
he pasted together the torn bits of the letter which
he had fished out of the scrap-basket, "which detectives use in studying forgeries. I don't know that it
has a name, although it might be called a 'rayograph.'
You see, all you have to do is to lay the thing you wish
to study flat here, and the system of mirrors and lenses
reflects it and enlarges it on a sheet."

He had lowered a rolled-up sheet of white at the

opposite end of the room, and there, in huge characters, stood forth plainly the writing of the note.

"This letter," he resumed, studying the enlargement carefully, "is likely to prove crucial. It's very queer. Collins says he didn't write it, and if he did he surely is a wonder at disguising his hand. I doubt if any one could disguise what the rayograph shows. Now, for instance, this is very important. Do you see how those strokes of the long letters are—well, wobbly? You'd never see that in the original, but when it is enlarged you see how plainly visible the tremors of the hand become? Try as you may, you can't conceal them. The fact is that the writer of this note suffered from a form of heart disease. Now let us look at the copy that Collins made at the Novella."

He placed the copy on the table of the rayograph. It was quite evident that the two had been written by entirely different persons. "I thought he was telling the truth," commented Craig, "by the surprised look on his face the moment I mentioned the note to Miss Blaisdell. Now I know he was. There is no such evidence of heart trouble in his writing as in the other. Of course that's all aside from what a study of the handwriting itself might disclose. They are not similar at all. But there is an important clue there. Find the writer of that note who has heart trouble, and we either have the murderer or some one close to the murderer."

I remembered the tremulousness of the little beauty-doctor, his third-rate artificial acting of fear for the reputation of the Novella, and I must confess

I agreed with O'Connor and Collins that it looked black for him. At one time I had suspected Collins himself, but now I could see perfectly why he had not concealed his anxiety to hush up his connection with the case, while at the same time his instinct as a lawyer, and I had almost added, lover, told him that justice must be done. I saw at once how, accustomed as he was to weigh evidence, he had immediately seen the justification for O'Connor's arrest of the Millefleurs.

"More than that," added Kennedy, after examining the fibres of the paper under a microscope, "all these notes are written on the same kind of paper. That first torn note to Miss Blaisdell was written right in the Novella and left so as to seem to have been sent in from outside."

It was early the following morning when Kennedy roused me with the remark: "I think I'll go up to the hospital. Do you want to come along? We'll stop for Barron on the way. There is a little experiment I want to try on that girl up there."

When we arrived, the nurse in charge of the ward told us that her patient had passed a fairly good night, but that now that the influence of the drug had worn off she was again restless and still repeating the words that she had said over and over before. Nor had she been able to give any clearer account of herself. Apparently she had been alone in the city, for although there was a news item about her in the morning papers, so far no relative or friend had called to identify her.

Kennedy had placed himself directly before her, listening intently to her ravings. Suddenly he managed to fix her eye, as if by a sort of hypnotic influence.

"Agnes!" he called in a sharp tone.

The name seemed to arrest her fugitive attention. Before she could escape from his mental grasp again he added: "Your date-book is full. Aren't you going to the Novella this morning?"

The change in her was something wonderful to see. It was as though she had come out of a trance. She sat up in bed and gazed about blankly.

"Yes, yes, I must go," she cried as if it were the most natural thing in the world. Then she realised the strange surroundings and faces. "Where is my hat—wh-where am I? What has happened?"

"You are all right," soothed Kennedy gently. "Now rest. Try to forget everything for a little while, and you will be all right. You are among friends."

As Kennedy led us out she fell back, now physically exhausted, on the pillow.

"I told you, Barron," he whispered, "that there was more to this case than you imagined. Unwittingly you brought me a very important contribution to a case of which the papers are full this morning, the case of the murdered actress, Blanche Blaisdell."

IV

The Beauty Shop

IT was only after a few hours that Kennedy thought it wise to try to question the poor girl at the hospital. Her story was simple enough in itself, but it certainly complicated matters considerably without throwing much light on the case. She had been busy because her day was full, and she had yet to dress the hair of Miss Blaisdell for her play that night. Several times she had been interrupted by impatient messages from the actress in her little dressing-booth, and one of the girls had already demolished the previous hair-dressing in order to save time. Once Agnes had run down for a few seconds to reassure her that she would be through in time.

She had found the actress reading a newspaper, and when Kennedy questioned her she remembered seeing a note lying on the dresser. "Agnes," Miss Blaisdell had said, "will you go into the writing-room and bring me some paper, a pen, and ink? I don't want to go in there this way. There's a dear good girl." Agnes had gone, though it was decidedly no part of her duty as one of the highest paid employés of the Novella. But they all envied the popular actress, and were ready to do anything for her. The next thing she remembered was finishing the coiffure she was working on and going to Miss Blaisdell.

There lay the beautiful actress. The light in the corridor had not been lighted yet, and it was dark. Her lips and mouth seemed literally to shine. Agnes called her, but she did not move; she touched her, but she was cold. Then she screamed and fled. That was the last she remembered.

"The little writing-room," reasoned Kennedy as we left the poor little hair-dresser quite exhausted by her narrative, "was next to the sanctum of Millefleur, where they found that bottle of ether phosphoré and the oil of turpentine. Some one who knew of that note or perhaps wrote it must have reasoned that an answer would be written immediately. That person figured that the note would be the next thing written and that the top envelope of the pile would be used. That person knew of the deadly qualities of too much phosphorised ether, and painted the gummed flap of the envelope with several grains of it. The reasoning held good, for Agnes took the top envelope with its poisoned flap to Miss Blaisdell. No, there was no chance about that. It was all clever, quick reasoning."

"But," I objected, "how about the oil of turpentine?"

"Simply to remove the traces of the poison. I think you will see why that was attempted before we get through."

Kennedy would say no more, but I was content because I could see that he was now ready to put his theories, whatever they were, to the final test. He spent the rest of the day working at the hospital with Dr. Barron, adjusting a very delicate piece of apparatus down in a special room in the basement. I saw it, but I had no idea what it was or what its use might be.

Close to the wall was a stereopticon which shot a beam of light through a tube to which I heard them refer as a galvanometer, about three feet distant. In front of this beam whirled a five-spindled wheel, governed by a chronometer which erred only a second a day. Between the poles of the galvanometer was stretched a slender thread of fused quartz plated with silver, only one one-thousandth of a millimetre in diameter, so tenuous that it could not be seen except in a bright light. It was a thread so slender that it might have been spun by a miscroscopic spider.

Three feet farther away was a camera with a moving film of sensitised material, the turning of which was regulated by a little flywheel. The beam of light focused on the thread in the galvanometer passed to the photographic film, intercepted only by the five spindles of the wheel, which turned once a second, thus marking the picture off into exact fifths of a second. The vibrations of the microscopic quartz thread were enormously magnified on the sensitive film by a lens and resulted in producing a long zigzag, wavy line. The whole was shielded by a wooden hood which permitted no light, except the slender ray, to strike it. The film revolved slowly across the field, its speed regulated by the flywheel, and all moved by an electric motor.

I was quite surprised, then, when Kennedy told me that the final tests which he was arranging were not to be held at the hospital at all, but in his laboratory, the scene of so many of his scientific triumphs over the cleverest of criminals.

While he and Dr. Barron were still fussing with the machine he despatched me on the rather ticklish errand of gathering together all those who had been at the Novella at the time and might possibly prove important in the case.

My first visit was to Hugh Dayton, whom I found in his bachelor apartment on Madison Avenue, apparently waiting for me. One of O'Connor's men had already warned him that any attempt to evade putting in an appearance when he was wanted would be of no avail. He had been shadowed from the moment that it was learned that he was a patient of Millefleur's and had been at the Novella that fatal afternoon. He seemed to realise that escape was impossible. Dayton was one of those typical young fellows, tall, with sloping shoulders and a carefully acquired English manner, whom one sees in scores on Fifth Avenue late in the afternoon. His face, which on the stage was forceful and attractive, was not prepossessing at close range. Indeed it showed too evident marks of excesses, both physical and moral, and his hand was none too steady. Still, he was an interesting personality, if not engaging.

I was also charged with delivering a note to Burke Collins at his office. The purport of it was, I knew, a request couched in language that veiled a summons that Mrs. Collins was of great importance in getting at the truth, and that if he needed an excuse himself for being present it was suggested that he appear as protecting his wife's interests as a lawyer. Kennedy

5

had added that I might tell him orally that he would pass over the scandal as lightly as possible and spare the feelings of both as much as he could. I was rather relieved when this mission was accomplished, for I had expected Collins to demur violently.

Those who gathered that night, sitting expectantly in the little armchairs which Kennedy's students used during his lectures, included nearly every one who could cast any light on what had happened at the Novella. Professor and Madame Millefleur were brought up from the house of detention, to which both O'Connor and Dr. Leslie had insisted that they be sent. Millefleur was still bewailing the fate of the Novella, and Madame had begun to show evidences of lack of the constant beautification which she was always preaching as of the utmost importance to her patrons. Agnes was so far recovered as to be able to be present, though I noticed that she avoided the Millefleurs and sat as far from them as possible.

Burke Collins and Mrs. Collins arrived together. I had expected that there would be an icy coolness if not positive enmity between them. They were not exactly cordial, though somehow I seemed to feel that now that the cause of estrangement was removed a tactful mutual friend might have brought about a reconciliation. Hugh Dayton swaggered in, his nervousness gone or at least controlled. I passed behind him once, and the odour that smote my olfactory sense told me too plainly that he had fortified himself with a stimulant on his way from the apartment to the laboratory. Of course O'Connor and Dr. Leslie were there, though in the background.

It was a silent gathering, and Kennedy did not attempt to relieve the tension even by small talk as he wrapped the forearms of each of us with cloths steeped in a solution of salt. Upon these cloths he placed little plates of German silver to which were attached wires which led back of a screen. At last he was ready to begin.

"The long history of science," he began as he emerged from behind the screen, "is filled with instances of phenomena, noted at first only for their beauty or mystery, which have been later proved to be of great practical value to mankind. A new example is the striking phenomenon of luminescence. Phosphorus, discovered centuries ago, was first merely a curiosity. Now it is used for many practical things, and one of the latest uses is as a medicine. It is a constituent of the body, and many doctors believe that the lack of it causes, and that its presence will cure, many ills. But it is a virulent and toxic drug, and no physician except one who knows his business thoroughly should presume to handle it. Whoever made a practice of using it at the Novella did not know his business, or he would have used it in pills instead of in the nauseous liquid. It is not with phosphorised ether as a medicine that we have to deal in this case. It is with the stuff as a poison, a poison administered by a demon."

Craig shot the word out so that it had its full effect on his little audience. Then he paused, lowered his voice, and resumed on a new subject.

"Up in the Washington Heights Hospital," he went on, "is an apparatus which records the secrets of the human heart. That is no figure of speech, but a cold scientific fact. This machine records every variation of the pulsations of the heart with such exquisite accuracy that it gives Dr. Barron, who is up there now, not merely a diagram of the throbbing organ of each of you seated here in my laboratory a mile away, but a sort of moving-picture of the emotions by which each heart here is swayed. Not only can Dr. Barron diagnose disease, but he can detect love, hate, fear, joy, anger, and remorse. This machine is known as the Einthoven 'string galvanometer,' invented by that famous Dutch physiologist of Leyden."

There was a perceptible movement in our little audience at the thought that the little wires that ran back of the screen from the arms of each were connected with this uncanny instrument so far away.

"It is all done by the electric current that the heart itself generates," pursued Kennedy, hammering home the new and startling idea. "That current is one of the feeblest known to science, for the dynamo that generates it is no ponderous thing of copper wire and steel castings. It is just the heart itself. The heart sends over the wire its own telltale record to the machine which registers it. The thing takes us all the way back to Galvani, who was the first to observe and study animal electricity. The heart makes only one three-thousandth of a volt of electricity at each beat. It would take over two hundred thousand men to light one of these incandescent lamps, two million or more to run a trolley-car. Yet just that slight little current is enough to sway the gossamer strand of quartz fibre up there at what we call the 'heart station.' So fine is this machine that the pulse-tracings produced by the sphygmograph, which I have used in other cases up to this time, are clumsy and inexact."

Again he paused as if to let the fear of discovery sink deep into the minds of all of us.

"This current, as I have said, passes from each one of you in turn over a wire and vibrates a fine quartz fibre up there in unison with each heart here. It is one of the most delicate bits of mechanism ever made, beside which the hairspring of a watch is coarse. Each of you in turn, is being subjected to this test. More than that, the record up there shows not only the beats of the heart but the successive waves of emotion that vary the form of those beats. Every normal individual gives what we call an 'electro-cardiogram,' which follows a certain type. The photographic film on which this is being recorded is ruled so that at the heart station Dr. Barron can read it. There are five waves to each heart-beat, which he letters P, Q, R, S, and T, two below and three above a base line on the film. They have all been found to represent a contraction of a certain portion of the heart. Any change of the height, width, or time of any one of those lines shows that there is some defect or change in the contraction of that part of the heart. Thus Dr. Barron, who has studied this thing carefully, can tell infallibly not only disease but emotion."

It seemed as if no one dared look at his neighbour, as if all were trying vainly to control the beating of their own hearts.

"Now," concluded Kennedy solemnly as if to force the last secret from the wildly beating heart of some one in the room, "it is my belief that the person who had access to the operating-room of the Novella was a person whose nerves were run down, and in addition to any other treatment that person was familiar with the ether phosphoré. This person knew Miss Blaisdell well, saw her there, knew she was there for the purpose of frustrating that person's own dearest hopes. That person wrote her the note, and knowing that she would ask for paper and an envelope in order to answer it, poisoned the flap of the envelope. Phosphorus is a remedy for hysteria, vexatious emotions, want of sympathy, disappointed and concealed affections—but not in the quantities that this person lavished on that flap. Whoever it was, not life, but death, and a ghastly death, was uppermost in that person's thoughts."

Agnes screamed. "I saw him take something and rub it on her lips, and the brightness went away. I —I didn't mean to tell, but, God help me, I must."

"Saw whom?" demanded Kennedy, fixing her eye as he had when he had called her back from aphasia.

"Him—Millefleur—Miller," she sobbed, shrinking back as if the very confession appalled her.

"Yes," added Kennedy coolly, "Miller did try to remove the traces of the poison after he discovered it, in order to protect himself and the reputation of the Novella."

The telephone bell tinkled. Craig seized the receiver.

"Yes, Barron, this is Kennedy. You received the

impulses all right? Good. And have you had time
to study the records? Yes? What's that? Number
seven? All right. I'll see you very soon and go over
the records again with you. Good-bye."

"One word more," he continued, now facing us.
"The normal heart traces its throbs in regular
rhythm. The diseased or overwrought heart throbs
in degrees of irregularity that vary according to the
trouble that affects it, both organic and emotional.
The expert like Barron can tell what each wave
means, just as he can tell what the lines in a spectrum mean. He can see the invisible, hear the inaudible, feel the intangible, with mathematical pre-
cision. Barron has now read the electro-cardiograms.
Each is a picture of the beating of the heart that made
it, and each smallest variation has a meaning to him.
Every passion, every emotion, every disease, is recorded with inexorable truth. The person with murder in his heart cannot hide it from the string galvanometer, nor can that person who wrote the false
note in which the very lines of the letters betray a
diseased heart hide that disease. The doctor tells me
that that person was number—"

Mrs. Collins had risen wildly and was standing before us with blazing eyes. "Yes," she cried, pressing
her hands on her breast as if it were about to burst
and tell the secret before her lips could frame the
words, "yes, I killed her, and I would follow her to
the end of the earth if I had not succeeded. She was
there, the woman who had stolen from me what was
more than life itself. Yes, I wrote the note, I poisoned the envelope. I killed her."

All the intense hatred that she had felt for that other woman in the days that she had vainly striven to equal her in beauty and win back her husband's love broke forth. She was wonderful, magnificent, in her fury. She was passion personified; she was fate, retribution.

Collins looked at his wife, and even he felt the spell. It was not crime that she had done; it was elemental justice.

For a moment she stood, silent, facing Kennedy. Then the colour slowly faded from her cheeks. She reeled.

Collins caught her and imprinted a kiss, the kiss that for years she had longed and striven for again. She looked rather than spoke forgiveness as he held her and showered them on her.

"Before Heaven," I heard him whisper into her ear, "with all my power as a lawyer I will free you from this."

Gently Dr. Leslie pushed him aside and felt her pulse as she dropped limply into the only easy chair in the laboratory.

"O'Connor," he said at length, "all the evidence that we really have hangs on an invisible thread of quartz a mile away. If Professor Kennedy agrees, let us forget what has happened here to-night. I will direct my jury to bring in a verdict of suicide. Collins, take good care of her." He leaned over and whispered so she could not hear. "I wouldn't promise her six weeks otherwise."

I could not help feeling deeply moved as the newly reunited Collinses left the laboratory together. Even the bluff deputy, O'Connor, was touched by it and under the circumstances did what seemed to him his higher duty with a tact of which I had believed him scarcely capable. Whatever the ethics of the case, he left it entirely to Dr. Leslie's coroner's jury to determine.

Burke Collins was already making hasty preparations for the care of his wife so that she might have the best medical attention to prolong her life for the few weeks or months before nature exacted the penalty which was denied the law.

"That's a marvellous piece of apparatus," I remarked, standing over the connections with the string galvanometer, after all had gone. "Just suppose the case had fallen into the hands of some of these old-fashioned detectives—"

"I hate post-mortems—on my own cases," interrupted Kennedy brusquely. "To-morrow will be time enough to clear up this mess. Meanwhile, let us get this thing out of our minds."

He clapped his hat on his head decisively and deliberately walked out of the laboratory, starting off at a brisk pace in the moonlight across the campus to the avenue where now the only sound was the noisy rattle of an occasional trolley car.

How long we walked I do not know. But I do know that for genuine relaxation after a long period of keen mental stress, there is nothing like physical exercise. We turned into our apartment, roused the sleepy hall-boy, and rode up.

"I suppose people think I never rest," remarked Kennedy, carefully avoiding any reference to the exciting events of the past two days. "But I do. Like every one else, I have to. When I am working hard on a case—well, I have my own violent reaction against it—more work of a different kind. Others choose white lights, red wines and blue feelings after-wards. But I find, when I reach that state, that the best anti-toxin is something that will chase the last case from your brain by getting you in trim for the next unexpected event."

He had sunk into an easy chair where he was run-ning over in his mind his own plans for the morrow.

"Just now I must recuperate by doing no work at all," he went on slowly undressing. "That walk was just what I needed. When the fever of dissipation comes on again, I'll call on you. You won't miss any-thing, Walter."

Like the famous Finnegan, however, he was on again and gone again in the morning. This time I had no misgivings, although I should have liked to accompany him, for on the library table he had scrawled a little note, "Studying East Side to-day. Will keep in touch with you. Craig."

My daily task of transcribing my notes was com-pleted and I thought I would run down to the *Star* to let the editor know how I was getting along on my assignment.

I had scarcely entered the door when the office boy thrust a message into my hand. It stopped me even before I had a chance to get as far as my own desk. It was from Kennedy at the laboratory and bore a time stamp that showed that it must have been re-ceived only a few minutes before I came in.

"Meet me at the Grand Central," it read, "immediately."

Without going further into the office, I turned and dropped down in the elevator to the subway. As quickly as an express could take me, I hurried up to the new station.

"Where away?" I asked breathlessly, as Craig met me at the entrance through which he had reasoned I would come. "The coast or Down East?"

"Woodrock," he replied quickly, taking my arm and dragging me down a ramp to the train that was just leaving for that fashionable suburb.

"Well," I queried eagerly, as the train started. "Why all this secrecy?"

"I had a caller this afternoon," he began, running his eye over the other passengers to see if we were observed. "She is going back on this train. I am not to recognise her at the station, but you and I are to walk to the end of the platform and enter a limousine bearing that number."

He produced a card on the back of which was written a number in six figures. Mechanically I glanced at the name as he handed the card to me. Craig was watching intently the expression on my face as I read, "Miss Yvonne Brixton."

"Since when were you admitted into society?" I gasped, still staring at the name of the daughter of the millionaire banker, John Brixton.

"She came to tell me that her father is in a virtual state of siege, as it were, up there in his own house," explained Kennedy in an undertone, "so much so that, apparently, she is the only person he felt he dared trust with a message to summon me. Practically everything he says or does is spied on; he can't even telephone without what he says being known."

"Siege?" I repeated incredulously. "Impossible. Why, only this morning I was reading about his negotiations with a foreign syndicate of bankers from southeastern Europe for a ten-million-dollar loan to relieve the money stringency there. Surely there must be some mistake in all this. In fact, as I recall it, one of the foreign bankers who is trying to interest him is that Count Wachtmann who, everybody says, is engaged to Miss Brixton, and is staying at the house at Woodrock. Craig, are you sure nobody is hoaxing you?"

"Read that," he replied laconically, handing me a piece of thin letter-paper such as is often used for foreign correspondence. "Such letters have been coming to Mr. Brixton, I understand, every day."

The letter was in a cramped foreign scrawl:

JOHN BRIXTON,
      Woodrock, New York.
   American dollars must not endanger the peace of Europe. Be warned in time. In the name of liberty and progress we have raised the standard of conflict without truce or quarter against reaction. If you and the American bankers associated with you take up these bonds you will never live to receive the first payment of interest.
                  THE RED BROTHERHOOD OF THE BALKANS.

I looked up inquiringly. "What is the Red Brotherhood?" I asked.

"As nearly as I can make out," replied Kennedy, "it seems to be a sort of international secret society.

I believe it preaches the gospel of terror and violence in the cause of liberty and union of some of the peoples of southeastern Europe. Anyhow, it keeps its secrets well. The identity of the members is a mystery, as well as the source of its funds, which, it is said, are immense."

"And they operate so secretly that Brixton can trust no one about him?" I asked.

"I believe he is ill," explained Craig. "At any rate, he evidently suspects almost every one about him except his daughter. As nearly as I could gather, however, he does not suspect Wachtmann himself. Miss Brixton seemed to think that there were some enemies of the Count at work. Her father is a secretive man. Even to her, the only message he would entrust was that he wanted to see me immediately."

At Woodrock we took our time in getting off the train. Miss Brixton, a tall, dark-haired, athletic girl just out of college, had preceded us, and as her own car shot out from the station platform we leisurely walked down and entered another bearing the number she had given Kennedy.

We seemed to be expected at the house. Hardly had we been admitted through the door from the porte-cochère, than we were led through a hall to a library at the side of the house. From the library we entered another door, then down a flight of steps which must have brought us below an open courtyard on the outside, under a rim of the terrace in front of the house for a short distance to a point where we descended three more steps.

At the head of these three steps was a great steel

and iron door with heavy bolts and a combination lock of a character ordinarily found only on a safe in a banking institution.

The door was opened, and we descended the steps, going a little farther in the same direction away from the side of the house. Then we turned at a right angle facing toward the back of the house but well to one side of it. It must have been, I figured out later, underneath the open courtyard. A few steps farther brought us to a fair-sized, vaulted room.

V

The Phantom Circuit

BRIXTON had evidently been waiting impatiently for our arrival. "Mr. Kennedy?" he inquired, adding quickly without waiting for an answer: "I am glad to see you. I suppose you have noticed the precautions we are taking against intruders? Yet it seems to be all of no avail. I can not be alone even here. If a telephone message comes to me over my private wire, if I talk with my own office in the city, it seems that it is known. I don't know what to make of it. It is terrible. I don't know what to expect next."

Brixton had been standing beside a huge mahogany desk as we entered. I had seen him before at a distance as a somewhat pompous speaker at banquets and the cynosure of the financial district. But there was something different about his looks now. He seemed to have aged, to have grown yellower. Even the whites of his eyes were yellow.

I thought at first that perhaps it might be the effect of the light in the centre of the room, a huge affair set in the ceiling in a sort of inverted hemisphere of glass, concealing and softening the rays of a powerful incandescent bulb which it enclosed. It was not the light that gave him the altered appearance, as I concluded from catching a casual confirmatory glance of perplexity from Kennedy himself.

"My personal physician says I am suffering from jaundice," explained Brixton. Rather than seeming to be offended at our notice of his condition he seemed to take it as a good evidence of Kennedy's keenness that he had at once hit on one of the things that were weighing on Brixton's own mind. "I feel pretty badly, too. Curse it," he added bitterly, "coming at a time when it is absolutely necessary that I should have all my strength to carry through a negotiation that is only a beginning, important not so much for myself as for the whole world. It is one of the first times New York bankers have had a chance to engage in big dealings in that part of the world. I suppose Yvonne has shown you one of the letters I am receiving?"

He rustled a sheaf of them which he drew from a drawer of his desk, and continued, not waiting for Kennedy even to nod:

"Here are a dozen or more of them. I get one or two every day, either here or at my town house or at the office."

Kennedy had moved forward to see them.

"One moment more," Brixton interrupted, still holding them. "I shall come back to the letters. That is not the worst. I've had threatening letters before. Have you noticed this room?"

We had both seen and been impressed by it.

"Let me tell you more about it," he went on. "It was designed especially to be, among other things, absolutely soundproof."

We gazed curiously about the strong room. It was beautifully decorated and furnished. On the walls was a sort of heavy, velvety green wall-paper. Exquisite hangings were draped about, and on the floor were thick rugs. In all I noticed that the prevailing tint was green.

"I had experiments carried out," he explained languidly, "with the object of discovering methods and means for rendering walls and ceilings capable of effective resistance to sound transmission. One of the methods devised involved the use under the ceiling or parallel to the wall, as the case might be, of a network of wire stretched tightly by means of pulleys in the adjacent walls and not touching at any point the surface to be protected against sound. Upon the wire network is plastered a composition formed of strong glue, plaster of Paris, and granulated cork, so as to make a flat slab, between which and the wall or ceiling is a cushion of confined air. The method is good in two respects: the absence of contact between the protective and protected surfaces and the colloid nature of the composition used. I have gone into the thing at length because it will make all the more remarkable what I am about to tell you."

Kennedy had been listening attentively. As Brixton proceeded I had noticed Kennedy's nostrils dilating almost as if he were a hound and had scented his quarry. I sniffed, too. Yes, there was a faint odour, almost as if of garlic in the room. It was unmistakable. Craig was looking about curiously, as if to discover a window by which the odour might have entered. Brixton, with his eyes following keenly every move, noticed him.

6

"More than that," he added quickly, "I have had the most perfect system of modern ventilation installed in this room, absolutely independent from that in the house."

Kennedy said nothing.

"A moment ago, Mr. Kennedy, I saw you and Mr. Jameson glancing up at the ceiling. Sound-proof as this room is, or as I believe it to be, I—I hear voices, voices from—not through, you understand, but from —that very ceiling. I do not hear them now. It is only at certain times when I am alone. They repeat the words in some of these letters—'You must not take up those bonds. You must not endanger the peace of the world. You will never live to get the interest.' Over and over I have heard such sentences spoken in this very room. I have rushed out and up the corridor. There has been no one there. I have locked the steel door. Still I have heard the voices. And it is absolutely impossible that a human being could get close enough to say them without my knowing and finding out where he is."

Kennedy betrayed by not so much as the motion of a muscle even a shade of a doubt of Brixton's incredible story. Whether because he believed it or because he was diplomatic, Craig took the thing at its face value. He moved a blotter so that he could stand on the top of Brixton's desk in the centre of the room. Then he unfastened and took down the glass hemisphere over the light.

"It is an Osram lamp of about a hundred candle-power, I should judge," he observed.

Apparently he had satisfied himself that there was

nothing concealed in the light itself. Laboriously, with such assistance as the memory of Mr. Brixton could give, he began tracing out the course of both the electric light and telephone wires that led down into the den.

Next came a close examination of the ceiling and side walls, the floor, the hangings, the pictures, the rugs, everything. Kennedy was tapping here and there all over the wall, as if to discover whether there was any such hollow sound as a cavity might make. There was none.

A low exclamation from him attracted my attention, though it escaped Brixton. His tapping had raised the dust from the velvety wall-paper wherever he had tried it. Hastily, from a corner where it would not be noticed, he pulled off a piece of the paper and stuffed it into his pocket. Then followed a hasty examination of the intake of the ventilating apparatus.

Apparently satisfied with his examination of things in the den, Craig now prepared to trace out the course of the telephone and light wires in the house. Brixton excused himself, asking us to join him in the library up-stairs after Craig had completed his investigation.

Nothing was discovered by tracing the lines back, as best we could, from the den. Kennedy therefore began at the other end, and having found the points in the huge cellar of the house where the main trunk and feed wires entered, he began a systematic search in that direction.

A separate line led, apparently, to the den, and

where this line feeding the Osram lamp passed near a dark storeroom in a corner Craig examined more closely than ever. Seemingly his search was rewarded, for he dived into the dark storeroom and commenced lighting matches furiously to discover what was there.

"Look, Walter," he exclaimed, holding a match so that I could see what he had unearthed. There, in a corner concealed by an old chest of drawers, stood a battery of five storage-cells connected with an instrument that looked very much like a telephone transmitter, a rheostat, and a small transformer coil.

"I suppose this is a direct-current lighting circuit," he remarked, thoughtfully regarding his find. "I think I know what this is, all right. Any amateur could do it, with a little knowledge of electricity and a source of direct current. The thing is easily constructed, the materials are common, and a wonderfully complicated result can be obtained. What's this?"

He had continued to poke about in the darkness as he was speaking. In another corner he had discovered two ordinary telephone receivers.

"Connected up with something, too, by George!" he ejaculated.

Evidently some one had tapped the regular telephone wires running into the house, had run extensions into the little storeroom, and was prepared to overhear everything that was said either to or by those in the house.

Further examination disclosed that there were two separate telephone systems running into Brixton's house. One, with its many extensions, was used by the household and by the housekeeper; the other was the private wire which led, ultimately, down into Brixton's den. No sooner had he discovered it than Kennedy became intensely interested. For the moment he seemed entirely to forget the electric-light wires and became absorbed in tracing out the course of the telephone trunk-line and its extensions. Continued search rewarded him with the discovery that both the household line and the private line were connected by hastily improvised extensions with the two receivers he had discovered in the out-of-the-way corner of a little dark storeroom.

"Don't disturb a thing," remarked Kennedy, cautiously picking up even the burnt matches he had dropped in his hasty search. "We must devise some means of catching the eavesdropper red handed. It has all the marks of being an inside job."

We had completed our investigation of the basement without attracting any attention, and Craig was careful to make it seem that in entering the library we came from the den, not from the cellar. As we waited in the big leather chairs Kennedy was sketching roughly on a sheet of paper the plan of the house, drawing in the location of the various wires.

The door opened. We had expected John Brixton. Instead, a tall, spare foreigner with a close-cropped moustache entered. I knew at once that it must be Count Wachtmann, although I had never seen him.

"Ah, I beg your pardon," he exclaimed in English which betrayed that he had been under good teachers in London. "I thought Miss Brixton was here."

"Count Wachtmann?" interrogated Kennedy, rising.

"The same," he replied easily, with a glance of inquiry at us.

"My friend and I are from the *Star*," said Kennedy.

"Ah! Gentlemen of the press?" He elevated his eyebrows the fraction of an inch. It was so politely contemptuous that I could almost have throttled him.

"We are waiting to see Mr. Brixton," explained Kennedy.

"What is the latest from the Near East?" Wachtmann asked, with the air of a man expecting to hear what he could have told you yesterday if he had chosen.

There was a movement of the portières, and a woman entered. She stopped a moment. I knew it was Miss Brixton. She had recognised Kennedy, but her part was evidently to treat him as a total stranger.

"Who are these men, Conrad?" she asked, turning to Wachtmann.

"Gentlemen of the press, I believe, to see your father, Yvonne," replied the count.

It was evident that it had not been mere newspaper talk about this latest rumored international engagement.

"How did you enjoy it?" he asked, noticing the title of a history which she had come to replace in the library.

"Very well—all but the assassinations and the intrigues," she replied with a little shudder.

He shot a quick, searching look at her face. "They

are a violent people—some of them," he commented quickly.

"You are going into town to-morrow?" I heard him ask Miss Brixton, as they walked slowly down the wide hall to the conservatory a few moments later.

"What do you think of him?" I whispered to Kennedy.

I suppose my native distrust of his kind showed through, for Craig merely shrugged his shoulders. Before he could reply Mr. Brixton joined us.

"There's another one—just came," he ejaculated, throwing a letter down on the library table. It was only a few lines this time:

"The bonds will not be subject to a tax by the government, they say. No—because if there is a war there won't be any government to tax them!"

The note did not appear to interest Kennedy as much as what he had discovered. "One thing is self-evident, Mr. Brixton," he remarked. "Some one inside this house is spying, is in constant communication with a person or persons outside. All the watchmen and Great Danes on the estate are of no avail against the subtle, underground connection that I believe exists. It is still early in the afternoon. I shall make a hasty trip to New York and return after dinner. I should like to watch with you in the den this evening."

"Very well," agreed Brixton. "I shall arrange to have you met at the station and brought here as secretly as I can."

He sighed, as if admitting that he was no longer master of even his own house.

Kennedy was silent during most of our return trip to New York. As for myself, I was deeply mired in an attempt to fathom Wachtmann. He baffled me. However, I felt that if there was indeed some subtle, underground connection between some one inside and some one outside Brixton's house, Craig would prepare an equally subtle method of meeting it on his own account. Very little was said by either of us on the journey up to the laboratory, or on the return to Woodrock. I realised that there was very little excuse for a commuter not to be well informed. I, at least, had plenty of time to exhaust the newspapers I had bought.

Whether or not we returned without being observed, I did not know, but at least we did find that the basement and dark storeroom were deserted, as we cautiously made our way again into the corner where Craig had made his enigmatical discoveries of the afternoon.

While I held a pocket flashlight Craig was busy concealing another instrument of his own in the little storeroom. It seemed to be a little black disk about as big as a watch, with a number of perforated holes in one face. Carelessly he tossed it into the top drawer of the chest under some old rubbish, shut the drawer tight and ran a flexible wire out of the back of the chest. It was a simple matter to lay the wire through some bins next the storeroom and then around to the passageway down to the subterranean den of Brixton. There Craig deposited a little black box about the size of an ordinary kodak.

For an hour or so we sat with Brixton. Neither

of us said anything, and Brixton was uncommunicatively engaged in reading a railroad report. Suddenly a sort of muttering, singing noise seemed to fill the room.

"There it is!" cried Brixton, clapping the book shut and looking eagerly at Kennedy.

Gradually the sound increased in pitch. It seemed to come from the ceiling, not from any particular part of the room, but merely from somewhere overhead. There was no hallucination about it. We all heard. As the vibrations increased it was evident that they were shaping themselves into words.

Kennedy had grasped the black box the moment the sound began and was holding two black rubber disks to his ears.

At last the sound from overhead became articulate. It was weird, uncanny. Suddenly a voice said distinctly: "Let American dollars beware. They will not protect American daughters."

Craig had dropped the two ear-pieces and was gazing intently at the Osram lamp in the ceiling. Was he, too, crazy?

"Here, Mr. Brixton, take these two receivers of the detectaphone," said Kennedy. "Tell me whether you can recognise the voice."

"Why, it's familiar," he remarked slowly. "I can't place it, but I've heard it before. Where is it? What is this thing, anyhow?"

"It is some one hidden in the storeroom in the basement," answered Craig. "He is talking into a very sensitive telephone transmitter and—"

"But the voice—here?" interrupted Brixton impatiently.

Kennedy pointed to the incandescent lamp in the ceiling. "The incandescent lamp," he said, "is not always the mute electrical apparatus it is supposed to be. Under the right conditions it can be made to speak exactly as the famous 'speaking-arc,' as it was called by Professor Duddell, who investigated it. Both the arc-light and the metal-filament lamp can be made to act as telephone receivers."

It seemed unbelievable, but Kennedy was positive. "In the case of the speaking-arc or 'arcophone,' as it might be called," he continued, "the fact that the electric arc is sensitive to such small variations in the current over a wide range of frequency has suggested that a direct-current arc might be used as a telephone receiver. All that is necessary is to superimpose a microphone current on the main arc current, and the arc reproduces sounds and speech distinctly, loud enough to be heard several feet. Indeed, the arc could be used as a transmitter, too, if a sensitive receiver replaced the transmitter at the other end. The things needed are an arc-lamp, an impedance coil, or small transformer-coil, a rheostat, and a source of energy. The alternating current is not adapted to reproduce speech, but the ordinary direct current is. Of course, the theory isn't half as simple as the apparatus I have described."

He had unscrewed the Osram lamp. The talking ceased immediately.

"Two investigators named Ort and Ridger have used a lamp like this as a receiver," he continued.

"They found that words spoken were reproduced in the lamp. The telephonic current variations superposed on the current passing through the lamp produce corresponding variations of heat in the filament, which are radiated to the glass of the bulb, causing it to expand and contract proportionately, and thus transmitting vibrations to the exterior air. Of course, in sixteen- and thirty-two-candle-power lamps the glass is too thick, and the heat variations are too feeble."

Who was it whose voice Brixton had recognised as familiar over Kennedy's hastily installed detectaphone? Certainly he must have been a scientist of no mean attainment. That did not surprise me, for I realised that from that part of Europe where this mystical Red Brotherhood operated some of the most famous scientists of the world had sprung.

A hasty excursion into the basement netted us nothing. The place was deserted.

We could only wait. With parting instructions to Brixton in the use of the detectaphone we said good night, were met by a watchman and escorted as far as the lodge safely.

Only one remark did Kennedy make as we settled ourselves for the long ride in the accommodation train to the city. "That warning means that we have two people to protect—both Brixton and his daughter."

Speculate as I might, I could find no answer to the mystery, nor to the question, which was also unsolved, as to the queer malady of Brixton himself, which his physician diagnosed as jaundice.

VI

The Detectaphone

FAR after midnight though it had been when we
had at last turned in at our apartment, Kennedy was up even earlier than usual in the morning.
I found him engrossed in work at the laboratory.

"Just in time to see whether I'm right in my guess
about the illness of Brixton," he remarked, scarcely
looking up at me.

He had taken a flask with a rubber stopper.
Through one hole in it was fitted a long funnel;
through another ran a glass tube, connecting with a
large U-shaped drying-tube filled with calcium chlo-
ride, which in turn connected with a long open tube
with an up-turned end.

Into the flask Craig dropped some pure granulated
zinc coated with platinum. Then he covered it with
dilute sulphuric acid through the funnel tube.
"That forms hydrogen gas," he explained, "which
passes through the drying-tube and the ignition-tube.
Wait a moment until all the air is expelled from the
tubes."

He lighted a match and touched it to the open up-
turned end. The hydrogen, now escaping freely, was
ignited with a pale-blue flame.

Next, he took the little piece of wall-paper I had
seen him tear off in the den, scraped off some powder

from it, dissolved it, and poured it into the funnel-tube.

Almost immediately the pale, bluish flame turned to bluish white, and white fumes were formed. In the ignition-tube a sort of metallic deposit appeared. Quickly he made one test after another. I sniffed. There was an unmistakable smell of garlic in the air.

"Arseniureted hydrogen," commented Craig. "This is the Marsh test for arsenic. That wall-paper in Brixton's den has been loaded down with arsenic, probably Paris green or Schweinfurth green, which is aceto-arsenite of copper. Every minute he is there he is breathing arseniureted hydrogen. Some one has contrived to introduce free hydrogen into the intake of his ventilator. That acts on the arsenic compounds in the wall-paper and hangings and sets free the gas. I thought I knew the smell the moment I got a whiff of it. Besides, I could tell by the jaundiced look of his face that he was being poisoned. His liver was out of order, and arsenic seems to accumulate in the liver."

"Slowly poisoned by minute quantities of gas," I repeated in amazement. "Some one in that Red Brotherhood is a diabolical genius. Think of it—poisoned wall-paper!"

It was still early in the forenoon when Kennedy excused himself, and leaving me to my own devices disappeared on one of his excursions into the underworld of the foreign settlements on the East Side. About the middle of the afternoon he reappeared. As far as I could learn all that he had found out was that the famous, or rather infamous, Professor Michael Kumanova, one of the leaders of the Red Brotherhood, was known to be somewhere in this country.

We lost no time in returning again to Woodrock late that afternoon. Craig hastened to warn Brixton of his peril from the contaminated atmosphere of the den, and at once a servant was set to work with a vacuum cleaner.

Carefully Craig reconnoitred the basement where the eavesdropping storeroom was situated. Finding it deserted, he quickly set to work connecting the two wires of the general household telephone with what looked very much like a seamless iron tube, perhaps six inches long and three inches in diameter. Then he connected the tube also with the private wire of Brixton in a similar manner.

"This is a special repeating-coil of high efficiency," he explained in answer to my inquiry. "It is absolutely balanced as to resistance, number of turns, and everything. I shall run this third line from the coil into Brixton's den, and then, if you like, you can accompany me on a little excursion down to the village where I am going to install another similar coil between the two lines at the local telephone central station opposite the railroad."

Brixton met us about eight o'clock that night in his now renovated den. Apparently, even the little change from uncertainty to certainty so far had had a tonic effect on him. I had, however, almost given up the illusion that it was possible for us to be even in the den without being watched by an unseen eye. It seemed to me that to one who could conceive of talking through an incandescent lamp seeing, even through steel and masonry, was not impossible.

Kennedy had brought with him a rectangular box of oak, in one of the large faces of which were two square holes. As he replaced the black camera-like box of the detectaphone with this oak box he remarked: "This is an intercommunicating telephone arrangement of the detectaphone. You see, it is more sensitive than anything of the sort ever made before. The arrangement of these little square holes is such as to make them act as horns or magnifiers of a double receiver. We can all hear at once what is going on by using this machine."

We had not been waiting long before a peculiar noise seemed to issue from the detectaphone. It was as though a door had been opened and shut hastily. Some one had evidently entered the storeroom. A voice called up the railroad station and asked for Michael Kronski, Count Wachtmann's chauffeur.

"It is the voice I heard last night," exclaimed Brixton. "By the Lord Harry, do you know, it is Janeff the engineer who has charge of the steam heating, the electric bells, and everything of the sort around the place. My own engineer—I'll land the fellow in jail before I'll—"

Kennedy raised his hand. "Let us hear what he has to say," remonstrated Craig calmly. "I suppose you have wondered why I didn't just go down there last night and grab the fellow. Well, you see now. It is my invariable rule to get the man highest up. This fellow is only one tool. Arrest him, and as

likely as not we should allow the big criminal to escape."

"Hello, Kronski!" came over the detectaphone.
"This is Janeff. How are things going?"

Wachtmann's chauffeur must have answered that
everything was all right.

"You knew that they had discovered the poisoned
wall-paper?" asked Janeff.

A long parley followed. Finally, Janeff repeated
what apparently had been his instructions. "Now,
let me see," he said. "You want me to stay here until the last minute so that I can overhear whether any
alarm is given for her? All right. You're sure it
is the nine-o'clock train she is due on? Very well.
I shall meet you at the ferry across the Hudson. I'll
start from here as soon as I hear the train come in.
We'll get the girl this time. That will bring Brixton to terms sure. You're right. Even if we fail
this time, we'll succeed later. Don't fail me. I'll
be at the ferry as soon as I can get past the guards
and join you. There isn't a chance of an alarm from
the house. I'll cut all the wires the last thing before
I leave. Good-bye."

All at once it dawned on me what they were planning—the kidnapping of Brixton's only daughter, to
hold her, perhaps, as a hostage until he did the bid-
ding of the gang. Wachtmann's chauffeur was doing it and using Wachtmann's car, too. Was Wachtmann a party to it?

What was to be done? I looked at my watch. It
was already only a couple of minutes of nine, when
the train would be due.

"If we could seize that fellow in the closet and start for the station immediately we might save Yvonne," cried Brixton, starting for the door.

"And if they escape you make them more eager than ever to strike a blow at you and yours," put in Craig coolly. "No, let us get this thing straight. I didn't think it was as serious as this, but I'm prepared to meet any emergency."

"But, man," shouted Brixton, "you don't suppose anything in the world counts beside her, do you?"

"Exactly the point," urged Craig. "Save her and capture them—both at once."

"How can you?" fumed Brixton. "If you attempt to telephone from here, that fellow Janeff will overhear and give a warning."

Regardless of whether Janeff was listening or not, Kennedy was eagerly telephoning to the Woodrock central down in the village. He was using the transmitter and receiver that were connected with the iron tube which he had connected to the two regular house lines.

"Have the ferry held at any cost," he was ordering. "Don't let the next boat go out until Mr. Brixton gets there, under any circumstances. Now put that to them straight, central. You know Mr. Brixton has just a little bit of influence around here, and somebody's head will drop if they let that boat go out before he gets there."

"Humph!" ejaculated Brixton. "Much good that will do. Why, I suppose our friend Janeff down in the storeroom knows it all now. Come on, let's grab him."

7

Nevertheless there was no sound from the detecta-. phone which would indicate that he had overheard and was spreading the alarm. He was there yet, for we could hear him clear his throat once or twice.

"No," replied Kennedy calmly, "he knows nothing about it. I didn't use any ordinary means to prepare against the experts who have brought this situation about. That message you heard me send went out over what we call the 'phantom circuit.'"

"The phantom circuit?" repeated Brixton, chafing at the delay.

"Yes, it seems fantastic at first, I suppose," pursued Kennedy calmly; "but, after all, it is in accordance with the laws of electricity. It's no use fretting and fuming, Mr. Brixton. If Janeff can wait, we'll have to do so, too. Suppose we should start and this Kronski should change his plans at the last minute? How would we find it out? By telepathy? Believe me, sir, it is better to wait here a minute and trust to the phantom circuit than to mere chance."

"But suppose he should cut the line," I put in.

Kennedy smiled. "I have provided for that, Walter, in the way I installed the thing. I took good care that we could not be cut off that way. We can hear everything ourselves, but we cannot be overheard. He knows nothing. You see, I took advantage of the fact that additional telephones or so-called phantom lines can be superposed on existing physical lines. It is possible to obtain a third circuit from two similar metallic circuits by using for each side of this third circuit the two wires of each of the other circuits in multiple. All three circuits are independent, too.

"The third telephone current enters the wires of the first circuit, as it were, and returns along the wires of the second circuit. There are several ways of doing it. One is to use retardation or choke-coils bridged across the two metallic circuits at both ends, with taps taken from the middle points of each. But the more desirable method is the one you saw me install this afternoon. I introduced repeating-coils into the circuits at both ends. Technically, the third circuit is then taken off from the mid-points of the secondaries or line windings of these repeating coils.

"The current on a long-distance line is alternating in character, and it passes readily through a repeating-coil. The only effect it has on the transmission is slightly reducing the volume. The current passes into the repeating-coil, then divides and passes through the two line wires. At the other end the halves balance, so to speak. Thus, currents passing over a phantom circuit don't set up currents in the terminal apparatus of the side circuits. Consequently, a conversation carried on over the phantom circuit will not be heard in either side circuit, nor does a conversation on one side circuit affect the phantom. We could all talk at once without interfering with each other."

"At any other time I should be more than interested," remarked Brixton grimly, curbing his impatience to be doing something.

"I appreciate that, sir," rejoined Kennedy. "Ah, here it is. I have the central down in the village.

Yes? They will hold the boat for us? Good.
Thank you. The nine-o'clock train is five minutes
late? Yes—what? Count Wachtmann's car is
there? Oh, yes, the train is just pulling in. I see.
Miss Brixton has entered his car alone. What's
that? His chauffeur has started the car without
waiting for the Count, who is coming down the platform?"

Instantly Kennedy was on his feet. He was dashing up the corridor and the stairs from the den and
down into the basement to the little storeroom.

We burst into the place. It was empty. Janeff
had cut the wires and fled. There was not a moment
to lose. Craig hastily made sure that he had not discovered or injured the phantom circuit.

"Call the fastest car you have in your garage, Mr.
Brixton," ordered Kennedy. "Hello, hello, central!
Get the lodge at the Brixton estate. Tell them if
they see the engineer Janeff going out to stop him.
Alarm the watchman and have the dogs ready.
Catch him at any cost, dead or alive."

A moment later Brixton's car raced around, and
we piled in and were off like a whirlwind. Already
we could see lights moving about and hear the baying
of dogs. Personally, I wouldn't have given much for
Janeff's chances of escape.

As we turned the bend in the road just before we
reached the ferry, we almost ran into two cars standing before the ferry house. It looked as though one
had run squarely in front of the other and blocked
it off. In the slip the ferry boat was still steaming
and waiting.

Beside the wrecked car a man was lying on the ground groaning, while another man was quieting a girl whom he was leading to the waiting-room of the ferry.

Brixton, weak though he was from his illness, leaped out of our car almost before we stopped and caught the girl in his arms.

"Father!" she exclaimed, clinging to him.

"What's this?" he demanded sternly, eying the man. It was Wachtmann himself.

"Conrad saved me from that chauffeur of his," explained Miss Brixton. "I met him on the train, and we were going to ride up to the house together. But before Conrad could get into the car this fellow, who had the engine running, started it. Conrad jumped into another car that was waiting at the station. He overtook us and dodged in front so as to cut the chauffeur off from the ferry."

"Curse that villain of a chauffeur," muttered Wachtmann, looking down at the wounded man.

"Do you know who he is?" asked Craig with a searching glance at Wachtmann's face.

"I ought to. His name is Kronski, and a blacker devil an employment bureau never furnished."

"Kronski? No," corrected Kennedy. "It is Professor Kumanova, whom you perhaps have heard of as a leader of the Red Brotherhood, one of the cleverest scientific criminals who ever lived. I think you'll have no more trouble negotiating your loan or your love affair, Count," added Craig, turning on his heel.

He was in no mood to receive the congratulations of the supercilious Wachtmann. As far as Craig was concerned, the case was finished, although I fancied from a flicker of his eye as he made some passing reference to the outcome that when he came to send in a bill to Brixton for his services he would not forget the high eyebrowed Count.

I followed in silence as Craig climbed into the Brixton car and explained to the banker that it was imperative that he should get back to the city immediately. Nothing would do but that the car must take us all the way back, while Brixton summoned another from the house for himself.

The ride was accomplished swiftly in record time. Kennedy said little. Apparently the exhilaration of the on-rush of cool air was quite in keeping with his mood, though for my part, I should have preferred something a little more relaxing of the nervous tension.

"We've been at it five days, now," I remarked wearily as I dropped into an easy chair in our own quarters. "Are you going to keep up this debauch?"

Kennedy laughed.

"No," he said with a twinkle of scientific mischief, "no, I'm going to sleep it off."

"Thank heaven!" I muttered.

"Because," he went on seriously, "that case interrupted a long series of tests I am making on the sensitiveness of selenium to light, and I want to finish them up soon. There's no telling when I shall be called on to use the information."

I swallowed hard. He really meant it. He was laying out more work for himself.

Next morning I fully expected to find that he had

gone. Instead he was preparing for what he called a quiet day in the laboratory.

"Now for some *real* work," he smiled. "Sometimes, Walter, I feel that I ought to give up this outside activity and devote myself entirely to research. It is so much more important."

I could only stare at him and reflect on how often men wanted to do something other than the very thing that nature had evidently intended them to do, and on how fortunate it was that we were not always free agents.

He set out for the laboratory and I determined that as long as he would not stop working, neither would I. I tried to write. Somehow I was not in the mood. I wrote *at* my story, but succeeded only in making it more unintelligible. I was in no fit condition for it.

It was late in the afternoon. I had made up my mind to use force, if necessary, to separate Kennedy from his study of selenium. My idea was that anything from the Metropolitan to the "movies" would do him good, and I had almost carried my point when a big, severely plain black foreign limousine pulled up with a rush at the laboratory door. A large man in a huge fur coat jumped out and the next moment strode into the room. He needed no introduction, for we recognised at once J. Perry Spencer, one of the foremost of American financiers and a trustee of the university.

With that characteristic directness which I have always thought accounted in large measure for his success, he wasted scarcely a word in coming straight

to the object of his visit. "Professor Kennedy," he
began, chewing his cigar and gazing about with evident interest at the apparatus Craig had collected
in his warfare of science with crime, "I have dropped
in here as a matter of patriotism. I want you to preserve to America those masterpieces of art and liter-
ature which I have collected all over the world during
many years. They are the objects of one of the most
curious pieces of vandalism of which I have ever
heard. Professor Kennedy," he concluded earnestly, "could I ask you to call on Dr. Hugo Lith,
the curator of my private museum, as soon as you can
possibly find it convenient?"

"Most assuredly, Mr. Spencer," replied Craig, with
a whimsical side glance at me that told without words
that this was better relaxation to him than either the
Metropolitan or the "movies." "I shall be glad to
see Dr. Lith at any time—right now, if it is convenient to him."

The millionaire connoisseur consulted his watch.
"Lith will be at the museum until six, at least. Yes,
we can catch him there. I have a dinner engagement
at seven myself. I can give you half an hour of the
time before then. If you're ready, just jump into
the car, both of you."

The museum to which he referred was a handsome
white marble building, in Renaissance, fronting on a
side street just off Fifth Avenue and in the rear of
the famous Spencer house, itself one of the show
places of that wonderful thoroughfare. Spencer had
built the museum at great cost simply to house those
treasures which were too dear to him to entrust to a

public institution. It was in the shape of a rectangle and planned with special care as to the lighting.

Dr. Lith, a rather stout, mild-eyed German savant, plunged directly into the middle of things as soon as we had been introduced. "It is a most remarkable affair, gentlemen," he began, placing for us chairs that must have been hundreds of years old. "At first it was only those objects in the museum that were green that were touched, like the collection of famous and historic French emeralds. But soon we found it was other things, too, that were missing—old Roman coins of gold, a collection of watches, and I know not what else until we have gone over the—"

"Where is Miss White?" interrupted Spencer, who had been listening somewhat impatiently.

"In the library, sir. Shall I call her?"

"No, I will go myself. I want her to tell her experience to Professor Kennedy exactly as she told it to me. Explain while I am gone how impossible it would be for a visitor to do one, to say nothing of all, of the acts of vandalism we have discovered."

VII

The Green Curse

THE American Medici disappeared into his main library, where Miss White was making a minute examination to determine what damage had been done in the realm over which she presided.

"Apparently every book with a green binding has been mutilated in some way," resumed Dr. Lith, "but that was only the beginning. Others have suffered, too, and some are even gone. It is impossible that any visitor could have done it. Only a few personal friends of Mr. Spencer are ever admitted here, and they are never alone. No, it is weird, mysterious."

Just then Spencer returned with Miss White. She was an extremely attractive girl, slight of figure, but with an air about her that all the imported gowns in New York could not have conferred. They were engaged in animated conversation, so much in contrast with the bored air with which Spencer had listened to Dr. Lith that even I noticed that the connoisseur was completely obliterated in the man, whose love of beauty was by no means confined to the inanimate. I wondered if it was merely his interest in her story that impelled Spencer. The more I watched the girl the more I was convinced that she knew that she was interesting to the millionaire.

"For example," Dr. Lith was saying, "the famous

collection of emeralds which has disappeared has always been what you Americans call 'hoodooed.' They have always brought ill luck, and, like many things of the sort to which superstition attaches, they have been 'banked,' so to speak, by their successive owners in museums."

"Are they salable; that is, could any one dispose of the emeralds or the other curios with reasonable safety and at a good price?"

"Oh, yes, yes," hastened Dr. Lith, "not as collections, but separately. The emeralds alone cost fifty thousand dollars. I believe Mr. Spencer bought them for Mrs. Spencer some years before she died. She did not care to wear them, however, and had them placed here."

I thought I noticed a shade of annoyance cross the face of the magnate. "Never mind that," he interrupted. "Let me introduce Miss White. I think you will find her story one of the most uncanny you have ever heard."

He had placed a chair for her and, still addressing us but looking at her, went on: "It seems that the morning the vandalism was first discovered she and Dr. Lith at once began a thorough search of the building to ascertain the extent of the depredations. The search lasted all day, and well into the night. I believe it was midnight before you finished?"

"It was almost twelve," began the girl, in a musical voice that was too Parisian to harmonize with her plain Anglo-Saxon name, "when Dr. Lith was down here in his office checking off the objects in the catalogue which were either injured or missing. I had been working in the library. The noise of something like a shade flapping in the wind attracted my attention. I listened. It seemed to come from the art-gallery, a large room up-stairs where some of the greatest masterpieces in this country are hung. I hurried up there.

"Just as I reached the door a strange feeling seemed to come over me that I was not alone in that room. I fumbled for the electric light switch, but in my nervousness could not find it. There was just enough light in the room to make out objects indistinctly. I thought I heard a low, moaning sound from an old Flemish copper ewer near me. I had heard that it was supposed to groan at night."

She paused and shuddered at her recollection, and looked about as if grateful for the flood of electric light that now illuminated everything. Spencer reached over and touched her arm to encourage her to go on. She did not seem to resent the touch.

"Opposite me, in the middle of the open floor," she resumed, her eyes dilated and her breath coming and going rapidly, "stood the mummy-case of Ka, an Egyptian priestess of Thebes, I think. The case was empty, but on the lid was painted a picture of the priestess! Such wonderful eyes! They seem to pierce right through your very soul. Often in the daytime I have stolen off to look at them. But at night—remember the hour of night, too—oh, it was awful, terrible. The lid of the mummy-case moved, yes, really moved, and seemed to float to one side. I could see it. And back of that carved and painted face with the piercing eyes was another face, a real face, real eyes, and they looked out at me with such hatred from the place that I knew was empty—"

She had risen and was facing us with wild terror written on her face as if in appeal for protection against something she was powerless to name. Spencer, who had not taken his hand off her arm, gently pressed her back into the easy chair and finished the story.

"She screamed and fainted. Dr. Lith heard it and rushed up-stairs. There she lay on the floor. The lid of the sarcophagus had really been moved. He saw it. Not a thing else had been disturbed. He carried her down here and revived her, told her to rest for a day or two, but—"

"I cannot, I cannot," she cried. "It is the fascination of the thing. It brings me back here. I dream of it. I thought I saw those eyes the other night. They haunt me. I fear them, and yet I would not avoid them, if it killed me to look. I must meet and defy the power. What is it? Is it a curse four thousand years old that has fallen on me?"

I had heard stories of mummies that rose from their sleep of centuries to tell the fate of some one when it was hanging in the balance, of mummies that groaned and gurgled and fought for breath, frantically beating with their swathed hands in the witching hours of the night. And I knew that the lure of these mummies was so strong for some people that they were drawn irresistibly to look upon and confer with them. Was this a case for the oculists, the spiritualists, the Egyptologists, or for a detective?

"I should like to examine the art gallery, in fact,

go over the whole museum," put in Kennedy in his most matter-of-fact tone.

Spencer, with a glance at his watch, excused himself, nodding to Dr. Lith to show us about, and with a good night to Miss White which was noticeable for its sympathy with her fears, said, "I shall be at the house for another half-hour at least, in case anything really important develops."

A few minutes later Miss White left for the night, with apparent reluctance, and yet, I thought, with just a little shudder as she looked back up the staircase that led to the art-gallery.

Dr. Lith led us into a large vaulted marble hall and up a broad flight of steps, past beautiful carvings and frescoes that I should have liked to stop and admire.

The art-gallery was a long room in the interior and at the top of the building, windowless but lighted by a huge double skylight each half of which must have been some eight or ten feet across. The light falling through this skylight passed through plate glass of marvellous transparency. One looked up at the sky as if through the air itself.

Kennedy ignored the gallery's profusion of priceless art for the time and went directly to the mummy-case of the priestess Ka.

"It has a weird history," remarked Dr. Lith. "No less than seven deaths, as well as many accidents, have been attributed to the malign influence of that greenish yellow coffin. You know the ancient Egyptians used to chant as they buried their sacred dead: 'Woe to him who injures the tomb. The dead shall point out the evildoer to the Devourer of the Under-world. Soul and body shall be destroyed.' "

It was indeed an awesome thing. It represented a woman in the robes of an Egyptian priestess, a woman of medium height, with an inscrutable face. The slanting Egyptian eyes did, as Miss White had said, almost literally stare through you. I am sure that any one possessing a nature at all affected by such things might after a few minutes gazing at them in self-hypnotism really convince himself that the eyes moved and were real. Even as I turned and looked the other way I felt that those penetrating eyes were still looking at me, never asleep, always keen and searching.

There was no awe about Kennedy. He carefully pushed aside the lid and peered inside. I almost expected to see some one in there. A moment later he pulled out his magnifying-glass and carefully examined the interior. At last he was apparently satisfied with his search. He had narrowed his attention down to a few marks on the stone, partly in the thin layer of dust that had collected on the bottom.

"This was a very modern and material reincarnation," he remarked, as he rose. "If I am not mistaken, the apparition wore shoes, shoes with nails in the heels, and nails that are not like those in American shoes. I shall have to compare the marks I have found with marks I have copied from shoe-nails in the wonderful collection of M. Bertillon. Offhand, I should say that the shoes were of French make."

The library having been gone over next without anything attracting Kennedy's attention particularly, he asked about the basement or cellar. Dr. Lith lighted the way, and we descended.

Down there were innumerable huge packing-cases which had just arrived from abroad, full of the latest consignment of art treasures which Spencer had purchased. Apparently Dr. Lith and Miss White had been so engrossed in discovering what damage had been done to the art treasures above that they had not had time to examine the new ones in the basement.

Kennedy's first move was to make a thorough search of all the little grated windows and a door which led out into a sort of little areaway for the removal of ashes and refuse. The door showed no evidence of having been tampered with, nor did any of the windows at first sight. A low exclamation from Kennedy brought us to his side. He had opened one of the windows and thrust his hand out against the grating, which had fallen on the outside pavement with a clang. The bars had been completely and laboriously sawed through, and the whole thing had been wedged back into place so that nothing would be detected at a cursory glance. He was regarding the lock on the window. Apparently it was all right; actually it had been sprung so that it was useless.

"Most persons," he remarked, "don't know enough about jimmies. Against them an ordinary door-lock or window-catch is no protection. With a jimmy eighteen inches long even an anæmic burglar can exert a pressure sufficient to lift two tons. Not one window in a thousand can stand that strain. The only use of locks is to keep out sneak-thieves and compel the modern scientific educated burglar to make a noise. But making a noise isn't enough here, at night. This place with all its fabulous treasures must be guarded constantly, now, every hour, as if the front door were wide open."

The bars replaced and the window apparently locked as before, Craig devoted his efforts to examining the packing cases in the basement. As yet apparently nothing down there had been disturbed. But while rummaging about, from an angle formed behind one of the cases he drew forth a cane, to all appearances an ordinary Malacca walking-stick. He balanced it in his hand a moment, then shook his head.

"Too heavy for a Malacca," he ruminated. Then an idea seemed to occur to him. He gave the handle a twist. Sure enough, it came off, and as it did so a bright little light flashed up.

"Well, what do you think of that?" he exclaimed. "For a scientific dark-lantern that is the neatest thing I have ever seen. An electric light cane, with a little incandescent lamp and a battery hidden in it. This grows interesting. We must at last have found the cache of a real gentleman burglar such as Bertillon says exists only in books. I wonder if he has anything else hidden back here."

He reached down and pulled out a peculiar little instrument—a single blue steel cylinder. He fitted a hard rubber cap snugly into the palm of his hand, and with the first and middle fingers encircled the cylinder over a steel ring near the other end.

A loud report followed, and a vase, just unpacked, at the opposite end of the basement was shattered as if by an explosion.

"Phew!" exclaimed Kennedy. "I didn't mean to do that. I knew the thing was loaded, but I had no idea the hair-spring ring at the end was so delicate as to shoot it off at a touch. It's one of those aristocratic little Apache pistols that one can carry in his vest pocket and hide in his hand. Say, but that stung! And back here is a little box of cartridges, too."

We looked at each other in amazement at the chance find. Apparently the vandal had planned a series of visits.

"Now, let me see," resumed Kennedy. "I suppose our very human but none the less mysterious intruder expected to use these again. Well, let him try. I'll put them back here for the present. I want to watch in the art-gallery to-night."

I could not help wondering whether, after all, it might not be an inside job and the fixing of the window merely a blind. Or was the vandal fascinated by the subtle influence of mysticism that so often seems to emanate from objects that have come down from the remote ages of the world? I could not help asking myself whether the story that Miss White had told was absolutely true. Had there been anything more than superstition in the girl's evident fright? She had seen something, I felt sure, for it was certain she was very much disturbed. But what was it she had really seen? So far all that Kennedy had found had proved that the reincarnation of the priestess Ka

had been very material. Perhaps the "reincarnation" had got in in the daytime and had spent the
hours until night in the mummy-case. It might well
have been chosen as the safest and least suspicious
hiding-place.

Kennedy evidently had some ideas and plans, for
no sooner had he completed arrangements with Dr.
Lith so that we could get into the museum that night
to watch, than he excused himself. Scarcely around
the corner on the next business street he hurried into
a telephone booth.

"I called up First Deputy O'Connor," he explained
as he left the booth a quarter of an hour later. "You
know it is the duty of two of O'Connor's men to visit
all the pawn-shops of the city at least once a week,
looking over recent pledges and comparing them with
descriptions of stolen articles. I gave him a list from
that catalogue of Dr. Lith's and I think that if any
of the emeralds, for instance, have been pawned his
men will be on the alert and will find it out."

We had a leisurely dinner at a near-by hotel, during
most of which time Kennedy gazed vacantly at his
food. Only once did he mention the case, and that
was almost as if he were thinking aloud.

"Nowadays," he remarked, "criminals are excep-
tionally well informed. They used to steal only
money and jewels; to-day it is famous pictures and
antiques also. They know something about the value
of antique bronze and marble. In fact, the spread of
a taste for art has taught the enterprising burglar
that such things are worth money, and he, in turn,
has educated up the receivers of stolen goods to pay

a reasonable percentage of the value of his artistic plunder. The success of the European art thief is enlightening the American thief. That's why I think we'll find some of this stuff in the hands of the professional fences."

It was still early in the evening when we returned to the museum and let ourselves in with the key that Dr. Lith had loaned Kennedy. He had been anxious to join us in the watch, but Craig had diplomatically declined, a circumstance that puzzled me and set me thinking that perhaps he suspected the curator himself.

We posted ourselves in an angle where we could not possibly be seen even if the full force of the electrolier were switched on. Hour after hour we waited. But nothing happened. There were strange and weird noises in plenty, not calculated to reassure one, but Craig was always ready with an explanation.

It was in the forenoon of the day after our long and unfruitful vigil in the art-gallery that Dr. Lith himself appeared at our apartment in a great state of perturbation.

"Miss White has disappeared," he gasped, in answer to Craig's hurried question. "When I opened the museum, she was not there as she is usually. Instead, I found this note."

He laid the following hastily written message on the table:

Do not try to follow me. It is the green curse that has pursued me from Paris. I cannot escape it, but I may prevent it from affecting others.

LUCILLE WHITE.

That was all. We looked at each other at a loss to
understand the enigmatic wording—"the green
curse."

"I rather expected something of the sort," observed
Kennedy. "By the way, the shoenails were French,
as I surmised. They show the marks of French heels.
It was Miss White herself who hid in the mummy-
case."

"Impossible," exclaimed Dr. Lith incredulously.
As for myself, I had learned that it was of no use being incredulous with Kennedy.

A moment later the door opened, and one of O'Connor's men came in bursting with news. Some of the
emeralds had been discovered in a Third Avenue
pawn-shop. O'Connor, mindful of the historic fate
of the Mexican Madonna and the stolen statue of the
Egyptian goddess Neith, had instituted a thorough
search with the result that at least part of the pilfered
jewels had been located. There was only one clue to
the thief, but it looked promising. The pawnbroker
described him as "a crazy Frenchman of an artist,"
tall, with a pointed black beard. In pawning the
jewels he had given the name of Edouard Delaverde,
and the city detectives were making a canvass of the
better known studios in hope of tracing him.

Kennedy, Dr. Lith and myself walked around to
the boarding-house where Miss White lived. There
was nothing about it, from the landlady to the gossip,
to distinguish it from scores of other places of the better sort. We had no trouble in finding out that Miss
White had not returned home at all the night before.
The landlady seemed to look on her as a woman of

mystery, and confided to us that it was an open secret that she was not an American at all, but a French
girl whose name, she believed, was really Lucille Le-
blanc—which, after all, was White. Kennedy made
no comment, but I wavered between the conclusions
that she had been the victim of foul play and that she
might be the criminal herself, or at least a member of
a band of criminals.

No trace of her could be found through the usual
agencies for locating missing persons. It was the
middle of the afternoon, however, when word came to
us that one of the city detectives had apparently located the studio of Delaverde. It was coupled with
the interesting information that the day before a
woman roughly answering the description of Miss
White had been seen there. Delaverde himself was
gone.

The building to which the detective took us was
down-town in a residence section which had remained
as a sort of little eddy to one side of the current of
business that had swept everything before it up-town.
It was an old building and large, and was entirely
given over to studios of artists.

Into one of the cheapest of the suites we were directed. It was almost bare of furniture and in a peculiarly shiftless state of disorder. A half-finished
picture stood in the centre of the room, and several
completed ones were leaning against the wall. They
were of the wildest character imaginable. Even the
conceptions of the futurists looked tame in compari-
son.

Kennedy at once began rummaging and exploring.

In a corner of a cupboard near the door he disclosed a row of dark-colored bottles. One was filled halfway with an emerald-green liquid.

He held it up to the light and read the label, "Absinthe."

"Ah," he exclaimed with evident interest, looking first at the bottle and then at the wild, formless pictures. "Our crazy Frenchman was an absintheur. I thought the pictures were rather the product of a disordered mind than of genius."

He replaced the bottle, adding: "It is only recently that our own government placed a ban on the importation of that stuff as a result of the decision of the Department of Agriculture that it was dangerous to health and conflicted with the pure food law. In France they call it the 'scourge,' the 'plague,' the 'enemy,' the 'queen of poisons.' Compared with other alcoholic beverages it has the greatest toxicity of all. There are laws against the stuff in France, Switzerland, and Belgium. It isn't the alcohol alone, although there is from fifty to eighty per cent. in it, that makes it so deadly. It is the absinthe, the oil of wormwood, whose bitterness has passed into a proverb. The active principle absinthin is a narcotic poison. The stuff creates a habit most insidious and difficult to break, a longing more exacting than hunger. It is almost as fatal as cocaine in its blasting effects on mind and body.

"Wormwood," he pursued, still rummaging about, "has a special affinity for the brain-cells and the nervous system in general. It produces a special affliction of the mind, which might be called absinthism.

Loss of will follows its use, brutishness, softening of the brain.   It gives rise to the wildest hallucinations. Perhaps that was why our absintheur chose first to destroy or steal all things green, as if there were some merit in the colour, when he might have made away with so many more valuable things.   Absintheurs have been known to perform some of the most intricate manœuvres, requiring great skill and the use of delicate tools.   They are given to disappearing, and have no memory of their actions afterward."

On an ink-spattered desk lay some books, including Lombroso's "Degenerate Man" and "Criminal Woman."   Kennedy glanced at them, then at a crumpled manuscript that was stuck into a pigeonhole.   It was written in a trembling, cramped, foreign hand, evidently part of a book, or an article.

"Oh, the wickedness of wealth!" it began.   "While millions of the poor toilers slave and starve and shiver, the slave-drivers of to-day, like the slave-drivers of ancient Egypt, spend the money wrung from the blood of the people in useless and worthless toys of art while the people have no bread, in old books while the people have no homes, in jewels while the people have no clothes.   Thousands are spent on dead artists, but a dollar is grudged to a living genius. Down with such art!   I dedicate my life to righting the wrongs of the proletariat.   *Vive l'anarchism!*"

The thing was becoming more serious.   But by far the most serious discovery in the now deserted studio was a number of large glass tubes in a corner, some broken, others not yet used and standing in rows as if waiting to be filled.   A bottle labelled "Sulphuric

Acid" stood at one end of a shelf, while at the other was a huge jar full of black grains, next a bottle of chlorate of potash. Kennedy took a few of the black grains and placed them on a metal ash-tray. He lighted a match. There was a puff and a little cloud of smoke.

"Ah," he exclaimed, "black gunpowder. Our absintheur was a bomb-maker, an expert perhaps. Let me see. I imagine he was making an explosive bomb, ingeniously contrived of five glass tubes. The centre one, I venture, contained sulphuric acid and chlorate of potash separated by a close-packed wad of cotton wool. Then the two tubes on each side probably contained the powder, and perhaps the outside tubes were filled with spirits of turpentine. When it is placed in position, it is so arranged that the acid in the center tube is uppermost and will thus gradually soak through the cotton wool and cause great heat and an explosion by contact with the potash. That would ignite the powder in the next tubes, and that would scatter the blazing turpentine, causing a terrific explosion and a widespread fire. With an imperative idea of vengeance, such as that manuscript discloses, either for his own wrongs as an artist or for the fancied wrongs of the people, what may this absintheur not be planning now? He has disappeared, but perhaps he may be more dangerous if found than if lost."

VIII

The Mummy Case

THE horrible thought occurred to me that perhaps he was not alone. I had seen Spencer's infatuation with his attractive librarian. The janitor of the studio-building was positive that a woman answering her description had been a visitor at the studio. Would she be used to get at the millionaire and his treasures? Was she herself part of the plot to victimise, perhaps kill, him? The woman had been much of an enigma to me at first. She was more so now. It was barely possible that she, too, was an absintheur, who had shaken off the curse for a time only to relapse into it again.

If there were any thoughts like these passing through Kennedy's mind he did not show it, at least not in the shape of hesitating in the course he had evidently mapped out to follow. He said little, but hurried off from the studio in a cab up-town again to the laboratory. A few minutes later we were speeding down to the museum.

There was not much time for Craig to work if he hoped to be ready for anything that might happen that night. He began by winding coil after coil of copper wire about the storeroom in the basement of the museum. It was not a very difficult matter to conceal it, so crowded was the room, or to lead the ends out through a window at the opposite side from that where the window had been broken open.

Up-stairs in the art-gallery he next installed several boxes such as those which I had seen him experimenting with during his tests of selenium on the afternoon when Mr. Spencer had first called on us. They were camera-like boxes, about ten inches long, three inches or so wide, and four inches deep.

One end was open, or at least looked as though the end had been shoved several inches into the interior of the box. I looked into one of the boxes and saw a slit in the wall that had been shoved in. Kennedy was busy adjusting the apparatus, and paused only to remark that the boxes contained two sensitive selenium surfaces balanced against two carbon resistances. There was also in the box a clockwork mechanism which Craig wound up and set ticking ever so softly. Then he moved a rod that seemed to cover the slit, until the apparatus was adjusted to his satisfaction, a delicate operation, judging by the care he took. Several of these boxes were installed, and by that time it was quite late.

Wires from the apparatus in the art-gallery also led outside, and these as well as the wires from the coils down in the basement he led across the bit of garden back of the Spencer house and up to a room on the top floor. In the upper room he attached the wires from the storeroom to what looked like a piece of crystal and a telephone receiver. Those from the art-gallery terminated in something very much like the apparatus which a wireless operator wears over his head.

Among other things which Craig had brought down from the laboratory was a package which he had not yet unwrapped. He placed it near the window, still wrapped. It was quite large, and must have weighed fifteen or twenty pounds. That done, he produced a tape-measure and began, as if he were a surveyor, to measure various distances and apparently to calculate the angles and distances from the window-sill of the Spencer house to the skylight, which was the exact centre of the museum. The straight distance, if I recall correctly, was in the neighborhood of four hundred feet.

These preparations completed, there was nothing left to do but to wait for something to happen. Spencer had declined to get alarmed about our fears for his own safety, and only with difficulty had we been able to dissuade him from moving heaven and earth to find Miss White, a proceeding which must certainly have disarranged Kennedy's carefully laid plans. So interested was he that he postponed one of the most important business conferences of the year, growing out of the anti-trust suits, in order to be present with Dr. Lith and ourselves in the little upper back room.

It was quite late when Kennedy completed his hasty arrangements, yet as the night advanced we grew more and more impatient for something to happen. Craig was apparently even more anxious than he had been the night before, when we watched in the art-gallery itself. Spencer was nervously smoking, lighting one cigar furiously from another until the air was almost blue.

Scarcely a word was spoken as hour after hour
Craig sat with the receiver to his ear, connected with
the coils down in the storeroom. "You might call
this an electric detective," he had explained to Spencer. "For example, if you suspected that anything
out of the way was going on in a room anywhere this
would report much to you even if you were miles
away. It is the discovery of a student of Thorne
Baker, the English electrical expert. He was experimenting with high-frequency electric currents, investigating the nature of the discharges used for elec-
trifying certain things. Quite by accident he found
that when the room on which he was experimenting
was occupied by some person his measuring-instru-
ments indicated that fact. He tested the degree of
variation by passing the current first through the
room and then through a sensitive crystal to a delicate telephone receiver. There was a distinct change
in the buzzing sound heard through the telephone
when the room was occupied or unoccupied. What
I have done is to wind single loops of plain wire on
each side of that room down there, as well as to wind
around the room a few turns of concealed copper wire.
These collectors are fitted to a crystal of car-
borundum and a telephone receiver."

We had each tried the thing and could hear a distinct buzzing in the receiver.

"The presence of a man or woman in that room
would be evident to a person listening miles away,"
he went on. "A high-frequency current is constantly
passing through that storeroom. That is what causes
that normal buzzing."

It was verging on midnight when Kennedy suddenly cried: "Here, Walter, take this receiver. You remember how the buzzing sounded. Listen. Tell me if you, too, can detect the change."

I clapped the receiver quickly to my ear. Indeed I could tell the difference. In place of the loud buzzing there was only a mild sound. It was slower and lower.

"That means," he said excitedly, "that some one has entered that pitch-dark storeroom by the broken window. Let me take the receiver back again. Ah, the buzzing is coming back. He is leaving the room. I suppose he has found the electric light cane and the pistol where he left them. Now, Walter, since you have become accustomed to this thing take it and tell me what you hear."

Craig had already seized the other apparatus connected with the art-gallery and had the wireless receiver over his head. He was listening with rapt attention, talking while he waited.

"This is an apparatus," he was saying, "that was devised by Dr. Fournier d'Albe, lecturer on physics at Birmingham University, to aid the blind. It is known as the optophone. What I am literally doing now is to *hear* light. The optophone translates light into sound by means of that wonderful little element, selenium, which in darkness is a poor conductor of electricity, but in light is a good conductor. This property is used in the optophone in transmitting an electric current which is interrupted by a special clockwork interrupter. It makes light and darkness audible in the telephone. This thing over my head is like a wireless telephone receiver, capable of detecting a current of even a quarter of a microampere."

We were all waiting expectantly for Craig to speak. Evidently the intruder was now mounting the stairs to the art-gallery.

"Actually I can hear the light of the stars shining in through that wonderful plate glass skylight of yours, Mr. Spencer," he went on. "A few moments ago when the moon shone through I could hear it, like the rumble of a passing cart. I knew it was the moon both because I could see that it must be shining in and because I recognised the sound. The sun would thunder like a passing express-train if it were daytime now. I can distinguish a shadow passing between the optophone and the light. A hand moved across in front of it would give a purring sound, and a glimpse out of a window in daylight would sound like a cinematograph reeling off a film.

"Ah, there he is." Craig was listening with intense excitement now. "Our intruder has entered the art-gallery. He is flashing his electric light cane about at various objects, reconnoitring. No doubt if I were expert enough and had had time to study it, I could tell you by the sound just what he is looking at."

"Craig," I interrupted, this time very excited myself, "the buzzing from the high-frequency current is getting lower and lower."

"By George, then, there is another of them," he replied. "I'm not surprised. Keep a sharp watch. Tell me the moment the buzzing increases again."

Spencer could scarcely control his impatience. It

had been a long time since he had been a mere spec-
tator, and he did not seem to relish being held in
check by anybody.

"Now that you are sure the vandal is there," he
cut in, his cigar out in his excitement, "can't we make
a dash over there and get him before he has a chance
to do any more damage? He might be destroying
thousands of dollars' worth of stuff while we are waiting here."

"And he could destroy the whole collection, building and all, including ourselves into the bargain, if
he heard so much as a whisper from us," added Kennedy firmly.

"That second person has left the storeroom, Craig,"
I put in. "The buzzing has returned again full
force."

Kennedy tore the wireless receiver from his ear.
"Here, Walter, never mind about that electric detective any more, then. Take the optophone. Describe
minutely to me just exactly what you hear."

He had taken from his pocket a small metal ball. I
seized the receiver from him and fitted it to my ear.
It took me several instants to accustom my ears to
the new sounds, but they were plain enough, and I
shouted my impressions of their variations. Kennedy
was busy at the window over the heavy package, from
which he had torn the wrapping. His back was
toward us, and we could not see what he was doing.

A terrific din sounded in my ears, almost splitting
my ear-drums. It was as though I had been suddenly
hurled into a magnified cave of the winds and a cat-
aract mightier than Niagara was thundering at me.

It was so painful that I cried out in surprise and involuntarily dropped the receiver to the floor.

"It was the switching on of the full glare of the electric lights in the art-gallery," Craig shouted. "The other person must have got up to the room quicker than I expected. Here goes."

A loud explosion took place, apparently on the very window-sill of our room. Almost at the same instant there was a crash of glass from the museum.

We sprang to the window, I expecting to see Kennedy injured, Spencer expecting to see his costly museum a mass of smoking ruins. Instead we saw nothing of the sort. On the window-ledge was a peculiar little instrument that looked like a miniature field-gun with an elaborate system of springs and levers to break the recoil.

Craig had turned from it so suddenly that he actually ran full tilt into us. "Come on," he cried breathlessly, bolting from the room, and seizing Dr. Lith by the arm as he did so. "Dr. Lith, the keys to the museum, quick! We must get there before the fumes clear away."

He was taking the stairs two at a time, dragging the dignified curator with him.

In fewer seconds than I can tell it we were in the museum and mounting the broad staircase to the art-gallery. An overpowering gas seemed to permeate everything.

"Stand back a moment," cautioned Kennedy as we neared the door. "I have just shot in here one of those asphyxiating bombs which the Paris police invented to war against the Apaches and the motor-car

9

bandits. Open all the windows back here and let the air clear. Walter, breathe as little of it as you can —but—come here—do you see?—over there, near the other door—a figure lying on the floor? Make a dash in after me and carry it out. There is just one thing more. If I am not back in a minute come in and try to get me."

He had already preceded me into the stifling fumes. With a last long breath of fresh air I plunged in after him, scarcely knowing what would happen to me. I saw the figure on the floor, seized it, and backed out of the room as fast as I could.

Dizzy and giddy from the fumes I had been forced to inhale, I managed to drag the form to the nearest window. It was Lucille White.

An instant later I felt myself unceremoniously pushed aside. Spencer had forgotten all about the millions of dollars' worth of curios, all about the suspicions that had been entertained against her, and had taken the half-conscious burden from me.

"This is the second time I have found you here, Edouard," she was muttering in her half-delirium, still struggling. "The first time—that night I hid in the mummy-case, you fled when I called for help. I have followed you every moment since last night to prevent this. Edouard, don't, *don't!* Remember I was—I am your wife. Listen to me. Oh, it is the absinthe that has spoiled your art and made it worthless, not the critics. It is not Mr. Spencer who has enticed me away, but you who drove me away, first from Paris, and now from New York. He has been only— No! No!—" she was shrieking now, her eyes wide open as she realised it was Spencer himself she saw leaning over her. With a great effort she seemed to rouse herself. "Don't stay. Run—run. Leave me. He has a bomb that may go off at any moment. Oh— oh—it is the curse of absinthe that pursues me. Will you not go? *Vite! Vite!*"

She had almost fainted and was lapsing into French, laughing and crying alternately, telling him to go, yet clinging to him.

Spencer paid no attention to what she had said of the bomb. But I did. The minute was up, and Kennedy was in there yet. I turned to rush in again to warn him at any peril.

Just then a half-conscious form staggered against me. It was Craig himself. He was holding the infernal machine of the five glass tubes that might at any instant blow us into eternity.

Overcome himself, he stumbled. The sinking sensation in my heart I can never describe. It was just a second that I waited for the terrific explosion that was to end it all for us, one long interminable second.

But it did not come.

Limp as I was with the shock, I dropped down beside him and bent over.

"A glass of water, Walter," he murmured, "and fan me a bit. I didn't dare trust myself to carry the thing complete, so I emptied the acid into the sarcophagus. I guess I must have stayed in there too long. But we are safe. See if you can drag out Delaverde. He is in there by the mummy-case."

Spencer was still holding Lucille, although she was much better in the fresh air of the hall. "I understand," he was muttering. "You have been following this fiend of a husband of yours to protect the museum and myself from him. Lucille, Lucille—look at me. You are mine, not his, whether he is dead or alive. I will free you from him, from the curse of the absinthe that has pursued you."

The fumes had cleared a great deal by this time. In the centre of the art-gallery we found a man, a tall, black-bearded Frenchman, crazy indeed from the curse of the green absinthe that had ruined him. He was scarcely breathing from a deadly wound in his chest. The hair-spring ring of the Apache pistol had exploded the cartridge as he fell.

Spencer did not even look at him, as he carried his own burden down to the little office of Dr. Lith.

"When a rich man marries a girl who has been earning her own living, the newspapers always distort it," he whispered aside to me a few minutes later. "Jameson, you're a newspaperman—I depend on you to get the facts straight this time."

Outside, Kennedy grasped my arm.

"You'll do that, Walter?" he asked persuasively. "Spencer is a client that one doesn't get every day. Just drop into the *Star* office and give them the straight story. I'll promise you I'll not take another case until you are free again to go on with me in it."

There was no denying him. As briefly as I could I rehearsed the main facts to the managing editor late that night. I was too tired to write it at length, yet I could not help a feeling of satisfaction as he exclaimed, "Great stuff, Jameson,—great."

"I know," I replied, "but this six-cylindered exist-ence for a week wears you out."

"My dear boy," he persisted, "if I had turned some one else loose on that story, he'd have been dead. Go to it—it's fine."

It was a bit of blarney, I knew. But somehow or other I liked it. It was just what I needed to en-courage me, and I hurried uptown promising myself a sound sleep at any rate.

"Very good," remarked Kennedy the next morn-ing, poking his head in at my door and holding up a copy of the *Star* into which a very accurate brief ac-count of the affair had been dropped at the last mo-ment. "I'm going over to the laboratory. See you there as soon as you can get over."

"Craig," I remarked an hour or so later as I saun-tered in on him, hard at work, "I don't see how you stand this feverish activity."

"Stand it?" he repeated, holding up a beaker to the light to watch a reaction. "It's my very life. Stand it? Why, man, if you want me to pass away—stop it. As long as it lasts, I shall be all right. Let it quit and I'll—I'll go back to research work," he laughed.

Evidently he had been waiting for me, for as he talked, he laid aside the materials with which he had been working and was preparing to go out.

"Then, too," he went on, "I like to be with people like Spencer and Brixton. For example, while I was waiting here for you, there came a call from Emery Pitts."

"Emery Pitts?" I echoed. "What does he want?"

"The best way to find out is—to find out," he answered simply. "It's getting late and I promised to be there directly. I think we'd better take a taxi."

A few minutes later we were ushered into a large Fifth Avenue mansion and were listening to a story which interested even Kennedy.

"Not even a blood spot has been disturbed in the kitchen. Nothing has been altered since the discovery of the murdered chef, except that his body has been moved into the next room."

Emery Pitts, one of the "thousand millionaires of steel," overwrought as he was by a murder in his own household, sank back in his easy-chair, exhausted.

Pitts was not an old man; indeed, in years he was in the prime of life. Yet by his looks he might almost have been double his age, the more so in contrast with Minna Pitts, his young and very pretty wife, who stood near him in the quaint breakfast-room and solicitously moved a pillow back of his head.

Kennedy and I looked on in amazement. We knew that he had recently retired from active business, giving as a reason his failing health. But neither of us had thought, when the hasty summons came early that morning to visit him immediately at his house, that his condition was as serious as it now appeared.

"In the kitchen?" repeated Kennedy, evidently not prepared for any trouble in that part of the house.

Pitts, who had closed his eyes, now reopened them slowly and I noticed how contracted were the pupils.

"Yes," he answered somewhat wearily, "my private kitchen which I have had fitted up. You know, I am on a diet, have been ever since I offered the one hundred thousand dollars for the sure restoration of youth. I shall have you taken out there presently."

He lapsed again into a half dreamy state, his head bowed on one hand resting on the arm of his chair. The morning's mail still lay on the table, some letters open, as they had been when the discovery had been announced. Mrs. Pitts was apparently much excited and unnerved by the gruesome discovery in the house.

"You have no idea who the murderer might be?" asked Kennedy, addressing Pitts, but glancing keenly at his wife.

"No," replied Pitts, "if I had I should have called the regular police. I wanted you to take it up before they spoiled any of the clues. In the first place we do not think it could have been done by any of the other servants. At least, Minna says that there was no quarrel."

"How could any one have got in from the outside?" asked Craig.

"There is a back way, a servants' entrance, but it is usually locked. Of course some one might have obtained a key to it."

Mrs. Pitts had remained silent throughout the dialogue. I could not help thinking that she suspected something, perhaps was concealing something. Yet each of them seemed equally anxious to have the marauder apprehended, whoever he might be.

"My dear," he said to her at length, "will you call some one and have them taken to the kitchen?"

IX

The Elixir of Life

A S Minna Pitts led us through the large mansion preparatory to turning us over to a servant she explained hastily that Mr. Pitts had long been ill and was now taking a new treatment under Dr. Thompson Lord. No one having answered her bell in the present state of excitement of the house, she stopped short at the pivoted door of the kitchen, with a little shudder at the tragedy, and stood only long enough to relate to us the story as she had heard it from the valet, Edward.

Mr. Pitts, it seemed, had wanted an early breakfast and had sent Edward to order it. The valet had found the kitchen a veritable slaughter-house, with the negro chef, Sam, lying dead on the floor. Sam had been dead, apparently, since the night before.

As she hurried away, Kennedy pushed open the door. It was a marvellous place, that antiseptic or rather aseptic kitchen, with its white tiling and enamel, its huge ice-box, and cooking-utensils for every purpose, all of the most expensive and modern make.

There were marks everywhere of a struggle, and by the side of the chef, whose body now lay in the next room awaiting the coroner, lay a long carving-knife with which he had evidently defended himself. On its blade and haft were huge coagulated spots of blood. The body of Sam bore marks of his having been clutched violently by the throat, and in his head was a single, deep wound that penetrated the skull in a most peculiar manner. It did not seem possible that a blow from a knife could have done it. It was a most unusual wound and not at all the sort that could have been made by a bullet.

As Kennedy examined it, he remarked, shaking his head in confirmation of his own opinion, "That must have been done by a Behr bulletless gun."

"A bulletless gun?" I repeated.

"Yes, a sort of pistol with a spring-operated device that projects a sharp blade with great force. No bullet and no powder are used in it. But when it is placed directly over a vital point of the skull so that the aim is unerring, a trigger lets a long knife shoot out with tremendous force, and death is instantaneous."

Near the door, leading to the courtyard that opened on the side street, were some spots of blood. They were so far from the place where the valet had discovered the body of the chef that there could be no doubt that they were blood from the murderer himself. Kennedy's reasoning in the matter seemed irresistible.

He looked under the table near the door, covered with a large light cloth. Beneath the table and behind the cloth he found another blood spot.

"How did that land there?" he mused aloud. "The table-cloth is bloodless."

Craig appeared to think a moment. Then he unlocked and opened the door. A current of air was created and blew the cloth aside.

"Clearly," he exclaimed, "that drop of blood was wafted under the table as the door was opened. The chances are all that it came from a cut on perhaps the hand or face of the murderer himself."

It seemed to be entirely reasonable, for the blood-stains about the room were such as to indicate that he had been badly cut by the carving-knife.

"Whoever attacked the chef must have been deeply wounded," I remarked, picking up the bloody knife and looking about at the stains, comparatively few of which could have come from the one deep fatal wound in the head of the victim.

Kennedy was still engrossed in a study of the stains, evidently considering that their size, shape, and location might throw some light on what had occurred. "Walter," he said finally, "while I'm busy here, I wish you would find that valet, Edward. I want to talk to him."

I found him at last, a clean-cut young fellow of much above average intelligence.

"There are some things I have not yet got clearly, Edward," began Kennedy. "Now where was the body, exactly, when you opened the door?"

Edward pointed out the exact spot, near the side of the kitchen toward the door leading out to the breakfast room and opposite the ice-box.

"And the door to the side street?" asked Kennedy, to all appearances very favorably impressed by the young man.

"It was locked, sir," he answered positively.

Kennedy was quite apparently considering the honesty and faithfulness of the servant. At last he leaned over and asked quickly, "Can I trust you?"

The frank, "Yes," of the young fellow was convincing enough.

"What I want," pursued Kennedy, "is to have some one inside this house who can tell me as much as he can see of the visitors, the messengers that come here this morning. It will be an act of loyalty to your employer, so that you need have no fear about that."

Edward bowed, and left us. While I had been seeking him, Kennedy had telephoned hastily to his laboratory and had found one of his students there. He had ordered him to bring down an apparatus which he described, and some other material.

While we waited Kennedy sent word to Pitts that he wanted to see him alone for a few minutes.

The instrument appeared to be a rubber bulb and cuff with a rubber bag attached to the inside. From it ran a tube which ended in another graduated glass tube with a thin line of mercury in it like a thermometer.

Craig adjusted the thing over the brachial artery of Pitts, just above the elbow.

"It may be a little uncomfortable, Mr. Pitts," he apologised, "but it will be for only a few minutes."

Pressure through the rubber bulb shut off the artery so that Kennedy could no longer feel the pulse at the wrist. As he worked, I began to see what he was after. The reading on the graded scale of the height of the column of mercury indicated, I knew, blood pressure. This time, as he worked, I noted also the flabby skin of Pitts as well as the small and sluggish pupils of his eyes.

He completed his test in silence and excused himself, although as we went back to the kitchen I was burning with curiosity.

"What was it?" I asked. "What did you discover?"

"That," he replied, "was a sphygmomanometer, something like the sphygmograph which we used once in another case. Normal blood pressure is 125 millimetres. Mr. Pitts shows a high pressure, very high. The large life insurance companies are now using this instrument. They would tell you that a high pressure like that indicates apoplexy. Mr. Pitts, young as he really is, is actually old. For, you know, the saying is that a man is as old as his arteries. Pitts has hardening of the arteries, arteriosclerosis —perhaps other heart and kidney troubles, in short pre-senility."

Craig paused: then added sententiously as if to himself: "You have heard the latest theories about old age, that it is due to microbic poisons secreted in the intestines and penetrating the intestinal walls? Well, in premature senility the symptoms are the same as in senility, only mental acuteness is not so impaired."

We had now reached the kitchen again. The student had also brought down to Kennedy a number of sterilised microscope slides and test-tubes, and from here and there in the masses of blood spots Kennedy was taking and preserving samples. He also took samples of the various foods, which he preserved in the sterilised tubes.

While he was at work Edward joined us cautiously.

"Has anything happened?" asked Craig.

"A message came by a boy for Mrs. Pitts," whispered the valet.

"What did she do with it?"

"Tore it up."

"And the pieces?"

"She must have hidden them somewhere."

"See if you can get them."

Edward nodded and left us.

"Yes," I remarked after he had gone, "it does seem as if the thing to do was to get on the trail of a person bearing wounds of some kind. I notice, for one thing, Craig, that Edward shows no such marks, nor does any one else in the house as far as I can see. If it were an 'inside job' I fancy Edward at least could clear himself. The point is to find the person with a bandaged hand or plastered face."

Kennedy assented, but his mind was on another subject. "Before we go we must see Mrs. Pitts alone, if we can," he said simply.

In answer to his inquiry through one of the servants she sent down word that she would see us immediately in her sitting-room. The events of the morning had quite naturally upset her, and she was, if anything, even paler than when we saw her before.

"Mrs. Pitts," began Kennedy, "I suppose you are aware of the physical condition of your husband?"

It seemed a little abrupt to me at first, but he in-tended it to be. "Why," she asked with real alarm, "is he so very badly?"

"Pretty badly," remarked Kennedy mercilessly, ob-serving the effect of his words. "So badly, I fear, that it would not require much more excitement like to-day's to bring on an attack of apoplexy. I should advise you to take especial care of him, Mrs. Pitts."

Following his eyes, I tried to determine whether the agitation of the woman before us was genuine or not. It certainly looked so. But then, I knew that she had been an actress before her marriage. Was she acting a part now?

"What do you mean?" she asked tremulously.

"Mrs. Pitts," replied Kennedy quickly, observing still the play of emotion on her delicate features, "some one, I believe, either regularly in or employed in this house or who had a ready means of access to it must have entered that kitchen last night. For what purpose, I can leave you to judge. But Sam surprised the intruder there and was killed for his faithfulness."

Her startled look told plainly that though she might have suspected something of the sort she did not think that any one else suspected, much less actually perhaps knew it.

"I can't imagine who it could be, unless it might be one of the servants," she murmured hastily; add-ing, "and there is none of them that I have any right to suspect."

She had in a measure regained her composure, and Kennedy felt that it was no use to pursue the conversation further, perhaps expose his hand before he was ready to play it.

"That woman is concealing something," remarked Kennedy to me as we left the house a few minutes later.

"She at least bears no marks of violence herself of any kind," I commented.

"No," agreed Craig, "no, you are right so far." He added: "I shall be very busy in the laboratory this afternoon, and probably longer. However, drop in at dinner time, and in the meantime, don't say a word to any one, but just use your position on the *Star* to keep in touch with anything the police authorities may be doing."

It was not a difficult commission, since they did nothing but issue a statement, the net import of which was to let the public know that they were very active, although they had nothing to report.

Kennedy was still busy when I rejoined him, a little late purposely, since I knew that he would be over his head in work.

"What's this—a zoo?" I asked, looking about me as I entered the sanctum that evening.

There were dogs and guinea pigs, rats and mice, a menagerie that would have delighted a small boy. It did not look like the same old laboratory for the investigation of criminal science, though I saw on a second glance that it was the same, that there was the usual hurly-burly of microscopes, test-tubes, and all the paraphernalia that were so mystifying at first but in the end under his skilful hand made the most complicated cases seem stupidly simple.

Craig smiled at my surprise. "I'm making a little study of intestinal poisons," he commented, "poisons produced by microbes which we keep under more or less control in healthy life. In death they are the little fellows that extend all over the body and putrefy it. We nourish within ourselves microbes which secrete very virulent poisons, and when those poisons are too much for us—well, we grow old. At least that is the theory of Metchnikoff, who says that old age is an infectious chronic, disease. Somehow," he added thoughtfully, "that beautiful white kitchen in the Pitts home had really become a factory for intestinal poisons."

There was an air of suppressed excitement in his manner which told me that Kennedy was on the trail of something unusual.

"Mouth murder," he cried at length, "that was what was being done in that wonderful kitchen. Do you know, the scientific slaying of human beings has far exceeded organised efforts at detection? Of course you expect me to say that; you think I look at such things through coloured glasses. But it is a fact, nevertheless.

"It is a very simple matter for the police to apprehend the common murderer whose weapon is a knife or a gun, but it is a different thing when they investigate the death of a person who has been the victim of the modern murderer who slays, let us say, with some kind of deadly bacilli. Authorities say, and I agree with them, that hundreds of murders are committed in this country every year and are not detected because the detectives are not scientists, while the slayers have used the knowledge of the scientists both to commit and to cover up the crimes. I tell you, Walter, a murder science bureau not only would clear up nearly every poison mystery, but also it would inspire such a wholesome fear among would-be murderers that they would abandon many attempts to take life."

He was as excited over the case as I had ever seen him. Indeed it was one that evidently taxed his utmost powers.

"What have you found?" I asked, startled.

"You remember my use of the sphygmomanometer?" he asked. "In the first place that put me on what seems to be a clear trail. The most dreaded of all the ills of the cardiac and vascular systems nowadays seems to be arterio-sclerosis, or hardening of the arteries. It is possible for a man of forty-odd, like Mr. Pitts, to have arteries in a condition which would not be encountered normally in persons under seventy years of age.

"The hard or hardening artery means increased blood pressure, with a consequent increased strain on the heart. This may lead, has led in this case, to a long train of distressing symptoms, and, of course, to ultimate death. Heart disease, according to statistics, is carrying off a greater percentage of persons than formerly. This fact cannot be denied, and it is attributed largely to worry, the abnormal rush of the life of to-day, and sometimes to faulty methods of eating and bad nutrition. On the surface, these natural causes might seem to be at work with Mr. Pitts. But, Walter, I do not believe it, I

10

do not believe it. There is more than that, here. Come, I can do nothing more to-night, until I learn more from these animals and the cultures which I have in these tubes. Let us take a turn or two, then dine, and perhaps we may get some word at our apartment from Edward."

It was late that night when a gentle tap at the door proved that Kennedy's hope had not been unfounded. I opened it and let in Edward, the valet, who produced the fragments of a note, torn and crumpled.

"There is nothing new, sir," he explained, "except that Mrs. Pitts seems more nervous than ever, and Mr. Pitts, I think, is feeling a little brighter."

Kennedy said nothing, but was hard at work with puckered brows at piecing together the note which Edward had obtained after hunting through the house. It had been thrown into a fireplace in Mrs. Pitts's own room, and only by chance had part of it been unconsumed. The body of the note was gone altogether, but the first part and the last part remained.

Apparently it had been written the very morning on which the murder was discovered.

It read simply, "I have succeeded in having Thornton declared . . . " Then there was a break. The last words were legible, and were, " . . . confined in a suitable institution where he can cause no future harm."

There was no signature, as if the sender had perfectly understood that the receiver would understand.

"Not difficult to supply some of the context, at any rate," mused Kennedy. "Whoever Thornton may be, some one has succeeded in having him declared 'insane,' I should supply. If he is in an institution near New York, we must be able to locate him. Edward, this is a very important clue. There is nothing else."

Kennedy employed the remainder of the night in obtaining a list of all the institutions, both public and private, within a considerable radius of the city where the insane might be detained.

The next morning, after an hour or so spent in the laboratory apparently in confirming some control tests which Kennedy had laid out to make sure that he was not going wrong in the line of inquiry he was pursuing, we started off in a series of flying visits to the various sanitaria about the city in search of an inmate named Thornton.

I will not attempt to describe the many curious sights and experiences we saw and had. I could readily believe that any one who spent even as little time as we did might almost think that the very world was going rapidly insane. There were literally thousands of names in the lists which we examined patiently, going through them all, since Kennedy was not at all sure that Thornton might not be a first name, and we had no time to waste on taking any chances.

It was not until long after dusk that, weary with the search and dust-covered from our hasty scouring of the country in an automobile which Kennedy had hired after exhausting the city institutions, we came to a small private asylum up in Westchester. I had almost been willing to give it up for the day, to start afresh on the morrow, but Kennedy seemed to feel that the case was too urgent to lose even twelve hours over.

It was a peculiar place, isolated, out-of-the-way, and guarded by a high brick wall that enclosed a pretty good sized garden.

A ring at the bell brought a sharp-eyed maid to the door.

"Have you—er—any one here named Thornton—er—?" Kennedy paused in such a way that if it were the last name he might come to a full stop, and if it were a first name he could go on.

"There is a Mr. Thornton who came yesterday," she snapped ungraciously, "but you can not see him. It's against the rules."

"Yes—yesterday," repeated Kennedy eagerly, ignoring her tartness. "Could I—" he slipped a crumpled treasury note into her hand—"could I speak to Mr. Thornton's nurse?"

The note seemed to render the acidity of the girl slightly alkaline. She opened the door a little further, and we found ourselves in a plainly furnished reception room, alone.

We might have been in the reception-room of a prosperous country gentleman, so quiet was it. There was none of the raving, as far as I could make out. that I should have expected even in a twentieth century Bedlam, no material for a Poe story of Dr. Tarr and Professor Feather.

At length the hall door opened, and a man entered, not a prepossessing man, it is true, with his large and powerful hands and arms and slightly bowed, almost bulldog legs. Yet he was not of that aggressive kind which would make a show of physical strength without good and sufficient cause.

"You have charge of Mr. Thornton?" inquired Kennedy.

"Yes," was the curt response.

"I trust he is all right here?"

"He wouldn't be here if he was all right," was the quick reply. "And who might you be?"

"I knew him in the old days," replied Craig evasively. "My friend here does not know him, but I was in this part of Westchester visiting and having heard he was here thought I would drop in, just for old time's sake. That is all."

"How did you know he was here?" asked the man suspiciously.

"I heard indirectly from a friend of mine, Mrs. Pitts."

"Oh."

The man seemed to accept the explanation at its face value.

"Is he very—very badly?" asked Craig with well-feigned interest.

"Well," replied the man, a little mollified by a good cigar which I produced, "don't you go a-telling her, but if he says the name Minna once a day it is a thousand times. Them drug-dopes has some strange delusions."

"Strange delusions?" queried Craig. "Why, what do you mean?"

"Say," ejaculated the man. "I don't know you. You come here saying you're friends of Mr. Thornton's. How do I know what you are?"

"Well," ventured Kennedy, "suppose I should also tell you I am a friend of the man who committed him."

"Of Dr. Thompson Lord?"

"Exactly. My friend here knows Dr. Lord very well, don't you, Walter?"

Thus appealed to I hastened to add, "Indeed I do." Then, improving the opening, I hastened: "Is this Mr. Thornton violent? I think this is one of the most quiet institutions I ever saw for so small a place."

The man shook his head.

"Because," I added, "I thought some drug fiends were violent and had to be restrained by force, often."

"You won't find a mark or a scratch on him, sir," replied the man. "That ain't our system."

"Not a mark or scratch on him," repeated Kennedy thoughtfully. "I wonder if he'd recognise me?"

"Can't say," concluded the man. "What's more, can't try. It's against the rules. Only your knowing so many he knows has got you this far. You'll have to call on a regular day or by appointment to see him, gentlemen."

There was an air of finality about the last statement that made Kennedy rise and move toward the door with a hearty "Thank you, for your kindness," and a wish to be remembered to "poor old Thornton."

As we climbed into the car he poked me in the ribs. "Just as good for the present as if we had seen him."

he exclaimed. "Drug-fiend, friend of Mrs. Pitts, committed by Dr. Lord, no wounds."

Then he lapsed into silence as we sped back to the city.

"The Pitts house," ordered Kennedy as we bowled along, after noting by his watch that it was after nine. Then to me he added, "We must see Mrs. Pitts once more, and alone."

We waited some time after Kennedy sent up word that he would like to see Mrs. Pitts. At last she appeared. I thought she avoided Kennedy's eye, and I am sure that her intuition told her that he had some revelation to make, against which she was steeling herself.

Craig greeted her as reassuringly as he could, but as she sat nervously before us, I could see that she was in reality pale, worn, and anxious.

"We have had a rather hard day," began Kennedy after the usual polite inquiries about her own and her husband's health had been, I thought, a little prolonged by him.

"Indeed?" she asked. "Have you come any closer to the truth?"

Kennedy met her eyes, and she turned away.

" Yes, Mr. Jameson and I have put in the better part of the day in going from one institution for the insane to another."

He paused. The startled look on her face told as plainly as words that his remark had struck home.

Without giving her a chance to reply, or to think of a verbal means of escape, Craig hurried on with an account of what we had done, saying nothing about the original letter which had started us on the search for Thornton, but leaving it to be inferred by her that he knew much more than he cared to tell.

"In short, Mrs. Pitts," he concluded firmly, "I do not need to tell you that I already know much about the matter which you are concealing."

The piling up of fact on fact, mystifying as it was to me who had as yet no inkling of what it was tending toward, proved too much for the woman who knew the truth, yet did not know how much Kennedy knew of it. Minna Pitts was pacing the floor wildly, all the assumed manner of the actress gone from her, yet with the native grace and feeling of the born actress playing unrestrained in her actions.

"You know only part of my story," she cried, fixing him with her now tearless eyes. "It is only a question of time when you will worm it all out by your uncanny, occult methods. Mr. Kennedy, I cast myself on you."

X

The Toxin of Death

THE note of appeal in her tone was powerful, but I could not so readily shake off my first suspicions of the woman. Whether or not she convinced Kennedy, he did not show.

"I was only a young girl when I met Mr. Thornton," she raced on. "I was not yet eighteen when we were married. Too late, I found out the curse of his life—and of mine. He was a drug fiend. From the very first life with him was insupportable. I stood it as long as I could, but when he beat me because he had no money to buy drugs, I left him. I gave myself up to my career on the stage. Later I heard that he was dead—a suicide. I worked, day and night, slaved, and rose in the profession—until, at last, I met Mr. Pitts."

She paused, and it was evident that it was with a struggle that she could talk so.

"Three months after I was married to him, Thornton suddenly reappeared, from the dead it seemed to me. He did not want me back. No, indeed. All he wanted was money. I gave him money, my own money, for I made a great deal in my stage days. But his demands increased. To silence him I have paid him thousands. He squandered them faster than ever. And finally, when it became unbearable,

151

I appealed to a friend. That friend has now succeeded in placing this man quietly in a sanitarium
for the insane."

"And the murder of the chef?" shot out Kennedy.

She looked from one to the other of us in alarm.
"Before God, I know no more of that than does Mr.
Pitts."

Was she telling the truth? Would she stop at anything to avoid the scandal and disgrace of the charge
of bigamy? Was there not something still that she
was concealing? She took refuge in the last resort
—tears.

Encouraging as it was to have made such progress,
it did not seem to me that we were much nearer,
after all, to the solution of the mystery. Kennedy,
as usual, had nothing to say until he was absolutely
sure of his ground. He spent the greater part of the
next day hard at work over the minute investiga-
tions of his laboratory, leaving me to arrange the details of a meeting he planned for that night.

There were present Mr. and Mrs. Pitts, the former
in charge of Dr. Lord. The valet, Edward, was also
there, and in a neighbouring room was Thornton in
charge of two nurses from the sanitarium. Thornton was a sad wreck of a man now, whatever he might
have been when his blackmail furnished him with an
unlimited supply of his favourite drugs.

"Let us go back to the very start of the case," began Kennedy when we had all assembled, "the murder of the chef, Sam."

It seemed that the mere sound of his voice electri-
fied his little audience. I fancied a shudder passed

over the slight form of Mrs. Pitts, as she must have
realised that this was the point where Kennedy had
left off, in his questioning her the night before.

"There is," he went on slowly, "a blood test so delicate that one might almost say that he could identify
a criminal by his very blood-crystals—the finger-
prints, so to speak, of his blood. It was by means
of these 'hemoglobin clues,' if I may call them so,
that I was able to get on the right trail. For the
fact is that a man's blood is not like that of any other
living creature. Blood of different men, of men and
women differ. I believe that in time we shall be able
to refine this test to tell the exact individual, too.

"What is this principle? It is that the hemoglobin or red colouring-matter of the blood forms
crystals. That has long been known, but working on
this fact Dr. Reichert and Professor Brown of the
University of Pennsylvania have made some wonderful discoveries.

"We could distinguish human from animal blood
before, it is true. But the discovery of these two
scientists takes us much further. By means of
blood-crystals we can distinguish the blood of man
from that of the animals and in addition that of white
men from that of negroes and other races. It is often
the only way of differentiating between various kinds
of blood.

"The variations in crystals in the blood are in part
of form and in part of molecular structure, the latter
being discovered only by means of the polarising
microscope. A blood-crystal is only one two-thou-
sand-two-hundred-and-fiftieth of an inch in length and

one nine-thousandth of an inch in breadth. And yet, minute as these crystals are, this discovery is of immense medico-legal importance. Crime may now be traced by blood-crystals."

He displayed on his table a number of enlarged micro-photographs. Some were labelled, "Characteristic crystals of white man's blood"; others "Crystallisation of negro blood"; still others, "Blood-crystals of the cat."

"I have here," he resumed, after we had all examined the photographs and had seen that there was indeed a vast amount of difference, "three characteristic kinds of crystals, all of which I found in the various spots in the kitchen of Mr. Pitts. There were three kinds of blood, by the infallible Reichert test."

I had been prepared for his discovery of two kinds, but three heightened the mystery still more.

"There was only a very little of the blood which was that of the poor, faithful, unfortunate Sam, the negro chef," Kennedy went on. "A little more, found far from his body, is that of a white person. But most of it is not human blood at all. It was the blood of a cat."

The revelation was startling. Before any of us could ask, he hastened to explain.

"It was placed there by some one who wished to exaggerate the struggle in order to divert suspicion. That person had indeed been wounded slightly, but wished it to appear that the wounds were very serious. The fact of the matter is that the carving-knife is spotted deeply with blood, but it is not human blood. It is the blood of a cat. A few years ago even a scientific detective would have concluded that a fierce hand-to-hand struggle had been waged and that the murderer was, perhaps, fatally wounded. Now, another conclusion stands, proved infallibly by this Reichert test. The murderer was wounded, but not badly. That person even went out of the room and returned later, probably with a can of animal blood, sprinkled it about to give the appearance of a struggle, perhaps thought of preparing in this way a plea of self-defence. If that latter was the case, this Reichert test completely destroys it, clever though it was."

No one spoke, but the same thought was openly in all our minds. Who was this wounded criminal?

I asked myself the usual query of the lawyers and the detectives— Who would benefit most by the death of Pitts? There was but one answer, apparently, to that. It was Minna Pitts. Yet it was difficult for me to believe that a woman of her ordinary gentleness could be here to-night, faced even by so great exposure, yet be so solicitous for him as she had been and then at the same time be plotting against him. I gave it up, determining to let Kennedy unravel it in his own way.

Craig evidently had the same thought in his mind, however, for he continued: "Was it a woman who killed the chef? No, for the third specimen of blood, that of the white person, was the blood of a man; not of a woman."

Pitts had been following closely, his unnatural eyes now gleaming. "You said he was wounded, you remember," he interrupted, as if casting about in his mind to recall some one who bore a recent wound. "Perhaps it was not a bad wound, but it was a wound, nevertheless, and some one must have seen it, must know about it. It is not three days."

Kennedy shook his head. It was a point that had bothered him a great deal.

"As to the wounds," he added in a measured tone, "although this occurred scarcely three days ago, there is no person even remotely suspected of the crime who can be said to bear on his hands or face others than old scars of wounds."

He paused. Then he shot out in quick staccato, "Did you ever hear of Dr. Carrel's most recent discovery of accelerating the healing of wounds so that those which under ordinary circumstances might take ten days to heal might be healed in twenty-four hours?"

Rapidly, now, he sketched the theory. "If the factors that bring about the multiplication of cells and the growth of tissues were discovered, Dr. Carrel said to himself, it would perhaps become possible to hasten artificially the process of repair of the body. Aseptic wounds could probably be made to cicatrise more rapidly. If the rate of reparation of tissue were hastened only ten times, a skin wound would heal in less than twenty-four hours and a fracture of the leg in four or five days.

"For five years Dr. Carrel has been studying the subject, applying various extracts to wounded tissues. All of them increased the growth of connective tissue, but the degree of acceleration varied greatly. In some cases it was as high as forty times the normal. Dr. Carrel's dream of ten times the normal was exceeded by himself."

Astounded as we were by this revelation, Kennedy did not seem to consider it as important as one that he was now hastening to show us. He took a few cubic centimetres of some culture which he had been preparing, placed it in a tube, and poured in eight or ten drops of sulphuric acid. He shook it.

"I have here a culture from some of the food that I found was being or had been prepared for Mr. Pitts. It was in the icebox."

Then he took another tube. "This," he remarked, "is a one-to-one-thousand solution of sodium nitrite."

He held it up carefully and poured three or four cubic centimetres of it into the first tube so that it ran carefully down the side in a manner such as to form a sharp line of contact between the heavier culture with the acid and the lighter nitrite solution.

"You see," he said, "the reaction is very clear cut if you do it this way. The ordinary method in the laboratory and the text-books is crude and uncertain."

"What is it?" asked Pitts eagerly, leaning forward with unwonted strength and noting the pink colour that appeared at the junction of the two liquids, contrasting sharply with the portions above and below.

"The ring or contact test for indol," Kennedy replied, with evident satisfaction. "When the acid and the nitrites are mixed the colour reaction is unsatisfactory. The natural yellow tint masks that pink tint, or sometimes causes it to disappear, if the tube is shaken. But this is simple, clear, delicate—unescapable. There was indol in that food of yours, Mr. Pitts."

"Indol?" repeated Pitts.

"Is," explained Kennedy, "a chemical compound—one of the toxins secreted by intestinal bacteria and responsible for many of the symptoms of senility. It used to be thought that large doses of indol might be consumed with little or no effect on normal man, but now we know that headache, insomnia, confusion, irritability, decreased activity of the cells, and intoxication are possible from it. Comparatively small doses over a long time produce changes in organs that lead to serious results.

"It is," went on Kennedy, as the full horror of the thing sank into our minds, "the indol- and phenol-producing bacteria which are the undesirable citizens of the body, while the lactic-acid producing germs check the production of indol and phenol. In my tests here to-day, I injected four one-hundredths of a grain of indol into a guinea-pig. The animal had sclerosis or hardening of the aorta. The liver, kidneys, and supra-renals were affected, and there was a hardening of the brain. In short, there were all the symptoms of old age."

We sat aghast. Indol! What black magic was this? Who put it in the food?

"It is present," continued Craig, "in much larger quantities than all the Metchnikoff germs could neutralise. What the chef was ordered to put into the food to benefit you, Mr. Pitts, was rendered valueless, and a deadly poison was added by what another—"

Minna Pitts had been clutching for support at the arms of her chair as Kennedy proceeded. She now threw herself at the feet of Emery Pitts.

"Forgive me," she sobbed. "I can stand it no longer. I had tried to keep this thing about Thornton from you. I have tried to make you happy and well—oh—tried so hard, so faithfully. Yet that old skeleton of my past which I thought was buried would not stay buried. I have bought Thornton off again and again, with money—my money—only to find him threatening again. But about this other thing, this poison, I am as innocent, and I believe Thornton is as—"

Craig laid a gentle hand on her lips. She rose wildly and faced him in passionate appeal.

"Who—who is this Thornton?" demanded Emery Pitts.

Quickly, delicately, sparing her as much as he could, Craig hurried over our experiences.

"He is in the next room," Craig went on, then facing Pitts added: "With you alive, Emery Pitts, this blackmail of your wife might have gone on, although there was always the danger that you might hear of it—and do as I see you have already done—forgive, and plan to right the unfortunate mistake. But with you dead, this Thornton, or rather some one using him, might take away from Minna Pitts her whole interest in your estate, at a word. The law, or your heirs at law, would never forgive as you would."

Pitts, long poisoned by the subtle microbic poison, stared at Kennedy as if dazed.

"Who was caught in your kitchen, Mr. Pitts, and
11

to escape detection, killed your faithful chef and covered his own traces so cleverly?" rapped out Kennedy. "Who would have known the new process of healing wounds? Who knew about the fatal properties of indol? Who was willing to forego a one-hundred-thousand-dollar prize in order to gain a fortune of many hundreds of thousands?"

Kennedy paused, then finished with irresistibly dramatic logic,

"Who else but the man who held the secret of Minna Pitts's past and power over her future so long as he could keep alive the unfortunate Thornton—the up-to-date doctor who substituted an elixir of death at night for the elixir of life prescribed for you by him in the daytime—Dr. Lord."

Kennedy had moved quietly toward the door. It was unnecessary. Dr. Lord was cornered and knew it. He made no fight. In fact, instantly his keen mind was busy outlining his battle in court, relying on the conflicting testimony of hired experts.

"Minna," murmured Pitts, falling back, exhausted by the excitement, on his pillows, "Minna—forgive? What is there to forgive? The only thing to do is to correct. I shall be well—soon now—my dear. Then all will be straightened out."

"Walter," whispered Kennedy to me, "while we are waiting, you can arrange to have Thornton cared for at Dr. Hodge's Sanitarium."

He handed me a card with the directions where to take the unfortunate man. When at last I had Thornton placed where no one else could do any harm through him, I hastened back to the laboratory.

Craig was still there, waiting alone.

"That Dr. Lord will be a tough customer," he remarked. "Of course you're not interested in what happens in a case after we have caught the criminal. But that often is really only the beginning of the fight. We've got him safely lodged in the Tombs now, however."

"I wish there was some elixir for fatigue," I remarked, as we closed the laboratory that night.

"There is," he replied. "A homeopathic remedy—more fatigue."

We started on our usual brisk roundabout walk to the apartment. But instead of going to bed, Kennedy drew a book from the bookcase.

"I shall read myself to sleep to-night," he explained, settling deeply in his chair.

As for me, I went directly to my room, planning that to-morrow I would take several hours off and catch up in my notes.

That morning Kennedy was summoned downtown and had to interrupt more important duties in order to appear before Dr. Leslie in the coroner's inquest over the death of the chef. Dr. Lord was held for the Grand Jury, but it was not until nearly noon that Craig returned.

We were just about to go out to luncheon, when the door buzzer sounded.

"A note for Mr. Kennedy," announced a man in a police uniform, with a blue anchor edged with white on his coat sleeve.

Craig tore open the envelope quickly with his forefinger. Headed "Harbour Police, Station No. 3,

Staten Island," was an urgent message from our old friend Deputy Commissioner O'Connor.

"I have taken personal charge of a case here that is sufficiently out of the ordinary to interest you," I read when Kennedy tossed the note over to me and nodded to the man from the harbour squad to wait for us. "The Curtis family wish to retain a private detective to work in conjunction with the police in investigating the death of Bertha Curtis, whose body was found this morning in the waters of Kill van Kull."

Kennedy and I lost no time in starting downtown with the policeman who had brought the note.

The Curtises, as we knew, were among the prominent families of Manhattan and I recalled having heard that at one time Bertha Curtis had been an actress, in spite of the means and social position of her family, from whom she had become estranged as a result.

At the station of the harbour police, O'Connor and another man, who was in a state of extreme excitement, greeted us almost before we had landed.

"There have been some queer doings about here," exclaimed the deputy as he grasped Kennedy's hand, "but first of all let me introduce Mr. Walker Curtis."

In a lower tone as we walked up the dock O'Connor continued, "He is the brother of the girl whose body the men in the launch at the station found in the Kill this morning. They thought at first that the girl had committed suicide, making it doubly sure by jumping into the water, but he will not believe it and,—well, if you'll just come over with us to the local undertaking establishment, I'd like to have you take a look at the body and see if your opinion coincides with mine.

"Ordinarily," pursued O'Connor, "there isn't much romance in harbour police work nowadays, but in this case some other elements seem to be present which are not usually associated with violent deaths in the waters of the bay, and I have, as you will see, thought it necessary to take personal charge of the investigation.

"Now, to shorten the story as much as possible, Kennedy, you know of course that the legislature at the last session enacted laws prohibiting the sale of such drugs as opium, morphine, cocaine, chloral and others, under much heavier penalties than before. The Health authorities not long ago reported to us that dope was being sold almost openly, without orders from physicians, at several scores of places and we have begun a crusade for the enforcement of the law. Of course you know how prohibition works in many places and how the law is beaten. The dope fiends seem to be doing the same thing with this law.

"Of course nowadays everybody talks about a 'system' controlling everything, so I suppose people would say that there is a 'dope trust.' At any rate we have run up against at least a number of places that seem to be banded together in some way, from the lowest down in Chinatown to one very swell joint uptown around what the newspapers are calling 'Crime Square.' It is not that this place is pandering to criminals or the women of the Tenderloin that interests us so much as that its patrons are men and women of fashionable society whose jangled nerves seem to demand a strong narcotic.

"This particular place seems to be a headquarters for obtaining them, especially opium and its derivatives.

"One of the frequenters of the place was this unfortunate girl, Bertha Curtis. I have watched her go in and out myself, wild-eyed, nervous, mentally and physically wrecked for life. Perhaps twenty-five or thirty persons visit the place each day. It is run by a man known as 'Big Jack' Clendenin who was once an actor and, I believe, met and fascinated Miss Curtis during her brief career on the stage. He has an attendant there, a Jap, named Nichi Moto, who is a perfect enigma. I can't understand him on any reasonable theory. A long time ago we raided the place and packed up a lot of opium, pipes, material and other stuff. We found Clendenin there, this girl, several others, and the Jap. I never understood just how it was but somehow Clendenin got off with a nominal fine and a few days later opened up again. We were watching the place, getting ready to raid it again and present such evidence that Clendenin couldn't possibly beat it, when all of a sudden along came this—this tragedy."

We had at last arrived at the private establishment which was doing duty as a morgue. The bedraggled form that had been bandied about by the tides all night lay covered up in the cold damp basement. Bertha Curtis had been a girl of striking beauty once. For a long time I gazed at the swollen features before I realised what it was that fascinated and puzzled me about her. Kennedy, however, after a casual glance had arrived at at least a part of her story.

"That girl," he whispered to me so that her brother could not hear, "has led a pretty fast life. Look at those nails, yellow and dark. It isn't a weak face, either. I wouldn't be surprised if the whole thing, the Oriental glamour and all that, fascinated her as much as the drug."

So far the case with its heartrending tragedy had all the earmarks of suicide.

XI

The Opium Joint

O'CONNOR drew back the sheet which covered her and in the calf of the leg disclosed an ugly bullet hole. Ugly as it was, however, it was anything but dangerous and seemed to indicate nothing as to the real cause of her death. He drew from his pocket a slightly misshapen bullet which had been probed from the wound and handed it to Kennedy, who examined both the wound and the bullet carefully. It seemed to be an ordinary bullet except that in the pointed end were three or four little round, very shallow wells or depressions only the minutest fraction of an inch deep.

"Very extraordinary," he remarked slowly. "No, I don't think this was a case of suicide. Nor was it a murder for money, else the jewels would have been taken."

O'Connor looked approvingly at me. "Exactly what I said," he exclaimed. "She was dead before her body was thrown into the water."

"No, I don't agree with you there," corrected Craig, continuing his examination of the body. "And yet it is not a case of drowning exactly, either."

"Strangled?" suggested O'Connor.

"By some jiu jitsu trick?" I put in, mindful of the queer-acting Jap at Clendenin's.

Kennedy shook his head.

"Perhaps the shock of the bullet wound rendered her unconscious and in that state she was thrown in," ventured Walker Curtis, apparently much relieved that Kennedy coincided with O'Connor in disagreeing with the harbour police as to the suicide theory.

Kennedy shrugged his shoulders and looked at the bullet again. "It is very extraordinary," was all he replied. "I think you said a few moments ago, O'Connor, that there had been some queer doings about here. What did you mean?"

"Well, as I said, the work of the harbour squad isn't ordinarily very remarkable. Harbour pirates aren't murderous as a rule any more. For the most part they are plain sneak thieves or bogus junk dealers who work with dishonest pier watchmen and crooked canal boat captains and lighter hands.

"But in this instance," continued the deputy, his face knitting at the thought that he had to confess another mystery to which he had no solution, "it is something quite different. You know that all along the shore on this side of the island are old, dilapidated and, some of them, deserted houses. For several days the residents of the neighbourhood have been complaining of strange occurrences about one place in particular which was the home of a wealthy family in a past generation. It is about a mile from here, facing the road along the shore, and has in front of it and across the road the remains of an old dock sticking out a few feet into the water at high tide.

"Now, as nearly as any one can get the story, there seems to have been a mysterious, phantom boat, very swift, without lights, and with an engine carefully muffled down which has been coming up to the old dock for the past few nights when the tide was high enough. A light has been seen moving on the dock, then suddenly extinguished, only to reappear again. Who carried it and why, no one knows. Any one who has tried to approach the place has had a scare thrown into him which he will not easily forget. For instance, one man crept up and though he did not think he was seen he was suddenly shot at from behind a tree. He felt the bullet pierce his arm, started to run, stumbled, and next morning woke up in the exact spot on which he had fallen, none the worse for his experience except that he had a slight wound that will prevent his using his right arm for some time for heavy work.

"After each visit of the phantom boat there is heard, according to the story of the few neighbours who have observed it, the tramp of feet up the overgrown stone walk from the dock and some have said that they heard an automobile as silent and ghostly as the boat. We have been all through the weird old house, but have found nothing there, except enough loose boards and shutters to account for almost any noise or combination of noises. However, no one has said there was anything there except the tramp of feet going back and forth on the old pavements outside. Two or three times shots have been heard, and on the dock where most of the alleged mysterious doings have taken place we have found one very new exploded shell of a cartridge."

Craig took the shell which O'Connor drew from

another pocket and trying to fit the bullet and the cartridge together remarked "both from a .44, probably one of those old-fashioned, long-barrelled makes."

"There," concluded O'Connor ruefully, "you know all we know of the thing so far."

"I may keep these for the present?" inquired Kennedy, preparing to pocket the shell and the bullet, and from his very manner I could see that as a matter of fact he already knew a great deal more about the case than the police. "Take us down to this old house and dock, if you please."

Over and over, Craig paced up and down the dilapidated dock, his keen eyes fastened to the ground, seeking some clue, anything that would point to the marauders. Real persons they certainly were, and not any ghostly crew of the bygone days of harbour pirates, for there was every evidence of some one who had gone up and down the walk recently, not once but many times.

Suddenly Kennedy stumbled over what looked like a sardine tin can, except that it had no label or trace of one. It was lying in the thick long matted grass by the side of the walk as if it had tumbled there and had been left unnoticed.

Yet there was nothing so very remarkable about it in itself. Tin cans were lying all about, those marks of decadent civilisation. But to Craig it had instantly presented an idea. It was a new can. The others were rusted.

He had pried off the lid and inside was a blackish, viscous mass.

"Smoking opium," Craig said at last.

We retraced our steps pondering on the significance of the discovery.

O'Connor had had men out endeavouring all day to get a clue to the motor car that had been mentioned in some of the accounts given by the natives. So far the best he had been able to find was a report of a large red touring car which crossed from New York on a late ferry. In it were a man and a girl as well as a chauffeur who wore goggles and a cap pulled down over his head so that he was practically unrecognisable. The girl might have been Miss Curtis and, as for the man, it might have been Clendenin. No one had bothered much with them; no one had taken their number; no one had paid any attention where they went after the ferry landed. In fact, there would have been no significance to the report if it had not been learned that early in the morning on the first ferry from the lower end of the island to New Jersey a large red touring car answering about the same description had crossed, with a single man and driver but no woman.

"I should like to watch here with you to-night, O'Connor," said Craig as we parted. "Meet us here. In the meantime I shall call on Jameson with his well-known newspaper connections in the white light district," here he gave me a half facetious wink, "to see what he can do toward getting me admitted to this gilded palace of dope up there on Forty-fourth Street."

After no little trouble Kennedy and I discovered our "hop joint" and were admitted by Nichi Moto, of whom we had heard. Kennedy gave me a final injunction to watch but to be very careful not to seem to watch.

Nichi Moto with an eye to business and not to our absorbing more than enough to whet our descriptive powers quickly conducted us into a large room where, on single bamboo couches or bunks, rather tastefully made, perhaps half a dozen habitués lay stretched at full length smoking their pipes in peace, or preparing them in great expectation from the implements on the trays before them.

Kennedy relieved me of the responsibility of cooking the opium by doing it for both of us and, incidentally, dropping a hint not to inhale it and to breathe as little of it as possible. Even then it made me feel badly, though he must have contrived in some way to get even less of the stuff than I. A couple of pipes, and Kennedy beckoned to Nichi.

"Where is Mr. Clendenin?" he asked familiarly. "I haven't seen him yet."

The Japanese smiled his engaging smile. "Not know," was all he said, and yet I knew the fellow at least knew better English, if not more facts.

Kennedy had about started on our faking a third "pipe" when a new, unexpected arrival beckoned excitedly to Nichi. I could not catch all that was said but two words that I did catch were "the boss" and "hop toy," the latter the word for opium. No sooner had the man disappeared without joining the smokers than Nichi seemed to grow very restless and anxious. Evidently he had received orders to do something. He seemed anxious to close the place and get away. I thought that some one might have given a tip that the place was to be raided, but Kennedy, who had been closer, had overheard more than I had and among other things he had caught the word, "meet him at the same place."

It was not long before we were all politely hustled out.

"At least we know this," commented Kennedy, as I congratulated myself on our fortunate escape, "Clendenin was not there, and there is something doing to-night, for he has sent for Nichi."

We dropped into our apartment to freshen up a bit against the long vigil that we knew was coming that night. To our surprise Walker Curtis had left a message that he wished to see Kennedy immediately and alone, and although I was not present I give the substance of what he said. It seemed that he had not wished to tell O'Connor for fear that it would get into the papers and cause an even greater scandal, but it had come to his knowledge a few days before the tragedy that his sister was determined to marry a very wealthy Chinese merchant, an importer of tea, named Chin Jung. Whether or not this had any bearing on the case he did not know. He thought it had, because for a long time, both when she was on the stage and later, Clendenin had had a great influence over her and had watched with a jealous eye the advances of every one else. Curtis was especially bitter against Clendenin.

As Kennedy related the conversation to me on our way over to Staten Island I tried to piece the thing together, but like one of the famous Chinese puzzles, it would not come out. I had to admit the possibility that it was Clendenin who might have quarrelled over her attachment to Chin Jung, even though I have never yet been able to understand what the fascination is that some Orientals have over certain American girls.

All that night we watched patiently from a vantage point of an old shed near both the house and the decayed pier. It was weird in the extreme, especially as we had no idea what might happen if we had success and saw something. But there was no reward for our patience. Absolutely nothing happened. It was as though they knew, whoever they were, that we were there. During the hours that passed O'Connor whiled away the time in a subdued whisper now and then in telling us of his experiences in Chinatown which he was now engaged in trying to clean up. From Chinatown, its dens, its gamblers and its tongs we drifted to the legitimate business interests there, and I, at least, was surprised to find that there were some of the merchants for whom even O'Connor had a great deal of respect. Kennedy evidently did not wish to violate in any way the confidence of Walker Curtis, and mention of the name of Chin Jung, but by a judicious question as to who the best men were in the Celestial settlement he did get a list of half a dozen or so from O'Connor. Chin Jung was well up in the list. However, the night wore away and still nothing happened.

It was in the middle of the morning when we were taking a snatch of sleep in our own rooms uptown that the telephone began to ring insistently. Kennedy, who was resting, I verily believe, merely out of consideration for my own human frailties, was at the receiver in an instant. It proved to be O'Connor. He had just gone back to his office at headquarters and there he had found a report of another murder.

"Who is it?" asked Kennedy, "and why do you connect it with this case?"

O'Connor's answer must have been a poser, judging from the look of surprise on Craig's face. "The Jap—Nichi Moto?" he repeated. "And it is the same sort of non-fatal wound, the same evidence of asphyxia, the same circumstances, even down to the red car reported by residents in the neighbourhood."

Nothing further happened that day except this thickening of the plot by the murder of the peculiar-acting Nichi. We saw his body and it was as O'Connor said.

"That fellow wasn't on the level toward Clendenin," Craig mused after we had viewed the second murder in the case. "The question is, who and what was he working for?"

There was as yet no hint of answer, and our only plan was to watch again that night. This time O'Connor, not knowing where the lightning would strike next, took Craig's suggestion and we determined to spend the time cruising about in the fastest of the police motor boats, while the force of watchers along the entire shore front of the city was quietly augmented and ordered to be extra vigilant.

O'Connor at the last moment had to withdraw and let us go alone, for the worst, and not the unexpected, happened in his effort to clean up Chinatown. The war between the old rivals, the Hep Sing Tong and the On Leong Tong, those ancient societies of trouble-makers in the little district, had broken out afresh during the day and three Orientals had been killed already.

It is not a particularly pleasant occupation cruising aimlessly up and down the harbour in a fifty-foot police boat, staunch and fast as she may be.

Every hour we called at a police post to report and to keep in touch with anything that might interest us. It came at about two o'clock in the morning and of all places, near the Battery itself. From the front of a ferry boat that ran far down on the Brooklyn side, what looked like two flashlights gleamed out over the water once, then twice.

"Headlights of an automobile," remarked Craig, scarcely taking more notice of it, for they might have simply been turned up and down twice by a late returning traveller to test them. We were ourselves near the Brooklyn shore. Imagine our surprise to see an answering light from a small boat in the river which was otherwise lightless. We promptly put out our own lights and with every cylinder working made for the spot where the light had flashed up on the river. There was something there all right and we went for it.

On we raced after the strange craft, the phantom that had scared Staten Island. For a mile or so we seemed to be gaining, but one of our cylinders began to miss—the boat turned sharply around a bend in the shore. We had to give it up as well as trying to overtake the ferry boat going in the opposite direction.

12

Kennedy's equanimity in our apparent defeat surprised me. "Oh, it's nothing, Walter," he said. "They slipped away to-night, but I have found the clue. To-morrow as soon as the Customs House is open you will understand. It all centres about opium."

At least a large part of the secret was cleared, too, as a result of Kennedy's visit to the Customs House. After years of fighting with the opium ring on the Pacific coast, the ring had tried to "put one over" on the revenue officers and smuggle the drug in through New York.

It did not take long to find the right man among the revenue officers to talk with. Nor was Kennedy surprised to learn that Nichi Moto had been in fact a Japanese detective, a sort of stool pigeon in Clendenin's establishment working to keep the government in touch with the latest scheme.

The finding of the can of opium on the scene of the murder of Bertha Curtis, and the chase after the lightless motor boat had at last placed Kennedy on the right track. With one of the revenue officers we made a quick trip to Brooklyn and spent the morning inspecting the ships from South American ports docked in the neighbourhood where the phantom boat had disappeared.

From ship to ship we journeyed until at last we came to one on which, down in the chain locker, we found a false floor with a locker under that. There was a compartment six feet square and in it lay, neatly packed, fourteen large hermetically sealed cylinders, each full of the little oblong tins such as Kennedy had picked up the other day—forty thousand dollars' worth of the stuff at one haul, to say nothing of the thousands that had already been landed at one place or another.

It had been a good day's work, but as yet it had not caught the slayer or cleared up the mystery of Bertha Curtis. Some one or something had had a power over the girl to lure her on. Was it Clendenin? The place in Forty-fourth Street, on inquiry, proved to be really closed as tight as a drum. Where was he?

All the deaths had been mysterious, were still mysterious. Bertha Curtis had carried her secret with her to the grave to which she had been borne, willingly it seemed, in the red car with the unknown companion and the goggled chauffeur. I found myself still asking what possible connection she could have with smuggling opium.

Kennedy, however, was indulging in no such speculations. It was enough for him that the scene had suddenly shifted and in a most unexpected manner. I found him voraciously reading practically everything that was being printed in the papers about the revival of the tong war.

"They say much about the war, but little about the cause," was his dry comment. "I wish I could make up my mind whether it is due to the closing of the joints by O'Connor, or the belief that one tong is informing on the other about opium smuggling."

Kennedy passed over all the picturesque features in the newspapers, and from it all picked out the one point that was most important for the case which he was working to clear up.   One tong used revolvers of a certain make; the other of a different make. The bullet which had killed Bertha Curtis and later Nichi Moto was from a pistol like that of the Hep Sings.

The difference in the makes of guns seemed at once to suggest something to Kennedy and instead of mixing actively in the war of the highbinders he retired to his unfailing laboratory, leaving me to pass the time gathering such information as I could.   Once I dropped in on him but found him unsociably surrounded by microscopes and a very sensitive arrangement for taking microphotographs.   Some of his negatives were nearly a foot in diameter, and might have been, for all I knew, pictures of the surface of the moon.

While I was there O'Connor came in.   Craig questioned him about the war of the tongs.

"Why," O'Connor cried, almost bubbling over with satisfaction, "this afternoon I was waited on by Chin Jung, you remember?—one of the leading merchants down there.   Of course you know that Chinatown doesn't believe in hurting business and it seems that he and some of the others like him are afraid that if the tong war is not hushed up pretty soon it will cost a lot—in money.   They are going to have an anniversary of the founding of the Chinese republic soon and of the Chinese New Year and they are afraid that if the war doesn't stop they'll be ruined."

"Which tong does he belong to?" asked Kennedy, still scrutinising a photograph through his lens.

"Neither," replied O'Connor.   "With his aid and

that of a Judge of one of our courts who knows the Chinaman like a book we. have had a conference this afternoon between the two tongs and the truce is restored again for two weeks."

"Very good," answered Kennedy, "but it doesn't catch the murderer of Bertha Curtis and the Jap. Where is Clendenin, do you suppose?"

"I don't know, but it at least leaves me free to carry on that case. What are all these pictures?"

"Well," began Kennedy, taking his glass from his eye and wiping it carefully, "a Paris crime specialist has formulated a system for identifying revolver bullets which is very like that of Dr. Bertillon for identifying human beings."

He picked up a handful of the greatly enlarged photographs. "These are photographs of bullets which he has sent me. The barrel of every gun leaves marks on the bullet that are always the same for the same barrel but never identical for two different barrels. In these big negatives every detail appears very distinctly and it can be decided with absolute certainty whether a given bullet was fired from a given revolver. Now, using this same method, I have made similar greatly enlarged photographs of the two bullets that have figured so far in this case. The bullet that killed Miss Curtis shows the same marks as that which killed Nichi."

He picked up another bunch of prints. "Now," he continued, "taking up the firing pin of a rifle or the hammer of a revolver, you may not know it but they are different in every case. Even among the same makes they are different, and can be detected.

"The cartridge in either a gun or revolver is struck at a point which is never in the exact centre or edge, as the case may be, but is always the same for the same weapon. Now the end of the hammer when examined with the microscope bears certain irregularities of marking different from those of every other gun and the shell fired in it is impressed with the particular markings of that hammer, just as paper is by type. On making microphotographs of firing pins or hammers, with special reference to the rounded ends and also photographs of the corresponding rounded depressions in the primers fired by them it is forced on any one that cartridges fired by each individual rifle or pistol can positively be identified.

"You will see on the edge of the photographs I have made a rough sketch calling attention to the 'L'-shaped mark which is the chief characteristic of this hammer, although there are other detailed markings which show well under the microscope but not well in a photograph. You will notice that the characters on the firing hammer are reversed on the cartridge in the same way that a metal type and the character printed by it are reversed as regards one another. Again, depressions on the end of the hammer become raised characters on the cartridge, and raised characters on the hammer become depressions on the cartridge.

"Look at some of these old photographs and you will see that they differ from this. They lack the 'L' mark. Some have circles, others a very different series of pits and elevations, a set of characters when examined and measured under the microscope utterly different from those in every other case. Each is unique, in its pits, lines, circles and irregularities. The laws of chance are as much against two of them having the same markings as they are against the thumb prints of two human subjects being identical. The firing-pin theory, which was used in a famous case in Maine, is just as infallible as the finger-print theory. In this case when we find the owner of the gun making an 'L' mark we shall have the murderer."

Something, I could see, was working on O'Connor's mind. "That's all right," he interjected, "but you know in neither case was the victim shot to death. They were asphyxiated."

"I was coming to that," rejoined Craig. "You recall the peculiar marking on the nose of those bullets? They were what is known as narcotic bullets, an invention of a Pittsburg scientist. They have the property of lulling their victims to almost instant slumber. A slight scratch from these sleep-producing bullets is all that is necessary, as it was in the case of the man who spied on the queer doings on Staten Island. The drug, usually morphia, is carried in tiny wells on the cap of the bullet, is absorbed by the system and acts almost instantly."

The door burst open and Walker Curtis strode in excitedly. He seemed surprised to see us all there, hesitated, then motioned to Kennedy that he wished to see him. For a few moments they talked and finally I caught the remark from Kennedy, "But, Mr. Curtis, I must do it. It is the only way."

Curtis gave a resigned nod and Kennedy turned to us. "Gentlemen," he said, "Mr. Curtis in going over

the effects of his sister has found a note from Clendenin which mentions another opium joint down in
Chinatown. He wished me to investigate privately,
but I have told him it would be impossible."

At the mention of a den in the district he was clean-
ing up O'Connor had pricked up his ears. "Where
is it?" he demanded.

Curtis mentioned a number on Doyer Street.

"The Amoy restaurant," ejaculated O'Connor, seizing the telephone. A moment later he was arranging with the captain at the Elizabeth Street station
for the warrants for an instant raid.

XII

The "Dope Trust"

A S we hurried into Chinatown from Chatham
Square we could see that the district was cele-
brating its holidays with long ropes of firecrackers,
and was feasting to reed discords from the pipes of
its most famous musicians, and was gay with the
hanging out of many sunflags, red with an eighteen-
rayed white sun in the blue union. Both the new
tong truce and the anniversary were more than cause
for rejoicing.

Hurried though it was, the raid on the Hep Sing
joint had been carefully prepared by O'Connor. The
house we were after was one of the oldest of the rook-
eries, with a gaudy restaurant on the second floor,
a curio shop on the street level, while in the
basement all that was visible was a view of a
huge and orderly pile of tea chests. A moment
before the windows of the dwellings above the restaurant had been full of people. All had faded away
even before the axes began to swing on the basement
door which had the appearance of a storeroom for
the shop above.

The flimsy outside door went down quickly. But
it was only a blind. Another door greeted the raid-
ers. The axes swung noisily and the crowbars tore
at the fortified, iron-clad, "ice box" door inside.

After breaking it down they had to claw their way through another just like it. The thick doors and tea chests piled up showed why no sounds of gambling and other practices ever were heard outside.

Pushing aside a curtain we were in the main room. The scene was one of confusion showing the hasty departure of the occupants.

Kennedy did not stop here. Within was still another room, for smokers, anything but like the fashionable place we had seen uptown. It was low, common, disgusting. The odour everywhere was offensive; everywhere was filth that should naturally breed disease. It was an inferno reeking with unwholesome sweat and still obscured with dense fumes of smoke.

Three tiers of bunks of hardwood were built along the walls. There was no glamour here; all was sordid. Several Chinamen in various stages of dazed indolence were jabbering in incoherent oblivion, a state I suppose of "Oriental calm."

There, in a bunk, lay Clendenin. His slow and uncertain breathing told of his being under the influence of the drug, and he lay on his back beside a "layout" with a half-cooked pill still in the bowl of his pipe.

The question was to wake him up. Craig began slapping him with a wet towel, directing us how to keep him roused. We walked him about, up and down, dazed, less than half sensible, dreaming, muttering, raving.

A hasty exclamation from O'Connor followed as he drew from the scant cushions of the bunk a long-barreled pistol, a .44 such as the tong leaders used, the same make as had shot Bertha Curtis and Nichi. Craig seized it and stuck it into his pocket.

All the gamblers had fled, all except those too drugged to escape. Where they had gone was indicated by a door leading up to the kitchen of the restaurant. Craig did not stop but leaped upstairs and then down again into a little back court by means of a fire-escape. Through a sort of short alley we groped our way, or rather through an intricate maze of alleys and a labyrinth of blind recesses. We were apparently back of a store on Pell Street.

It was the work of only a moment to go through another door and into another room, filled with smoky, dirty, unpleasant, fetid air. This room, too, seemed to be piled with tea chests. Craig opened one. There lay piles and piles of opium tins, a veritable fortune in the drug.

Mysterious pots and pans, strainers, wooden vessels, and testing instruments were about. The odour of opium in the manufacture was unmistakable, for smoking opium is different from the medicinal drug. There it appeared the supplies of thousands of smokers all over the country were stored and prepared. In a corner a mass of the finished product lay weltering in a basin like treacle. In another corner was the apparatus for remaking yen-shee or once-smoked opium. This I felt was at last the home of the "dope trust," as O'Connor had once called it, the secret realm of a real opium king, the American end of the rich Shanghai syndicate.

A door opened and there stood a Chinaman, stoical, secretive, indifferent, with all the Oriental cunning and cruelty hall-marked on his face. Yet there was a fascination and air of Eastern culture about him in spite of that strange and typical Oriental depth of intrigue and cunning that shone through, great characteristics of the East.

No one said a word as Kennedy continued to ransack the place. At last under a rubbish heap he found a revolver wrapped up loosely in an old sweater. Quickly, under the bright light, Craig drew Clendenin's pistol, fitted a cartridge into it and fired at the wall. Again into the second gun he fitted another and a second shot rang out.

Out of his pocket came next the small magnifying glass and two unmounted microphotographs. He bent down over the exploded shells.

"There it is," cried Craig scarcely able to restrain himself with the keenness of his chase, "there it is— the mark like an 'L.' This cartridge bears the one mark, distinct, not possible to have been made by any other pistol in the world. None of the Hep Sings, all with the same make of weapons, none of the gunmen in their employ, could duplicate that mark."

"Some bullets," reported a policeman who had been rummaging further in the rubbish.

"Be careful, man," cautioned Craig. "They are doped. Lay them down. Yes, this is the same gun that fired the shot at Bertha Curtis and Nichi Moto —fired narcotic bullets in order to stop any one who interfered with the opium smuggling, without killing the victim."

"What's the matter?" asked O'Connor, arriving

breathless from the gambling room after hearing the shots. The Chinaman stood, still silent, impassive. At sight of him O'Connor gasped out, "Chin Jung!"

"Real tong leader," added Craig, "and the murderer of the white girl to whom he was engaged. This is the goggled chauffeur of the red car that met the smuggling boat, and in which Bertha Curtis rode, unsuspecting, to her death."

"And Clendenin?" asked Walker Curtis, not comprehending.

"A tool—poor wretch. So keen had the hunt for him become that he had to hide in the only safe place, with the coolies of his employer. He must have been in such abject terror that he has almost smoked himself to death."

"But why should the Chinaman shoot my sister?" asked Walker Curtis amazed at the turn of events.

"Your sister," replied Craig, almost reverently, "wrecked though she was by the drug, was at last conscience stricken when she saw the vast plot to debauch thousands of others. It was from her that the Japanese detective in the revenue service got his information—and both of them have paid the price. But they have smashed the new opium ring—we have captured the ring-leaders of the gang."

Out of the maze of streets, on Chatham Square again, we lost no time in mounting to the safety of the elevated station before some murderous tong member might seek revenge on us.

The celebration in Chinatown was stilled. It was as though the nerves of the place had been paralysed by our sudden, sharp blow.

A downtown train took me to the office to write a "beat," for the *Star* always made a special feature of the picturesque in Chinatown news. Kennedy went uptown.

Except for a few moments in the morning, I did not see Kennedy again until the following afternoon, for the tong war proved to be such an interesting feature that I had to help lay out and direct the assignments covering its various details.

I managed to get away again as soon as possible, however, for I knew that it would not be long before some one else in trouble would commandeer Kennedy to untangle a mystery, and I wanted to be on the spot when it started.

Sure enough, it turned out that I was right. Seated with him in our living room, when I came in from my hasty journey uptown in the subway, was a man, tall, thick-set, with a crop of closely curling dark hair, a sharp, pointed nose, ferret eyes, and a reddish moustache, curled at the ends. I had no difficulty in deciding what he was, if not who he was. He was the typical detective who, for the very reason that he looked the part, destroyed much of his own usefulness.

"We have lost so much lately at Trimble's," he was saying, "that it is long past the stage of being merely interesting. It is downright serious—for me, at least. I've got to make good or lose my job. And I'm up against one of the cleverest shoplifters that ever entered a department-store, apparently. Only Heaven knows how much she has got away with in various departments so far, but when it comes to lifting valuable things like pieces of jewelry which run into the thousands, that is too much."

At the mention of the name of the big Trimble store I had recognised at once what the man was, and it did not need Kennedy's rapid-fire introduction of Michael Donnelly to tell me that he was a department store detective.

"Have you no clue, no suspicions?" inquired Kennedy.

"Well, yes, suspicions," measured Donnelly slowly. "For instance, one day not long ago a beautifully dressed and refined-looking woman called at the jewellery department and asked to see a diamond necklace which we had just imported from Paris. She seemed to admire it very much, studied it, tried it on, but finally went away without making up her mind. A couple of days later she returned and asked to see it again. This time there happened to be another woman beside her who was looking at some pendants. The two fell to talking about the necklace, according to the best recollection of the clerk, and the second woman began to examine it critically. Again the prospective buyer went away. But this time after she had gone, and when he was putting the things back into the safe, the clerk examined the necklace, thinking that perhaps a flaw had been discovered in it which had decided the woman against it. It was a replica in paste; probably substituted by one of these clever and smartly dressed women for the real necklace."

Before Craig had a chance to put another question, the buzzer on our door sounded, and I admitted a dapper, soft-spoken man of middle size, who might have been a travelling salesman or a bookkeeper. He pulled a card from his case and stood facing us, evidently in doubt how to proceed.

"Professor Kennedy?" he asked at length, balancing the pasteboard between his fingers.

"Yes," answered Craig. "What can I do for you?"

"I am from Shorham, the Fifth Avenue jeweller, you know," he began brusquely, as he handed the card to Kennedy. "I thought I'd drop in to consult you about a peculiar thing that happened at the store recently, but if you are engaged, I can wait. You see, we had on exhibition a very handsome pearl dog-collar, and a few days ago two women came to—"

"Say," interrupted Kennedy, glancing from the card to the face of Joseph Bentley, and then at Donnelly. "What is this—a gathering of the clans? There seems to be an epidemic of shoplifting. How much were you stung for?"

"About twenty thousand altogether," replied Bentley with rueful frankness. "Why? Has some one else been victimised, too?"

XIII

The Kleptomaniac

QUICKLY Kennedy outlined, with Donnelly's permission, the story we had just heard. The two store detectives saw the humour of the situation, as well as the seriousness of it, and fell to comparing notes.

"The professional as well as the amateur shoplifter has always presented to me an interesting phase of criminality," remarked Kennedy tentatively, during a lull in their mutual commiseration. "With thousands of dollars' worth of goods lying unprotected on the counters, it is really no wonder that some are tempted to reach out and take what they want."

"Yes," explained Donnelly, "the shop-lifter is the department-store's greatest unsolved problem. Why, sir, she gets more plunder in a year than the burglar. She's costing the stores over two million dollars. And she is at her busiest just now with the season's shopping in full swing. It's the price the stores have to pay for displaying their goods, but we have to do it, and we are at the mercy of the thieves. I don't mean by that the occasional shoplifter who, when she gets caught, confesses, cries, pleads, and begs to return the stolen article. They often get off. It is the regulars who get the two million, those known to the police, whose pictures are, many of them, in the Rogues' Gallery, whose careers and haunts are known to every probation officer. They are getting away with loot that means for them a sumptuous living."

"Of course we are not up against the same sort of swindlers that you are," put in Bentley, "but let me tell you that when the big jewelers do get up against anything of the sort they are up against it hard."

"Have you any idea who it could be?" asked Kennedy, who had been following the discussion keenly.

"Well, some idea," spoke up Donnelly. "From what Bentley says I wouldn't be surprised to find that it was the same person in both cases. Of course you know how rushed all the stores are just now. It is much easier for these light-fingered individuals to operate during the rush than at any other time. In the summer, for instance, there is almost no shoplifting at all. I thought that perhaps we could discover this particular shoplifter by ordinary means, that perhaps some of the clerks in the jewellery department might be able to identify her. We found one who said that he thought he might recognise one of the women if he saw her again. Perhaps you did not know that we have our own little rogues' gallery in most of the big department-stores. But there didn't happen to be anything there that he recognised. So I took him down to Police Headquarters. Through plate after plate of pictures among the shoplifters in the regular Rogues' Gallery the clerk went. At last he came to one picture that caused him to stop. 'That is one of the women I saw in the store that day,' he said. 'I'm sure of it.'"

Donnelly produced a copy of the Bertillon picture.

"What?" exclaimed Bentley, as he glanced at it and then at the name and history on the back. "Annie Grayson? Why, she is known as the queen of shoplifters. She has operated from Christie's in London to the little curio-shops of San Francisco. She has worked under a dozen aliases and has the art of alibi down to perfection. Oh, I've heard of her many times before. I wonder if she really is the person we're looking for. They say that Annie Grayson has forgotten more about shoplifting than the others will ever know."

"Yes," continued Donnelly, "and here's the queer part of it. The clerk was ready to swear that he had seen the woman in the store at some time or other, but whether she had been near the counter where the necklace was displayed was another matter. He wasn't so sure about that."

"Then how did she get it?" I asked, much interested.

"I don't say that she did get it," cautioned Donnelly. "I don't know anything about it. That is why I am here consulting Professor Kennedy."

"Then who did get it, do you think?" I demanded.

"We have a great deal of very conflicting testimony from the various clerks," Donnelly continued. "Among those who are known to have visited the department and to have seen the necklace is another woman, of an entirely different character, well known in the city." He glanced sharply at us, as if to impress us with what he was about to say, then he leaned over and almost whispered the name. "As nearly as I can gather out of the mass of evidence, Mrs. William Willoughby, the wife of the broker down in Wall Street, was the last person who was seen looking at the diamonds."

The mere breath of such a suspicion would have been enough, without his stage-whisper method of imparting the information. I felt that it was no wonder that, having even a suspicion of this sort, he should be in doubt how to go ahead and should wish Kennedy's advice. Ella Willoughby, besides being the wife of one of the best known operators in high-class stocks and bonds, was well known in the society columns of the newspapers. She lived in Glenclair, where she was a leader of the smarter set at both the church and the country club. The group who preserved this neat balance between higher things and the world, the flesh and the devil, I knew to be a very exclusive group, which, under the calm suburban surface, led a sufficiently rapid life. Mrs. Willoughby, in addition to being a leader, was a very striking woman and a beautiful dresser, who set a fast pace for the semi-millionaires who composed the group.

Here indeed was a puzzle at the very start of the case. It was in all probability Mrs. Willoughby who had looked at the jewels in both cases. On the other hand, it was Annie Grayson who had been seen on at least one occasion, yet apparently had had nothing whatever to do with the missing jewels, at least not so far as any tangible evidence yet showed. More than that, Donnelly vouchsafed the information that he had gone further and that some of the men working under him had endeavoured to follow the movements of the two women and had found what looked to be a curious crossing of trails. Both of them, he had found, had been in the habit of visiting, while shopping, the same little tea-room on Thirty-third Street, though no one had ever seen them together there, and the coincidence might be accounted for by the fact that many Glenclair ladies on shopping expeditions made this tea-room a sort of rendezvous. By inquiring about among his own fraternity Donnelly had found that other stores also had reported losses recently, mostly of diamonds and pearls, both black and white.

Kennedy had been pondering the situation for some time, scarcely uttering a word. Both detectives were now growing restless, waiting for him to say something. As for me, I knew that if anything were said or done it would be in Kennedy's own good time. I had learned to have implicit faith and confidence in him, for I doubt if Craig could have been placed in a situation where he would not know just what to do after he had looked over the ground.

At length he leisurely reached across the table for the suburban telephone book, turned the pages quickly, snapped it shut, and observed wearily and, as it seemed, irrelevantly: "The same old trouble again about accurate testimony. I doubt whether if I should suddenly pull a revolver and shoot Jameson, either of you two men could give a strictly accurate account of just what happened."

No one said anything, as he raised his hands from

his habitual thinking posture with finger-tips together, placed both hands back of his head, and leaned back facing us squarely.

"The first step," he said slowly, "must be to arrange a 'plant.' As nearly as I can make out the shoplifters or shoplifter, whichever it may prove to be, have no hint that any one is watching them yet. Now, Donnelly, it is still very early. I want you to telephone around to the newspapers, and either in the Trimble advertisements or in the news columns have it announced that your jewellery department has on exhibition a new and special importation of South African stones among which is one—let me see, let's call it the 'Kimberley Queen.' That will sound attractive. In the meantime find the largest and most perfect paste jewel in town and have it fixed up for exhibition and labelled the Kimberley Queen. Give it a history if you can; anything to attract attention. I'll see you in the morning. Good-night, and thank you for coming to me with this case."

It was quite late, but Kennedy, now thoroughly interested in following the chase, had no intention of waiting until the morrow before taking action on his own account. In fact he was just beginning the evening's work by sending Donnelly off to arrange the "plant." No less interested in the case than himself, I needed no second invitation, and in a few minutes we were headed from our rooms toward the laboratory, where Kennedy had apparatus to meet almost any conceivable emergency. From a shelf in the corner he took down an oblong oak box, perhaps eighteen inches in length, in the front of which was set a circular metal disk with a sort of pointer and dial. He lifted the lid of the box, and inside I could see two shiny caps which in turn he lifted, disclosing what looked like two good-sized spools of wire. Apparently satisfied with his scrutiny, he snapped the lid shut and wrapped up the box carefully, consigning it to my care, while he hunted some copper wire.

From long experience with Kennedy I knew better than to ask what he had in mind to do. It was enough to know that he had already, in those few minutes of apparent dreaming while Donnelly and Bentley were fidgeting for words, mapped out a complete course of action.

We bent our steps toward the under-river tube, which carried a few late travellers to the railroad terminal where Kennedy purchased tickets for Glenclair. I noticed that the conductor on the suburban train eyed us rather suspiciously as though the mere fact that we were not travelling with commutation tickets at such an hour constituted an offence. Although I did not yet know the precise nature of our adventure, I remembered with some misgiving that I had read of police dogs in Glenclair which were uncomfortably familiar with strangers carrying bundles. However, we got along all right, perhaps because the dogs knew that in a town of commuters every one was privileged to carry a bundle.

"If the Willoughbys had been on a party line," remarked Craig as we strode up Woodridge Avenue trying to look as if it was familiar to us, "we might have arranged this thing by stratagem. As it is, we shall have to resort to another method, and perhaps better, since we shall have to take no one into our confidence."

The avenue was indeed a fine thoroughfare, lined on both sides with large and often imposing mansions, surrounded with trees and shrubbery, which served somewhat to screen them. We came at last to the Willoughby house, a sizable colonial residence set up on a hill. It was dark, except for one dim light in an upper story. In the shadow of the hedge, Craig silently vaulted the low fence and slipped up the terraces, as noiselessly as an Indian, scarcely crackling a twig or rustling a dead leaf on the ground. He paused as he came to a wing on the right of the house.

I had followed more laboriously, carrying the box and noting that he was not looking so much at the house as at the sky, apparently. It did not take long to fathom what he was after. It was not a star-gazing expedition; he was following the telephone wire that ran in from the street to the corner of the house near which we were now standing. A moment's inspection showed him where the wire was led down on the outside and entered through the top of a window.

Quickly he worked, though in a rather awkward position, attaching two wires carefully to the telephone wires. Next he relieved me of the oak box with its strange contents, and placed it under the porch where it was completely hidden by some lattice-work which extended down to the ground on this side. Then he attached the new wires from the telephone to it and hid the connecting wires as best he could behind the swaying runners of a vine. At last, when he had finished to his satisfaction, we retraced our steps, to find that our only chance of getting out of town that night was by trolley that landed us, after many changes, in our apartment in New York, thoroughly convinced of the disadvantages of suburban detective work.

Nevertheless the next day found us out sleuthing about Glenclair, this time in a more pleasant rôle. We had a newspaper friend or two out there who was willing to introduce us about without asking too many questions. Kennedy, of course, insisted on beginning at the very headquarters of gossip, the country club.

We spent several enjoyable hours about the town, picking up a good deal of miscellaneous and useless information. It was, however, as Kennedy had suspected. Annie Grayson had taken up her residence in an artistic little house on one of the best side streets of the town. But her name was no longer Annie Grayson. She was Mrs. Maud Emery, a dashing young widow of some means, living in a very quiet but altogether comfortable style, cutting quite a figure in the exclusive suburban community, a leading member of the church circle, an officer of the Civic League, prominent in the women's club, and popular with those to whom the established order of things was so perfect that the only new bulwark of their rights was an anti-suffrage society. In fact, every one was talking of the valuable social acquisition in the person of this attractive young woman who entertained lavishly and was bracing up an otherwise drooping season. No one knew much about her, but then, that was not necessary. It was enough to accept one whose opinions and actions were not subversive of the social order in any way.

The Willoughbys, of course, were among the most prominent people in the town. William Willoughby was head of the firm of Willoughby & Walton, and it was the general opinion that Mrs. Willoughby was the head of the firm of Ella & William Willoughby. The Willoughbys were good mixers, and were spoken well of even by the set who occupied the social stratum just one degree below that in which they themselves moved. In fact, when Mrs. Willoughby had been severely injured in an automobile accident during the previous summer Glenclair had shown real solicitude for her and had forgotten a good deal of its artificiality in genuine human interest.

Kennedy was impatiently waiting for an opportunity to recover the box which he had left under the Willoughby porch. Several times we walked past the house, but it was not until nightfall that he considered it wise to make the recovery. Again we slipped silently up the terraces. It was the work of only a moment to cut the wires, and in triumph Craig bore off the precious oak box and its batteries.

He said little on our journey back to the city, but the moment we had reached the laboratory he set the box on a table with an attachment which seemed to be controlled by pedals operated by the feet.

"Walter," he explained, holding what looked like an earpiece in his hand, "this is another of those new little instruments that scientific detectives to-day are using. A poet might write a clever little verse entitled, 'The telegraphone'll get you, if you don't watch out.' This is the latest improved telegraphone, a little electromagnetic wizard in a box, which we detectives are now using to take down and 'can' telephone conversations and other records. It is based on an entirely new principle in every way different from the phonograph. It was discovered by an inventor several years ago, while experimenting in telephony.

"There are no disks or cylinders of wax, as in the phonograph, but two large spools of extremely fine steel wire. The record is not made mechanically on a cylinder, but electromagnetically on this wire. Small portions of magnetism are imparted to fractions of the steel wire as it passes between two carbon electric magnets. Each impression represents a sound wave. There is no apparent difference in the wire, no surface abrasion or other change, yet each particle of steel undergoes an electromagnetic transformation by which the sound is indelibly imprinted on it until it is wiped out by the erasing magnet. There are no cylinders to be shaved; all that is needed to use the wire again is to pass a magnet over it, automatically erasing any previous record that you do not wish to preserve. You can dictate into it, or, with this plug in, you can record a telephone conversation on it. Even rust or other deterioration of the steel wire by time will not affect this electromagnetic registry of sound. It can be read as long as steel will last. It is as effective for long distances as for short, and there is wire enough on one of these spools for thirty minutes of uninterrupted record."

Craig continued to tinker tantalisingly with the machine.

"The principle on which it is based," he added, "is that a mass of tempered steel may be impressed with and will retain magnetic fluxes varying in density and in sign in adjacent portions of its mass. There are no indentations on the wire or the steel disk. Instead there is a deposit of magnetic impulse on the wire, which is made by connecting up an ordinary telephone transmitter with the electromagnets and talking through the coil. The disturbance set up in the coils by the vibration of the diaphragm of the transmitter causes a deposit of magnetic impulse on the wire, the coils being connected with dry batteries. When the wire is again run past these coils, with a receiver such as I have here in circuit with the coils, a light vibration is set up in the receiver diaphragm which reproduces the sound of speech."

He turned a switch and placed an ear-piece over his head, giving me another connected with it. We listened eagerly. There were no foreign noises in the machine, no grating or thumping sounds, as he controlled the running off of the steel wire by means of a foot-pedal.

We were listening to everything that had been said over the Willoughby telephone during the day. Several local calls to tradesmen came first, and these we passed over quickly. Finally we heard the following conversation:

"Hello. Is that you, Ella? Yes, this is Maud. Good-morning. How do you feel to-day?"

"Good-morning, Maud. I don't feel very well. I have a splitting headache."

"Oh, that's too bad, dear. What are you doing for it?"

"Nothing—yet. If it doesn't get better I shall have Mr. Willoughby call up Dr. Guthrie."

"Oh, I hope it gets better soon. You poor creature, don't you think a little trip into town might make you feel better? Had you thought of going to-day?"

"Why, no. I hadn't thought of going in. Are you going?"

"Did you see the Trimble ad. in the morning paper?"

"No, I didn't see the papers this morning. My head felt too bad."

"Well, just glance at it. It will interest you. They have the Kimberley Queen, the great new South African diamond on exhibition there."

"They have? I never heard of it before, but isn't that interesting. I certainly would like to see it. Have you ever seen it?"

"No, but I have made up my mind not to miss a sight of it. They say it is wonderful. You'd better come along. I may have something interesting to tell you, too."

"Well, I believe I will go. Thank you, Maud, for suggesting it. Perhaps the little change will make me feel better. What train are you going to take? The ten-two? All right, I'll try to meet you at the station. Good-bye, Maud."

"Good-bye, Ella."

Craig stopped the machine, ran it back again and repeated the record. "So," he commented at the conclusion of the repetition, "the 'plant' has taken root. Annie Grayson has bitten at the bait."

A few other local calls and a long-distance call from Mr. Willoughby cut short by his not finding his wife at home followed. Then there seemed to have been nothing more until after dinner. It was a call by Mr. Willoughby himself that now interested us.

"Hello! hello! Is that you, Dr. Guthrie? Well, Doctor, this is Mr. Willoughby talking. I'd like to make an appointment for my wife to-morrow."

"Why, what's the trouble, Mr. Willoughby? Nothing serious, I hope."

"Oh, no, I guess not. But then I want to be sure, and I guess you can fix her up all right. She complains of not being able to sleep and has been having pretty bad headaches now and then."

"Is that so? Well, that's too bad. These women and their headaches—even as a doctor they puzzle me. They often go away as suddenly as they come. However, it will do no harm to see me."

"And then she complains of noises in her ears, seems to hear things, though as far as I can make out, there is nothing—at least nothing that I hear."

"Um-m, hallucinations in hearing, I suppose. Any dizziness?"

"Why, yes, a little once in a while."

"How is she now?"

"Well, she's been into town this afternoon and is pretty tired, but she says she feels a little better for the excitement of the trip."

"Well, let me see. I've got to come down Woodridge Avenue to see a patient in a few minutes anyhow. Suppose I just drop off at your place?"

"That will be fine. You don't think it is anything
serious, do you, Doctor?"

"Oh, no. Probably it's her nerves. Perhaps a little rest would do her good. We'll see."

The telegraphone stopped, and that seemed to be
the last conversation recorded. So far we had
learned nothing very startling, I thought, and was
just a little disappointed. Kennedy seemed well satisfied, however.

Our own telephone rang, and it proved to be Donnelly on the wire. He had been trying to get Kennedy
all day, in order to report that at various times his
men at Trimble's had observed Mrs. Willoughby and
later Annie Grayson looking with much interest at
the Kimberley Queen, and other jewels in the exhibit.
There was nothing more to report.

"Keep it on view another day or two," ordered
Kennedy. "Advertise it, but in a quiet way. We
don't want too many people interested. I'll see you
in the morning at the store—early."

"I think I'll just run back to Glenclair again to-
night," remarked Kennedy as he hung up the receiver.
"You needn't bother about coming, Walter. I want
to see Dr. Guthrie a moment. You remember him?
We met him to-day at the country club, a kindly looking, middle-aged fellow?"

I would willingly have gone back with him, but I
felt that I could be of no particular use. While he
was gone I pondered a good deal over the situation.

Twice, at least, previously some one had pilfered jewellery from stores, leaving in its place worthless imitations. Twice the evidence had been so conflicting that no one could judge of its value. What reason, I asked myself, was there to suppose that it would be different now? No shoplifter in her senses was likely to lift the great Kimberley Queen gem with the eagle eyes of clerks and detectives on her, even if she did not discover that it was only a paste jewel. And if Craig gave the woman, whoever she was, a good opportunity to get away with it, it would be a case of the same conflicting evidence; or worse, no evidence.

Yet the more I thought of it, the more apparent to me was it that Kennedy must have thought the whole thing out before. So far all that had been evident was that he was merely preparing a "plant." Still, I meant to caution him when he returned that one could not believe his eyes, certainly not his ears, as to what might happen, unless he was unusually skilful or lucky. It would not do to rely on anything so fallible as the human eye or ear, and I meant to impress it on him. What, after all, had been the net result of our activities so far? We had found next to nothing. Indeed, it was all a greater mystery than ever.

It was very late when Craig returned, but I gathered from the still fresh look on his face that he had been successful in whatever it was he had had in mind when he made the trip.

"I saw Dr. Guthrie," he reported laconically, as we prepared to turn in. "He says that he isn't quite sure but that Mrs. Willoughby may have a touch of vertigo. At any rate, he has consented to let me come out to-morrow with him and visit her as a specialist in nervous diseases from New York. I had to tell him just enough about the case to get him interested, but that will do no harm. I think I'll set this alarm an hour ahead. I want to get up early to-morrow, and if I shouldn't be here when you wake, you'll find me at Trimble's."

XIV

The Crimeometer

THE alarm wakened me all right, but to my surprise Kennedy had already gone, ahead of it. I dressed hurriedly, bolted an early breakfast, and made my way to Trimble's. He was not there, and I had about concluded to try the laboratory, when I saw him pulling up in a cab from which he took several packages. Donnelly had joined us by this time, and together we rode up in the elevator to the jewelry department. I had never seen a department-store when it was empty, but I think I should like to shop in one under those conditions. It seemed incredible to get into the elevator and go directly to the floor you wanted.

The jewelry department was in the front of the building on one of the upper floors, with wide windows through which the bright morning light streamed attractively on the glittering wares that the clerks were taking out of the safes and disposing to their best advantage. The store had not opened yet, and we could work unhampered.

From his packages, Kennedy took three black boxes. They seemed to have an opening in front, while at one side was a little crank, which, as nearly as I could make out, was operated by clockwork released by an electric contact. His first problem seemed to be to dispose the boxes to the best advantage at various angles about the counter where the Kimberley Queen was on exhibition. With so much bric-à-brac and other large articles about, it did not appear to be very difficult to conceal the boxes, which were perhaps four inches square on the ends and eight inches deep. From the boxes with the clockwork attachment at the side he led wires, centring at a point at the interior end of the aisle where we could see but would hardly be observed by any one standing at the jewelry counter.

Customers had now begun to arrive, and we took a position in the background, prepared for a long wait. Now and then Donnelly casually sauntered past us. He and Craig had disposed the store detectives in a certain way so as to make their presence less obvious, while the clerks had received instructions how to act under the circumstance that a suspicious person was observed.

Once when Donnelly came up he was quite excited. He had just received a message from Bentley that some of the stolen property, the pearls, probably, from the dog collar that had been taken from Shorham's, had been offered for sale by a "fence" known to the police as a former confederate of Annie Grayson.

"You see, that is one great trouble with them all," he remarked, with his eye roving about the store in search of anything irregular. "A shoplifter rarely becomes a habitual criminal until after she passes the age of twenty-five. If they pass that age without quitting, there is little hope of their getting right again, as you see. For by that time they have long since begun to consort with thieves of the other sex."

The hours dragged heavily, though it was a splendid chance to observe at leisure the psychology of the shopper who looked at much and bought little, the uncomfortableness of the men who had been dragged to the department store slaughter to say "Yes" and foot the bills, a kaleidoscopic throng which might have been interesting if we had not been so intent on only one matter.

Kennedy grasped my elbow in vise-like fingers. Involuntarily I looked down at the counter where the Kimberley Queen reposed in all the trappings of genuineness. Mrs. Willoughby had arrived again.

We were too far off to observe distinctly just what was taking place, but evidently Mrs. Willoughby was looking at the gem. A moment later another woman sauntered casually up to the counter. Even at a distance I recognised Annie Grayson. As nearly as I could make out they seemed to exchange remarks. The clerk answered a question or two, then began to search for something apparently to show them. Every one about them was busy, and, obedient to instructions from Donnelly, the store detectives were in the background.

Kennedy was leaning forward watching as intently as the distance would permit. He reached over and pressed the button near him.

After a minute or two the second woman left, followed shortly by Mrs. Willoughby herself. We hurried over to the counter, and Kennedy seized the box containing the Kimberley Queen. He examined it carefully. A flaw in the paste jewel caught his eye.

"There has been a substitution here," he cried. "See! The paste jewel which we used was flawless; this has a little carbon spot here on the side."

"One of my men has been detailed to follow each of them," whispered Donnelly. "Shall I order them to bring Mrs. Willoughby and Annie Grayson to the superintendent's office and have them searched?"

"No," Craig almost shouted. "That would spoil everything. Don't make a move until I get at the real truth of this affair."

The case was becoming more than ever a puzzle to me, but there was nothing left for me to do but to wait until Kennedy was ready to accompany Dr. Guthrie to the Willoughby house. Several times he tried to reach the doctor by telephone, but it was not until the middle of the afternoon that he succeeded.

"I shall be quite busy the rest of the afternoon, Walter," remarked Craig, after he had made his appointment with Dr. Guthrie. "If you will meet me out at the Willoughbys' at about eight o'clock, I shall be much obliged to you."

I promised, and tried to devote myself to catching up with my notes, which were always sadly behind when Kennedy had an important case. I did not succeed in accomplishing much, however.

Dr. Guthrie himself met me at the door of the beautiful house on Woodridge Avenue and with a hearty handshake ushered me into the large room in the right wing outside of which we had placed the telegraphone two nights before. It was the library.

We found Kennedy arranging an instrument in the

music-room which adjoined the library. From what
little knowledge I have of electricity I should have
said it was, in part at least, a galvanometer, one of
those instruments which register the intensity of
minute electric currents. As nearly as I could make
out, in this case the galvanometer was so arranged
that its action swung to one side or the other a little
concave mirror hung from a framework which rested
on the table. Directly in front of it was an electric
light, and the reflection of the light was caught in
the mirror and focused by its concavity upon a point
to one side of the light. Back of it was a long strip
of ground glass and an arrow point, attached to which
was a pen which touched a roll of paper.

On the large table in the library itself Kennedy had
placed in the centre a transverse board partition, high
enough so that two people seated could see each
other's faces and converse over it, but could not see
each other's hands. On one side of the partition
were two metal domes which were fixed to a board
set on the table. On the other side, in addition to
space on which he could write, Kennedy had arranged
what looked like one of these new miniature moving-
picture apparatuses operated by electricity. Indeed,
I felt that it must be that, for directly in front of it,
hanging on the wall, in plain view of any one seated
on the side of the table containing the metal domes,
was a large white sheet.

The time for the experiment, whatever its nature
might be, had at last arrived, and Dr. Guthrie introduced Mr. and Mrs. Willoughby to us as specialists
whom he had persuaded with great difficulty to come

down from New York. Mr. Willoughby he requested
to remain outside until after the tests. She seemed
perfectly calm as she greeted us, and looked with
curiosity at the paraphernalia which Kennedy had
installed in her library. Kennedy, who was putting
some finishing touches on it, was talking in a low
voice to reassure her.

"If you will sit here, please, Mrs. Willoughby, and
place your hands on these two brass domes—there,
that's it. This is just a little arrangement to test
your nervous condition. Dr. Guthrie, who understands it, will take his position outside in the music-
room at that other table. Walter, just switch off
that light, please.

"Mrs. Willoughby, I may say that in testing, say,
the memory, we psychologists have recently developed
two tests, the event test, where something is made to
happen before a person's eyes and later he is asked
to describe it, and the picture test, where a picture
is shown for a certain length of time, after which the
patient is also asked to describe what was in the
picture. I have endeavoured to combine these two
ideas by using the moving-picture machine which you
see here. I am going to show three reels of films."

As nearly as I could make out Kennedy had turned
on the light in the lantern on his side of the table.
As he worked over the machine, which for the present
served to distract Mrs. Willoughby's attention from
herself, he was asking her a series of questions.
From my position I could see that by the light of
the machine he was recording both the questions and
the answers, as well as the time registered to the

fifth of a second by a stop-watch. Mrs. Willoughby could not see what he was doing under the pretence of working over his little moving-picture machine.

He had at last finished the questioning. Suddenly, without any warning, a picture began to play on the sheet. I must say that I was startled myself. It represented the jewelry counter at Trimble's, and in it I could see Mrs. Willoughby herself in animated conversation with one of the clerks. I looked intently, dividing my attention between the picture and the woman. But so far as I could see there was nothing in this first film that incriminated either of them.

Kennedy started on the second without stopping. It was practically the same as the first, only taken from a different angle.

He had scarcely run it half through when Dr. Guthrie opened the door.

"I think Mrs. Willoughby must have taken her hands off the metal domes," he remarked; "I can get no record out here."

I had turned when he opened the door, and now I caught a glimpse of Mrs. Willoughby standing, her hands pressed tightly to her head as if it were bursting, and swaying as if she would faint. I do not know what the film was showing at this point, for Kennedy with a quick movement shut it off and sprang to her side.

"There, that will do, Mrs. Willoughby. I see that you are not well," he soothed. "Doctor, a little something to quiet her nerves. I think we can complete our work merely by comparing notes. Call Mr. Willoughby, Walter. There, sir, if you will take charge of your wife and perhaps take her for a turn or two in the fresh air, I think we can tell you in a few moments whether her condition is in any way serious or not."

Mrs. Willoughby was on the verge of hysterics as her husband supported her out of the room. The door had scarcely shut before Kennedy threw open a window and seemed to beckon into the darkness. As if from nowhere, Donnelly and Bentley sprang up and were admitted.

Dr. Guthrie had now returned from the music-room, bearing a sheet of paper on which was traced a long irregular curve at various points on which marginal notes had been written hastily.

Kennedy leaped directly into the middle of things with his characteristic ardour. "You recall," he began, "that no one seemed to know just who took the jewels in both the cases you first reported? 'Seeing is believing,' is an old saying, but in the face of such reports as you detectives gathered it is in a fair way to lose its force. And you were not at fault, either, for modern psychology is proving by experiments that people do not see even a fraction of the things they confidently believe they see.

"For example, a friend of mine, a professor in a Western university, has carried on experiments with scores of people and has not found one who could give a completely accurate description of what he had seen, even in the direct testimony; while under the influence of questions, particularly if they were at all leading, witnesses all showed extensive inaccuracies in one or more particulars, and that even though they are in a more advantageous position for giving reports than were your clerks who were not prepared. Indeed, it is often a wonder to me that witnesses of ordinary events who are called upon in court to relate what they saw after a considerable lapse of time are as accurate as they are, considering the questioning they often go through from interested parties, neighbours and friends, and the constant and often biased rehearsing of the event. The court asks the witness to tell the truth, the whole truth, and nothing but the truth. How can he? In fact, I am often surprised that there is such a resemblance between the testimony and the actual facts of the case!

"But I have here a little witness that never lies, and, mindful of the fallibility of ordinary witnesses, I called it in. It is a new, compact, little motion camera which has just been perfected to do automatically what the big moving-picture making cameras do."

He touched one of the little black boxes such as we had seen him install in the jewelry department at Trimble's.

"Each of these holds one hundred and sixty feet of film," he resumed, "enough to last three minutes, taking, say, sixteen pictures to the foot and running about one foot a second. You know that less than ten or eleven pictures a second affect the retina as separate, broken pictures. The use of this compact little motion camera was suggested to me by an ingenious but cumbersome invention recently offered to the police in Paris—the installation on the clock-towers in various streets of cinematograph appa-

ratus directed by wireless.   The motion camera as a
detective has now proved its value.   I have here three
films taken at Trimble's, from different angles, and
they clearly show exactly what actually occurred
while Mrs. Willoughby and Annie Grayson were
looking at the Kimberley Queen."

He paused as if analysing the steps in his own
mind.   "The telegraphone gave me the first hint of
the truth," he said.   "The motion camera brought me
a step nearer, but without this third instrument, while
I should have been successful, I would not have got
at the whole truth."

He was fingering the apparatus on the library table
connected with that in the music-room.   "This is the
psychometer for testing mental aberrations," he explained.   "The scientists who are using it to-day are
working, not with a view to aiding criminal juris-
prudence, but with the hope of making such discoveries that the mental health of the race may be bet-
tered.   Still, I believe that in the study of mental
diseases these men are furnishing the knowledge upon
which future criminologists will build to make the
detection of crime an absolute certainty.   Some day
there will be no jury, no detectives, no witnesses, no
attorneys.   The state will merely submit all suspects
to tests of scientific instruments like these, and as
these instruments can not make mistakes or tell lies
their evidence will be conclusive of guilt or innocence.

"Already the psychometer is an actual working
fact.   No living man can conceal his emotions from
the uncanny instrument.   He may bring the most gi-

gantic of will-powers into play to conceal his inner feelings and the psychometer will record the very work which he makes this will-power do.

"The machine is based upon the fact that experiments have proved that the human body's resistance to an electrical current is increased with the increase of the emotions. Dr. Jung, of Zurich, thought that it would be a very simple matter to record these varying emotions, and the psychometer is the result—simple and crude to-day compared with what we have a right to expect in the future.

"A galvanometer is so arranged that its action swings a mirror from side to side, reflecting a light. This light falls on a ground-glass scale marked off into centimetres, and the arrow is made to follow the beam of light. A pen pressing down on a metal drum carrying a long roll of paper revolved by machinery records the variations. Dr. Guthrie, who had charge of the recording, simply sat in front of the ground glass and with the arrow point followed the reflection of the light as it moved along the scale, in this way making a record on the paper on the drum, which I see he is now holding in his hand.

"Mrs. Willoughby, the subject, and myself, the examiner, sat here, facing each other over this table. Through those metal domes on which she was to keep her hands she received an electric current so weak that it could not be felt even by the most sensitive nerves. Now with every increase in her emotion, either while I was putting questions to her or showing her the pictures, whether she showed it outwardly or not, she increased her body's resistance to the current that was being passed in through her hands. The increase was felt by the galvanometer connected by wires in the music-room, the mirror swung, the light travelled on the scale, the arrow was moved by Dr. Guthrie, and her varying emotions were recorded indelibly upon the revolving sheet of paper, recorded in such a way as to show their intensity and reveal to the trained scientist much of the mental condition of the subject."

Kennedy and Dr. Guthrie now conversed in low tones. Once in a while I could catch a scrap of the conversation—"not an epileptic," "no abnormal conformation of the head," "certain mental defects," "often the result of sickness or accident."

"Every time that woman appeared there was a most peculiar disturbance," remarked Dr. Guthrie as Kennedy took the roll of paper from him and studied it carefully.

At length the light seemed to break through his face.

"Among the various kinds of insanity," he said, slowly measuring his words, "there is one that manifests itself as an irresistible impulse to steal. Such terms as neuropath and kleptomaniac are often regarded as rather elegant names for contemptible excuses invented by medical men to cover up stealing. People are prone to say cynically, 'Poor man's sins; rich man's diseases.' Yet kleptomania does exist, and it is easy to make it seem like crime when it is really persistent, incorrigible, and irrational stealing. Often it is so great as to be incurable. Cases have been recorded of clergymen who were kleptomaniacs and in one instance a dying victim stole the snuff-box of his confessor.

"It is the pleasure and excitement of stealing, not the desire for the object stolen, which distinguishes the kleptomaniac from the ordinary thief. Usually the kleptomaniac is a woman, with an insane desire to steal for the mere sake of stealing. The morbid craving for excitement which is at the bottom of so many motiveless and useless crimes, again and again has driven apparently sensible men and women to ruin and even to suicide. It is a form of emotional insanity, not loss of control of the will, but perversion of the will. Some are models in their lucid intervals, but when the mania is on them they cannot resist. The very act of taking constitutes the pleasure, not possession. One must take into consideration many things, for such diseases as kleptomania belong exclusively to civilisation; they are the product of an age of sensationalism. Naturally enough, woman, with her delicately balanced nervous organisation, is the first and chief offender."

Kennedy had seated himself at the table and was writing hastily. When he had finished, he held the papers in his hand to dry.

He handed one sheet each to Bentley and Donnelly. We crowded about. Kennedy had simply written out two bills for the necklace and the collar of pearls.

"Send them in to Mr. Willoughby," he added. "I think he will be glad to pay them to hush up the scandal."

We looked at each other in amazement at the revelation.

"But what about Annie Grayson?" persisted Donnelly.

"I have taken care of her," responded Kennedy laconically. "She is already under arrest. Would you like to see why?"

A moment later we had all piled into Dr. Guthrie's car, standing at the door.

At the cosy little Grayson villa we found two large-eyed detectives and a very angry woman waiting impatiently. Heaped up on a table in the living room was a store of loot that readily accounted for the ocular peculiarity of the detectives.

The jumble on the table contained a most magnificent collection of diamonds, sapphires, ropes of pearls, emeralds, statuettes, and bronze and ivory antiques, books in rare bindings, and other baubles which wealth alone can command. It dazzled our eyes as we made a mental inventory of the heap. Yet it was a most miscellaneous collection. Beside a pearl collar with a diamond clasp were a pair of plain leather slippers and a pair of silk stockings. Things of value and things of no value were mixed as if by a lunatic. A beautiful neck ornament of carved coral lay near a half-dozen common linen handkerchiefs. A strip of silk hid a valuable collection of antique jewellery. Besides diamonds and precious stones by the score were gold and silver ornaments, silks, satins, laces, draperies, articles of virtu, plumes, even cutlery and bric-à-brac. All this must have been the result of countless excursions to the stores of New York and innumerable clever thefts.

We could only look at each other in amazement

and wonder at the defiance written on the face of Annie Grayson.

"In all this strange tangle of events," remarked Kennedy, surveying the pile with obvious satisfaction, "I find that the precise instruments of science have told me one more thing. Some one else discovered Mrs. Willoughby's weakness, led her on, suggested opportunities to her, used her again and again, profited by her malady, probably to the extent of thousands of dollars. My telegraphone record hinted at that. In some way Annie Grayson secured the confidence of Mrs. Willoughby. The one took for the sake of taking; the other received for the sake of money. Mrs. Willoughby was easily persuaded by her new friend to leave here what she had stolen. Besides, having taken it, she had no further interest in it.

"The rule of law is that every one is responsible who knows the nature and consequences of his act. We have absolute proof that you, Annie Grayson, although you did not actually commit any of the thefts yourself, led Mrs. Willoughby on and profited by her. Dr. Guthrie will take care of the case of Mrs. Willoughby. But the law must deal with you for playing on the insanity of a kleptomaniac—the cleverest scheme yet of the queen of shoplifters."

As Kennedy turned nonchalantly from the detectives who had seized Annie Grayson, he drew a little red folder from his pocket.

"You see, Walter," he smiled, "how soon one gets into a habit? I'm almost a regular commuter, now. You know, they are always bringing out these little red folders just when things grow interesting."

I glanced over his shoulder. He was studying the local timetable.

"We can get the last train from Glenclair if we hurry," he announced, stuffing the folder back into his pocket. "They will take her to Newark by trolley, I suppose. Come on."

We made our hasty adieux and escaped as best we could the shower of congratulations.

"Now for a rest," he said, settling back into the plush covered seat for the long ride into town, his hat down over his eyes and his legs hunched up against the back of the next seat. Across in the tube and uptown in a nighthawk cab we went and at last we were home for a good sleep.

"This promises to be an off-day," Craig remarked, the next morning over the breakfast table. "Meet me in the forenoon and we'll take a long, swinging walk. I feel the need of physical exercise."

"A mark of returning sanity!" I exclaimed.

I had become so used to being called out on the unexpected, now, that I almost felt that some one might stop us on our tramp. Nothing of the sort happened, however, until our return.

Then a middle-aged man and a young girl, heavily veiled, were waiting for Kennedy, as we turned in from the brisk finish in the cutting river wind along the Drive.

"Winslow is my name, sir," the man began, rising nervously as we entered the room, "and this is my only daughter, Ruth."

Kennedy bowed and we waited for the man to proceed. He drew his hand over his forehead which was

15

moist with perspiration in spite of the season. Ruth Winslow was an attractive young woman, I could see at a glance, although her face was almost completely hidden by the thick veil.

"Perhaps, Ruth, I had better—ah—see these gentlemen alone?" suggested her father gently.

"No, father," she answered in a tone of forced bravery, "I think not. I can stand it. I must stand it. Perhaps I can help you in telling about the—the case."

Mr. Winslow cleared his throat.

"We are from Goodyear, a little mill-town," he proceeded slowly, "and as you doubtless can see we have just arrived after travelling all day."

"Goodyear," repeated Kennedy slowly as the man paused. "The chief industry, of course, is rubber, I suppose."

"Yes," assented Mr. Winslow, "the town centres about rubber. Our factories are not the largest but are very large, nevertheless, and are all that keep the town going. It is on rubber, also, I fear, that the tragedy which I am about to relate hangs. I suppose the New York papers have had nothing to say of the strange death of Bradley Cushing, a young chemist in Goodyear who was formerly employed by the mills but had lately set up a little laboratory of his own?"

Kennedy turned to me. "Nothing unless the late editions of the evening papers have it," I replied.

"Perhaps it is just as well," continued Mr. Winslow. "They wouldn't have it straight. In fact, no one has it straight yet. That is why we have come to you. You see, to my way of thinking Bradley Cushing was on the road to changing the name of the town from Goodyear to Cushing. He was not the inventor of synthetic rubber about which you hear nowadays, but he had improved the process so much that there is no doubt that synthetic rubber would soon have been on the market cheaper and better than the best natural rubber from Para.

"Goodyear is not a large place, but it is famous for its rubber and uses a great deal of raw material. We have sent out some of the best men in the business, seeking new sources in South America, in Mexico, in Ceylon, Malaysia and the Congo. What our people do not know about rubber is hardly worth knowing, from the crude gum to the thousands of forms of finished products. Goodyear is a wealthy little town, too, for its size. Naturally all its investments are in rubber, not only in our own mills but in companies all over the world. Last year several of our leading citizens became interested in a new concession in the Congo granted to a group of American capitalists, among whom was Lewis Borland, who is easily the local magnate of our town. When this group organised an expedition to explore the region preparatory to taking up the concession, several of the best known people in Goodyear accompanied the party and later subscribed for large blocks of stock.

"I say all this so that you will understand at the start just what part rubber plays in the life of our little community. You can readily see that such being the case, whatever advantage the world at large might gain from cheap synthetic rubber would scarcely benefit those whose money and labour had been expended on the assumption that rubber would be scarce and dear. Naturally, then, Bradley Cushing was not precisely popular with a certain set in Goodyear. As for myself, I am frank to admit that I might have shared the opinion of many others regarding him, for I have a small investment in this Congo enterprise myself. But the fact is that Cushing, when he came to our town fresh from his college fellowship in industrial chemistry, met my daughter."

Without taking his eyes off Kennedy, he reached over and patted the gloved hand that clutched the arm of the chair alongside his own. "They were engaged and often they used to talk over what they would do when Bradley's invention of a new way to polymerise isoprene, as the process is called, had solved the rubber question and had made him rich. I firmly believe that their dreams were not day dreams, either. The thing was done. I have seen his products and I know something about rubber. There were no impurities in his rubber."

Mr. Winslow paused. Ruth was sobbing quietly.

"This morning," he resumed hastily, "Bradley Cushing was found dead in his laboratory under the most peculiar circumstances. I do not know whether his secret died with him or whether some one has stolen it. From the indications I concluded that he had been murdered."

Such was the case as Kennedy and I heard it then.

Ruth looked up at him with tearful eyes wistful with pain, "Would Mr. Kennedy work on it?" There was only one answer.

XV

The Vampire

AS we sped out to the little mill-town on the last train, after Kennedy had insisted on taking us all to a quiet little restaurant, he placed us so that Miss Winslow was furthest from him and her father nearest. I could hear now and then scraps of their conversation as he resumed his questioning, and knew that Mr. Winslow was proving to be a good observer.

"Cushing used to hire a young fellow of some scientific experience, named Strong," said Mr. Winslow as he endeavoured to piece the facts together as logically as it was possible to do. "Strong used to open his laboratory for him in the morning, clean up the dirty apparatus, and often assist him in some of his experiments. This morning when Strong approached the laboratory at the usual time he was surprised to see that though it was broad daylight there was a light burning. He was alarmed and before going in looked through the window. The sight that he saw froze him. There lay Cushing on a workbench and beside him and around him pools of coagulating blood. The door was not locked, as we found afterward, but the young man did not stop to enter. He ran to me and, fortunately, I met him at our door. I went back.

"We opened the unlocked door. The first thing, as I recall it, that greeted me was an unmistakable odour of oranges. It was a very penetrating and very peculiar odour. I didn't understand it, for there seemed to be something else in it besides the orange smell. However, I soon found out what it was, or at least Strong did. I don't know whether you know anything about it, but it seems that when you melt real rubber in the effort to reduce it to carbon and hydrogen, you get a liquid substance which is known as isoprene. Well, isoprene, according to Strong, gives out an odour something like ether. Cushing, or some one else, had apparently been heating isoprene. As soon as Strong mentioned the smell of ether I recognised that that was what made the smell of oranges so peculiar.

"However, that's not the point. There lay Cushing on his back on the workbench, just as Strong had said. I bent over him, and in his arm, which was bare, I saw a little gash made by some sharp instrument and laying bare an artery, I think, which was cut. Long spurts of blood covered the floor for some distance around and from the veins in his arm, which had also been severed, a long stream of blood led to a hollow in the cement floor where it had collected. I believe that he bled to death."

"And the motive for such a terrible crime?" queried Craig.

Mr. Winslow shook his head helplessly. "I suppose there are plenty of motives," he answered slowly, "as many motives as there are big investments in rubber-producing ventures in Goodyear."

"But have you any idea who would go so far to protect his investments as to kill?" persisted Kennedy.

Mr. Winslow made no reply. "Who," asked Kennedy, "was chiefly interested in the rubber works where Cushing was formerly employed?"

"The president of the company is the Mr. Borland whom I mentioned," replied Mr. Winslow. "He is a man of about forty, I should say, and is reputed to own a majority of the—"

"Oh, father," interrupted Miss Winslow, who had caught the drift of the conversation in spite of the pains that had been taken to keep it away from her, "Mr. Borland would never dream of such a thing. It is wrong even to think of it."

"I didn't say that he would, my dear," corrected Mr. Winslow gently. "Professor Kennedy asked me who was chiefly interested in the rubber works and Mr. Borland owns a majority of the stock." He leaned over and whispered to Kennedy, "Borland is a visitor at our home, and between you and me, he thinks a great deal of Ruth."

I looked quickly at Kennedy, but he was absorbed in looking out of the car window at the landscape which he did not and could not see.

"You said there were others who had an interest in outside companies," cross-questioned Kennedy. "I take it that you mean companies dealing in crude rubber, the raw material, people with investments in plantations and concessions, perhaps. Who are they? Who were the men who went on that expedition to the Congo with Borland which you mentioned?"

"Of course, there was Borland himself," answered Winslow. "Then there was a young chemist named Lathrop, a very clever and ambitious fellow who succeede̅ Cushing when he resigned from the works, and Dr. Harris, who was persuaded to go because of his friendship for Borland. After they took up the concession I believe all of them put money into it, though how much I can't say."

I was curious to ask whether there were any other visitors at the Winslow house who might be rivals for Ruth's affections, but there was no opportunity.

Nothing more was said until we arrived at Goodyear.

We found the body of Cushing lying in a modest little mortuary chapel of an undertaking establishment on the main street. Kennedy at once began his investigation by discovering what seemed to have escaped others. About the throat were light discolourations that showed that the young inventor had been choked by a man with a powerful grasp, although the fact that the marks had escaped observation led quite obviously to the conclusion that he had not met his death in that way, and that the marks probably played only a minor part in the tragedy.

Kennedy passed over the doubtful evidence of strangulation for the more profitable examination of the little gash in the wrist.

"The radial artery has been cut," he mused.

A low exclamation from him brought us all bending over him as he stooped and examined the cold form. He was holding in the palm of his hand a little piece of something that shone like silver. It was in the form of a minute hollow cylinder with two grooves on it, a cylinder so tiny that it would scarcely have slipped over the point of a pencil.

"Where did you find it?" I asked eagerly.

He pointed to the wound. "Sticking in the severed end of a piece of vein," he replied, half to himself, "cuffed over the end of the radial artery which had been severed, and done so neatly as to be practically hidden. It was done so cleverly that the inner linings of the vein and artery, the endothelium as it is called, were in complete contact with each other."

As I looked at the little silver thing and at Kennedy's face, which betrayed nothing, I felt that here indeed was a mystery. What new scientific engine of death was that little hollow cylinder?

"Next I should like to visit the laboratory," he remarked simply.

Fortunately, the laboratory had been shut and nothing had been disturbed except by the undertaker and his men who had carried the body away. Strong had left word that he had gone to Boston, where, in a safe deposit box, was a sealed envelope in which Cushing kept a copy of the combination of his safe, which had died with him. There was, therefore, no hope of seeing the assistant until the morning.

Kennedy found plenty to occupy his time in his minute investigation of the laboratory. There, for instance, was the pool of blood leading back by a thin dark stream to the workbench and its terrible figure, which I could almost picture to myself lying there through the silent hours of the night before, with its life blood slowly oozing away, unconscious, powerless to save itself. There were spurts of arterial blood on the floor and on the nearby laboratory furniture, and beside the workbench another smaller and isolated pool of blood.

On a table in a corner by the window stood a microscope which Cushing evidently used, and near it a box of fresh sterilised slides. Kennedy, who had been casting his eye carefully about taking in the whole laboratory, seemed delighted to find the slides. He opened the box and gingerly took out some of the little oblong pieces of glass, on each of which he dropped a couple of minute drops of blood from the arterial spurts and the venous pools on the floor.

Near the workbench were circular marks, much as if some jars had been set down there. We were watching him, almost in awe at the matter of fact manner in which he was proceeding in what to us was nothing but a hopeless enigma, when I saw him stoop and pick up a few little broken pieces of glass. There seemed to be blood spots on the glass, as on other things, but particularly interesting to him.

A moment later I saw that he was holding in his hand what were apparently the remains of a little broken vial which he had fitted together from the pieces. Evidently it had been used and dropped in haste.

"A vial for a local anesthetic," he remarked. "This is the sort of thing that might be injected into an arm or leg and deaden the pain of a cut, but that is all.

It wouldn't affect the consciousness or prevent any one from resisting a murderer to the last. I doubt if that had anything directly to do with his death, or perhaps even that this is Cushing's blood on it."

Unlike Winslow I had seen Kennedy in action so many times that I knew it was useless to speculate. But I was fascinated, for the deeper we got into the case, the more unusual and inexplicable it seemed. I gave that end of it up, but the fact that Strong had gone to secure the combination of the safe suggested to me to examine that article. There was certainly no evidence of robbery or even of an attempt at robbery there.

"Was any doctor called?" asked Kennedy.

"Yes," he replied. "Though I knew it was of no use I called in Dr. Howe, who lives up the street from the laboratory. I should have called Dr. Harris, who used to be my own physician, but since his return from Africa with the Borland expedition, he has not been in very good health and has practically given up his practice. Dr. Howe is the best practising physician in town, I think."

"We shall call on him to-morrow," said Craig, snapping his watch, which already marked far after midnight.

Dr. Howe proved, the next day, to be an athletic-looking man, and I could not help noticing and admiring his powerful frame and his hearty handshake, as he greeted us when we dropped into his office with a card from Winslow.

The doctor's theory was that Cushing had committed suicide.

"But why should a young man who had invented a new method of polymerising isoprene, who was going to become wealthy, and was engaged to a beautiful young girl, commit suicide?"

The doctor shrugged his shoulders. It was evident that he, too, belonged to the "natural rubber set" which dominated Goodyear.

"I haven't looked into the case very deeply, but I'm not so sure that he had the secret, are you?"

Kennedy smiled. "That is what I'd like to know. I suppose that an expert like Mr. Borland could tell me, perhaps?"

"I should think so."

"Where is his office?" asked Craig. "Could you point it out to me from the window?"

Kennedy was standing by one of the windows of the doctor's office, and as he spoke he turned and drew a little field glass from his pocket. "Which end of the rubber works is it?"

Dr. Howe tried to direct him but Kennedy appeared unwarrantably obtuse, requiring the doctor to raise the window, and it was some moments before he got his glasses on the right spot.

Kennedy and I thanked the doctor for his courtesy and left the office.

We went at once to the office of Dr. Harris, to whom Winslow had also given us cards. We found him an anæmic man, half asleep. Kennedy tentatively suggested the murder of Cushing.

"Well, if you ask me my opinion," snapped out the doctor, "although I wasn't called into the case, from what I hear, I'd say that he was murdered."

"Some seem to think it was suicide," prompted Kennedy.

"People who have brilliant prospects and are engaged to pretty girls don't usually die of their own accord," rasped Harris.

"So you think he really did have the secret of artificial rubber?" asked Craig.

"Not artificial rubber. Synthetic rubber. It was the real thing, I believe."

"Did Mr. Borland and his new chemist Lathrop believe it, too?"

"I can't say. But I should surely advise you to see them." The doctor's face was twitching nervously.

"Where is Borland's office?" repeated Kennedy, again taking from his pocket the field glass and adjusting it carefully by the window.

"Over there," directed Harris, indicating the corner of the works to which we had already been directed.

Kennedy had stepped closer to the window before him and I stood beside him looking out also.

"The cut was a very peculiar one," remarked Kennedy, still adjusting the glasses. "An artery and a vein had been placed together so that the endothelium, or inner lining of each, was in contact with the other, giving a continuous serous surface. Which window did you say was Borland's? I wish you'd step to the other window and raise it, so that I can be sure. I don't want to go wandering all over the works looking for him."

"Yes," the doctor said as he went, leaving him standing beside the window from which he had been directing us, "yes, you surely should see Mr. Borland. And don't forget that young chemist of his, Lathrop, either. If I can be of any more help to you, come back again."

It was a long walk through the village and factory yards to the office of Lewis Borland, but we were amply repaid by finding him in and ready to see us. Borland was a typical Yankee, tall, thin, evidently predisposed to indigestion, a man of tremendous mental and nervous energy and with a hidden wiry strength.

"Mr. Borland," introduced Kennedy, changing his tactics and adopting a new rôle, "I've come down to you as an authority on rubber to ask you what your opinion is regarding the invention of a townsman of yours named Cushing."

"Cushing?" repeated Borland in some surprise. "Why—"

"Yes," interrupted Kennedy, "I understand all about it. I had heard of his invention in New York and would have put some money into it if I could have been convinced. I was to see him to-day, but of course, as you were going to say, his death prevents it. Still, I should like to know what you think about it."

"Well," Borland added, jerking out his words nervously, as seemed to be his habit, "Cushing was a bright young fellow. He used to work for me until he began to know too much about the rubber business."

"Do you know anything about his scheme?" insinuated Kennedy.

"Very little, except that it was not patented yet, I believe, though he told every one that the patent was applied for and he expected to get a basic patent in some way without any interference."

"Well," drawled Kennedy, affecting as nearly as possible the air of a promoter, "if I could get his assistant, or some one who had authority to be present, would you, as a practical rubber man, go over to his laboratory with me? I'd join you in making an offer to his estate for the rights to the process, if it seemed any good."

"You're a cool one," ejaculated Borland, with a peculiar avaricious twinkle in the corners of his eyes. "His body is scarcely cold and yet you come around proposing to buy out his invention and—and, of all persons, you come to me."

"To you?" inquired Kennedy blandly.

"Yes, to me. Don't you know that synthetic rubber would ruin the business system that I have built up here?"

Still Craig persisted and argued.

"Young man," said Borland rising at length as if an idea had struck him, "I like your nerve. Yes, I will go. I'll show you that I don't fear any competition from rubber made out of fusel oil or any other old kind of oil." He rang a bell and a boy answered. "Call Lathrop," he ordered.

The young chemist, Lathrop, proved to be a bright and active man of the new school, though a good deal of a rubber stamp. Whenever it was compatible with science and art, he readily assented to every proposition that his employer laid down.

Kennedy had already telephoned to the Winslows and Miss Winslow had answered that Strong had returned from Boston. After a little parleying, the second visit to the laboratory was arranged and Miss Winslow was allowed to be present with her father, after Kennedy had been assured by Strong that the gruesome relics of the tragedy would be cleared away.

It was in the forenoon that we arrived with Borland and Lathrop. I could not help noticing the cordial manner with which Borland greeted Miss Winslow. There was something obtrusive even in his sympathy. Strong, whom we met now for the first time, seemed rather suspicious of the presence of Borland and his chemist, but made an effort to talk freely without telling too much.

"Of course you know," commenced Strong after proper urging, "that it has long been the desire of chemists to synthesise rubber by a method that will make possible its cheap production on a large scale. In a general way I know what Mr. Cushing had done, but there are parts of the process which are covered in the patents applied for, of which I am not at liberty to speak yet."

"Where are the papers in the case, the documents showing the application for the patent, for instance?" asked Kennedy.

"In the safe, sir," replied Strong.

Strong set to work on the combination which he had obtained from the safe deposit vault. I could see that Borland and Miss Winslow were talking in a low tone.

"Are you sure that it is a fact?" I overheard him

ask, though I had no idea what they were talking about.

"As sure as I am that the Borland Rubber Works are a fact," she replied.

Craig also seemed to have overheard, for he turned quickly. Borland had taken out his penknife and was moistening the blade carefully preparing to cut into a piece of the synthetic rubber. In spite of his expressed scepticism, I could see that he was eager to learn what the product was really like.

Strong, meanwhile, had opened the safe and was going over the papers. A low exclamation from him brought us around the little pile of documents. He was holding a will in which nearly everything belonging to Cushing was left to Miss Winslow.

Not a word was said, although I noticed that Kennedy moved quickly to her side, fearing that the shock of the discovery might have a bad effect on her, but she took it with remarkable calmness. It was apparent that Cushing had taken the step of his own accord and had said nothing to her about it.

"What does anything amount to?" she said tremulously at last. "The dream is dead without him in it."

"Come," urged Kennedy gently. "This is enough for to-day."

An hour later we were speeding back to New York. Kennedy had no apparatus to work with out at Goodyear and could not improvise it. Winslow agreed to keep us in touch with any new developments during the few hours that Craig felt it was necessary to leave the scene of action.

16

Back again in New York, Craig took a cab directly for his laboratory, leaving me marooned with instructions not to bother him for several hours. I employed the time in a little sleuthing on my own account, endeavouring to look up the records of those involved in the case. I did not discover much, except an interview that had been given at the time of the return of his expedition by Borland to the *Star,* in which he gave a graphic description of the dangers from disease that they had encountered.

I mention it because, though it did not impress me much when I read it, it at once leaped into my mind when the interminable hours were over and I rejoined Kennedy. He was bending over a new microscope.

"This is a rubber age, Walter," he began, "and the stories of men who have been interested in rubber often sound like fiction."

He slipped a slide under the microscope, looked at it and then motioned to me to do the same. "Here is a very peculiar culture which I have found in some of that blood," he commented. "The germs are much larger than bacteria and they can be seen with a comparatively low power microscope swiftly darting between the blood cells, brushing them aside, but not penetrating them as some parasites, like that of malaria, do. Besides, spectroscope tests show the presence of a rather well-known chemical in that blood."

"A poisoning, then?" I ventured. "Perhaps he suffered from the disease that many rubber workers get from the bisulphide of carbon. He must have done a good deal of vulcanising of his own rubber, you know."

"No," smiled Craig enigmatically, "it wasn't that. It was an arsenic derivative. Here's another thing. You remember the field glass I used?"

He had picked it up from the table and was pointing at a little hole in the side, that had escaped my notice before. "This is what you might call a right-angled camera. I point the glass out of the window and while you think I am looking through it I am really focusing it on you and taking your picture standing there beside me and out of my apparent line of vision. It would deceive the most wary."

Just then a long-distance call from Winslow told us that Borland had been to call on Miss Ruth and, in as kindly a way as could be, had offered her half a million dollars for her rights in the new patent. At once it flashed over me that he was trying to get control of and suppress the invention in the interests of his own company, a thing that has been done hundreds of times. Or could it all have been part of a conspiracy? And if it was his conspiracy, would he succeed in tempting his friend, Miss Winslow, to fall in with this glittering offer?

Kennedy evidently thought, also, that the time for action had come, for without a word he set to work packing his apparatus and we were again headed for Goodyear.

XVI

The Blood Test

WE arrived late at night, or rather in the morning, but in spite of the late hour Kennedy was up early urging me to help him carry the stuff over to Cushing's laboratory. By the middle of the morning he was ready and had me scouring about town collecting his audience, which consisted of the Winslows, Borland and Lathrop, Dr. Howe, Dr. Harris, Strong and myself. The laboratory was darkened and Kennedy took his place beside an electric moving picture apparatus.

The first picture was different from anything any of us had ever seen on a screen before. It seemed to be a mass of little dancing globules. "This," explained Kennedy, "is what you would call an educational moving picture, I suppose. It shows normal blood corpuscles as they are in motion in the blood of a healthy man. Those little round cells are the red corpuscles and the larger irregular cells are the white corpuscles."

He stopped the film. The next picture was a sort of enlarged and elongated house fly, apparently, of sombre grey color, with a narrow body, thick proboscis and wings that overlapped like the blades of a pair of shears.

"This," he went on, "is a picture of the now well-known tse-tse fly found over a large area of Africa. It has a bite something like a horse-fly and is a perfect blood-sucker. Vast territories of thickly populated, fertile country near the shores of lakes and rivers are now depopulated as a result of the death-dealing bite of these flies, more deadly than the blood-sucking, vampirish ghosts with which, in the middle ages, people supposed night air to be inhabited. For this fly carries with it germs which it leaves in the blood of its victims, which I shall show next."

A new film started.

"Here is a picture of some blood so infected. Notice that worm-like sheath of undulating membrane terminating in a slender whip-like process by which it moves about. That thing wriggling about like a minute electric eel, always in motion, is known as the trypanosome.

"Isn't this a marvellous picture? To see the micro-organism move, evolve and revolve in the midst of normal cells, uncoil and undulate in the fluids which they inhabit, to see them play hide and seek with the blood corpuscles and clumps of fibrin, turn, twist, and rotate as if in a cage, to see these deadly little trypanosomes moving back and forth in every direction displaying their delicate undulating membranes and shoving aside the blood cells that are in their way while by their side the leucocytes, or white corpuscles, lazily extend or retract their pseudopods of protoplasm. To see all this as it is shown before us here is to realise that we are in the presence of an unknown world, a world infinitesimally small, but as real and as complex as that about us. With the cinematograph and the ultra-microscope we can see what no other forms of photography can reproduce.

"I have secured these pictures so that I can better mass up the evidence against a certain person in this room. For in the blood of one of you is now going on the fight which you have here seen portrayed by the picture machine. Notice how the blood corpuscles in this infected blood have lost their smooth, glossy appearance, become granular and incapable of nourishing the tissues. The trypanosomes are fighting with the normal blood cells. Here we have the lowest group of animal life, the protozoa, at work killing the highest, man."

Kennedy needed nothing more than the breathless stillness to convince him of the effectiveness of his method of presenting his case.

"Now," he resumed, "let us leave this blood-sucking, vampirish tse-tse fly for the moment. I have another revelation to make."

He laid down on the table under the lights, which now flashed up again, the little hollow silver cylinder.

"This little instrument," Kennedy explained, "which I have here is known as a canula, a little canal, for leading off blood from the veins of one person to another—in other words, blood transfusion. Modern doctors are proving themselves quite successful in its use.

"Of course, like everything, it has its own peculiar dangers. But the one point I wish to make is this: In the selection of a donor for transfusion, people fall into definite groups. Tests of blood must be made first to see whether it 'agglutinates,' and in this respect there are four classes of persons. In our case this matter had to be neglected. For, gentlemen, there were two kinds of blood on that laboratory floor, and they do not agglutinate. This, in short, was what actually happened. An attempt was made to transfuse Cushing's blood as donor to another person as recipient. A man suffering from the disease caught from the bite of the tse-tse fly—the deadly sleeping sickness so well known in Africa —has deliberately tried a form of robbery which I believe to be without parallel. He has stolen the blood of another!

"He stole it in a desperate attempt to stay an incurable disease. This man had used an arsenic compound called atoxyl, till his blood was filled with it and its effects on the trypanosomes nil. There was but one wild experiment more to try—the stolen blood of another."

Craig paused to let the horror of the crime sink into our minds.

"Some one in the party which went to look over the concession in the Congo contracted the sleeping sickness from the bites of those blood-sucking flies. That person has now reached the stage of insanity, and his blood is full of the germs and overloaded with atoxyl.

"Everything had been tried and had failed. He was doomed. He saw his fortune menaced by the discovery of the way to make synthetic rubber. Life and money were at stake. One night, nerved up by a fit of insane fury, with a power far beyond what one would expect in his ordinary weakened condition, he saw a light in Cushing's laboratory. He stole in

stealthily. He seized the inventor with his momentarily superhuman strength and choked him. As
they struggled he must have shoved a sponge soaked
with ether and orange essence under his nose. Cushing went under.

"Resistance overcome by the anesthetic, he dragged
the now insensible form to the work bench. Frantically he must have worked. He made an incision
and exposed the radial artery, the pulse. Then he
must have administered a local anesthetic to himself
in his arm or leg. He secured a vein and pushed the
cut end over this little canula. Then he fitted the
artery of Cushing over that and the blood that was,
perhaps, to save his life began flowing into his de-
pleted veins.

"Who was this madman? I have watched the actions of those whom I suspected when they did not
know they were being watched. I did it by using
this neat little device which looks like a field glass,
but is really a camera that takes pictures of things
at right angles to the direction in which the glass
seems to be pointed. One person, I found, had a
wound on his leg, the wrapping of which he adjusted
nervously when he thought no one was looking. He
had difficulty in limping even a short distance to open
a window."

Kennedy uncorked a bottle and the subtle odor of
oranges mingled with ether stole through the room.

"Some one here will recognize that odour immediately. It is the new orange-essence vapour anesthetic, a mixture of essence of orange with ether and
chloroform. The odour hidden by the orange which

lingered in the laboratory, Mr. Winslow and Mr. Strong, was not isoprene, but really ether.

"I am letting some of the odour escape here because in this very laboratory it was that the thing took place, and it is one of the well-known principles of psychology that odours are powerfully suggestive. In this case the odour now must suggest the terrible scene of the other night to some one before me. More than that, I have to tell that person that the blood transfusion did not and could not save him. His illness is due to a condition that is incurable and cannot be altered by transfusion of new blood. That person is just as doomed to-day as he was before he committed—"

A figure was groping blindly about. The arsenic compounds with which his blood was surcharged had brought on one of the attacks of blindness to which users of the drug are subject. In his insane frenzy he was evidently reaching desperately for Kennedy himself. As he groped he limped painfully from the soreness of his wound.

"Dr. Harris," accused Kennedy, avoiding the mad rush at himself, and speaking in a tone that thrilled us, "you are the man who sucked the blood of Cushing into your own veins and left him to die. But the state will never be able to exact from you the penalty of your crime. Nature will do that too soon for justice. Gentlemen, this is the murderer of Bradley Cushing, a maniac, a modern scientific vampire."

I regarded the broken, doomed man with mingled pity and loathing, rather than with the usual feelings one has toward a criminal.

"Come," said Craig. "The local authorities can take care of this case now."

He paused just long enough for a word of comfort to the poor, broken-hearted girl. Ruth Winslow answered with a mute look of gratitude and despair. In fact, in the confusion we were only too glad to escape any more such mournful congratulations.

"Well," Craig remarked, as we walked quickly down the street, "if we have to wait here for a train, I prefer to wait in the railroad station. I have done my part. Now my only interest is to get away before they either offer me a banquet or lynch me."

Actually, I think he would have preferred the novelty of dealing with a lynching party, if he had had to choose between the two.

We caught a train soon, however, and fortunately it had a diner attached. Kennedy whiled away the time between courses by reading the graft exposures in the city.

As we rolled into the station late in the afternoon, he tossed aside the paper with an air of relief.

"Now for a quiet evening in the laboratory," he exclaimed, almost gleefully.

By what stretch of imagination he could call that recreation, I could not see. But as for quietness, I needed it, too. I had fallen wofully behind in my record of the startling events through which he was conducting me. Consequently, until late that night I pecked away at my typewriter trying to get order out of the chaos of my hastily scribbled notes. Under ordinary circumstances, I remembered, the morrow would have been my day of rest on the *Star*. I had gone far enough with Kennedy to realise that on this assignment there was no such thing as rest.

"District Attorney Carton wants to see me immediately at the Criminal Courts Building, Walter," announced Kennedy, early the following morning.

Clothed, and as much in my right mind as possible after the arduous literary labours of the night before, I needed no urging, for Carton was an old friend of all the newspaper men. I joined Craig quickly in a hasty ride down-town in the rush hour.

On the table before the square-jawed, close-cropped, fighting prosecutor, whom I knew already after many a long and hard-fought campaign both before and after election, lay a little package which had evidently come to him in the morning's mail by parcel-post.

"What do you suppose is in that, Kennedy?" he asked, tapping it gingerly. "I haven't opened it yet, but I think it's a bomb. Wait—I'll have a pail of water sent in here so that you can open it, if you will. You understand such things."

"No—no," hastened Kennedy, "that's exactly the wrong thing to do. Some of these modern chemical bombs are set off in precisely that way. No. Let me dissect the thing carefully. I think you may be right. It does look as if it might be an infernal machine. You see the evident disguise of the roughly written address?"

Carton nodded, for it was that that had excited his suspicion in the first place. Meanwhile, Kennedy, without further ceremony, began carefully to remove the wrapper of brown Manila paper, preserving everything as he did so. Carton and I instinctively backed away.   Inside, Craig had disclosed an oblong wooden box.

"I realise that opening a bomb is dangerous busi-ness," he pursued slowly, engrossed in his work and almost oblivious to us, "but I think I can take a chance safely with this fellow. The dangerous part is what might be called drawing the fangs. No bombs are exactly safe toys to have around until they are wholly destroyed, and before you can say you have destroyed one, it is rather a ticklish business to take out the dangerous element."

He had removed the cover in the deftest manner without friction, and seemingly without disturbing the contents in the least. I do not pretend to know how he did it; but the proof was that we could see him still working from our end of the room.

On the inside of the cover was roughly drawn a skull and cross-bones, showing that the miscreant who sent the thing had at least a sort of grim humour. For, where the teeth should have been in the skull were innumerable match-heads. Kennedy picked them out with as much *sang-froid* as if he were not playing jackstraws with life and death.

Then he removed the explosive itself and the vari-ous murderous slugs and bits of metal embedded in it, carefully separating each as if to be labelled "Ex-hibit A," "B," and so on for a class in bomb dissec-tion.   Finally, he studied the sides and bottom of the box.

"Evidence of chlorate-of-potash mixture," Ken-nedy muttered to himself, still examining the bomb.

"The inside was a veritable arsenal—a very unusual and clever construction."

"My heavens!" breathed Carton. "I would rather go through a campaign again."

XVII

The Bomb Maker

WE stared at each other in blank awe, at the various parts, so innocent looking in the heaps on the table, now safely separated, but together a combination ticket to perdition.

"Who do you suppose could have sent it?" I blurted out when I found my voice, then, suddenly recollecting the political and legal fight that Carton was engaged in at the time, I added, "The white slavers?"

"Not a doubt," he returned laconically. "And," he exclaimed, bringing down both hands vigorously in characteristic emphasis on the arms of his office chair, "I've got to win this fight against the vice trust, as I call it, or the whole work of the district attorney's office in clearing up the city will be discredited —to say nothing of the risk the present incumbent runs at having such grateful friends about the city send marks of their affection and esteem like this."

I knew something already of the situation, and Carton continued thoughtfully: "All the powers of vice are fighting a last-ditch battle against me now. I think I am on the trail of the man or men higher up in this commercialised-vice business—and it is a business, big business, too. You know, I suppose, that they seem to have a string of hotels in the city, of the worst character. There is nothing that they will stop at to protect themselves. Why, they are using gangs of thugs to terrorise any one who informs on them. The gunmen, of course, hate a snitch worse than poison. There have been bomb outrages, too— nearly a bomb a day lately—against some of those who look shaky and seem to be likely to do business with my office. But I'm getting closer all the time."

"How do you mean?" asked Kennedy.

"Well, one of the best witnesses, if I can break him down by pressure and promises, ought to be a man named Haddon, who is running a place in the Fifties, known as the Mayfair. Haddon knows all these people. I can get him in half an hour if you think it worth while—not here, but somewhere uptown, say at the Prince Henry."

Kennedy nodded. We had heard of Haddon before, a notorious character in the white-light district. A moment later Carton had telephoned to the Mayfair and had found Haddon.

"How did you get him so that he is even considering turning state's evidence?" asked Craig.

"Well," answered Carton slowly, "I suppose it was partly through a cabaret singer and dancer, Loraine Keith, at the Mayfair. You know you never get the truth about things in the underworld except in pieces. As much as any one, I think we have been able to use her to weave a web about him. Besides, she seems to think that Haddon has treated her shamefully. According to her story, he seems to have been lavishing everything on her, but lately, for some reason, has deserted her. Still, even in her jealousy she does not accuse any other woman of winning him away."

"Perhaps it is the opposite—another man winning her," suggested Craig dryly.

"It's a peculiar situation," shrugged Carton. "There is another man. As nearly as I can make out there is a fellow named Brodie who does a dance with her. But he seems to annoy her, yet at the same time exercises a sort of fascination over her."

"Then she is dancing at the Mayfair yet?" hastily asked Craig.

"Yes. I told her to stay, not to excite suspicion."

"And Haddon knows?"

"Oh, no. But she has told us enough about him already so that we can worry him, apparently, just as what he can tell us would worry the others interested in the hotels. To tell the truth, I think she is a drug fiend. Why, my men tell me that they have seen her take just a sniff of something and change instantly—become a willing tool."

"That's the way it happens," commented Kennedy.

"Now, I'll go up there and meet Haddon," resumed Carton. "After I have been with him long enough to get into his confidence, suppose you two just happen along."

Half an hour later Kennedy and I sauntered into the Prince Henry, where Carton had made the appointment in order to avoid suspicion that might arise if he were seen with Haddon at the Mayfair.

The two men were waiting for us—Haddon, by contrast with Carton, a weak-faced, nervous man, with bulgy eyes.

"Mr. Haddon," introduced Carton, "let me present a couple of reporters from the *Star*—off duty, so that we can talk freely before them, I can assure you. Good fellows, too, Haddon."

The hotel and cabaret keeper smiled a sickly smile and greeted us with a covert, questioning glance.

"This attack on Mr. Carton has unnerved me," he shivered. "If any one dares to do that to him, what will they do to me?"

"Don't get cold feet, Haddon," urged Carton. "You'll be all right. I'll swing it for you."

Haddon made no reply. At length he remarked: "You'll excuse me for a moment. I must telephone to my hotel."

He entered a booth in the shadow of the back of the café, where there was a slot-machine pay-station. "I think Haddon has his suspicions," remarked Carton, "although he is too prudent to say anything yet."

A moment later he returned. Something seemed to have happened. He looked less nervous. His face was brighter and his eyes clearer. What was it, I wondered? Could it be that he was playing a game with Carton and had given him a double cross? I was quite surprised at his next remark.

"Carton," he said confidently, "I'll stick."

"Good," exclaimed the district attorney, as they fell into a conversation in low tones.

"By the way," drawled Kennedy, "I must telephone to the office in case they need me."

He had risen and entered the same booth.

Haddon and Carton were still talking earnestly. It was evident that, for some reason, Haddon had lost his former halting manner. Perhaps, I reasoned, the

17

bomb episode had, after all, thrown a scare into him, and he felt that he needed protection against his own associates, who were quick to discover such dealings as Carton had forced him into. I rose and lounged back to the booth and Kennedy.

"Whom did he call?" I whispered, when Craig emerged perspiring from the booth, for I knew that that was his purpose.

Craig glanced at Haddon, who now seemed absorbed in talking to Carton. "No one," he answered quickly. "Central told me there had not been a call from this pay-station for half an hour."

"No one?" I echoed almost incredulously. "Then what did he do? Something happened, all right."

Kennedy was evidently engrossed in his own thoughts, for he said nothing.

"Haddon says he wants to do some scouting about," announced Carton, when we rejoined them. "There are several people whom he says he might suspect. I've arranged to meet him this afternoon to get the first part of this story about the inside working of the vice trust, and he will let me know if anything develops then. You will be at your office?"

"Yes, one or the other of us," returned Craig, in a tone which Haddon could not hear.

In the meantime we took occasion to make some inquiries of our own about Haddon and Loraine Keith. They were evidently well known in the select circle in which they travelled. Haddon had many curious characteristics, chief of which to interest Kennedy was his speed mania. Time and again he had been arrested for exceeding the speed limit in taxi-cabs and in a car of his own, often in the past with Loraine Keith, but lately alone.

It was toward the close of the afternoon that Carton called up hurriedly. As Kennedy hung up the receiver, I read on his face that something had gone wrong.

"Haddon has disappeared," he announced, "mysteriously and suddenly, without leaving so much as a clue. It seems that he found in his office a package exactly like that which was sent to Carton earlier in the day. He didn't wait to say anything about it, but left. Carton is bringing it over here."

Perhaps a quarter of an hour later, Carton himself deposited the package on the laboratory table with an air of relief. We looked eagerly. It was addressed to Haddon at the Mayfair in the same disguised handwriting and was done up in precisely the same fashion.

"Lots of bombs are just scare bombs," observed Craig. "But you never can tell."

Again Kennedy had started to dissect.

"Ah," he went on, "this is the real thing, though, only a little different from the other. A dry battery gives a spark when the lid is slipped back. See, the explosive is in a steel pipe. Sliding the lid off is supposed to explode it. Why, there is enough explosive in this to have silenced a dozen Haddons."

"Do you think he could have been kidnapped or murdered?" I asked. "What is this, anyhow—gang-war?"

"Or perhaps bribed?" suggested Carton.

"I can't say," ruminated Kennedy. "But I can say

this: that there is at large in this city a man of great mechanical skill and practical knowledge of electricity and explosives. He is trying to make sure of hiding something from exposure. We must find him."

"And especially Haddon," Carton added quickly. "He is the missing link. His testimony is absolutely essential to the case I am building up."

"I think I shall want to observe Loraine Keith without being observed," planned Kennedy, with a hasty glance at his watch. "I think I'll drop around at this Mayfair I have heard so much about. Will you come?"

"I'd better not," refused Carton. "You know they all know me, and everything quits wherever I go. I'll see you soon."

As we drove in a cab over to the Mayfair, Kennedy said nothing. I wondered how and where Haddon had disappeared. Had the powers of evil in the city learned that he was weakening and hurried him out of the way at the last moment? Just what had Loraine Keith to do with it? Was she in any way responsible? I felt that there were, indeed, no bounds to what a jealous woman might dare.

Beside the ornate grilled doorway of the carriage entrance of the Mayfair stood a gilt-and-black easel with the words, "Tango Tea at Four." Although it was considerably after that time, there was a line of taxi-cabs before the place and, inside, a brave array of late-afternoon and early-evening revellers. The public dancing had ceased, and a cabaret had taken its place.

We entered and sat down at one of the more inconspicuous of the little round tables. On a stage, at one side, a girl was singing one of the latest syncopated airs.

"We'll just stick around a while, Walter," whispered Craig. "Perhaps this Loraine Keith will come in."

Behind us, protected both by the music and the rustle of people coming and going, a couple talked in low tones. Now and then a word floated over to me in a language which was English, sure enough, but not of a kind that I could understand.

"Dropped by a flatty," I caught once, then something about a "mouthpiece," and the "bulls," and "making a plant."

"A dip—pickpocket—and his girl, or gun-moll, as they call them," translated Kennedy. "One of their number has evidently been picked up by a detective and he looks to them for a good lawyer, or mouthpiece."

Besides these two there were innumerable other interesting glimpses into the life of this meeting-place for the half-and underworlds. A motion in the audience attracted me, as if some favourite performer were about to appear, and I heard the "gun-moll" whisper, "Loraine Keith."

There she was, a petite, dark-haired, snappy-eyed girl, *chic,* well groomed, and gowned so daringly that every woman in the audience envied and every man craned his neck to see her better. Loraine wore a tight-fitting black dress, slashed to the knee. In fact, everything was calculated to set her off at best advantage, and on the stage, at least, there was some-thing *recherché* about her. Yet, there was also something gross about her, too.

Accompanying her was a nervous-looking fellow whose washed-out face was particularly unattractive. It seemed as if the bone in his nose was going, due to the shrinkage of the blood-vessels. Once, just be-fore the dance began, I saw him rub something on the back of his hand, raise it to his nose, and sniff. Then he took a sip of a liqueur.

The dance began, wild from the first step, and as it developed, Kennedy leaned over and whispered, "The *danse des Apaches*."

It was acrobatic. The man expressed brutish pas-sion and jealousy; the woman, affection and fear. It seemed to tell a story—the struggle of love, the love of the woman against the brutal instincts of the thug, her lover. She was terrified as well as fascinated by him in his mad temper and tremendous superhuman strength. I wondered if the dance portrayed the fact.

The music was a popular air with many rapid changes, but through all there was a constant rhythm which accorded well with the abandon of the swaying dance. Indeed, I could think of nothing so much as of Bill Sykes and Nancy as I watched these two.

It was the fight of two frenzied young animals. He would approach stealthily, seize her, and whirl her about, lifting her to his shoulder. She was agile, do-cile, and fearful. He untied a scarf and passed it about her; she leaned against it, and they whirled gid-dily about. Suddenly, it seemed that he became jeal-ous. She would run; he follow and catch her. She

would try to pacify him; he would become more en-
raged. The dance became faster and more furious.
His violent efforts seemed to be to throw her to the
floor, and her streaming hair now made it seem more
like a fight than a dance. The audience hung breathless. It ended with her dropping exhausted, a proper
finale to this lowest and most brutal dance.

Panting, flushed, with an unnatural light in their
eyes, they descended to the audience and, scorning
the roar of applause to repeat the performance, sat
at a little table.

I saw a couple of girls come over toward the man.

"Give us a deck, Coke," said one, in a harsh voice.

He nodded. A silver quarter gleamed momentarily
from hand to hand, and he passed to one girl stealthily a small white-paper packet. Others came to him,
both men and women. It seemed to be an established
thing.

"Who is that?" asked Kennedy, in a low tone, of
the pickpocket back of us.

"Coke Brodie," was the laconic reply.

"A cocaine fiend?"

"Yes, and a lobbygow for the grapevine system of
selling the dope under this new law."

"Where does he get the supply to sell?" asked Kennedy, casually.

The pickpocket shrugged his shoulders.

"No one knows, I suppose," Kennedy commented
to me. "But he gets it in spite of the added restric-
tions and peddles it in little packets, adulterated,
and at a fabulous price for such cheap stuff. The
habit is spreading like wildfire. It is a fertile means

of recruiting the inmates in the vice-trust hotels. A veritable epidemic it is, too. Cocaine is one of the most harmful of all habit-forming drugs. It used to be a habit of the underworld, but now it is creeping up, and gradually and surely reaching the higher strata of society. One thing that causes its spread is the ease with which it can be taken. It requires no smoking-dens, no syringe, no paraphernalia—only the drug itself."

Another singer had taken the place of the dancers. Kennedy leaned over and whispered to the dip.

"Say, do you and your gun-moll want to pick up a piece of change to get that mouthpiece I heard you talking about?"

The pickpocket looked at Craig suspiciously.

"Oh, don't worry; I'm all right," laughed Craig. "You see that fellow, Coke Brodie? I want to get something on him. If you will frame that sucker to get away with a whole front, there's a fifty in it."

The dip looked, rather than spoke, his amazement. Apparently Kennedy satisfied his suspicions.

"I'm on," he said quickly. "When he goes, I'll follow him. You keep behind us, and we'll deliver the goods."

"What's it all about?" I whispered.

"Why," he answered, "I want to get Brodie, only I don't want to figure in the thing so that he will know me or suspect anything but a plain hold-up. They will get him; take everything he has. There must be something on that man that will help us."

Several performers had done their turns, and the supply of the drug seemed to have been exhausted.

Brodie rose and, with a nod to Loraine, went out, unsteadily, now that the effect of the cocaine had worn off. One wondered how this shuffling person could ever have carried through the wild dance. It was not Brodie who danced. It was the drug.

The dip slipped out after him, followed by the woman. We rose and followed also. Across the city Brodie slouched his way, with an evident purpose, it seemed, of replenishing his supply and continuing his round of peddling the stuff.

He stopped under the brow of a thickly populated tenement row on the upper East Side, as though this was his destination. There he stood at the gate that led down to a cellar, looking up and down as if wondering whether he was observed. We had slunk into a doorway.

A woman coming down the street, swinging a chatelaine, walked close to him, spoke, and for a moment they talked.

"It's the gun-moll," remarked Kennedy. "She's getting Brodie off his guard. This must be the root of that grapevine system, as they call it."

Suddenly from the shadow of the next house a stealthy figure sprang out on Brodie. It was our dip, a dip no longer but a regular stick-up man, with a gun jammed into the face of his victim and a broad hand over his mouth. Skilfully the woman went through Brodie's pockets, her nimble fingers missing not a thing.

"Now—beat it," we heard the dip whisper hoarsely, "and if you raise a holler, we'll get you right, next time."

Brodie fled as fast as his weakened nerves would permit his shaky limbs to move. As he disappeared, the dip sent something dark hurtling over the roof of the house across the street and hurried toward us.

"What was that?" I asked.

"I think it was the pistol on the end of a stout cord. That is a favourite trick of the gunmen after a job. It destroys at least a part of the evidence. You can't throw a gun very far alone, you know. But with it at the end of a string you can lift it up over the roof of a tenement. If Brodie squeals to a copper and these people are caught, they can't hold them under the pistol law, anyhow."

The dip had caught sight of us, with his ferret eyes, in the doorway. Quickly Kennedy passed over the money in return for the motley array of objects taken from Brodie. The dip and his gun-moll disappeared into the darkness as quickly as they had emerged.

There was a curious assortment—the paraphernalia of a drug fiend, old letters, a key, and several other useless articles. The pickpocket had retained the money from the sale of the dope as his own particular honorarium.

"Brodie has led us up to the source of his supply," remarked Kennedy, thoughtfully regarding the stuff. "And the dip has given us the key to it. Are you game to go in?"

A glance up and down the street showed it still deserted. We wormed our way in the shadow to the cellar before which Brodie had stood. The outside door was open. We entered, and Craig stealthily struck a match, shading it in his hands.

At one end we were confronted by a little door of mystery, barred with iron and held by an innocent enough looking padlock. It was this lock, evidently, to which the key fitted, opening the way into the subterranean vault of brick and stone.

Kennedy opened it and pushed back the door. There was a little square compartment, dark as pitch and delightfully cool and damp. He lighted a match, then hastily blew it out and switched on an electric bulb which it disclosed.

"Can't afford risks like that here," he exclaimed, carefully disposing of the match, as our eyes became accustomed to the light.

On every side were pieces of gas-pipe, boxes, and paper, and on shelves were jars of various materials. There was a work-table littered with tools, pieces of wire, boxes, and scraps of metal.

"My word!" exclaimed Kennedy, as he surveyed the curious scene before us, "this is a regular bomb factory—one of the most amazing exhibits that the history of crime has ever produced."

XVIII

The "Coke" Fiend

I FOLLOWED him in awe as he made a hasty inventory of what we had discovered. There were as many as a dozen finished and partly finished infernal machines of various sizes and kinds, some of tremendous destructive capacity. Kennedy did not even attempt to study them. All about were high explosives, chemicals, dynamite. There was gunpowder of all varieties, antimony, blasting-powder, mercury cyanide, chloral hydrate, chlorate of potash, samples of various kinds of shot, some of the outlawed soft-nosed dumdum bullets, cartridges, shells, pieces of metal purposely left with jagged edges, platinum, aluminum, iron, steel—a conglomerate mass of stuff that would have gladdened an anarchist.

Kennedy was examining a little quartz-lined electric furnace, which was evidently used for heating soldering-irons and other tools. Everything had been done, it seemed, to prevent explosions. There were no open lights and practically no chance for heat to be communicated far among the explosives. Indeed, everything had been arranged to protect the operator himself in his diabolical work.

Kennedy had switched on the electric furnace, and from the various pieces of metal on the table selected several. These he was placing together in a peculiar manner, and to them he attached some copper wire which lay in a corner in a roll.

Under the work-table, beneath the furnace, one could feel the warmth of the thing slightly. Quickly he took the curious affair, which he had hastily shaped, and fastened it under the table at that point, then led the wires out through a little barred window to an air-shaft, the only means of ventilation of the place except the door.

While he was working I had been gingerly inspecting the rest of the den. In a corner, just beside the door, I had found a set of shelves and a cabinet. On both were innumerable packets done up in white paper. I opened one and found it contained several pinches of a white, crystalline substance.

"Little portions of cocaine," commented Kennedy, when I showed him what I had found. "In the slang of the fiends, 'decks.' "

On the top of the cabinet he discovered a little enamelled box, much like a snuff-box, in which were also some of the white flakes. Quickly he emptied them out and replaced them with others from jars which had not been made up into packets.

"Why, there must be hundreds of ounces of the stuff here, to say nothing of the various things they adulterate it with," remarked Kennedy. "No wonder they are so careful when it is a felony even to have it in your possession in such quantities. See how careful they are about the adulteration, too. You could never tell except from the effect whether it was the pure or only a few-per-cent.-pure article."

Kennedy took a last look at the den, to make sure that nothing had been disturbed that would arouse suspicion.

"We may as well go," he remarked. "To-morrow, I want to be free to make the connection outside with that wire in the shaft."

Imagine our surprise, the next morning, when a tap at our door revealed Loraine Keith herself.

"Is this Professor Kennedy?" she asked, gazing at us with a half-wild expression which she was making a tremendous effort to control. "Because if it is, I have something to tell him that may interest Mr. Carton."

We looked at her curiously. Without her make-up she was pallid and yellow in spots, her hands trembling, cold, and sweaty, her eyes sunken and glistening, with pupils dilated, her breathing short and hurried, restless, irresolute, and careless of her personal appearance.

"Perhaps you wonder how I heard of you and why I have come to you," she went on. "It is because I have a confession to make. I saw Mr. Haddon just before he was—kidnapped."

She seemed to hesitate over the word.

"How did you know I was interested?" asked Kennedy keenly.

"I heard him mention your name with Mr. Carton's."

"Then he knew that I was more than a reporter for the *Star*," remarked Kennedy. "Kidnapped, you say? How?"

She shot a glance half of suspicion, half of frankness, at us.

"That's what I must confess. Whoever did it must have used me as a tool. Mr. Haddon and I used to be good friends—I would be yet."

There was evident feeling in her tone which she did not have to assume. "All I remember yesterday was that, after lunch, I was in the office of the Mayfair when he came in. On his desk was a package. I don't know what has become of it. But he gave one look at it, seemed to turn pale, then caught sight of me. 'Loraine,' he whispered, 'we used to be good friends. Forgive me for turning you down. But you don't understand. Get me away from here—come with me—call a cab.'

"Well, I got into the cab with him. We had a chauffeur whom we used to have in the old days. We drove furiously, avoiding the traffic men. He told the driver to take us to my apartment—and—and that is the last I remember, except a scuffle in which I was dragged from the cab on one side and he on the other."

She had opened her handbag and taken from it a little snuff-box, like that which we had seen in the den.

"I—I can't go on," she apologised, "without this stuff."

"So you are a cocaine fiend, also?" remarked Kennedy.

"Yes, I can't help it. There is an indescribable excitement to do something great, to make a mark, that goes with it. It's soon gone, but while it lasts I can sing and dance, do anything until every part of my body begins crying for it again. I was full of the stuff when this happened yesterday; had taken too much, I guess."

The change in her after she had snuffed some of the crystals was magical. From a quivering wretch she had become now a self-confident neurasthenic.

"You know where that stuff will land you, I presume?" questioned Kennedy.

"I don't care," she laughed hollowly. "Yes, I know what you are going to tell me. Soon I'll be hunting for the cocaine bug, as they call it, imagining that in my skin, under the flesh, are worms crawling, perhaps see them, see the little animals running around and biting me. Oh, you don't know. There are two souls to the cocainist. One is tortured by the suffering which the stuff brings; the other laughs at the fears and pains. But it brings such thoughts! It stimulates my mind, makes it work without, against my will, gives me such visions—oh, I can not go on. They would kill me if they knew I had come to you. Why have I? Has not Haddon cast me off? What is he to me, now?"

It was evident that she was growing hysterical. I wondered whether, after all, the story of the kidnapping of Haddon might not be a figment of her brain, simply an hallucination due to the drug.

"They?" inquired Kennedy, observing her narrowly. "Who?"

"I can't tell. I don't know. Why did I come? Why did I come?"

She was reaching again for the snuff-box, but Kennedy restrained her.

"Miss Keith," he remarked, "you are concealing something from me. There is some one," he paused a moment, "whom you are shielding."

"No, no," she cried. "He was taken. Brodie had nothing to do with it, nothing. That is what you mean. I know. This stuff increases my sensitiveness. Yet I hate Coke Brodie—oh—let me go. I am all unstrung. Let me see a doctor. To-night, when I am better, I will tell all."

Loraine Keith had torn herself from him, had instantly taken a pinch of the fatal crystals, with that same ominous change from fear to self-confidence. What had been her purpose in coming at all? It had seemed at first to implicate Brodie, but she had been quick to shield him when she saw that danger. I wondered what the fascination might be which the wretch exercised over her.

"To-night—I will see you to-night," she cried, and a moment later she was gone, as unexpectedly as she had come.

I looked at Kennedy blankly.

"What was the purpose of that outburst?" I asked.

"I can't say," he replied. "It was all so incoherent that, from what I know of drug fiends, I am sure she had a deep-laid purpose in it all. It does not change my plans."

Two hours later we had paid a deposit on an empty flat in the tenement-house in which the bomb-maker had his headquarters, and had received a key to the

18

apartment from the janitor. After considerable difficulty, owing to the narrowness of the air-shaft, Kennedy managed to pick up the loose ends of the wire which had been led out of the little window at the base of the shaft, and had attached it to a couple of curious arrangements which he had brought with him. One looked like a large taximeter from a motor cab; the other was a diminutive gas-metre, in looks at least. Attached to them were several bells and lights.

He had scarcely completed installing the thing, whatever it was, when a gentle tap at the door startled me. Kennedy nodded, and I opened it. It was Carton.

"I have had my men watching the Mayfair," he announced. "There seems to be a general feeling of alarm there, now. They can't even find Loraine Keith. Brodie, apparently, has not shown up in his usual haunts since the episode of last night."

"I wonder if the long arm of this vice trust could have reached out and gathered them 'in, too?" I asked.

"Quite likely," replied Carton, absorbed in watching Kennedy. "What's this?"

A little bell had tinkled sharply, and a light had flashed up on the attachments to the apparatus.

"Nothing. I was just testing it to see if it works. It does, although the end which I installed down below was necessarily only a makeshift. It is not this red light with the shrill bell that we are interested in. It is the green light and the low-toned bell. This is a thermopile."

"And what is a thermopile?" queried Carton.

"For the sake of one who has forgotten his physics," smiled Kennedy, "I may say this is only another illustration of how all science ultimately finds practical application. You probably have forgotten that when two half-rings of dissimilar metals are joined together and one is suddenly heated or chilled, there is produced at the opposite connecting point a feeble current which will flow until the junctures are both at the same temperature. You might call this a thermo-electric thermometer, or a telethermometer, or a microthermometer, or any of a dozen names."

"Yes," I agreed mechanically, only vaguely guessing at what he had in mind.

"The accurate measurement of temperature is still a problem of considerable difficulty," he resumed, adjusting the thermometer. "A heated mass can impart vibratory motion to the ether which fills space, and the wave-motions of ether are able to reproduce in other bodies motions similar to those by which they are caused. At this end of the line I merely measure the electromotive force developed by the difference in temperature of two similar thermo-electric junctions, opposed. We call those junctions in a thermopile 'couples,' and by getting the recording instruments sensitive enough, we can measure one one-thousandth of a degree.

"Becquerel was the first, I believe, to use this property. But the machine which you see here was one recently invented for registering the temperature of sea water so as to detect the approach of an iceberg.

I saw no reason why it should not be used to measure heat as well as cold.

"You see, down there I placed the couples of the thermopile beneath the electric furnace on the table. Here I have the mechanism operated by the feeble current from the thermopile, opening and closing switches, and actuating bells and lights. Then, too, I have the recording instrument. The thing is fundamentally very simple and is based on well-known phenomena. It is not uncertain and can be tested at any time, just as I did then, when I showed a slight fall in temperature. Of course it is not the slight changes I am after, not the gradual but the sudden changes in temperature."

"I see," said Carton. "If there is a drop, the current goes one way and we see the red light; a rise and it goes the other, and we see a green light."

"Exactly," agreed Kennedy. "No one is going to approach that chamber down-stairs as long as he thinks any one is watching, and we do not know where they are watching. But the moment any sudden great change is registered, such as turning on that electric furnace, we shall know it here."

It must have been an hour that we sat there discussing the merits of the case and speculating on the strange actions of Loraine Keith.

Suddenly the red light flashed out brilliantly.

"What's that?" asked Carton quickly.

"I can't tell, yet," remarked Kennedy. "Perhaps it is nothing at all. Perhaps it is a draught of cold air from opening the door. We shall have to wait and see."

We bent over the little machine, straining our eyes and ears to catch the visual and audible signals which it gave.

Gradually the light faded, as the thermopile adjusted itself to the change in temperature.

Suddenly, without warning, a low-toned bell rang before us and a bright-green light flashed up.

"That can have only one meaning," cried Craig excitedly. "Some one is down there in that inferno—perhaps the bomb-maker himself."

The bell continued to ring and the light to glow, showing that whoever was there had actually started the electric furnace. What was he preparing to do? I felt that, even though we knew there was some one there, it did us little good. I, for one, had no relish for the job of bearding such a lion in his den.

We looked at Kennedy, wondering what he would do next. From the package in which he had brought the two registering machines he quietly took another package, wrapped up, about eighteen inches long and apparently very heavy. As he did so he kept his attention fixed on the telethermometer. Was he going to wait until the bomb-maker had finished what he had come to accomplish?

It was perhaps fifteen minutes after our first alarm that the signals began to weaken.

"Does that mean that he has gone—escaped?" inquired Carton anxiously.

"No. It means that his furnace is going at full power and that he has forgotten it. It is what I am waiting for. Come on."

Seizing the package as he hurried from the room,

Kennedy dashed out on the street and down the outside cellar stairs, followed by us.

He paused at the thick door and listened. Apparently there was not a sound from the other side, except a whir of a motor and a roar which might have been from the furnace. Softly he tried the door. It was locked on the inside.

Was the bomb-maker there still? He must be. Suppose he heard us. Would he hesitate a moment to send us all to perdition along with himself?

How were we to get past that door? Really, the deathlike stillness on the other side was more mysterious than would have been the detonation of some of the criminal's explosive.

Kennedy had evidently satisfied himself on one point. If we were to get into that chamber we must do it ourselves, and we must do it quickly.

From the package which he carried he pulled out a stubby little cylinder, perhaps eighteen inches long, very heavy, with a short stump of a lever projecting from one side. Between the stonework of a chimney and the barred door he laid it horizontally, jamming in some pieces of wood to wedge it tighter.

Then he began to pump on the handle vigorously. The almost impregnable door seemed slowly to bulge. Still there was no sign of life from within. Had the bomb-maker left before we arrived?

"This is my scientific sledge-hammer," panted Kennedy, as he worked the little lever backward and forward more quickly—"a hydraulic ram. There is no swinging of axes or wielding of crowbars necessary in breaking down an obstruction like this, nowadays. Such things are obsolete. This little jimmy, if you want to call it that, has a power of ten tons. That ought to be enough."

It seemed as if the door were slowly being crushed in before the irresistible ten-ton punch of the hydraulic ram.

Kennedy stopped. Evidently he did not dare to crush the door in altogether. Quickly he released the ram and placed it vertically. Under the now-yawning doorjamb he inserted a powerful claw of the ram and again he began to work the handle.

A moment later the powerful door buckled, and Kennedy deftly swung it outward so that it fell with a crash on the cellar floor.

As the noise reverberated, there came a sound of a muttered curse from the cavern. Some one was there.

We pressed forward.

On the floor, in the weird glare of the little furnace, lay a man and a woman, the light playing over their ghastly, set features.

Kennedy knelt over the man, who was nearest the door.

"Call a doctor, quick," he ordered, reaching over and feeling the pulse of the woman, who had half fallen out of her chair. "They will be all right soon. They took what they thought was their usual adulterated cocaine—see, here is the box in which it was. Instead, I filled the box with the pure drug. They'll come around. Besides, Carton needs both of them in his fight."

"Don't take any more," muttered the woman, half

conscious. "There's something wrong with it, Haddon."

I looked more closely at the face in the half-darkness.

It was Haddon himself.

"I knew he'd come back when the craving for the drug became intense enough," remarked Kennedy.

Carton looked at Kennedy in amazement. Haddon was the last person in the world whom he had evidently expected to discover here.

"How—what do you mean?"

"The episode of the telephone booth gave me the first hint. That is the favourite stunt of the drug fiend—a few minutes alone, and he thinks no one is the wiser about his habit. Then, too, there was the story about his speed mania. That is a frequent failing of the cocainist. The drug, too, was killing his interest in Loraine Keith—that is the last stage.

"Yet under its influence, just as with his lobbygow and lieutenant, Brodie, he found power and inspiration. With him it took the form of bombs to protect himself in his graft."

"He can't—escape this time—Loraine. We'll leave it—at his house—you know—Carton—"

We looked quickly at the work-table. On it was a gigantic bomb of clockwork over which Haddon had been working. The cocaine which was to have given him inspiration had, thanks to Kennedy, overcome him.

Beside Loraine Keith were a suit-case and a Gladstone. She had evidently been stuffing the corners full of their favourite nepenthe, for, as Kennedy reached down and turned over the closely packed woman's finery and the few articles belonging to Haddon, innumerable packets from the cabinet dropped out.

"Hulloa—what's this?" he exclaimed, as he came to a huge roll of bills and a mass of silver and gold coin. "Trying to double-cross us all the time. That was her clever game—to give him the hours he needed to gather what money he could save and make a clean getaway. Even cocaine doesn't destroy the interest of men and women in that," he concluded, turning over to Carton the wealth which Haddon had amassed as one of the meanest grafters of the city of graft.

Here was a case which I could not help letting the *Star* have immediately. Notes or no notes, it was local news of the first order. Besides, anything that concerned Carton was of the highest political significance.

It kept me late at the office and I overslept. Consequently I did not see much of Craig the next morning, especially as he told me he had nothing special, having turned down a case of a robbery of a safe, on the ground that the police were much better fitted to catch ordinary yeggmen than he was. During the day, therefore, I helped in directing the following up of the Haddon case for the *Star*.

Then, suddenly, a new front page story crowded this one of the main headlines. With a sigh of relief, I glanced at the new thriller, found it had something to do with the Navy Department, and that it came from as far away as Washington. There was no reason now why others could not carry on the graft story, and I left, not unwillingly. My special work just now was keeping on the trail of Kennedy, and I was glad to go back to the apartment and wait for him.

"I suppose you saw that despatch from Washington in this afternoon's papers?" he queried, as he came in, tossing a late edition of the *Record* down on my desk.

Across the front page extended a huge black scare-head: "NAVY'S MOST VITAL SECRET STOLEN."

"Yes," I shrugged, "but you can't get me much excited by what the rewrite men on the *Record* say."

"Why?" he asked, going directly into his own room.

"Well," I replied, glancing through the text of the story, "the actual facts are practically the same as in the other papers. Take this, for instance, 'On the night of the celebration of the anniversary of the battle of Manila there were stolen from the Navy Department plans which the *Record* learns exclusively represent the greatest naval secret in the world.' So much for that paragraph—written in the office. Then it goes on:

"The whole secret-service machinery of the Government has been put in operation. No one has been able to extract from the authorities the exact secret which was stolen, but it is believed to be an invention which will revolutionise the structure and construction of the most modern monster battleships. Such knowledge, it is said, in the hands of experts might prove fatal in almost any fight in which our newer ships met others of about equal fighting power, as with it marksmen might direct a shot that would disable our ships.

"It is the opinion of the experts that the theft was executed by a skilled draughtsman or other civilian employé. At any rate,

the thief knew what to take and its value. There is, at least,
one nation, it is asserted, which faces the problem of bringing
its ships up to the standard of our own to which the plans would
be very valuable.

"The building had been thrown open to the public for the display of fireworks on the Monument grounds before it. The plans
are said to have been on one of the draughting-tables, drawn upon
linen to be made into blue-prints. They are known to have been
on the tables when the draughting-room was locked for the night.

"The room is on the third floor of the Department and has a
balcony looking out on the Monument. Many officers and officials
had their families and friends on the balcony to witness the celebration, though it is not known that any one was in the draughting-room itself. All were admitted to the building on passes.
The plans were tacked to a draughting-board in the room, but
when it was opened in the morning the linen sheet was gone, and
so were the thumb-tacks. The plans could readily have been
rolled into a small bundle and carried under a coat or wrap.

"While the authorities are trying to minimise the actual loss,
it is believed that this position is only an attempt to allay the
great public concern."

I paused. "Now then," I added, picking up one
of the other papers I had brought up-town myself, "take the *Express*. It says that the plans were
important, but would have been made public in a few
months, anyhow. Here:

"The theft—or mislaying, as the Department hopes it will prove
to be—took place several days ago. Official confirmation of the
report is lacking, but from trustworthy unofficial sources it is
learned that only unimportant parts of plans are missing, pre-
sumably minor structural details of battle-ship construction, and
other things of a really trivial character, such as copies of naval
regulations, etc.

"The attempt to make a sensational connection between the
loss and a controversy which is now going on with a foreign
government is greatly to be deplored and is emphatically asserted
to be utterly baseless. It bears traces of the jingoism of those
'interests' which are urging naval increases.

"There is usually very little about a battle-ship that is not known before her keel is laid, or even before the signing of the contracts. At any rate, when it is asserted that the plans represent the *dernier cri* in some form of war preparation, it is well to remember that a 'last cry' is last only until there is a later. Naval secrets are few, anyway, and as it takes some years to apply them, this loss cannot be of superlative value to any one. Still, there is, of course, a market for such information in spite of the progress toward disarmament, but the rule in this case will be the rule as in a horse trade, '*Caveat emptor.*'"

"So there you are," I concluded. "You pay your penny for a paper, and you take your choice."

"And the *Star,*" inquired Kennedy, coming to the door and adding with an aggravating grin, "the infallible?"

"The *Star,*" I replied, unruffled, "hits the point squarely when it says that whether the plans were of immediate importance or not, the real point is that if they could be stolen, really important things could be taken also. For instance, 'The thought of what the thief might have stolen has caused much more alarm than the knowledge of what he has succeeded in taking.' I think it is about time those people in Washington stopped the leak if—"

The telephone rang insistently.

"I think that's for me," exclaimed Craig, bounding out of his room and forgetting his quiz of me. "Hello—yes—is that you, Burke? At the Grand Central—half an hour—all right. I'm bringing Jameson. Good-bye."

Kennedy jammed down the receiver on the hook.

XIX

The Submarine Mystery

"THE *Star* was not far from right, Walter," he added seriously. "If the battleship plans could be stolen, other things could be—other things were. You remember Burke of the secret service? I'm going up to Lookout Hill on the Connecticut shore of the Sound with him to-night. The rewrite men on the *Record* didn't have the facts, but they had accurate imaginations. The most vital secret that any navy ever had, that would have enabled us in a couple of years to whip the navies of the world combined against us, has been stolen."

"And that is?" I asked.

"The practical working-out of the newest of sciences, the science of telautomatics."

"Telautomatics?" I repeated.

"Yes. There is something weird, fascinating about the very idea. I sit up here safely in this room, turning switches, pressing buttons, depressing levers. Ten miles away a vehicle, a ship, an aeroplane, a submarine obeys me. It may carry enough of the latest and most powerful explosive that modern science can invent, enough, if exploded, to rival the worst of earthquakes. Yet it obeys my will. It goes where I direct it. It explodes where I want it.

And it wipes off the face of the earth anything which I want annihilated.

"That's telautomatics, and that is what has been stolen from our navy and dimly sensed by you clever newspaper men, from whom even the secret service can't quite hide everything. The publication of the rumour alone that the government knows it has lost something has put the secret service in a hole. What might have been done quietly and in a few days has got to be done in the glare of the limelight and with the blare of a brass band—and it has got to be done right away, too. Come on, Walter. I've thrown together all we shall need for one night—and it doesn't include any pajamas, either."

A few minutes later we met our friend Burke of the secret service at the new terminal. He had wired Kennedy earlier in the day saying that he would be in New York and would call him up.

"The plans, as I told you in my message," began Burke, when we had seated ourselves in a compartment of the Pullman, "were those of Captain Shirley, covering the wireless-controlled submarine. The old captain is a thoroughbred, too. I've known him in Washington. Comes of an old New England family with plenty of money but more brains. For years he has been working on this science of radio-telautomatics, has all kinds of patents, which he has dedicated to the United States, too. Of course the basic, pioneer patents are not his. His work has been in the practical application of them. And, Kennedy, there are some secrets about his latest work that he has not patented; he has given them outright to the

Navy Department, because they are too valuable even to patent."

Burke, who liked a good detective tale himself, seemed pleased at holding Kennedy spellbound.

"For instance," he went on, "he has on the bay up here a submarine which can be made into a crewless dirigible. He calls it the *Turtle,* I believe, because that was the name of the first American submarine built by Dr. Bushnell during the Revolution, even before Fulton."

"You have theories of your own on the case?" asked Craig.

"Well, there are several possibilities. You know there are submarine companies in this country, bitter rivals. They might like to have those plans. Then, too, there are foreign governments."

He paused. Though he said nothing, I felt that there was no doubt what he hinted at. At least one government occurred to me which would like the plans above all others.

"Once some plans of a submarine were stolen, I recall," ruminated Kennedy. "But that theft, I am satisfied, was committed in behalf of a rival company."

"But, Kennedy," exclaimed Burke, "it was bad enough when the plans were stolen. Now Captain Shirley wires me that some one must have tampered with his model. It doesn't work right. He even believes that his own life may be threatened. And there is scarcely a real clue," he added dejectedly. "Of course we are watching all the employés who had access to the draughting-room and tracing everybody who was in the building that night. I have a complete list of them. There are three or four who will bear watching. For instance, there is a young attaché of one of the embassies, named Nordheim."

"Nordheim!" I echoed, involuntarily. I had expected an Oriental name.

"Yes, a German. I have been looking up his record, and I find that once he was connected in some way with the famous Titan Iron Works, at Kiel, Germany. We began watching him day before yesterday, but suddenly he disappeared. Then, there is a society woman in Washington, a Mrs. Bayard Brainard, who was at the Department that night. We have been trying to find her. To-day I got word that she was summering in the cottage colony across the bay from Lookout Hill. At any rate, I had to go up there to see the captain, and I thought I'd kill a whole flock of birds with one stone. The chief thought, too, that if you'd take the case with us you had best start on it up there. Next, you will no doubt want to go back to Washington with me."

Lookout Hill was the name of the famous old estate of the Shirleys, on a point of land jutting out into Long Island Sound and with a neighbouring point enclosing a large, deep, safe harbour. On the highest ground of the estate, with a perfect view of both harbour and sound, stood a large stone house, the home of Captain Shirley, of the United States navy, retired.

Captain Shirley, a man of sixty-two or three, bronzed and wiry, met us eagerly.

"So this is Professor Kennedy; I'm glad to meet

you, sir," he welcomed, clasping Craig's hand in both of his—a fine figure as he stood erect in the light of the *portecochère.* "What's the news from Washington, Burke? Any clues?"

"I can hardly tell," replied the secret service man, with assumed cheerfulness. "By the way, you'll have to excuse me for a few minutes while I run back into town on a little errand. Meanwhile, Captain, will you explain to Professor Kennedy just how things are? Perhaps he'd better begin by seeing the *Turtle* herself."

Burke had not waited longer than to take leave.

"The Turtle," repeated the captain, leading the way into the house. "Well, I did call it that at first. But I prefer to call it the *Z99.* You know the first submarines, abroad at least, were sometimes called A1, A2, A3, and so on. They were of the diving, plunging type, that is, they submerged on an inclined keel, nose down, like the Hollands. Then came the B type, in which the hydroplane appeared; the C type, in which it was more prominent, and a D type, where submergence is on a perfectly even keel, somewhat like our Lakes. Well, this boat of mine is a last word—the *Z99.* Call it the *Turtle,* if you like."

We were standing for a moment in a wide Colonial hall in which a fire was crackling in a huge brick fireplace, taking the chill off the night air.

"Let me give you a demonstration, first," added the captain. "Perhaps *Z99* will work—perhaps not."

There was an air of disappointment about the old veteran as he spoke, uncertainly now, of what a short time ago he had known to be a certainty and one of

19

the greatest it had ever been given the inventive mind of man to know.

A slip of a girl entered from the library, saw us, paused, and was about to turn back. Silhouetted against the curtained door, there was health, animation, gracefulness, in every line of her wavy chestnut hair, her soft, sparkling brown eyes, her white dress and hat to match, which contrasted with the healthy glow of tan on her full neck and arms, and her dainty little white shoes, ready for anything from tennis to tango.

"My daughter Gladys, Professor Kennedy and Mr. Jameson," introduced the captain. "We are going to try the *Z99* again, Gladys."

A moment later we four were walking to the edge of the cliff where Captain Shirley had a sort of workshop and signal-station.

He lighted the gas, for Lookout Hill was only on the edge of the town and boasted gas, electricity, and all modern improvements, as well as the atmosphere of old New England.

"The *Z99* is moored just below us at my private dock," began the captain. "I have a shed down there where we usually keep her, but I expected you, and she is waiting, thoroughly overhauled. I have signalled to my men—fellows I can trust, too, who used to be with me in the navy—to cast her off. There— now we are ready."

The captain turned a switch. Instantly a couple of hundred feet below us, on the dark and rippling water, a light broke forth. Another signal, and the light changed.

It was moving.

"The principle of the thing," said Captain Shirley, talking to us but watching the moving light intently, "briefly, is that I use the Hertzian waves to actuate relays on the *Z99*. That is, I send a child with a message, the grown man, through the relay, so to speak, does the work. So, you see, I can sit up here and send my little David out anywhere to strike down a huge Goliath.

"I won't bore you, yet, with explanations of my radio-combinator, the telecommutator, the aerial coherer relay, and the rest of the technicalities of wireless control of dirigible, self-propelled vessels. They are well known, beginning with pioneers like Wilson and Gardner in England, Roberts in Australia, Wirth and Lirpa in Germany, Gabet in France, and Tesla, Edison, Sims, and the younger Hammond in our own country.

"The one thing, you may not know, that has kept us back while wireless telegraphy has gone ahead so fast is that in wireless we have been able to discard coherers and relays and use detectors and microphones in their places. But in telautomatics we have to keep the coherer. That has been the barrier. The coherer until recently has been spasmodic, until we had Hammond's mercury steel-disc coherer and now my own. Why," he cried, "we are just on the threshold, now, of this great science which Tesla has named telautomatics—the electric arm that we can stretch out through space to do our work and fight our battles."

It was not difficult to feel the enthusiasm of the captain over an invention of such momentous possibilities, especially as the *Z99* was well out in the harbour now and we could see her flashing her red and green signal-lights back to us.

"You see," the captain resumed, "I have twelve numbers here on the keys of this radio-combinator—forward, back, stop propeller motor, rudder right, rudder left, stop steering motor, light signals front, light signals rear, launch torpedoes, and so on. The idea is that of a delayed contact. The machinery is always ready, but it delays a few seconds until the right impulse is given, a purely mechanical problem. I take advantage of the delay to have the message repeated by a signal back to me. I can even change it, then. You can see for yourself that it really takes no experience to run the thing when all is going right. Gladys has done it frequently herself. All you have to do is to pay attention, and press the right key for the necessary change. It is when things go wrong that even an expert like myself—confound it —there's something wrong!"

The *Z99* had suddenly swerved. Captain Shirley's brow knitted. We gathered around closer, Gladys next to her father and leaning anxiously over the transmitting apparatus.

"I wanted to turn her to port yet she goes to starboard, and signals starboard, too. There—now—she has stopped altogether. What do you think of that?"

Gladys stroked the old seafarer's hand gently, as he sat silently at the table, peering with contracted brows out into the now brilliantly moonlit night.

Shirley looked up at his daughter, and the lines

on his face relaxed as though he would hide his disappointment from her eager eyes.

"Confound that light! What's the matter with it?" he exclaimed, changing the subject, and glancing up at the gas-fixture.

Kennedy had already been intently looking at the Welsbach burner overhead, which had been flickering incessantly.

"That gas company!" added the Captain, shaking his head in disgust, and showing annoyance over a trivial thing to hide deep concern over a greater, as some men do. "I shall use the electricity altogether after this contract with the company expires. I suppose you literary men, Mr. Jameson, would call that the light that failed."

There was a forced air about his attempt to be facetious that did not conceal, but rather accentuated, the undercurrent of feelings in him.

"On the contrary," broke in Kennedy, "I shouldn't be surprised to find that it is the light that succeeded."

"How do you mean?"

"I wouldn't have said anything about it if you hadn't noticed it yourself. In fact, I may be wrong. It suggests something to me, but it will need a good deal of work to verify it, and then it may not be of any significance. Is that the way the *Z99* has behaved always lately?"

"Yes, but I know that she hasn't broken down of herself," Captain Shirley asserted. "It never did before, not since I perfected that new coherer. And now it always does, perhaps fifteen or twenty minutes after I start her out."

Shirley was watching the lights as they serpentined their way to us across the nearly calm water of the bay, idly toying with the now useless combinator.

"Wait here," he said, rising hurriedly. "I must send my motor-boat out there to pick her up and tow her in."

He was gone down the flight of rustic steps on the face of the cliff before we could reply.

"I wish father wouldn't take it to heart so," murmured Gladys. "Sometimes I fear that success or failure of this boat means life or death to him."

"That is exactly why we are here," reassured Kennedy, turning earnestly to her, "to help him to settle this thing at once. This is a beautiful spot," he added, as we stood on the edge of the cliff and looked far out over the tossing waves of the sound.

"What is on that other point?" asked Kennedy, turning again toward the harbour itself.

"There is a large cottage colony there," she replied. "Of course many of the houses are still closed so early in the season, but it is a beautiful place in the summer. The hotel over there is open now, though."

"You must have a lively time when the season is at its height," ventured Kennedy. "Do you know a cottager there, a Mrs. Brainard?"

"Oh, yes, indeed. I have known her in Washington for some time."

"No doubt the cottagers envy you your isolation here," remarked Kennedy, turning and surveying the beautifully kept grounds. "I should think it would be pleasant, too, to have an old Washington friend here."

"It is. We often invite our friends over for lawn-parties and other little entertainments. Mrs. Brainard has just arrived and has only had time to return my first visit to her, but I expect we shall have some good times this summer."

It was evident, at least, that Gladys was not concealing anything about her friend, whether there was any suspicion or not of her.

We had gone into the house to await the return of Captain Shirley. Burke had just returned, his face betraying that he was bursting with news.

"She's here, all right," he remarked in an undertone to Kennedy, "in the Stamford cottage—quite an outfit. French chauffeur, two Japanese servants, maids, and all."

"The Stamford cottage?" repeated Gladys. "Why, that is where Mrs. Brainard lives."

She gave a startled glance at Kennedy, as she suddenly seemed to realise that both he and the secret-service man had spoken about her friend.

"Yes," said Burke, noting on the instant the perfect innocence of her concern. "What do you know about Mrs. Brainard? Who, where is, Mr. Brainard?"

"Dead, I believe," Gladys hesitated. "Mrs. Brainard has been well known in Washington circles for years. Indeed, I invited her with us the night of the Manila display."

"And Mr. Nordheim?" broke in Burke.

"N-no," she hesitated. "He was there, but I don't know as whose guest."

"Did he seem very friendly with Mrs. Brainard?" pursued the detective.

I thought I saw a shade of relief pass over her face as she answered, "Yes." I could only interpret it that perhaps Nordheim had been attentive to Gladys herself and that she had not welcomed his attentions.

"I may as well tell you," she said, at length. "It is no secret in our set, and I suppose you would find it out soon, anyhow. It is said that he is engaged to Mrs. Brainard—that is all."

"Engaged?" repeated Burke. "Then that would account for his being at the hotel here. At least, it would offer an excuse."

Gladys was not slow to note the stress that Burke laid on the last word.

"Oh, impossible," she began hurriedly, "impossible that he could have known anything about this other matter. Why, she told me he was to sail suddenly for Germany and came up here for a last visit before he went, and to arrange to come back on his return. Oh, he could know nothing—impossible."

"Why impossible?" persisted Burke. "They have submarines in Germany, don't they? And rival companies, too."

"Who have rival companies?" inquired a familiar voice. It was Captain Shirley, who had returned out of breath from his long climb up the steps from the shore.

"The Germans. I was speaking of an attaché named Nordheim."

"Who is Nordheim?" inquired the captain.

"You met him at the Naval building, that night, don't you remember?" replied Gladys.

"Oh, yes, I believe I do—dimly. He was the man who seemed so devoted to Mrs. Brainard."

"I think he is, too, father," she replied hastily. "He has been suddenly called to Berlin and planned to spend the last few days here, at the hotel, so as to be near her. She told me that he had been ordered back to Washington again before he sailed and had had to cut his visit short."

"When did you first notice the interference with the *Turtle?*" asked Burke. "I received your message this morning."

"Yesterday morning was the first," replied the captain.

"He arrived the night before and did not leave until yesterday afternoon," remarked Burke.

"And we arrived to-night," put in Craig quietly. "The interference is going on yet."

"Then the Japs," I cut in, at last giving voice to the suspicion I had of the clever little Orientals.

"They could not have stolen the plans," asserted Burke, shaking his head. "No, Nordheim and Mrs. Brainard were the only ones who could have got into the draughting-room the night of the Manila celebration."

"Burke," said Kennedy, rising, "I wish you would take me into town. There are a few messages I would like to send. You will excuse us, Captain, for a few hours? Good evening, Miss Shirley." As he bowed I heard Kennedy add to her: "Don't worry about your father. Everything will come out all right soon."

Outside, in the car which Burke had hired, Craig added: "Not to town. That was an excuse not to alarm Miss Shirley too much over her friend. Take us over past the Stamford cottage, first."

The Stamford cottage was on the beach, between the shore front and the road. It was not a new place, but was built in the hideous style of some thirty years ago with all sorts of little turned and knobby orna- ments. We paused down the road a bit, though not long enough to attract attention. There were lights on every floor of the cottage, although most of the neighbouring cottages were dark.

"Well protected by lightning-rods," remarked Ken- nedy, as he looked the Stamford cottage over nar- rowly. "We might as well drive on. Keep an eye on the hotel, Burke. It may be that Nordheim intends to return, after all."

"Assuming that he has left," returned the secret- service man.

"But you said he had left," said Kennedy. "What do you mean?"

"I hardly know myself," wearily remarked Burke, on whom the strain of the case, to which we were still fresh, had begun to tell. "I only know that I called up Washington after I heard he had been at the hotel, and no one at our headquarters knew that he had re- turned. They may have fallen down, but they were to watch both his rooms and the embassy."

"H-m," mused Kennedy. "Why didn't you say that before?"

"Why, I assumed that he had gone back, until you told me there was interference to-night, too. Now, until I can locate him definitely I'm all at sea—that's all."

It was now getting late in the evening, but Kennedy had evidently no intention of returning yet to Lookout Hill. We paused at the hotel, which was in the centre of the cottage colony, and flanked by a hill that ran back of the colony diagonally and from which a view of both the hotel and the cottages could be obtained. Burke's inquiries developed the fact that Nordheim had left very hurriedly and in some agitation. "To tell you the truth," confided the clerk, with whom Burke had ingratiated himself, "I thought he acted like a man who was watched."

Late as it was, Kennedy insisted on motoring to the railroad station and catching the last train to New York. As there seemed to be nothing that I could do at Lookout Hill, I accompanied him on the long and tedious ride, which brought us back to the city in the early hours of the morning.

We stopped just long enough to run up to the laboratory and to secure a couple of little instruments which looked very much like small incandescent lamps in a box. Then, by the earliest train from New York, we returned to Lookout Hill, with only such sleep as Kennedy had predicted, snatched in the day coaches of the trains and during a brief wait in the station.

A half-hour's freshening up with a dip in the biting cold water of the bay, breakfast with Captain Shirley and Miss Gladys, and a return to the excitement of

the case, had to serve in place of rest. Burke disappeared, after a hasty conference with Kennedy, pre-
sumably to watch Mrs. Brainard, the hotel, and the
Stamford cottage to see who went in and out.

"I've had the *Z99* brought out of its shed," remarked the captain, as we rose from the breakfast-
table. "There was nothing wrong as far as I could
discover last night or by a more careful inspection
this morning. I'd like to have you take a look at
her now, in the daylight."

"I was about to suggest," remarked Kennedy, as
we descended the steps to the shore, "that perhaps,
first, it might be well to take a short run in her with
the crew, just to make sure that there is nothing
wrong with the machinery."

"A good idea," agreed the captain.

We came to the submarine, lying alongside the dock
and looking like a huge cigar. The captain preceded
us down the narrow hatchway, and I followed Craig.
The deck was cleared, the hatch closed, and the vessel
sealed.

XX

The Wireless Detector

REMEMBERING Jules Verne's enticing picture of life on the palatial *Nautilus*, I may as well admit that I was not prepared for a real submarine. My first impression, as I entered the hold, was that of discomfort and suffocation. I felt, too, that I was too close to too much whirring machinery. I gazed about curiously. On all sides were electrical devices and machines to operate the craft and the torpedoes. I thought, also, that the water outside was uncomfortably close; one could almost feel it. The *Z99* was low roofed, damp, with an intricate system of rods, controls, engines, tanks, stop-cocks, compasses, gauges—more things than it seemed the human mind, to say nothing of wireless, could possibly attend to at once.

"The policy of secrecy which governments keep in regard to submarines," remarked the captain, running his eye over everything at once, it seemed, "has led them to be looked upon as something mysterious. But whatever you may think of telautomatics, there is really no mystery about an ordinary submarine."

I did not agree with our "Captain Nemo," as, the examination completed, he threw in a switch. The motor started. The *Z99* hummed and trembled. The fumes of gasoline were almost suffocating at first, in

spite of the prompt ventilation to clear them off.
There was no escape from the smell. I had heard of
"gasoline heart," but the odour only made me sick
and dizzy. Like most novices, I suppose, I was suffering excruciating torture. Not so, Kennedy. He
got used to it in no time; indeed, seemed to enjoy the
very discomfort.

I felt that there was only one thing necessary to add
to it, and that was the odour of cooking. Cooking,
by the way, on a submarine is uncertain and disagreeable. There was a little electric heater, I found,
which might possibly have heated enough water for
one cup of coffee at a time.

In fact, space was economised to the utmost. Only
the necessaries of life were there. Every inch that
could be spared was given over to machinery. It
was everywhere, compact, efficient—everything for
running the boat under water, guiding it above and
below, controlling its submersion, compressing air,
firing torpedoes, and a thousand other things. It
was wonderful as it was. But when one reflected
that all could be done automatically, or rather telau-
tomatically, it was simply astounding.

"You see," observed Captain Shirley, "when she
is working automatically neither the periscope nor the
wireless-mast shows. The wireless impulses are carried down to her from an inconspicuous float which
trails along the surface and carries a short aerial
with a wire running down, like a mast, forming practically invisible antennæ."

As he was talking the boat was being "trimmed"
by admitting water as ballast into the proper tanks.

"The *Z99*," he went on, "is a submersible, not a diving, submarine. That is to say, the rudder guides it and changes the angle of the boat. But the hydroplanes pull it up and down, two pairs of them set fore and aft of the centre of gravity. They lift or lower the boat bodily on an even keel, not by plunging and diving. I will now set the hydroplanes at ten degrees down and the horizontal rudder two degrees up, and the boat will submerge to a depth of thirty feet and run constant at that depth."

He had shut off the gasoline motor and started the storage-battery electric motor, which was used when running submerged. The great motors gave out a strange, humming sound. The crew conversed in low, constrained tones. There was a slightly perceptible jar, and the boat seemed to quiver just a bit from stem to stern. In front of Shirley was a gauge which showed the depth of submergence and a spirit-level which showed any inclination.

"Submerged," he remarked, "is like running on the surface under dense-fog conditions."

I did not agree with those who have said there is no difference running submerged or on the surface. Under way on the surface was one thing. But when we dived it was most unpleasant. I had been reassured at the start when I heard that there were ten compressed-air tanks under a pressure of two thousand pounds to the square inch. But only once before had I breathed compressed air and that was when one of our cases once took us down into the tunnels below the rivers of New York. It was not a new sensation, but at fifty feet depth I felt a little tingling all over my body, a pounding of the ear-drums, and just a trace of nausea.

Kennedy smiled as I moved about. "Never mind, Walter," he said. "I know how you feel on a first trip. One minute you are choking from lack of oxygen, then in another part of the boat you are exhilarated by too much of it. Still," he winked, "don't forget that it is regulated."

"Well," I returned, "all I can say is that if war is hell, a submarine is war."

I had, however, been much interested in the things about me. Forward, the torpedo-discharge tubes and other apparatus about the little doors in the vessel's nose made it look somewhat like the shield used in boring a tunnel under compressed air.

"Ordinary torpedo-boats use the regular automobile torpedo," remarked Captain Shirley, coming ubiquitously up behind me. "I improve on that. I can discharge the telautomobile torpedo, and guide it either from the boat, as we are now, or from the land station where we were last night, at will."

There was something more than pride in his manner. He was deadly in earnest about his invention.

We had come over to the periscope, the "eye" of the submarine when she is running just under the surface, but of no use that we were below. "Yes," he remarked, in answer to my half-spoken question, "that is the periscope. Usually there is one fixed to look ahead and another that is movable, in order to take in what is on the sides and in the rear. I have both of those. But, in addition, I have the universal periscope, the eye that sees all around, three hundred and sixty degrees—a very clever application of an annular prism with objectives, condenser, and two eyepieces of low and high power."

A call from one of the crew took him into the stern to watch the operation of something, leaving me to myself, for Kennedy was roaming about on a still hunt for anything that might suggest itself. The safety devices, probably more than any other single thing, interested me, for I had read with peculiar fascination of the great disasters to the *Lutin,* the *Pluviöse,* the *Farfardet,* the *A8,* the *Foca,* the *Kambala,* the Japanese *No 6,* the German *U3,* and others.

Below us I knew there was a keel that could be dropped, lightening the boat considerably. Also, there was the submarine bell, immersed in a tank of water, with telephone receivers attached by which one could "listen in," for example, before rising, say, from sixty feet to twenty feet, and thus "hear" the hulls of other ships. The bell was struck by means of air pressure, and was the same as that used for submarine signalling on ships. Water, being dense, is an excellent conductor of sound. Even in the submarine itself, I could hear the muffled clang of the gong.

Then there were buoys which could be released and would fly to the surface, carrying within them a telephone, a light, and a whistle. I knew also something of the explosion dangers on a submarine, both from the fuel oil used when running on the surface, and from the storage batteries used when running submerged. Once in a while a sailor would take from a jar a piece of litmus paper and expose it, showing only a slight discolouration due to carbon dioxide.

20

That was the least of my troubles. For a few moments, also, the white mice in a cage interested me. White mice were carried because they dislike the odour of gasoline and give warning of any leakage by loud squeals.

The fact was that there was so much of interest that, the first discomfort over, I was, like Kennedy, beginning really to enjoy the trip.

I was startled suddenly to hear the motors stop. There was no more of that interminable buzzing. The *Z99* responded promptly to the air pressure that was forcing the water out of the tanks. The gauge showed that we were gradually rising on an even keel. A man sprang up the narrow hatchway and opened the cover through which we could see a little patch of blue sky again. The gasoline motor was started, and we ran leisurely back to the dock. The trip was over—safely. As we landed I felt a sense of gladness to get away from that feeling of being cut off from the world. It was not fear of death or of the water, as nearly as I could analyse it, but merely that terrible sense of isolation from man and nature as we know it.

A message from Burke was waiting for Kennedy at the wharf. He read it quickly, then handed it to Captain Shirley and myself.

Have just received a telegram from Washington. Great excitement at the embassy. Cipher telegram has been despatched to the Titan Iron Works. One of my men in Washington reports a queer experience. He had been following one of the members of the embassy staff, who saw he was being shadowed, turned suddenly on the man, and exclaimed, "Why are you hounding us still?" What do you make of it? No trace yet of Nordheim.

BURKE.

The lines in Craig's face deepened in thought as he folded the message and remarked abstractedly, "She works all right when you are aboard." Then he recalled himself. "Let us try her again without a crew."

Five minutes later we had ascended to the aerial conning-tower, and all was in readiness to repeat the trial of the night before. Vicious and sly the *Z99* looked in the daytime as she slipped off, under the unseen guidance of the wireless, with death hidden under her nose. Just as during the first trial we had witnessed, she began by fulfilling the highest expectations. Straight as an arrow she shot out of the harbour's mouth, half submerged, with her periscope sticking up and bearing the flag proudly flapping, leaving behind a wake of white foam.

She turned and re-entered the harbour, obeying Captain Shirley's every whim, twisting in and out of the shipping much to the amazement of the old salts, who had never become used to the weird sight. She cut a figure eight, stopped, started again.

Suddenly I could see by the look on Captain Shirley's face that something was wrong. Before either of us could speak, there was a spurt of water out in the harbour, a cloud of spray, and the *Z99* sank in a mass of bubbles. She had heeled over and was resting on the mud and ooze of the harbour bottom. The water had closed over her, and she was gone.

Instantly all the terrible details of the sinking of the *Lutin* and other submarines flashed over me. I fancied I could see on the *Z99* the overturned accumulators. I imagined the stifling fumes, the strug-

gle for breath in the suddenly darkened hull. Almost as if it had happened half an hour ago, I saw it.

"Thank God for telautomatics," I murmured, as the
thought swept over me of what we had escaped. "No
one was aboard her, at least."

Chlorine was escaping rapidly from the overturned
storage batteries, for a grave danger lurks in the
presence of sea water, in a submarine, in combination with any of the sulphuric acid. Salt water
and sulphuric acid produce chlorine gas, and a pint
of it inside a good-sized submarine would be sufficient
to render unconscious the crew of a boat. I began to
realise the risks we had run, which my confidence in
Captain Shirley had minimised. I wondered whether
hydrogen in dangerous quantities might not be given
off, and with the short-circuiting of the batteries perhaps explode. Nothing more happened, however.
All kinds of theories suggested themselves. Perhaps
in some way the gasoline motor had been started while
the boat was depressed, the "gas" had escaped, combined with air, and a spark had caused an explosion.
There were so many possibilities that it staggered
me. Captain Shirley sat stunned.

Yet here was the one great question, Whence had
come the impulse that had sent the famous *Z99* to
her fate?

"Could it have been through something internal?"
I asked. "Could a current from one of the batteries
have influenced the receiving apparatus?"

"No," replied the captain mechanically. "I have
a secret method of protecting my receiving instruments from such impulses within the hull."

Kennedy was sitting silently in the corner, oblivious to us up to this point.

"But not to impulses from outside the hull," he broke in.

Unobserved, he had been bending over one of the little instruments which had kept us up all night and had cost a tedious trip to New York and back.

"What's that?" I asked.

"This? This is a little instrument known as the audion, a wireless electric-wave detector."

"Outside the hull?" repeated Shirley, still dazed.

"Yes," cried Kennedy excitedly. "I got my first clue from that flickering Welsbach mantle last night. Of course it flickered from the wireless we were using, but it kept on. You know in the gas-mantle there is matter in a most mobile and tenuous state, very sensitive to heat and sound vibrations.

"Now, the audion, as you see, consists of two platinum wings, parallel to the plane of a bowed filament of an incandescent light in a vacuum. It was invented by Dr. Lee DeForest to detect wireless. When the light is turned on and the little tantalum filament glows, it is ready for business.

"It can be used for all systems of wireless—singing spark, quenched spark, arc sets, telephone sets; in fact, it will detect a wireless wave from whatever source it is sent. It is so susceptible that a man with one attached to an ordinary steel-rod umbrella on a rainy night can pick up wireless messages that are being transmitted within some hundreds of miles radius."

The audion buzzed.

"There—see? Our wireless is not working. But with the audion you can see that some wireless is, and a fairly near and powerful source it is, too."

Kennedy was absorbed in watching the audion.

Suddenly he turned and faced us. He had evidently reached a conclusion. "Captain," he cried, "can you send a wireless message? Yes? Well, this is to Burke. He is over there back of the hotel on the hill with some of his men. He has one there who understands wireless, and to whom I have given another audion. Quick, before this other wireless cuts in on us again. I want others to get the message as well as Burke. Send this: 'Have your men watch the railroad station and every road to it. Surround the Stamford cottage. There is some wireless interference from that direction.'"

As Shirley, with a half-insane light in his eyes, flashed the message mechanically through space, Craig rose and signalled to the house. Under the *portecochére* I saw a waiting automobile, which an instant later tore up the broken-stone path and whirled around almost on two wheels near the edge of the cliff. Glowing with health and excitement, Gladys Shirley was at the wheel herself. In spite of the tenseness of the situation, I could not help stopping to admire the change in the graceful, girlish figure of the night before, which was now all lithe energy and alertness in her eager devotion to carrying out the minutest detail of Kennedy's plan to aid her father.

"Excellent, Miss Shirley," exclaimed Kennedy, "but when I asked Burke to have you keep a car in readiness, I had no idea you would drive it yourself."

"I like it," she remonstrated, as he offered to take the wheel. "Please—please—let me drive. I shall go crazy if I'm not doing something. I saw the *Z99* go down. What was it? Who—"

"Captain," called Craig. "Quick—into the car. We must hurry. To the Stamford house, Miss Shirley. No one can get away from it before we arrive. It is surrounded."

Everything was quiet, apparently, about the house as our wild ride around the edge of the harbour ended under the deft guidance of Gladys Shirley. Here and there, behind a hedge or tree, I could see a lurking secret-service man. Burke joined us from behind a barn next door.

"Not a soul has gone in or out," he whispered. "There does not seem to be a sign of life there."

Craig and Burke had by this time reached the broad veranda. They did not wait to ring the bell, but carried the door down literally off its hinges. We followed closely.

A scream from the drawing-room brought us to a halt. It was Mrs. Brainard, tall, almost imperial in her loose morning gown, her dark eyes snapping fire at the sudden intrusion. I could not tell whether she had really noticed that the house was watched or was acting a part.

"What does this mean?" she demanded. "What—Gladys—you—"

"Florence—tell them—it isn't so—is it? You don't know a thing about those plans of father's that were—stolen—that night."

"Where is Nordheim?" interjected Burke quickly, a little of his "third degree" training getting the upper hand.

"Nordheim?"

"Yes—you know. Tell me. Is he here?"

"Here? Isn't it bad enough to hound him, without hounding me, too? Will you merciless detectives drive us all from place to place with your brutal suspicions?"

"Merciless?" inquired Burke, smiling with sarcasm. "Who has been hounding him?"

"You know very well what I mean," she repeated, drawing herself up to her full height and patting Gladys's hand to reassure her. "Read that message on the table."

Burke picked up a yellow telegram dated New York, two days before.

It was as I feared when I left you. The secret service must have rummaged my baggage both here and at the hotel. They have taken some very vaulable papers of mine.

"Secret service—rummage baggage?" repeated Burke, himself now in perplexity. "That is news to me. We have rummaged no trunks or bags, least of all Nordheim's. In fact, we have never been able to find them at all."

"Upstairs, Burke—the servants' quarters," interrupted Craig impatiently. "We are wasting time here."

Mrs. Brainard offered no protest. I began to think that the whole thing was indeed a surprise to her, and that she had, in fact, been reading, instead of making a studied effort to appear surprised at our intrusion.

Room after room was flung open without finding any one, until we reached the attic, which had been finished off into several rooms. One door was closed. Craig opened it cautiously. It was pitch dark in spite of the broad daylight outside. We entered gingerly.

On the floor lay two dark piles of something. My foot touched one of them. I drew back in horror at the feeling. It was the body of a man.

Kennedy struck a light, and as he bent over in its little circle of radiance, he disclosed a ghastly scene.

"Hari-kiri!" he ejaculated. "They must have got my message to Burke and have seen that the house was surrounded."

The two Japanese servants had committed suicide.

"Wh-what does it all mean?" gasped Mrs. Brainard, who had followed us upstairs with Gladys.

Burke's lip curled slightly and he was about to speak.

"It means," hastened Kennedy, "that you have been double crossed, Mrs. Brainard. Nordheim stole those plans of Captain Shirley's submarine for his Titan Iron Works. Then the Japs stole them from his baggage at the hotel. He thought the secret service had them. The Japs waited here just long enough to try the plans against the Z99 herself—to destroy Captain Shirley's work by his own method of destruction. It was clever, clever. It would make his labours seem like a failure and would discourage others from keeping up the experiments. They had planned to steal a march on the world. Every time the *Z99* was out they worked up here with their improvised wireless until they found the wave-length Shirley was using. It took fifteen or twenty minutes, but they managed, finally, to interfere so that they sent the submarine to the bottom of the harbour. Instead of being the criminal, Burke, Mrs. Brainard is the victim, the victim both of Nordheim and of her servants."

Craig had thrown open a window and had dropped down on his knees before a little stove by which the room was heated. He was poking eagerly in a pile of charred paper and linen.

"Shirley," he cried, "your secret is safe, even though the duplicate plans were stolen. There will be no more interference."

The Captain seized Craig by both hands and wrung them like the handle of a pump.

"Oh, thank you—thank you—thank you," cried Gladys, running up and almost dancing with joy at the change in her father. "I—I could almost—kiss you!"

"I could let you," twinkled Craig, promptly, as she blushed deeply. "Thank you, too, Mrs. Brainard," he added, turning to acknowledge her congratulations also. "I am glad I have been able to be of service to you."

"Won't you come back to the house for dinner?" urged the Captain.

Kennedy looked at me and smiled. "Walter," he said, "this is no place for two old bachelors like us."

Then turning, he added, "Many thanks, sir,—but,

seriously, last night we slept principally in day coaches. Really I must turn the case over to Burke now and get back to the city to-night early."

They insisted on accompanying us to the station, and there the congratulations were done all over again.

"Why," exclaimed Kennedy, as we settled ourselves in the Pullman after waving a final good-bye, "I shall be afraid to go back to that town again. I—I almost did kiss her!"

Then his face settled into its usual stern lines, although softened, I thought. I am sure that it was not the New England landscape, with its quaint stone fences, that he looked at out of the window, but the recollection of the bright dashing figure of Gladys Shirley.

It was seldom that a girl made so forcible an impression on Kennedy, I know, for on our return he fairly dived into work, like the *Z99* herself, and I did not see him all the next day until just before dinner time. Then he came in and spent half an hour restoring his acid-stained fingers to something like human semblance.

He said nothing about his research work of the day, and I was just about to remark that a day had passed without its usual fresh alarum and excursion, when a tap on the door buzzer was followed by the entrance of our old friend Andrews, head of the Great Eastern Life Insurance Company's own detective service.

"Kennedy," he began, "I have a startling case for you. Can you help me out with it?"

As he sat down heavily, he pulled from his immense

black wallet some scraps of paper and newspaper cuttings.

"You recall, I suppose," he went on, unfolding the papers without waiting for an answer, "the recent death of young Montague Phelps, at Woodbine, just outside the city?"

Kennedy nodded. The death of Phelps, about ten days before, had attracted nation-wide attention because of the heroic fight for life he had made against what the doctors admitted had puzzled them—a new and baffling manifestation of coma. They had laboured hard to keep him awake, but had not succeeded, and after several days of lying in a comatose state he had finally succumbed. It was one of those strange but rather frequent cases of long sleeps reported in the newspapers, although it was by no means one which might be classed as record-breaking.

The interest in Phelps lay, a great deal, in the fact that the young man had married the popular dancer, Anginette Petrovska, a few months previously. His honeymoon trip around the world had suddenly been interrupted, while the couple were crossing Siberia, by the news of the failure of the Phelps banking-house in Wall Street and the practical wiping-out of his fortune. He had returned, only to fall a victim to a greater misfortune.

"A few days before his death," continued Andrews, measuring his words carefully, "I, or rather the Great Eastern, which had been secretly investigating the case, received this letter. What do you think of it?"

He spread out on the table a crumpled note in a palpably disguised handwriting:

To Whom it May Concern:

You would do well to look into the death of Montague Phelps, Jr. I accuse no one, assert nothing. But when a young man, apparently in the best of health, drops off so mysteriously and even the physician in the case can give no very convincing information, that case warrants attention. I know what I know.

                                                      An Outsider.

XXI

The Ghouls

"H-M," mused Kennedy, weighing the contents of the note carefully, "one of the family, I'll be bound—unless the whole thing is a hoax. By the way, who else is there in the immediate family?"

"Only a brother, Dana Phelps, younger and somewhat inclined to wildness, I believe. At least, his father did not trust him with a large inheritance, but left most of his money in trust. But before we go any further, read that."

Andrews pulled from the papers a newspaper cutting on which he had drawn a circle about the following item. As we read, he eyed us sharply.

PHELPS TOMB DESECRATED

Last night, John Shaughnessy, a night watchman employed by the town of Woodbine, while on his rounds, was attracted by noises as of a violent struggle near the back road in the Woodbine Cemetery, on the outskirts of the town. He had varied his regular rounds because of the recent depredations of motor-car yeggmen who had timed him in pulling off several jobs lately.

As he hurried toward the large mausoleum of the Phelps family, he saw two figures slink away in opposite directions in the darkness. One of them, he asserts positively, seemed to be a woman in black, the other a man whom he could not see clearly. They readily eluded pursuit in the shadows, and a moment later he heard the whir of a high-powered car, apparently bearing them away.

At the tomb there was every evidence of a struggle. Things had been thrown about; the casket had been broken open, but the body of Montague Phelps, Jr., which had been interred there about ten days ago, was not touched or mutilated.

It was a shocking and extraordinary violation. Shaughnessy believes that some personal jewels may have been buried with Phelps and that the thieves were after them, that they fought over the loot, and in the midst of the fight were scared away.

The vault is of peculiar construction, a costly tomb in which repose the bodies of the late Montague Phelps, Sr., of his wife, and now of his eldest son. The raid had evidently been carefully planned to coincide with a time when Shaughnessy would ordinarily have been on the other side of the town. The entrance to the tomb had been barred, but during the commotion the ghouls were surprised and managed to escape without accomplishing their object and leaving no trace.

Mrs. Phelps, when informed of the vandalism, was shocked, and has been in a very nervous state since the tomb was forced open. The local authorities seem extremely anxious that every precaution should be taken to prevent a repetition of the ghoulish visit to the tomb, but as yet the Phelps family has taken no steps.

"Are you aware of any scandal, any skeleton in the closet in the family?" asked Craig, looking up.

"No—not yet," considered Andrews. "As soon as I heard of the vandalism, I began to wonder what could have happened in the Phelps tomb, as far as our company's interests were concerned. You see, that was yesterday. To-day this letter came along," he added, laying down a second very dirty and wrinkled note beside the first. It was quite patently written by a different person from the first; its purport was different, indeed quite the opposite of the other. "It was sent to Mrs. Phelps," explained Andrews, "and she gave it out herself to the police."

Do not show this to the police. Unless you leave $5000 in gold
in the old stump in the swamp across from the cemetery, you will
have reason to regret it. If you respect the memory of the dead,
do this, and do it quietly.

BLACK HAND.

"Well," I ejaculated, "that's cool. What threat
could be used to back this demand on the Phelpses?"

"Here's the situation," resumed Andrews, puffing
violently on his inevitable cigar and toying with the
letters and clippings. "We have already held up
payment of the half-million dollars of insurance to
the widow as long as we can consistently do so. But
we must pay soon, scandal or not, unless we can get
something more than mere conjecture."

"You are already holding it up?" queried Craig.

"Yes. You see, we investigate thoroughly every
suspicious death. In most cases, no body is found.
This case is different in that respect. There is a body,
and it is the body of the insured, apparently. But a
death like this, involving the least mystery, receives
careful examination, especially if, as in this case, it
has recently been covered by heavy policies. My
work has often served to reverse the decision of doctors and coroners' juries.

"An insurance detective, as you can readily appreciate, Kennedy, soon comes to recognise the characteristics in the crimes with which he deals. For example, writing of the insurance plotted for rarely pre-
cedes the conspiracy to defraud. That is, I know of
few cases in which a policy originally taken out in
good faith has subsequently become the means of a
swindle.

"In outright-murder cases, the assassin induces the

victim to take out insurance in his favour. In suicide cases, the insured does so himself. Just after
his return home, young Phelps, who carried fifty thousand dollars already, applied for and was granted
one of the largest policies we have ever written—half
a million."

"Was it incontestible without the suicide clause?"
asked Kennedy.

"Yes," replied Andrews, "and suicide is the first
and easiest theory. Why, you have no idea how common the crime of suicide for the sake of the life insurance is becoming. Nowadays, we insurance men
almost believe that every one who contemplates end-
ing his existence takes out a policy so as to make his
life, which is useless to him, a benefit, at least, to some
one—and a nightmare to the insurance detective."

"I know," I cut in, for I recalled having been rather
interested in the Phelps case at the time, "but I
thought the doctors said finally that death was due to
heart failure."

"Doctor Forden who signed the papers said so,"
corrected Andrews. "Heart failure—what does that
mean? As well say breath failure, or nerve failure.
I'll tell you what kind of failure I think it was. It
was money failure. Hard times and poor investments
struck Phelps before he really knew how to handle
his small fortune. It called him home and—pouf!—
he is off—to leave to his family a cool half-million by
his death. But did he do it himself or did some one
else do it? That's the question."

"What is your theory," inquired Kennedy absently,
"assuming there is no scandal hidden in the life of

21

Phelps before or after he married the Russian dancer?"

"I don't know, Kennedy," confessed Andrews. "I have had so many theories and have changed them so rapidly that all I lay claim to believing, outside of the bald facts that I have stated, is that there must have been some poison. I rather sense it, feel that there is no doubt of it, in fact. That is why I have come to you. I want you to clear it up, one way or another. The company has no interest except in getting at the truth."

"The body is really there?" asked Kennedy. "You saw it?"

"It was there no later than this afternoon, and in an almost perfect state of preservation, too."

Kennedy seemed to be looking at and through Andrews as if he would hypnotise the truth out of him. "Let me see," he said quickly. "It is not very late now. Can we visit the mausoleum to-night?"

"Easily. My car is down-stairs. Woodbine is not far, and you'll find it a very attractive suburb, aside from this mystery."

Andrews lost no time in getting us out to Woodbine, and on the fringe of the little town, one of the wealthiest around the city, he deposited us at the least likely place of all, the cemetery. A visit to a cemetery is none too enjoyable even on a bright day. In the early night it is positively uncanny. What was gruesome in the daylight became doubly so under the shroud of darkness.

We made our way into the grounds through a gate, and I, at least, even with all the enlightenment of modern science, could not restrain a weird and creepy sensation.

"Here is the Phelps tomb," directed Andrews, pausing beside a marble structure of Grecian lines and pulling out a duplicate key of a new lock which had been placed on the heavy door of grated iron. As we entered, it was with a shudder at the damp odour of decay. Kennedy had brought his little electric bull's-eye, and, as he flashed it about, we could see at a glance that the reports had not been exaggerated. Everything showed marks of a struggle. Some of the ornaments had been broken, and the coffin itself had been forced open.

"I have had things kept just as we found them," explained Andrews.

Kennedy peered into the broken coffin long and attentively. With a little effort I, too, followed the course of the circle of light. The body was, as Andrews had said, in an excellent, indeed a perfect, state of preservation. There were, strange to say, no marks of decay.

"Strange, very strange," muttered Kennedy to himself.

"Could it have been some medical students, body-snatchers?" I asked musingly. "Or was it simply a piece of vandalism? I wonder if there could have been any jewels buried with him, as Shaughnessy said? That would make the motive plain robbery."

"There were no jewels," said Andrews, his mind not on the first part of my question, but watching Kennedy intently.

Craig had dropped on his knees on the damp, mildewed floor, and bringing his bull's-eye close to the stones, was examining some spots here and there.

"There could not have been any substitution?" I whispered, with my mind still on the broken coffin. "That would cover up the evidence of a poisoning, you know."

"No," replied Andrews positively, "although bodies can be obtained cheaply enough from a morgue, ostensibly for medical purposes. No, that is Phelps, all right."

"Well, then," I persisted, "body-snatchers, medical students?"

"Not likely, for the same reason," he rejected.

We bent over closer to watch Kennedy. Apparently he had found a number of round, flat spots with little spatters beside them. He was carefully trying to scrape them up with as little of the surrounding mould as possible.

Suddenly, without warning, there was a noise outside, as if a person were moving through the underbrush. It was fearsome in its suddenness. Was it human or wraith? Kennedy darted to the door in time to see a shadow glide silently away, lost in the darkness of the fine old willows. Some one had approached the mausoleum for a second time, not knowing we were there, and had escaped. Down the road we could hear the purr of an almost silent motor.

"Somebody is trying to get in to conceal something here," muttered Kennedy, stifling his disappointment at not getting a closer view of the intruder.

"Then it was not a suicide," I exclaimed. "It was a murder!"

Craig shook his head sententiously. Evidently he was not prepared yet to talk.

With another look at the body in the broken casket he remarked: "To-morrow I want to call on Mrs. Phelps and Doctor Forden, and, if it is possible to find him, Dana Phelps. Meanwhile, Andrews, if you and Walter will stand guard here, there is an apparatus which I should like to get from my laboratory and set up here before it is too late."

It was far past the witching hour of midnight, when graveyards proverbially yawn, before Craig returned in the car. Nothing had happened in the meantime except those usual eery noises that one may hear in the country at night anywhere. Our visitor of the early evening seemed to have been scared away for good.

Inside the mausoleum, Kennedy set up a peculiar machine which he attached to the electric-light circuit in the street by a long wire which he ran loosely over the ground. Part of the apparatus consisted of an elongated box lined with lead, to which were several other attachments, the nature of which I did not understand, and a crank-handle.

"What's that?" asked Andrews curiously, as Craig set up a screen between the apparatus and the body.

"This is a calcium-tungsten screen," remarked Kennedy, adjusting now what I know to be a Crookes' tube on the other side of the body itself, so that the order was: the tube, the body, the screen, and the oblong box. Without a further word we continued to watch him.

At last, the apparatus adjusted apparently to his

satisfaction, he brought out a jar of thick white liquid and a bottle of powder.

"Buttermilk and a couple of ounces of bismuth sub-carbonate," he remarked, as he mixed some in a glass, and with a pump forced it down the throat of the body, now lying so that the abdomen was almost flat against the screen.

He turned a switch and the peculiar bluish efful-gence, which always appears when a Crookes' tube is being used, burst forth, accompanied by the droning of his induction-coil and the welcome smell of ozone produced by the electrical discharge in the almost fetid air of the tomb. Meanwhile, he was gradually turning the handle of the crank attached to the oblong box. He seemed so engrossed in the delicateness of the operation that we did not question him, in fact did not move. For Andrews, at least, it was enough to know that he had succeeded in enlisting Ken-nedy's services.

Well along toward morning it was before Kennedy had concluded his tests, whatever they were, and had packed away his paraphernalia.

"I'm afraid it will take me two or three days to get at this evidence, even now," he remarked, impa-tient at even the limitations science put on his activ-ity. We had started back for a quick run to the city and rest. "But, anyhow, it will give us a chance to do some investigating along other lines."

Early the next day, in spite of the late session of the night before, Kennedy started me with him on a second visit to Woodbine. This time he was armed with a letter of introduction from Andrews to Mrs. Phelps.

She proved to be a young woman of most extraordinary grace and beauty, with a superb carriage such as only years of closest training under the best dancers of the world could give. There was a peculiar velvety softness about her flesh and skin, a witching stoop to her shoulders that was decidedly continental, and in her deep, soulful eyes a half-wistful look that was most alluring. In fact, she was as attractive a widow as the best Fifth Avenue dealers in mourning goods could have produced.

I knew that 'Ginette Phelps had been, both as dancer and wife, always the centre of a group of actors, artists, and men of letters as well as of the world and affairs. The Phelpses had lived well, although they were not extremely wealthy, as fortunes go. When the blow fell, I could well fancy that the loss of his money had been most serious to young Montague, who had showered everything as lavishly as he was able upon his captivating bride.

Mrs. Phelps did not seem to be overjoyed at receiving us, yet made no open effort to refuse.

"How long ago did the coma first show itself?" asked Kennedy, after our introductions were completed. "Was your husband a man of neurotic tendency, as far as you could judge?"

"Oh, I couldn't say when it began," she answered, in a voice that was soft and musical and under perfect control. "The doctor would know that better. No, he was not neurotic, I think."

"Did you ever see Mr. Phelps take any drugs—
not habitually, but just before this sleep came
on?"

Kennedy was seeking his information in a manner
and tone that would cause as little offence as possible.
"Oh, no," she hastened. "No, never—absolutely."

"You called in Dr. Forden the last night?"

"Yes, he had been Montague's physician many years
ago, you know."

"I see," remarked Kennedy, who was thrusting
about aimlessly to get her off her guard. "By the
way, you know there is a great deal of gossip about
the almost perfect state of preservation of the body,
Mrs. Phelps. I see it was not embalmed."

She bit her lip and looked at Kennedy sharply.

"Why, why do you and Mr. Andrews worry me?
Can't you see Doctor Forden?"

In her annoyance I fancied that there was a sur-
prising lack of sorrow. She seemed preoccupied. I
could not escape the feeling that she was putting some
obstacle in our way, or that from the day of the discovery of the vandalism, some one had been making
an effort to keep the real facts concealed. Was she
shielding some one? It flashed over me that perhaps,
after all, she had submitted to the blackmail and had
buried the money at the appointed place. There
seemed to be little use in pursuing the inquiry, so we
excused ourselves, much, I thought, to her relief.

We found Doctor Forden, who lived on the same
street as the Phelpses several squares away, most fortunately at home. Forden was an extremely interesting man, as is, indeed, the rule with physicians,

I could not but fancy, however, that his hearty as-
surance that he would be glad to talk freely on the
case was somewhat forced.

"You were sent for by Mrs. Phelps, that last night,
I believe, while Phelps was still alive?" asked Kennedy.

"Yes. During the day it had been impossible to
arouse him, and that night, when Mrs. Phelps and the
nurse found him sinking even deeper into the comatose state, I was summoned again. He was beyond
hope then. I did everything I could, but he died a
few moments after I arrived."

"Did you try artificial respiration?" asked Kennedy.

"N-no," replied Forden. "I telephoned here for
my respirator, but by the time it arrived at the house
it was too late. Nothing had been omitted while he
was still struggling with the spark of life. When
that went out what was the use?"

"You were his personal physician?"

"Yes."

"Had you ever noticed that he took any drug?"

Doctor Forden shot a quick glance at Kennedy.
"Of course not. He was not a drug fiend."

"I didn't mean that he was addicted to any drug.
But had he taken anything lately, either of his own
volition or with the advice or knowledge of any one
else?"

"Of course not."

"There's another strange thing I wish to ask your
opinion about," pursued Kennedy, not to be rebuffed.
"I have seen his body. It is in an excellent state of

preservation, almost lifelike. And yet I understand, or at least it seems, that it was not embalmed."

"You'll have to ask the undertaker about that," answered the doctor brusquely.

It was evident that he was getting more and more constrained in his answers. Kennedy did not seem to mind it, but to me it seemed that he must be hiding something. Was there some secret which medical ethics kept locked in his breast? Kennedy had risen and excused himself.

The interviews had not resulted in much, I felt, yet Kennedy did not seem to care. Back in the city again, he buried himself in his laboratory for the rest of the day, most of the time in his dark room, where he was developing photographic plates or films, I did not know which.

During the afternoon Andrews dropped in for a few moments to report that he had nothing to add to what had already developed. He was not much impressed by the interviews.

"There's just one thing I want to speak about, though," he said at length, unburdening his mind. "That tomb and the swamp, too, ought to be watched. Last night showed me that there seems to be a regular nocturnal visitor and that we cannot depend on that town night watchman to scare him off. Yet if we watch up there, he will be warned and will lie low. How can we watch both places at once and yet remain hidden?"

Kennedy nodded approval of the suggestion. "I'll fix that," he replied, anxious to return to his photographic labours. "Meet me, both of you, on the road from the station at Woodbine, just as it is getting dusk." Without another word he disappeared into the dark room.

We met him that night as he had requested. He had come up to Woodbine in the baggage-car of the train with a powerful dog, for all the world like a huge, grey wolf.

"Down, Schaef," he ordered, as the dog began to show an uncanny interest in me. "Let me introduce my new dog-detective," he chuckled. "She has a wonderful record as a police-dog."

We were making our way now through the thickening shadows of the town to the outskirts. "She's a German sheep-dog, a *Schäferhund*," he explained. "For my part, it is the English bloodhound in the open country and the sheep-dog in the city and the suburbs."

Schaef seemed to have many of the characteristics of the wild, prehistoric animal, among them the full, upright ears of the wild dog which are such a great help to it. She was a fine, alert, upstanding dog, hardy, fierce, and literally untiring, of a tawny light brown like a lioness, about the same size and somewhat of the type of the smooth-coated collie, broad of chest and with a full brush of tail.

Untamed though she seemed, she was perfectly under Kennedy's control, and rendered him absolute and unreasoning obedience.

At the cemetery we established a strict watch about the Phelps mausoleum and the swamp which lay across the road, not a difficult thing to do as far as concealment went, owing to the foliage. Still, for the same reason, it was hard to cover the whole ground. In the shadow of a thicket we waited. Now and then we could hear Schaef scouting about in the underbrush, crouching and hiding, watching and guarding.

As the hours of waiting in the heavily laden night air wore on, I wondered whether our vigil in this weird place would be rewarded. The soughing of the night wind in the evergreens, mournful at best, was doubly so now. Hour after hour we waited patiently.

At last there was a slight noise from the direction opposite the mausoleum and toward the swamp next to the cemetery.

Kennedy reached out and drew us back into the shadow deeper. "Some one is prowling about, approaching the mausoleum on that side, I think," he whispered.

Instantly there recurred to me the thought I had had earlier in the day that perhaps, after all, the five thousand dollars of hush money, for whatever purpose it might be extorted, had been buried in the swamp by Mrs. Phelps in her anxiety. Had that been what she was concealing? Perhaps the blackmailer had come to reconnoitre, and, if the money was there, to take it away.

Schaef, who had been near us, was sniffing eagerly. From our hiding-place we could just see her. She had heard the sounds, too, even before we had, and for an instant stood with every muscle tense.

Then, like an arrow, she darted into the underbrush. An instant later, the sharp crack of a revolver rang out. Schaef kept right on, never stopping a second, except, perhaps, for surprise.

"Crack!" almost in her face came a second spit of fire in the darkness, and a bullet crashed through the leaves and buried itself in a tree with a ping. The intruder's marksmanship was poor, but the dog paid no attention to it.

"One of the few animals that show no fear of gun-fire," muttered Kennedy, in undisguised admiration.

"*G-r-r-r,*" we heard from the police-dog.

"She has made a leap at the hand that holds the gun," cried Kennedy, now rising and moving rapidly in the same direction. "She has been taught that a man once badly bitten in the hand is nearly out of the fight."

We followed, too. As we approached we were just in time to see Schaef running in and out between the legs of a man who had heard us approach and was hastily making tracks for the road. As he tripped, she lunged for his back.

Kennedy blew shrilly on a police whistle. Reluctantly, Schaef let go. One could see that with all her canine instinct she wanted to "get" that man. Her jaws were open, as, with longing eyes, she stood over the prostrate form in the grass. The whistle was a signal, and she had been taught to obey unquestioningly.

"Don't move until we get to you, or you are a dead man," shouted Kennedy, pulling an automatic as he ran. "Are you hurt?"

There was no answer, but as we approached, the man moved, ever so little, through curiosity to see his pursuers.

Schaef shot forward. Again the whistle sounded

and she dropped back. We bent over to seize him as Kennedy secured the dog.

"She's a devil," ground out the prone figure on the grass.

"Dana Phelps!" exclaimed Andrews, as the man turned his face toward us. "What are you doing, mixed up in this?"

Suddenly there was a movement in the rear, toward the mausoleum itself. We turned, but it was too late. Two dark figures slunk through the gloom, bearing something between them. Kennedy slipped the leash off Schaef and she shot out like a unchained bolt of lightning.

There was the whir of a high-powered machine which must have sneaked up with the muffler on during the excitement. They had taken a desperate chance and had succeeded. They were gone!

XXII

The X-Ray "Movies"

STILL holding Dana Phelps between us, we hurried toward the tomb and entered. While our attention had been diverted in the direction of the swamp, the body of Montague Phelps had been stolen.

Dana Phelps was still deliberately brushing off his clothes. Had he been in league with them, executing a flank movement to divert our attention? Or had it all been pure chance?

"Well?" demanded Andrews.

"Well?" replied Dana.

Kennedy said nothing, and I felt that, with our capture, the mystery seemed to have deepened rather than cleared.

As Andrews and Phelps faced each other, I noticed that the latter was now and then endeavouring to cover his wrist, where the dog had torn his coat sleeve.

"Are you hurt badly?" inquired Kennedy.

Dana said nothing, but backed away. Kennedy advanced, insisting on looking at the wounds. As he looked he disclosed a semicircle of marks.

"Not a dog bite," he whispered, turning to me and fumbling in his pocket. "Besides, those marks are a couple of days old. They have scabs on them."

He had pulled out a pencil and a piece of paper, and, unknown to Phelps, was writing in the darkness. I

leaned. over. Near the point, in the tube through
which the point for writing was, protruded a small
accumulator and tiny electric lamp which threw a little disc of light, so small that it could be hidden by
the hand, yet quite sufficient to guide Craig in moving
the point of his pencil for the proper formation of
whatever he was recording on the surface of the paper.

"An electric-light pencil," he remarked laconically,
in an undertone.

"Who were the others?" demanded Andrews of
Dana.

There was a pause as though he were debating
whether or not to answer at all. "I don't know," he
said at length. "I wish I did."

"You don't know?" queried Andrews, with incre-
dulity.

"No. I say I wish I did know. You and your dog
interrupted me just as I was about to find out, too."

We looked at each other in amazement. Andrews
was frankly skeptical of the coolness of the young
man. Kennedy said nothing for some moments.

"I see you don't want to talk," he put in shortly.

"Nothing to talk about," grunted Dana, in disgust.

"Then why are you here?"

"Nothing but conjecture. No facts, only suspicions," said Dana, half to himself.

"You expect us to believe that?" insinuated Andrews.

"I can't help what you believe. That is the fact."

"And you were not with them?"

"No."

"You'll be within call, if we let you go now, any time that we want you?" interrupted Kennedy, much to the surprise of Andrews.

"I shall stay in Woodbine as long as there is any hope of clearing up this case. If you want me, I suppose I shall have to stay anyhow, even if there is a clue somewhere else."

"I'll take your word for it," offered Kennedy.

"I'll give it."

I must say that I rather liked the young chap, although I could make nothing out of him.

As Dana Phelps disappeared down the road, Andrews turned to Kennedy. "What did you do that for?" he asked, half critically.

"Because we can watch him, anyway," answered Craig, with a significant glance at the now empty casket. "Have him shadowed, Andrews. It may lead to something and it may not. But in any case don't let him get out of reach."

"Here we are in a worse mystery than ever," grumbled Andrews. "We have caught a prisoner, but the body is gone, and we can't even show that he was an accomplice."

"What were you writing?" I asked Craig, endeavouring to change the subject to one more promising.

"Just copying the peculiar shape of those marks on Phelps' arm. Perhaps we can improve on the finger-print method of identification. Those were the marks of human teeth."

He was glancing casually at his sketch as he displayed it to us. I wondered whether he really ex-

22

pected to obtain proof of the identity of at least one of the ghouls by the tooth-marks.

"It shows eight teeth, one of them decayed," he remarked. "By the way, there's no use watching here any longer. I have some more work to do in the laboratory which will keep me another day. To-morrow night I shall be ready. Andrews, in the mean time I leave the shadowing of Dana to you, and with the help of Jameson I want you to arrange to have all those connected with the case at my laboratory to-morrow night without fail."

Andrews and I had to do some clever scheming to bring pressure to bear on the various persons interested to insure their attendance, now that Craig was ready to act. Of course there was no difficulty in getting Dana Phelps. Andrews's shadows reported nothing in his actions of the following day that indicated anything. Mrs. Phelps came down to town by train and Doctor Forden motored in. Andrews even took the precaution to secure Shaughnessy and the trained nurse, Miss Tracy, who had been with Montague Phelps during his illness but had not contributed anything toward untangling the case. Andrews and myself completed the little audience.

We found Kennedy heating a large mass of some composition such as dentists use in taking impressions of the teeth.

"I shall be ready in a moment," he excused himself, still bending over his Bunsen flame. "By the way, Mr. Phelps, if you will permit me."

He had detached a wad of the softened material. Phelps, taken by surprise, allowed him to make an impression of his teeth, almost before he realised what Kennedy was doing. The precedent set, so to speak, Kennedy approached Doctor Forden. He demurred, but finally consented. Mrs. Phelps followed, then the nurse, and even Shaughnessy.

With a quick glance at each impression, Kennedy laid them aside to harden.

"I am ready to begin," he remarked at length, turning to a peculiar looking instrument, something like three telescopes pointing at a centre in which was a series of glass prisms.

"These five senses of ours are pretty dull detectives sometimes," Kennedy began. "But I find that when we are able to call in outside aid we usually find that there are no more mysteries."

He placed something in a test-tube in line before one of the barrels of the telescopes, near a brilliant electric light.

"What do you see, Walter?" he asked, indicating an eyepiece.

I looked. "A series of lines," I replied. "What is it?"

"That," he explained, "is a spectroscope, and those are the lines of the absorption spectrum. Each of those lines, by its presence, denotes a different substance. Now, on the pavement of the Phelps mausoleum I found, you will recall, some roundish spots. I have made a very diluted solution of them which is placed in this tube.

"The applicability of the spectroscope to the differentiation of various substances is too well known to need explanation. Its value lies in the exact nature of the evidence furnished. Even the very dilute solution which I have been able to make of the material scraped from these spots gives characteristic absorption bands between the D and E lines, as they are called. Their wave-lengths are between 5774 and 5390. It is such a distinct absorption spectrum that it is possible to determine with certainty that the fluid actually contains a certain substance, even though the microscope might fail to give sure proof. Blood—human blood—that was what those stains were."

He paused. "The spectra of the blood pigments," he added, "of the extremely minute quantities of blood and the decomposition products of hemoglobin in the blood are here infallibly shown, varying very distinctly with the chemical changes which the pigments may undergo."

Whose blood was it? I asked myself. Was it of some one who had visited the tomb, who was surprised there or surprised some one else there? I was hardly ready for Kennedy's quick remark.

"There were two kinds of blood there. One was contained in the spots on the floor all about the mausoleum. There are marks on the arm of Dana Phelps which he probably might say were made by the teeth of my police-dog, Schaef. They are human tooth-marks, however. He was bitten by some one in a struggle. It was his blood on the floor of the mausoleum. Whose were the teeth?"

Kennedy fingered the now set impressions, then resumed: "Before I answer that question, what else does the spectroscope show? I found some spots near the coffin, which has been broken open by a heavy object.   It had slipped and had injured the body of Montague Phelps.   From the injury some drops had oozed.   My spectroscope tells me that that, too, is blood.   The blood and other muscular and nervous fluids of the body had remained in an aqueous condition instead of becoming pectous.   That is a remarkable circumstance."

It flashed over me what Kennedy had been driving at in his inquiry regarding embalming.   If the poisons of the embalming fluid had not been injected, he had now clear proof regarding anything his spectroscope discovered.

"I had expected to find a poison, perhaps an alkaloid," he continued slowly, as he outlined his discoveries by the use of one of the most fascinating branches of modern science, spectroscopy.   "In cases of poisoning by these substances, the spectroscope often has obvious advantages over chemical methods, for minute amounts will produce a well-defined spectrum. The spectroscope 'spots' the substance, to use a police idiom, the moment the case is turned over to it. There was no poison there."   He had raised his voice to emphasise the startling revelation.   "Instead, I found an extraordinary amount of the substance and products of glycogen.   The liver, where this substance is stored, is literally surcharged in the body of Phelps."

He had started his moving-picture machine.

"Here I have one of the latest developments in the moving-picture art," he resumed, "an X-ray moving picture, a feat which was until recently visionary, a science now in its infancy, bearing the formidable names of bioröntgenography, or kinematoradiography."

Kennedy was holding his little audience breathless as he proceeded. I fancied I could see Anginette Phelps give a little shudder at the prospect of looking into the very interior of a human body. But she was pale with the fascination of it. Neither Forden nor the nurse looked to the right or to the left. Dana Phelps was open-eyed with wonder.

"In one X-ray photograph, or even in several," continued Kennedy, "it is difficult to discover slight motions. Not so in a moving picture. For instance, here I have a picture which will show you a living body in all its moving details."

On the screen before us was projected a huge shadowgraph of a chest and abdomen. We could see the vertebræ of the spinal column, the ribs, and the various organs.

"It is difficult to get a series of photographs directly from a fluorescent screen," Kennedy went on. "I overcome the difficulty by having lenses of sufficient rapidity to photograph even faint images on that screen. It is better than the so-called serial method, by which a number of separate X-ray pictures are taken and then pieced together and rephotographed to make the film. I can focus the X-rays first on the screen by means of a special quartz objective which I have devised. Then I take the pictures.

"Here, you see, are the lungs in slow or rapid respiration. There is the rhythmically beating heart, distinctly pulsating in perfect outline. There is the liver, moving up and down with the diaphragm, the intestines, and the stomach. You can see the bones moving with the limbs, as well as the inner visceral life. All that is hidden to the eye by the flesh is now made visible in striking manner."

Never have I seen an audience at the "movies" so thrilled as we were now, as Kennedy swayed our interest at his will. I had been dividing my attention between Kennedy and the extraordinary beauty of the famous Russian dancer. I forgot Anginette Phelps entirely.

Kennedy placed another film in the holder.

"You are now looking into the body of Montague Phelps," he announced suddenly.

We leaned forward eagerly. Mrs. Phelps gave a half-suppressed gasp. What was the secret hidden in it?

There was the stomach, a curved sack something like a bagpipe or a badly made boot, with a tiny canal at the toe connecting it with the small intestine. There were the heart and lungs.

"I have rendered the stomach visible," resumed Kennedy, "made it 'metallic,' so to speak, by injecting a solution of bismuth in buttermilk, the usual method, by which it becomes more impervious to the X-rays and hence darker in the skiagraph. I took these pictures not at the rate of fourteen or so a second, like the others, but at intervals of a few seconds. I did that so that, when I run them off, I get a sort of compressed moving picture. What you see in a short space of time actually took much longer to occur. I could have either kind of picture, but I prefer the latter.

"For, you will take notice that there is movement here—of the heart, of the lungs, of the stomach—faint, imperceptible under ordinary circumstances, but nevertheless, movement."

He was pointing at the lungs. "A single peristaltic contraction takes place normally in a very few seconds. Here it takes minutes. And the stomach. Notice what the bismuth mixture shows. There is a very slow series of regular wave-contractions from the fundus to the pylorus. Ordinarily one wave takes ten seconds to traverse it; here it is so slow as almost to be unnoticed."

What was the implication of his startling, almost gruesome, discovery? I saw it clearly, yet hung on his words, afraid to admit even to myself the logical interpretation of what I saw.

"Reconstruct the case," continued Craig excitedly. "Mr. Phelps, always a *bon vivant* and now so situated by marriage that he must be so, comes back to America to find his personal fortune—gone.

"What was left? He did as many have done. He took out a new large policy on his life. How was he to profit by it? Others have committed suicide, have died to win. Cases are common now where men have ended their lives under such circumstances by swallowing bichloride-of-mercury tablets, a favourite method, it seems, lately.

"But Phelps did not want to die to win. Life was too sweet to him. He had another scheme." Kennedy dropped his voice.

"One of the most fascinating problems in speculation as to the future of the race under the influence of science is that of suspended animation. The usual attitude is one of reserve or scepticism. There is no necessity for it. Records exist of cases where vital functions have been practically suspended, with no food and little air. Every day science is getting closer to the control of metabolism. In the trance the body functions are so slowed as to simulate death. You have heard of the Indian fakirs who bury themselves alive and are dug up days later? You have doubted it. But there is nothing improbable in it.

"Experiments have been made with toads which have been imprisoned in porous rock where they could get the necessary air. They have lived for months in a stupor. In impervious rock they have died. Frozen fish can revive; bears and other animals hibernate. There are all gradations from ordinary sleep to the torpor of death. Science can slow down almost to a standstill the vital processes so that excretions disappear and respiration and heart-beat are almost *nil*.

"What the Indian fakir does in a cataleptic condition may be duplicated. It is not incredible that they may possess some vegetable extract by which they perform their as yet unexplained feats of prolonged living burial. For, if an animal free from disease is subjected to the action of some chemical and physical agencies which have the property of reducing to the extreme limit the motor forces and nervous stimulus, the body of even a warm-blooded animal may be brought down to a condition so closely resembling death that the most careful examination may fail to detect any signs of life. The heart will continue working regularly at low tension, supplying muscles and other parts with sufficient blood to sustain molecular life, and the stomach would naturally react to artificial stimulus. At any time before decomposition of tissue has set in, the heart might be made to resume its work and life come back.

"Phelps had travelled extensively. In Siberia he must undoubtedly have heard of the Buriats, a tribe of natives who hibernate, almost like the animals, during the winters, succumbing to a long sleep known as the 'leshka.' He must have heard of the experiments of Professor Bakhmetieff, who studied the Buriats and found that they subsisted on foods rich in glycogen, a substance in the liver which science has discovered makes possible life during suspended animation. He must have heard of 'anabiose,' as the famous Russian calls it, by which consciousness can be totally removed and respiration and digestion cease almost completely."

"But—the body—is gone!" some one interrupted. I turned. It was Dana Phelps, now leaning forward in wide-eyed excitement.

"Yes," exclaimed Craig. "Time was passing rapidly. The insurance had not been paid. He had expected to be revived and to disappear with Anginette Phelps long before this. Should the confederates of Phelps wait? They did not dare. To wait longer might be to sacrifice him, if indeed they had not taken a long chance already. Besides, you yourself had your suspicions and had written the insurance company hinting at murder."

Dana nodded, involuntarily confessing.

"You were watching them, as well as the insurance investigator, Mr. Andrews. It was an awful dilemma. What was to be done? He must be resuscitated at any risk.

"Ah—an idea! Rifle the grave—that was the way to solve it. That would still leave it possible to collect the insurance, too. The blackmail letter about the five thousand dollars was only a blind, to lay on the mythical Black Hand the blame for the desecration. Brought into light, humidity, and warmth, the body would recover consciousness and the life-functions resume their normal state after the anabiotic coma into which Phelps had drugged himself.

"But the very first night the supposed ghouls were discovered. Dana Phelps, already suspicious regarding the death of his brother, wondering at the lack of sentiment which Mrs. Phelps showed, since she felt that her husband was not really dead—Dana was there. His suspicions were confirmed, he thought. Montague had been, in reality, murdered, and his murderers were now making away with the evidence. He fought with the ghouls, yet apparently, in the darkness, he did not discover their identity. The struggle was bitter, but they were two to one. Dana was bitten by one of them. Here are the marks of teeth—teeth—of a woman."

Anginette Phelps was sobbing convulsively. She had risen and was facing Doctor Forden with outstretched hands.

"Tell them!" she cried wildly.

Forden seemed to have maintained his composure only by a superhuman effort.

"The—body is—at my office," he said, as we faced him with deathlike stillness. "Phelps had told us to get him within ten days. We did get him, finally. Gentlemen, you, who were seeking murderers, are, in effect, murderers. You kept us away two days too long. It was too late. We could not revive him. Phelps is really dead!"

"The deuce!" exclaimed Andrews, "the policy is incontestible!"

As he turned to us in disgust, his eyes fell on Anginette Phelps, sobered down by the terrible tragedy and nearly a physical wreck from real grief.

"Still," he added hastily, "we'll pay without a protest."

She did not even hear him. It seemed that the butterfly in her was crushed, as Dr. Forden and Miss Tracy gently led her away.

They had all left, and the laboratory was again in its normal state of silence, except for the occasional step of Kennedy as he stowed away the apparatus he had used.

"I must say that I was one of the most surprised in the room at the outcome of that case," I confessed at length. "I fully expected an arrest."

He said nothing, but went on methodically restoring his apparatus to its proper place.

"What a peculiar life you lead, Craig," I pursued reflectively. "One day it is a case that ends with such a bright spot in our lives as the recollection of the Shirleys; the next goes to the other extreme of gruesomeness and one can hardly think about it with-

out a shudder. And then, through it all, you go with
the high speed power of a racing motor."

"That last case appealed to me, like many others,"
he ruminated, "just because it was so unusual, so
gruesome, as you call it."

He reached into the pocket of his coat, hung over
the back of a chair.

"Now, here's another most unusual case, apparently.
It begins, really, at the other end, so to speak, with
the conviction, begins at the very place where we detectives send a man as the last act of our little
dramas."

"What?" I gasped, "another case before even this
one is fairly cleaned up? Craig—you are impossible.
You get worse instead of better."

"Read it," he said, simply. Kennedy handed me a
letter in the angular hand affected by many women.
It was dated at Sing Sing, or rather Ossining. Craig
seemed to appreciate the surprise which my face must
have betrayed at the curious combination of circumstances.

"Nearly always there is the wife or mother of a condemned man who lives in the shadow of the prison,"
he remarked quietly, adding, "where she can look
down at the grim walls, hoping and fearing."

I said nothing, for the letter spoke for itself.

I have read of your success as a scientific detective and hope
that you will pardon me for writing to you, but it is a matter
of life or death for one who is dearer to me than all the world.

Perhaps you recall reading of the trial and conviction of my
husband, Sanford Godwin, at East Point. The case did not attract much attention in New York papers, although he was defended by an able lawyer from the city.

Since the trial, I have taken up my residence here in Ossining in order to be near him. As I write I can see the cold, grey walls of the state prison that holds all that is dear to me. Day after day, I have watched and waited, hoped against hope. The courts are so slow, and lawyers are so technical. There have been executions since I came here, too—and I shudder at them. Will this appeal be denied, also?

My husband was accused of murdering by poison—hemlock, they alleged—his adoptive parent, the retired merchant, Parker Godwin, whose family name he took when he was a boy. After the death of the old man, a later will was discovered in which my husband's inheritance was reduced to a small annuity. The other heirs, the Elmores, asserted, and the state made out its case on the assumption, that the new will furnished a motive for killing old Mr. Godwin, and that only by accident had it been discovered.

Sanford is innocent. He could not have done it. It is not in him to do such a thing. I am only a woman, but about some things I know more than all the lawyers and scientists, and I *know* that he is innocent.

I cannot write all. My heart is too full. Cannot you come and advise me? Even if you cannot take up the case to which I have devoted my life, tell me what to do. I am enclosing a check for expenses, all I can spare at present.

Sincerely yours,

NELLA GODWIN.

"Are you going?" I asked, watching Kennedy as he tapped the check thoughtfully on the desk.

"I can hardly resist an appeal like that," he replied, absently replacing the check in the envelope with the letter.

XXIII

The Death House

IN the early forenoon, we were on our way by train "up the river" to Sing Sing, where, at the station, a line of old-fashioned cabs and red-faced cabbies greeted us, for the town itself is hilly.

The house to which we had been directed was on the hill, and from its windows one could look down on the barracks-like pile of stone with the evil little black-barred slits of windows, below and perhaps a quarter of a mile away.

There was no need to be told what it was. Its very atmosphere breathed the word "prison." Even the ugly clutter of tall-chimneyed workshops did not destroy it. Every stone, every grill, every glint of a sentry's rifle spelt "prison."

Mrs. Godwin was a pale, slight little woman, in whose face shone an indomitable spirit, unconquered even by the slow torture of her lonely vigil. Except for such few hours that she had to engage in her simple household duties, with now and then a short walk in the country, she was always watching that bleak stone house of atonement.

Yet, though her spirit was unconquered, it needed no physician to tell one that the dimming of the lights at the prison on the morning set for the execution would fill two graves instead of one. For she had come to know that this sudden dimming of the corridor lights, and then their almost as sudden flaring-up, had a terrible meaning, well known to the men inside. Hers was no less an agony than that of the men in the curtained cells, since she had learned that when the lights grow dim at dawn at Sing Sing, it means that the electric power has been borrowed for just that little while to send a body straining against the straps of the electric chair, snuffing out the life of a man.

To-day she had evidently been watching in both directions, watching eagerly the carriages as they climbed the hill, as well as in the direction of the prison.

"How can I ever thank you, Professor Kennedy," she greeted us at the door, keeping back with difficulty the tears that showed how much it meant to have any one interest himself in her husband's case.

There was that gentleness about Mrs. Godwin that comes only to those who have suffered much.

"It has been a long fight," she began, as we talked in her modest little sitting-room, into which the sun streamed brightly with no thought of the cold shadows in the grim building below. "Oh, and such a hard, heartbreaking fight! Often it seems as if we had exhausted every means at our disposal, and yet we shall never give up. Why cannot we make the world see our case as we see it? Everything seems to have conspired against us—and yet I cannot, I will not believe that the law and the science that have condemned him are the last words in law and science."

"You said in your letter that the courts were so slow and the lawyers so—"

"Yes, so cold, so technical. They do not seem to

realise that a human life is at stake. With them it is almost like a game in which we are the pawns. And sometimes I fear, in spite of what the lawyers say, that without some new evidence, it—it will go hard with him."

"You have not given up hope in the appeal?" asked Kennedy gently.

"It is merely on technicalities of the law," she replied with quiet fortitude, "that is, as nearly as I can make out from the language of the papers. Our lawyer is Salo Kahn, of the big firm of criminal lawyers, Smith, Kahn & Smith."

"A good lawyer," encouraged Kennedy.

"Yes, I know. He has done all that lawyers can do. But the evidence was—what you would call, scientific—absolutely. Three expert chemists testified for the people that they found the alkaloid, conine, in the body. You see, I have thought and rethought, read and reread the case so much that I can talk like a—a man about it. Yes, they found the alkaloid in the body and try as he did there was no way that Mr. Kahn could shake their testimony. The jury believed them.

"And yet, oh, Professor Kennedy, is there nothing higher than this cold science of theirs? It cannot be —it cannot be. Sanford has told me the truth, and I know I would know if he had not been telling me what was true."

It was splendid, this exhibition of a woman's faithfulness, of this wife fighting against such tremendous weight of odds, fighting his fight, daring both law and science in her intrepid belief in him.

23

"Conine," mused Kennedy, half to himself. I could not tell whether he was thinking of what he repeated or of the little woman.

"Yes, the active principle of hemlock," she went on. "That was what the experts discovered, they swore. In the pure state, I believe, it is more poisonous than anything except the cyanides. And it was absolutely scientific evidence. They repeated the tests in court. There was no doubt of it. But, oh, he did not do it. Some one else did it. He did not—he could not."

Kennedy said nothing for a few minutes, but from his tone when he did speak it was evident that he was deeply touched.

"Since our marriage we lived with old Mr. Godwin in the historic Godwin House at East Point," she resumed, as he renewed his questioning. "Sanford—that was my husband's real last name until he came as a boy to work for Mr. Godwin in the office of the factory and was adopted by his employer—Sanford and I kept house for him.

"About a year ago he began to grow feeble and seldom went to the factory, which Sanford managed for him. One night Mr. Godwin was taken suddenly ill. I don't know how long he had been ill before we heard him groaning, but he died almost before we could summon a doctor. There was really nothing suspicious about it, but there had always been a great deal of jealousy of my husband in the town and especially among the few distant relatives of Mr. Godwin. What must have started as an idle, gossipy rumour developed into a serious charge that my husband had hastened his old guardian's death.

"The original will—*the* will, I call it—had been placed in the safe of the factory several years ago. But when the gossip in the town grew bitter, one day when we were out, some private detectives entered the house with a warrant—and they did actually find a will, another will about which we knew nothing, dated later than the first and hidden with some papers in the back of a closet, or sort of fire proof box, built into the wall of the library. The second will was iden-tical with the first in language except that its terms were reversed and instead of being the residuary lega-tee, Sanford was given a comparatively small annuity, and the Elmores were made residuary legatees instead of annuitants."

"And who are these Elmores?" asked Kennedy curi-ously.

"There are three, two grandnephews and a grand-niece, Bradford, Lambert, and their sister Miriam."

"And they live—"

"In East Point, also. Old Mr. Godwin was not very friendly with his sister, whose grandchildren they were. They were the only other heirs living, and al-though Sanford never had anything to do with it, I think they always imagined that he tried to prejudice the old man against them."

"I shall want to see the Elmores, or at least some one who represents them, as well as the district at-torney up there who conducted the case. But now that I am here, I wonder if it is possible that I could bring any influence to bear to see your husband?"

Mrs. Godwin sighed.

"Once a month," she replied, "I leave this window,

walk to the prison, where the warden is very kind to me, and then I can see Sanford. Of course there are bars between us besides the regular screen. But I can have an hour's talk, and in those talks he has described to me exactly every detail of his life in the —the prison. We have even agreed on certain hours when we think of each other. In those hours I know almost what he is thinking." She paused to collect herself. "Perhaps there may be some way if I plead with the warden. Perhaps—you may be considered his counsel now—you may see him."

A half hour later we sat in the big registry room of the prison and talked with the big-hearted, big-handed warden. Every argument that Kennedy could summon was brought to bear. He even talked over long distance with the lawyers in New York. At last the rules were relaxed and Kennedy was admitted on some technicality as counsel. Counsel can see the condemned as often as necessary.

We were conducted down a flight of steps and past huge steel-barred doors, along corridors and through the regular prison until at last we were in what the prison officials called the section for the condemned. Every one else calls this secret heart of the grim place, the death house.

It is made up of two rows of cells, some eighteen or twenty in all, a little more modern in construction than the twelve hundred archaic caverns that pass for cells in the main prison.

At each end of the corridor sat a guard, armed, with eyes never off the rows of cells day or night.

In the wall, on one side, was a door—the little green

door—the door from the death house to the death chamber.

While Kennedy was talking to the prisoner, a guard volunteered to show me the death chamber and the "chair." No other furniture was there in the little brick house of one room except this awful chair, of yellow oak with broad, leather straps. There it stood, the sole article in the brightly varnished room of about twenty-five feet square with walls of clean blue, this grim acolyte of modern scientific death. There were the wet electrodes that are fastened to the legs through slits in the trousers at the calves; above was the pipe-like fixture, like a gruesome helmet of leather that fits over the head, carrying the other electrode.

Back of the condemned was the switch which lets loose a lethal store of energy, and back of that the prison morgue where the bodies are taken. I looked about. In the wall to the left toward the death house was also a door, on this side yellow. Somehow I could not get from my mind the fascination of that door—the threshold of the grave.

Meanwhile Kennedy sat in the little cage and talked with the convicted man across the three-foot distance between cell and screen. I did not see him at that time, but Kennedy repeated afterward what passed, and it so impressed me that I will set it down as if I had been present.

Sanford Godwin was a tall, ashen-faced man, in the prison pallor of whose face was written the determination of despair, a man in whose blue eyes was a queer, half-insane light of hope. One knew that if it had not been for the little woman at the window at the top of the hill, the hope would probably long ago have faded. But this man knew she was always there, thinking, watching, eagerly planning in aid of any new scheme in the long fight for freedom.

"The alkaloid was present, that is certain," he told Kennedy. "My wife has told you that. It was scientifically proved. There is no use in attacking that."

Later on he remarked: "Perhaps you think it strange that one in the very shadow of the death chair"—the word stuck in his throat—"can talk so impersonally of his own case. Sometimes I think it is not my case, but some one else's. And then—that door."

He shuddered and turned away from it. On one side was life, such as it was; on the other, instant death. No wonder he pleaded with Kennedy.

"Why, Walter," exclaimed Craig, as we walked back to the warden's office to telephone to town for a car to take us up to East Point, "whenever he looks out of that cage he sees it. He may close his eyes— and still see it. When he exercises, he sees it. Thinking by day and dreaming by night, it is always there. Think of the terrible hours that man must pass, knowing of the little woman eating her heart out. Is he really guilty? I must find out. If he is not, I never saw a greater tragedy than this slow, remorseless approach of death, in that daily, hourly shadow of the little green door."

East Point was a queer old town on the upper Hudson, with a varying assortment of industries. Just outside, the old house of the Godwins stood on a bluff overlooking the majestic river. Kennedy had wanted to see it before any one suspected his mission, and a note from Mrs. Godwin to a friend had been sufficient.

Carefully he went cver the deserted and now half-wrecked house, for the authorities had spared nothing in their search for poison, even going over the garden and the lawns in the hope of finding some of the poisonous shrub, hemlock, which it was contended had been used to put an end to Mr. Godwin.

As yet nothing had been done to put the house in order again and, as we walked about, we noticed a pile of old tins in the yard which had not been removed.

Kennedy turned them over with his stick. Then he picked one up and examined it attentively.

"H-m—a blown can," he remarked.

"Blown?" I repeated.

"Yes. When the contents of a tin begin to deteriorate they sometimes give off gases which press out the ends of the tin. You can see how these ends bulge."

Our next visit was to the district attorney, a young man, Gordon Kilgore, who seemed not unwilling to discuss the case frankly.

"I want to make arrangements for disinterring the body," explained Kennedy. "Would you fight such a move?"

"Not at all, not at all," he answered brusquely. "Simply make the arrangements through Kahn. I shall interpose no objection. It is the strongest, most impregnable part of the case, the discovery of the poison. If you can break that down you will do more than any one else has dared to hope. But it can't be done. The proof was too strong. Of course it is none of my business, but I'd advise some other point of attack."

I must confess to a feeling of disappointment when Kennedy announced after leaving Kilgore that, for the present, there was nothing more to be done at East Point until Kahn had made the arrangements for reopening the grave.

We motored back to Ossining, and Kennedy tried to be reassuring to Mrs. Godwin.

"By the way," he remarked, just before we left, "you used a good deal of canned goods at the Godwin house, didn't you?"

"Yes, but not more than other people, I think," she said.

"Do you recall using any that were—well, perhaps not exactly spoiled, but that had anything peculiar about them?"

"I remember once we thought we found some cans that seemed to have been attacked by mice—at least they smelt so, though how mice could get through a tin can we couldn't see."

"Mice?" queried Kennedy. "Had a mousey smell? That's interesting. Well, Mrs. Godwin, keep up a good heart. Depend on me. What you have told me to-day has made me more than interested in your case. I shall waste no time in letting you know when anything encouraging develops."

Craig had never had much patience with red tape that barred the way to the truth, yet there were times when law and legal procedure had to be respected, no matter how much they hampered, and this was one of them. The next day the order was obtained permitting the opening again of the grave of old Mr. Godwin. The body was exhumed, and Kennedy set about his examination of what secrets it might hide.

Meanwhile, it seemed to me that the suspense was terrible. Kennedy was moving slowly, I thought. Not even the courts themselves could have been more deliberate. Also, he was keeping much to himself.

Still, for another whole day, there was the slow, inevitable approach of the thing that now, I, too, had come to dread—the handing down of the final decision on the appeal.

Yet what could Craig do otherwise, I asked myself. I had become deeply interested in the case by this time and spent the time reading all the evidence, hundreds of pages of it. It was cold, hard, brutal, scientific fact, and as I read I felt that hope faded for the ashen-faced man and the pallid little woman. It seemed the last word in science. Was there any way of escape?

Impatient as I was, I often wondered what must have been the suspense of those to whom the case meant everything.

"How are the tests coming along?" I ventured one night, after Kahn had arranged for the uncovering of the grave.

It was now two days since Kennedy had gone up to East Point to superintend the exhumation and had returned to the city with the materials which had caused him to keep later hours in the laboratory than I had ever known even the indefatigable Craig to spend on a stretch before.

He shook his head doubtfully.

"Walter," he admitted, "I'm afraid I have reached the limit on the line of investigation I had planned at the start."

I looked at him in dismay. "What then?" I managed to gasp.

"I am going up to East Point again to-morrow to look over that house and start a new line. You can go."

No urging was needed, and the following day saw us again on the ground. The house, as I have said, had been almost torn to pieces in the search for the will and the poison evidence. As before, we went to it unannounced, and this time we had no difficulty in getting in. Kennedy, who had brought with him a large package, made his way directly to a sort of drawing-room next to the large library, in the closet of which the will had been discovered.

He unwrapped the package and took from it a huge brace and bit, the bit a long, thin, murderous looking affair such as might have come from a burglar's kit. I regarded it much in that light.

"What's the lay?" I asked, as he tapped over the walls to ascertain of just what they were composed.

Without a word he was now down on his knees, drilling a hole in the plaster and lath. When he struck an obstruction he stopped, removed the bit, inserted another, and began again.

"Are you going to put in a detectaphone?" I asked again.

He shook his head. "A detectaphone wouldn't be of any use here," he replied. "No one is going to do any talking in that room."

Again the brace and bit were at work. At last the wall had been penetrated, and he quickly removed every trace from the other side that would have attracted attention to a little hole in an obscure corner of the flowered wall-paper.

Next, he drew out what looked like a long putty-blower, perhaps a foot long and three-eighths of an inch in diameter.

"What's that?" I asked, as he rose after carefully inserting it.

"Look through it," he replied simply, still at work on some other apparatus he had brought.

I looked. In spite of the smallness of the opening at the other end, I was amazed to find that I could see nearly the whole room on the other side of the wall.

"It's a detectascope," he explained, "a tube with a fish-eye lens which I had an expert optician make for me."

"A fish-eye lens?" I repeated.

"Yes. The focus may be altered in range so that any one in the room may be seen and recognised and any action of his may be detected. The original of this was devised by Gaillard Smith, the adapter of the detectaphone. The instrument is something like the cytoscope, which the doctors use to look into the human interior. Now, look through it again. Do you see the closet?"

Again I looked. "Yes," I said, "but will one of us have to watch here all the time?"

He had been working on a black box in the meantime, and now he began to set it up, adjusting it to the hole in the wall which he enlarged on our side.

"No, that is my own improvement on it. You remember once we used a quick-shutter camera with an electric attachment, which moved the shutter on the contact of a person with an object in the room? Well, this camera has that quick shutter. But, in addition, I have adapted to the detectascope an invention by Professor Robert Wood, of Johns Hopkins. He has devised a fish-eye camera that 'sees' over a radius of one hundred and eighty degrees— not only straight in front, but over half a circle, every point in that room.

"You know the refracting power of a drop of water. Since it is a globe, it refracts the light which reaches it from all directions. If it is placed like the lens of a camera, as Dr. Wood tried it, so that one-half of it catches the light, all the light caught will be refracted through it. Fishes, too, have a wide range of vision. Some have eyes that see over half a circle. So the lens gets its name. Ordinary cameras, because of the flatness of their lenses, have a range of only a few degrees, the widest in use, I believe, taking in only ninety-six, or a little more than a quarter of a circle. So, you see, my detectascope has a range almost twice as wide as that of any other."

Though I did not know what he expected to discover and knew that it was useless to ask, the thing seemed very interesting. Craig did not pause, however, to enlarge on the new machine, but gathered up his tools and announced that our next step would be a visit to a lawyer whom the Elmores had retained as their personal counsel to look after their interests, now that the district attorney seemed to have cleared up the criminal end of the case.

Hollins was one of the prominent attorneys of East Point, and before the election of Kilgore as prosecutor had been his partner. Unlike Kilgore, we found him especially uncommunicative and inclined to resent our presence in the case as intruders.

The interview did not seem to me to be productive of anything. In fact, it seemed as if Craig were giving Hollins much more than he was getting.

"I shall be in town over night," remarked Craig. "In fact, I am thinking of going over the library up at the Godwin house soon, very carefully." He spoke casually. "There may be, you know, some finger-prints on the walls around that closet which might prove interesting."

A quick look from Hollins was the only answer. In fact, it was seldom that he uttered more than a monosyllable as we talked over the various aspects of the case.

A half-hour later, when he had left and had gone to the hotel, I asked Kennedy suspiciously, "Why did you expose your hand to Hollins, Craig?"

He laughed. "Oh, Walter," he remonstrated, "don't you know that it is nearly always useless to look for finger-prints, except under some circumstances, even a few days afterward? This is months, not days. Why on iron and steel they last with tolerable certainty only a short time, and not much longer on silver, glass, or wood. But they are seldom permanent unless they are made with ink or blood or something that leaves a more or less indelible mark. That was a 'plant.' "

"But what do you expect to gain by it?"

"Well," he replied enigmatically, "no one is necessarily honest."

It was late in the afternoon when Kennedy again visited the Godwin house and examined the camera. Without a word he pulled the detectascope from the wall and carried the whole thing to the developing-room of the local photographer.

There he set to work on the film and I watched him in silence. He seemed very much excited as he watched the film develop, until at last he held it up, dripping, to the red light.

"Some one has entered that room this afternoon and attempted to wipe off the walls and woodwork of that closet, as I expected," he exclaimed.

"Who was it?" I asked, leaning over.

Kennedy said nothing, but pointed to a figure on the film. I bent closer. It was the figure of a woman.

"Mirian!" I exclaimed in surprise.

XXIV

The Final Day

I LOOKED aghast at him. If it had been either Bradford or Lambert, both of whom we had come to know since Kennedy had interested himself in the case, or even Hollins or Kilgore, I should not have been surprised. But Miriam!

"How could she have any connection with the case?" I asked incredulously.

Kennedy did not attempt to explain. "It is a fatal mistake, Walter, for a detective to assume that he knows what anybody would do in any given circumstances. The only safe course for him is to find out what the persons in question did do. People are always doing the unexpected. This is a case of it, as you see. I am merely trying to get back at facts. Come; I think we might as well not stay over night, after all. I should like to drop off on the way back to the city to see Mrs. Godwin."

As we rode up the hill I was surprised to see that there was no one at the window, nor did any one seem to pay attention to our knocking at the door.

Kennedy turned the knob quickly and strode in.

Seated in a chair, as white as a wraith from the grave, was Mrs. Godwin, staring straight ahead, seeing nothing, hearing nothing.

"What's the matter?' demanded Kennedy, leaping to her side and grasping her icy hand.

The stare on her face seemed to change slightly as she recognised him.

"Walter—some water—and a little brandy—if there is any. Tell me—what has happened?"

From her lap a yellow telegram had fluttered to the floor, but before he could pick it up, she gasped, "The appeal—it has been denied." Kennedy picked up the paper. It was a message, unsigned, but not from Kahn, as its wording and in fact the circumstances plainly showed.

"The execution is set for the week beginning the fifth," she continued, in the same hollow, mechanical voice. "My God—that's next Monday!"

She had risen now and was pacing the room.

"No! I'm not going to faint. I wish I could. I wish I could cry. I wish I could do something. Oh, those Elmores—they must have sent it. No one would have been so cruel but they."

She stopped and gazed wildly out of the window at the prison. Neither of us knew what to say for the moment.

"Many times from this window," she cried, "I have seen a man walk out of that prison gate. I always watch to see what he does, though I know it is no use. If he stands in the free air, stops short, and looks up suddenly, taking a long look at every house —I hope. But he always turns for a quick, backward look at the prison and goes half running down the hill. They always stop in that fashion, when the steel door opens outward. Yet I have always looked and hoped. But I can hope no more—no more. The last chance is gone."

"No—not the last chance," exclaimed Craig, springing to her side lest she should fall. Then he added gently, "You must come with me to East Point —immediately."

"What—leave him here—alone—in the last days? No—no—no. Never. I must see him. I wonder if they have told him yet."

It was evident that she had lost faith in Kennedy, in everybody, now.

"Mrs. Godwin," he urged. "Come—you must. It is a last chance."

Eagerly he was pouring out the story of the discovery of the afternoon by the little detectascope.

"Miriam?" she repeated, dazed. "She—know anything—it can't be. No—don't raise a false hope now."

"It is the last chance," he urged again. "Come. There is not an hour to waste now."

There was no delay, no deliberation about Kennedy now. He had been forced out into the open by the course of events, and he meant to take advantage of every precious moment.

Down the hill our car sped to the town, with Mrs. Godwin still protesting, but hardly realising what was going on. Regardless of tolls, Kennedy called up his laboratory in New York and had two of his most careful students pack up the stuff which he described minutely to be carried to East Point immediately by train. Kahn, too, was at last found and summoned to meet us there, also.

24

Miles never seemed longer than they did to us as we tore over the country from Ossining to East Point, a silent party, yet keyed up by an excitement that none of us had ever felt before.

Impatiently we awaited the arrival of the men from Kennedy's laboratory, while we made Mrs. Godwin as comfortable as possible in a room at the hotel. In one of the parlours Kennedy was improvising a laboratory as best he could. Meanwhile, Kahn had arrived, and together we were seeking those whose connection with, or interest in, the case made necessary their presence.

It was well along toward midnight before the hasty conference had been gathered; besides Mrs. Godwin, Salo Kahn, and ourselves, the three Elmores, Kilgore, and Hollins.

Strange though it was, the room seemed to me almost to have assumed the familiar look of the laboratory in New York. There was the same clutter of tubes and jars on the tables, but above all that same feeling of suspense in the air which I had come to associate with the clearing up of a case. There was something else in the air, too. It was a peculiar mousey smell, disagreeable, and one which made it a relief to have Kennedy begin in a low voice to tell why he had called us together so hastily.

"I shall start," announced Kennedy, "at the point where the state left off—with the proof that Mr. Godwin died of conine, or hemlock poisoning. Conine, as every chemist knows, has a long and well-known history. It was the first alkaloid to be synthesised. Here is a sample, this colourless, oily fluid. No doubt you have noticed the mousey odour in this room. As little as one part of conine to fifty thousand of water gives off that odour—it is characteristic.

"I have proceeded with extraordinary caution in my investigation of this case," he went on. "In fact, there would have been no value in it, otherwise, for the experts for the people seem to have established the presence of conine in the body with absolute certainty."

He paused and we waited expectantly.

"I have had the body exhumed and have repeated the tests. The alkaloid which I discovered had given precisely the same results as in their tests."

My heart sank. What was he doing—convicting the man over again?

"There is one other test which I tried," he continued, "but which I can not take time to duplicate tonight. It was testified at the trial that conine, the active principle of hemlock, is intensely poisonous. No chemical antidote is known. A fifth of a grain has serious results; a drop is fatal. An injection of a most minute quantity of real conine will kill a mouse, for instance, almost instantly. But the conine which I have isolated in the body is inert!"

It came like a bombshell to the prosecution, so bewildering was the discovery.

"Inert?" cried Kilgore and Hollins almost together. "It can't be. You are making sport of the best chemical experts that money could obtain. Inert? Read the evidence—read the books."

"On the contrary," resumed Craig, ignoring the

interruption, "all the reactions obtained by the experts have been duplicated by me. But, in addition, I tried this one test which they did not try. I repeat: the conine isolated in the body is inert."

We were too perplexed to question him.

"Alkaloids," he continued quietly, "as you know, have names that end in 'in' or 'ine'—morphine, strychnine, and so on. Now there are two kinds of alkaloids which are sometimes called vegetable and animal. Moreover, there is a large class of which we are learning much which are called the ptomaines—from *ptoma,* a corpse. Ptomaine poisoning, as every one knows, results when we eat food that has begun to decay.

"Ptomaines are chemical compounds of an alkaloidal nature formed in protein substances during putrefaction. They are purely chemical bodies and differ from the toxins. There are also what are called leucomaines, formed in living tissues, and when not given off by the body they produce auto-intoxication.

"There are more than three score ptomaines, and half of them are poisonous. In fact, illness due to eating infected foods is much more common than is generally supposed. Often there is only one case in a number of those eating the food, due merely to that person's inability to throw off the poison. Such cases are difficult to distinguish. They are usually supposed to be gastro-enteritis. Ptomaines, as their name shows, are found in dead bodies. They are found in all dead matter after a time, whether it is decayed food or a decaying corpse.

"No general reaction is known by which the ptomaines can be distinguished from the vegetable alkaloids. But we know that animal alkaloids always develop either as a result of decay of food or of the decay of the body itself."

At one stroke Kennedy had reopened the closed case and had placed the experts at sea.

"I find that there is an animal conine as well as the true conine," he hammered out. "The truth of this matter is that the experts have confounded vegetable conine with cadaveric conine. That raises an interesting question. Assuming the presence of conine, where did it come from?"

He paused and began a new line of attack. "As the use of canned goods becomes more and more extensive, ptomaine poisoning is more frequent. In canning, the cans are heated. They are composed of thin sheets of iron coated with tin, the seams pressed and soldered with a thin line of solder. They are filled with cooked food, sterilised, and closed. The bacteria are usually all killed, but now and then, the apparatus does not work, and they develop in the can. That results in a 'blown can'—the ends bulge a little bit. On opening, a gas escapes, the food has a bad odour and a bad taste. Sometimes people say that the tin and lead poison them; in practically all cases the poisoning is of bacterial, not metallic, origin. Mr. Godwin may have died of poisoning, probably did. But it was ptomaine poisoning. The blown cans which I have discovered would indicate that."

I was following him closely, yet though this

seemed to explain a part of the case, it was far from explaining all.

"Then followed," he hurried on, "the development of the usual ptomaines in the body itself. These, I may say, had no relation to the cause of death itself. The putrefactive germs began their attack. Whatever there may have been in the body before, certainly they produced a cadaveric ptomaine conine. For many animal tissues and fluids, especially if somewhat decomposed, yield not infrequently compounds of an oily nature with a mousey odour, fuming with hydrochloric acid and in short, acting just like conine. There is ample evidence, I have found, that conine or a substance possessing most, if not all, of its properties is at times actually produced in animal tissues by decomposition. And the fact is, I believe, that a number of cases have arisen, in which the poisonous alkaloid was at first supposed to have been discovered which were really mistakes."

The idea was startling in the extreme. Here was Kennedy, as it were, overturning what had been considered the last word in science as it had been laid down by the experts for the prosecution, opinions so impregnable that courts and juries had not hesitated to condemn a man to death.

"There have been cases," Craig went on solemnly, "and I believe this to be one, where death has been pronounced to have been caused by wilful administration of a vegetable alkaloid, which toxicologists would now put down as ptomaine-poisoning cases. Innocent people have possibly already suffered and may in the future. But medical experts—" he laid especial stress on the word—"are much more alive to the danger of mistake than formerly. This was a case where the danger was not considered, either through carelessness, ignorance, or prejudice.

"Indeed, ptomaines are present probably to a greater or less extent in every organ which is submitted to the toxicologist for examination. If he is ignorant of the nature of these substances, he may easily mistake them for vegetable alkaloids. He may report a given poison present when it is not present. It is even yet a new line of inquiry which has only recently been followed, and the information is still comparatively small and inadequate.

"It is very difficult, perhaps impossible, for the chemist to state absolutely that he has detected true conine. Before he can do it, the symptoms and the post-mortem appearance must agree; analysis must be made before, not after, decomposition sets in, and the amount of the poison found must be sufficient to experiment with, not merely to react to a few usual tests.

"What the experts asserted so positively, I would not dare to assert. Was he killed by ordinary ptomaine poisoning, and had conine, or rather its double, developed first in his food along with other ptomaines that were not inert? Or did the cadaveric conine develop only in the body after death? Chemistry alone can not decide the question so glibly as the experts did. Further proof must be sought. Other sciences must come to our aid."

I was sitting next to Mrs. Godwin. As Kennedy's words rang out, her hand, trembling with emotion, pressed my arm. I turned quickly to see if she needed assistance. Her face was radiant. All the fees for big cases in the world could never have compensated Kennedy for the mute, unrestrained gratitude which the little woman shot at him.

Kennedy saw it, and in the quick shifting of his eyes to my face, I read that he relied on me to take care of Mrs. Godwin while he plunged again into the clearing up of the mystery.

"I have here the will—the second one," he snapped out, turning and facing the others in the room.

Craig turned a switch in an apparatus which his students had brought from New York. From a tube on the table came a peculiar bluish light.

"This," he explained, "is a source of ultraviolet rays. They are not the bluish light which you see, but rays contained in it which you can not see.

"Ultraviolet rays have recently been found very valuable in the examination of questioned documents. By the use of a lens made of quartz covered with a thin film of metallic silver, there has been developed a practical means of making photographs by the invisible rays of light above the spectrum—these ultraviolet rays. The quartz lens is necessary, because these rays will not pass through ordinary glass, while the silver film acts as a screen to cut off the ordinary light rays and those below the spectrum. By this means, most white objects are photographed black and even transparent objects like glass are black.

"I obtained the copy of this will, but under the condition from the surrogate that absolutely nothing must be done to it to change a fibre of the paper or a line of a letter. It was a difficult condition. While there are chemicals which are frequently resorted to for testing the authenticity of disputed decuments such as wills and deeds, their use frequently injures or destroys the paper under test. So far as I could determine, the document also defied the microscope.

"But ultraviolet photography does not affect the document tested in any way, and it has lately been used practically in detecting forgeries. I have photographed the last page of the will with its signatures, and here it is. What the eye itself can not see, the invisible light reveals."

He was holding the document and the copy, just an instant, as if considering how to announce with best effect what he had discovered.

"In order to unravel this mystery," he resumed, looking up and facing the Elmores, Kilgore, and Hollins squarely, "I decided to find out whether any one had had access to that closet where the will was hidden. It was long ago, and there seemed to be little that I could do. I knew it was useless to look for finger-prints.

"So I used what we detectives now call the law of suggestion. I questioned closely one who was in touch with all those who might have had such access. I hinted broadly at seeking finger-prints which might lead to the identity of one who had entered the house unknown to the Godwins, and placed a document where private detectives would subsequently find it under suspicious circumstances.

"Naturally, it would seem to one who was guilty of such an act, or knew of it, that there might, after all, be finger-prints. I tried it. I found out through this little tube, the detectascope, that one really entered the room after that, and tried to wipe off any supposed finger-prints that might still remain. That settled it. The second will was a forgery, and the person who entered that room so stealthily this afternoon knows that it is a forgery."

As Kennedy slapped down on the table the film from his camera, which had been concealed, Mrs. Godwin turned her now large and unnaturally bright eyes and met those of the other woman in the room.

"Oh—oh—heaven help us—me, I mean!" cried Miriam, unable to bear the strain of the turn of events longer. "I knew there would be retribution—I knew —I knew—"

Mrs. Godwin was on her feet in a moment.

"Once my intuition was not wrong though all science and law was against me," she pleaded with Kennedy. There was a gentleness in her tone that fell like a soft rain on the surging passions of those who had wronged her so shamefully. "Professor Kennedy, Miriam could not have forged—"

Kennedy smiled. "Science was not against you, Mrs. Godwin. Ignorance was against you. And your intuition does not go contrary to science this time, either."

It was a splendid exhibition of fine feeling which Kennedy waited to have impressed on the Elmores, as though burning it into their minds.

"Miriam Elmore knew that her brothers had forged a will and hidden it. To expose them was to convict them of a crime. She kept their secret, which was the secret of all three. She even tried to hide the finger-prints which would have branded her brothers.

"For ptomaine poisoning had unexpectedly hastened the end of old Mr. Godwin. Then gossip and the 'scientists' did the rest. It was accidental, but Bradford and Lambert Elmore were willing to let events take their course and declare genuine the forgery which they had made so skilfully, even though it convicted an innocent man of murder and killed his faithful wife. As soon as the courts can be set in motion to correct an error of science by the truth of later science, Sing Sing will lose one prisoner from the death house and gain two forgers in his place."

Mrs. Godwin stood before us, radiant. But as Kennedy's last words sank into her mind, her face clouded.

"Must—must it be an eye for an eye and a tooth for a tooth?" she pleaded eagerly. "Must that grim prison take in others, even if my husband goes free?"

Kennedy looked at her long and earnestly, as if to let the beauty of her character, trained by its long suffering, impress itself on his mind indelibly.

He shook his head slowly.

"I'm afraid there is no other way, Mrs. Godwin," he said gently taking her arm and leaving the others to be dealt with by a constable whom he had dozing in the hotel lobby.

"Kahn is going up to Albany to get the pardon—there can be no doubt about it now," he added. "Mrs. Godwin, if you care to do so, you may stay here at the hotel, or you may go down with us on the midnight train as far as Ossining. I will wire ahead for a conveyance to meet you at the station. Mr. Jameson and I must go on to New York."

"The nearer I am to Sanford now, the happier I shall be," she answered, bravely keeping back the tears of happiness.

The ride down to New York, after our train left Ossining, was accomplished in a day coach in which our fellow passengers slept in every conceivable attitude of discomfort.

Yet late, or rather early, as it was, we found plenty of life still in the great city that never sleeps. Tired, exhausted, I was at least glad to feel that finally we were at home.

"Craig," I yawned, as I began to throw off my clothes, "I'm ready to sleep a week."

There was no answer.

I looked up at him almost resentfully. He had picked up the mail that lay under our letter slot and was going through it as eagerly as if the clock registered P. M. instead of A. M.

"Let me see," I mumbled sleepily, checking over my notes, "how many days have we been at it?"

I turned the pages slowly, after the manner in which my mind was working.

"It was the twenty-sixth when you got that letter from Ossining," I calculated, "and to-day makes the thirtieth. My heavens—is there still another day of it? Is there no rest for the wicked?"

Kennedy looked up and laughed.

He was pointing at the calendar on the desk before him.

"There are only thirty days in the month," he remarked slowly.

"Thank the Lord," I exclaimed.   "I'm all in!"

He tipped his desk-chair back and bit the amber of his meerchaum contemplatively.

"But to-day is the first," he drawled, turning the leaf on the calendar with just a flicker of a smile.

THE END